JESTER:

Memoirs of a Retired Hippie

From San Francisco Hippie to Road Nomad:
experiencing life on the highways of America
and north to Alaska

WARREN TROY

PO Box 221974 Anchorage, Alaska 99522-1974
books@publicationconsultants.com—www.publicationconsultants.com

ISBN 978-1-59433-305-7
eBook ISBN 978-1-59433-306-4
Library of Congress Catalog Card Number: 2012940459

Manufactured in the United States of America.

Dedication

To my wife, brother and daughter for their support and encouragement.

Introduction

*I*have decided to put on paper the rambling memories of the man I know as Jester. He told me the name was given to him many years ago, because of a hat he used to have, multi-colored and pointed, with bells on it, the sort of headgear medieval court jesters used to wear. He said he only wore it a few times to be funny, but the nickname stuck and he took it for his own. After he had regaled me with a number of stories about where and how he had lived, the name seemed less strange, and more appropriate for the times.

I met Jester down by the Carson River outside Carson City, Nevada, near the end of summer, 2001. I had been living in Carson City for six years, working in a local casino as a dealer, and exploring the desert and canyons around the city in my free time. I've always been a bit of a desert rat, and this area with its rich mining history held my interest.

The part of the river where I met Jester is a popular camping area, peaceful, with cottonwoods and willows along the riverbanks. Often, there are transients squatting there. People living on the road, outside the mainstream of society use it when they are traveling through this part of Nevada, until someone complains about them making a mess or acting badly, probably hassling a local for money or food, and the local authorities tell them to move on.

I was roaming around in the sagebrush at an old mine site near the river, with a metal detector I had just bought, when someone close behind me said in a low, gravelly voice, "Trippy looking treasure finder, man."

Caught off guard, I spun around to see before me a man about six feet tall, with a full salt-and-pepper beard. He wore old but clean clothes, and

5

had piercing blue eyes with a sparkle of amusement in them, behind thick-lens, wire-frame glasses.

He seemed pleased to have caught me by surprise, but I sensed no hostility coming from him. After checking him out for a few seconds, I decided he was safe, so I told him it wasn't nice, sneaking up on people, especially out in the desert, where all kinds of characters are known to be. I figured a mental poke at him was okay, and it was, but I added a grin after I spoke to show I had taken the situation as I thought it was intended, a harmless game. He smiled back, showing teeth that were clean, but fewer than a full set.

He asked me if I knew the history of the area we were in. I told him it was called Brunswick Canyon and had been actively used during the Comstock mining era.

He said if I wanted to, I could come sit with him at his campsite, have a cup of coffee, and fill him in on the canyon's history. In return, he'd tell me a few stories he was sure I'd never heard before.

Intrigued and up for a cup, I told him I would, but we should at least exchange names. I introduced myself, and he gave his name as Jester. I say gave, because the way he said it made it seem like he was giving me a gift, and it was my choice to open it or not. I responded by asking where the name had come from, and he told me why he was called Jester. I didn't know it yet, but the seed had been sown for many tales to come.

He had a comfortable camp on the riverbank, set up unobtrusively among the willows. There were folding chairs, a small camp table, and a Coleman stove with an old-fashioned coffee pot heating on it. He had a clean, older Dodge pick-up truck with a full-sized camper on back. The striped awning on the camper's side provided shade.

I told him he seemed to be a seasoned camper, and he said he had been on the road for twenty-five years more or less, and ought to know by now how to do it right. I stood there considering what living for so long on the road would be like, until he offered me a chair and a cup of coffee, and we began talking.

After I told him what I knew about Brunswick Canyon, the mine sites and stamp mills, how mule-drawn wagons brought in the ore to use the river for power to process it, and how a small gauge railroad eventually ran through it, he said he figured it was his turn to tell me some things.

For the next several hours, Jester told me about experiences which had happened to and around him many years ago, during a time most people are scarcely familiar with or remember at all.

I sat there in the same mindset I get into when reading a book so interesting, I can't put it down. Reluctantly, I finally told him I had to head back to town, but would he be staying by the river for a while?

"Long as the weather holds," he said "then I'm going down to Temecula, California to visit a friend I haven't seen in way too long, if he's still around doing his thing."

I was going to offer him some money, thinking he might need it, but something made me hold back. As if reading my thoughts, Jester said it would be far out if I brought some smokes and some ground coffee next time I came.

By now, the slang he used while relating his tales was growing on me, and didn't sound as affected as it had at first. I figured it was just the way he normally talked, though coming from a guy a few years older than my own father, it sounded strange and out of place.

I asked if he wanted me to bring a few beers, too. His face grew instantly serious, but the smile and relaxed look I already recognized as his normal expression came right back again. "No, man, it's cool. Never touch the stuff anymore."

Over the next few months, I went to visit Jester as often as I could. I even called in sick a couple of times from my job, when I thought he might be leaving soon.

I sat for hours at his campsite, usually in the morning or early afternoon, often remaining until evening, kicking back in his camp. Occasionally, there were other people there when I arrived, most of them around his age, kicking back and talking, occasionally laughing and nodding their heads, but they would quiet down once I was there.

Jester always held center stage, rambling on, one story turning into another, his memory bouncing back and forth in time, tossing up things for him to tell. By the time I had heard the first bunch of stories, I understood why his memory functioned as it did. He was definitely not a straight-line thinker.

Though his thoughts were often scattered, I found Jester to be a treasure trove of fascinating remembrances about a time gone by, when a bold social experiment took place in San Francisco, California, eventually spreading all over America and ultimately the world. It may not have accomplished what the original hippies wanted it to in the end, but it's likely the people who started the movement didn't have a clear idea of what they actually intended to accomplish.

Later in our get-togethers, as he described the events of his life after the hippie scene was over, I could clearly see how the philosophy proclaimed during that time had affected his life, even in his later years.

I asked him early on if I could tape his stories so I wouldn't lose them to faulty memory. He told me he thought it would be cool.

"There aren't many of us left from the mellow yellow times, man. If you want to record what I say, I'll get to be the trip master one more time, and maybe someone else will get to hear what happened."

I have to say at this point, I was strongly affected by this fascinating, all-too-short episode in my life. I have had a few adventures as many people do, things which stand out in my mind. But, listening to Jester relating what had happened to him over the last thirty-five years overwhelmed me at times. When listening to him, I was drawn into the stories, but I initially assumed there was a fair amount of B.S. involved for my entertainment. I later came to realize, mostly by gut feeling, except for small changes brought on by time and memory lapse, he was indeed telling me his life as it had actually occurred.

When writing down his episodes, I would find myself immersed in them, as the form my writing has taken probably suggests. For this I ask the reader to allow me some leeway. Perhaps you too will become involved in his stories to the same degree.

So, for what it's worth, here are Jester's stories as he told them to me, slightly altered for the sake of clarity, but all his, nonetheless.

Section One

I graduated from high school in 1965. It had been a bummer, really boring. I was never much interested in anything except football and a few friendly girls. Most of the other kids seemed cool with cruising through school, not getting much from their time there, happy to get done with classes so they could hang out with their friends.

The town I lived in was a drag too. It was a normal Southern California suburb: smog, concrete, and lots of typical lowbrow stuff. 'Course, I got into the usual teenage trouble: getting caught smoking in school, drinking beer after a football game, coming home too late, typical lightweight stuff.

Nope, going to high school didn't turn me on. But, I knew when I turned eighteen I wanted to find my own life somewhere else, and it happened, though in ways I never would have expected.

Yeah, my personal evolution as a freethinking, individual human being was already starting, man. Life was going to get far out; I just didn't know it yet.

About a month after being released from school in the summer of '65, I decided to visit my brother who was studying English lit at San Francisco State College. He was always the brainy one, but he was cool, too.

My brother had a thing for the beatniks, who were all faded out by the Mid Sixties. Like them, he enjoyed listening to and discussing jazz. I guess it was why he chose San Francisco State. He told me a lot of the beatniks who still existed were in S.F.

I decided to hitchhike up there. Not owning a car made it an easy choice. My parents freaked of course, so I knew it was the cool thing to do. I filled a small pack with personal stuff and headed out. My first ride got me to the edge of East L.A., which was not as dangerous a place for white boys to stand on street corners hitching as it is now. I got a lift from a large, beefy old white man in a Chevy wagon, who was heading north up Highway 99. Smooth and fast Highway 5 didn't exist yet.

After we had ridden quite a ways in silence, this guy says, "So tell me son, what kind of work do you do?"

"Oh, I don't have a job right now."

"You don't work?"

"Nope, going up to see my brother. He's studying at San Francisco State College."

He immediately brought his car to a tire-squealing halt on the blacktop divider at the Saugus-Newhall turnoff. There was nothing there, only the turnoff, and the highway heading north.

With his face bright red and his eyes bulging, he yelled at me, "NO DEADBEAT BROTHER OF ANY SAN FRANCISCO WEIRDO IS GONNA RIDE IN MY CAR! GET OUT!"

I did, remembering barely in time to grab my pack. He roared off north up the highway, and there I was, shocked by his reaction, the July sun beating down, with nowhere to go for shade and still be in a good place to stand for a ride. People kept rushing by at sixty-five to seventy, not caring if I was melting out there.

I stood suffering for a couple of hours. I'm looking north when I hear this strange whirring-ticking sound right behind me. I turn, and here's this heavy-looking Highway Patrol cruiser right up on me, with a real classic trooper sitting behind the wheel, flattop, sunglasses, and no trace of a smile.

Now dig it: I was clean cut, like most normal high school kids. I had on a short-sleeved cotton shirt, levis and sneakers, and a short haircut, so I figured I was gonna be okay, maybe get a ride up the road a ways with this kind officer. Yeah, right!

He has me get in the car, I tell him the whole story, all the details, (I hadn't learned yet, man). He sits there silent as a statue, head turned around, listening to me babble in the back seat.

When I was all through, he tells me hitching on this highway is illegal, asks me for I.D., writes me out a fat ticket for hitchhiking on the Interstate, and takes me over to old Highway 99, saying it would be safer for me. He didn't mention hardly anybody used old 99 anymore!

I stood right where he left me for about three hours without even seeing a car, but at least there were a few trees on the side of the old patched blacktop, so I had a little shade. Finally, a shiny, green VW Beetle pulls up, and this neat-looking dude, maybe in his forties, asks me where I'm going. Playing it safe, I tell him I'm going to San Francisco to get a job on the docks. He said he was going to S.F. too, so I hop in, grateful for miracles. I was so beat from the hot sun, I dozed off almost immediately.

I woke up a few minutes later with this jerk's hand on my leg. It freaked me out, and I felt like punching him, but not wanting to get dumped back off on the road, I gently moved his hand off me and told him I was tired, and if he'd wait until we got to San Francisco, we could have a good time. It seemed to satisfy him, and I could feel the Beetle pick up speed.

We stopped once to eat in some small town. We sat, with him giving me the eye across the table and local people flashing us knowing looks. What a downer. Hey man, it was Central California, 1965, just out of the dark ages, and it could have been Iowa or Arkansas, you dig? I was only eighteen, and not worldly, but I was learning fast.

When we got to the city late in the evening, I waited for the first reasonable stop we came to, grabbed my pack from the backseat, jumped out of the car, yelled something about what he could do to himself, and took off. Not exactly the most laid-back journey, but I had made it to San Francisco, The City by the Bay.

I wanted to see my brother, but was so amazed and impressed at being in Frisco, which my brother thought was the greatest city on earth and had described it to me in glowing and wild word pictures, I decided to find China Town, get some Chinese food, and stay up all night exploring the streets.

I took a trolley car from Market Street and O'Farrell up to Washington Street in China Town, and got off. I will always remember the smell of the overheated wood blocks the trolley used for brakes. The sweet aroma became fused into my wide-open brain cells as THE San Francisco smell, and even now, all I have to do is think of that scent, and my mind is filled with it.

"What an incredible city," I thought, as I wandered. "Here it is the middle of the Twentieth Century, and I'm in a major city, riding an electric trolley car running on rails with a clanging bell announcing its existence."

Hopping off at Washington Street, I walked about a block and went into a classy-looking place called the Golden Dragon. It had the most delicious Chinese food, freshly made. It was the first time I'd ever had octopus. I'd ordered the house special chow mien, which had tiny octopuses all through it. After I got myself to try one, I couldn't get enough.

My exotic meal over, I went into a souvenir shop where I bought a groovy small incense burner in the shape of an elephant with a howdah on top, and some of those little cones of sandalwood incense.

Then I walked all the way down a very steep street to some tourist shops by the piers, and bought a large chocolate bar at Ghirardelli's, just before they closed. I took another trolley car back up and over the hilly street. It was a groovy trip.

What a city. San Francisco, city of Kerouac, Ginsburg, and Burroughs. Walking around an area called North Beach, I discovered there were still some beatniks floating around. Only later did I realize, besides being writers and musicians, they were drug- and booze-using whackos. My kind of people, I was to discover.

Yeah, I spent the whole night walking around, from North Beach back down to Lower Market Street, then up to the Castro District, which wasn't like it is now, center of the gay community, not in those days. The Castro Theatre used to be a family movie house, but not anymore.

I tell you, man, there was a heavy-duty, special thing about the atmosphere of San Francisco. I could feel it right away. It felt like the whole place was surrounded by a force field from a sci-fi story. The air was different, you know? It felt like something unique was about to happen, and things weren't the same as most places. Later, I was sure of it!

At five o'clock in the morning, I found my brother's pad, on Duboce Street right across from the San Francisco Mint. I stood there full of obnoxious youthful enthusiasm and adrenalin, banging on the door 'til some sleepy-eyed, great-looking girl opened it.

She asked in a cranky voice, "Who are you, and what do you want?"

"I came to see my brother," I answered, knowing I had probably blown it.

My brother came to the door. "Oh, wow, couldn't you have called first?"

He went back in, and a moment later returned with some money. "Here's five bucks. Go down to the coffee shop on the corner of Duboce off Market and get some steak and eggs or pancakes or something, and come back in a couple of hours. Hey, wait a minute, here, take this with you." He handed me a book, Kerouac's On the Road, and shut the door in my face.

I could have felt bad about my brother running me off, but getting some breakfast sounded good.

Turned out the ham was dry and the eggs runny, but the home-fried potatoes were perfect and soaked up the eggs. The coffee flowed, and the book kept boredom away. I was turned on by the characters in the book and their free-living ways.

The coffee shop had an OPEN ALL NIGHT sign in the window, and it looked like all sorts of people came into the place. I wanted to finish *On the Road*, but I ended up pretending to read the book, because watching all the people in the place was a lot more interesting. I eyed them from over the top edge of the book's pages, trying to be sneaky, but finally I put the book down and sat checking out all the interesting customers.

Sitting there with all these characters, I knew I was a long ways from home, and glad of it. It was fascinating. The waitress came over for the fifth or sixth time to refill my coffee cup and said, "First time in San Fran, Honey?"

"Uh, yeah, it is. Visiting my brother."

"No other city like it. Been working in this place for almost twenty years. The jokers who come in here are the best cheap entertainment there is. Enjoy yourself."

She was right. Some could barely keep their heads up to eat, and I now know they were probably nodding out on smack or some other downer drugs, while others could barely sit still enough to enjoy their meal.

I saw all kinds of clothing from regular to funky and freaky, and some who were dressed in costumes from another place and time. There was even a tux and evening gown combo over by a window. Some who I figured might be students or just deep thinkers ordered food, but ended up letting it sit and get cold while they ranted and raved on about who knows what. I wondered if they'd remember what they had discussed by the time they were done.

But then, this tall, skinny black man came in with two chicks. I couldn't stop staring. He had on a purple striped jump suit with these thick-heeled shoes, heavy gold chains and rings, a white broad-brimmed hat with a large purple feather in it, and oversized, red sunglasses. The girls were dressed brightly, but skimpily, with all their stuff hanging out.

After I had been watching them for a couple of minutes, this same wild-looking man gets up, walks over and leans down, taking his sunglasses off to reveal scary-looking, bloodshot eyes. "Boy, didn't your momma tell you it isn't polite to stare? Better be steppin' off before I have to make an attitude adjustment on you!"

After the few seconds it took for me to recover, I said lamely, "Sorry, I didn't mean to stare."

"It's cool, my man, my natural brilliance must have caught you unawares," and he puts out this wide smile revealing numerous solid-gold teeth, before rejoining his two giggling girls.

What a trip! I finished up, and headed back to my brother's pad.

The girl was gone, and my brother let me in. The apartment was cool. He told me the building was built around the turn of the century. The ceiling had these embossed tin panels, and there was heavy wooden framing around the old-fashioned windows. He said he loved living there because it felt like living in another time.

We sat drinking coffee, which I didn't need after the gallon I had drunk at the diner, and talked about things, his school, people, and the city. We rapped happily for hours. My brother and I really dug visiting. This was the first time we had been together away from home and the folks. It was neat. Two brothers out on our own.

But, when we got back from getting a take-out pizza for dinner the second night, the phone rang. It was Mom. I had gotten a military induction notice the day after I had left, and I had to come home and deal with it. My whole adventure had instantly come to an end. Apparently the force field around San Francisco wasn't invulnerable after all.

The pizza didn't seem quite as tasty after the call, but after dinner my brother said he had something to make me feel better. First he swore me to secrecy. Then he reached into the back of his refrigerator's tiny freezer compartment and pulled out a bag of strange, dried, grassy-looking stuff. He rolled some into a home-made cigarette, and lit it up. He inhaled it deeply, and holding it in for a long time, he started coughing like crazy. "Here man, try it," he said in a strained voice. It didn't seem to hurt him, except for the coughing. I asked him if it was marijuana.

At this point, Jester stopped his story and gave me a long, deep look. He asked me if talk about drugs and other such stuff was going to turn me off. "It's a major happening in the stories I'm going to tell you. I had drugs in my life for a long time, so if you don't want to hear about it, I don't want to get you all bummed out. I've been totally clean for many years now, and wouldn't want you to think I'm recommending anything I'm gonna talk about as being cool for anybody else, 'cause I don't. It's just how it was, man."

I told him I understood this would be a part of it, and it was necessary to tell. Jester collected himself, and continued on.

When I asked my brother if it was marijuana, he started this ridiculous, cackling laughter. I thought he had gone nuts. He told me to suck some smoke in and hold it a while, so I did. For a minute, nothing seemed any different. My brother sat at the kitchen table taking a few more hits and watching me. All of a sudden it was as if a switch went on in my head, and things changed. I mean, colors were brighter, everything around me appeared a little different, and anything either of us said was really funny.

I started laughing for no particular reason, told my brother I didn't know why I was laughing, and then we were both laughing. We couldn't stop until the person living above him started banging on the floor.

About an hour later, we went walking and laughing together down the street to the corner store for Rocky Road ice cream and Oreos, I think it was. Life would definitely never be the same.

In the morning before he headed to school, my brother gave me some money so I could get a bus ticket home, told me how to get to the Greyhound station, and we parted ways.

The last night at my brother's was the beginning of many amazing trips for me, and also probably the ruination of my life as a typical productive member of society. As far as drug use was concerned I had turned a corner, and just wanted to keep on keepin' on. I didn't start experiencing drugs to escape anything. I was just curious, and enjoyed the new and different sensations drugs offered.

At first, I started smoking marijuana with people in my hometown area, after I had returned from the visit with my brother. I also took several acid trips with friends from high school.

The first acid trip I took was truly an amazing event. Like so many other things, the first time is the most memorable, and it sets the pattern for future experiences.

Since coming back from San Francisco, I had been seeing a girl I had known since my junior year of high school. Her first name, no lie, was Berry, Berry Howard. She was an intelligent and pretty girl, but was also messed up, probably because she was such a curious person, wanting to know all about life, while her mother was an uptight, suppressive woman who kept her daughter on a short leash all the time. The situation was very rough on Berry. She was already drinking when I met her as a junior. Her mother didn't care for me, and when I was visiting at their house, she would give me looks, as if she knew I was only there for one thing, getting into Berry's shorts.

Berry's mom had given her husband one child, which I guess she figured was her wifely duty, after which she kicked him out of their bed for the remainder of their short-lived marriage.

Berry's rebellion against her mom's frosty ways got me laid for the first time.

One summer day when my folks were at work, Berry came over acting upset. She kept complaining about her mom hounding her. She asked for a shot of booze out of my folks' supply, drank it down, walked into my room, and took all her clothes off. I stood there gawking, totally unprepared for this.

She said, "Are you gonna get going or am I?" She stayed. But it was the only time we ever did it during our high school days. I don't even think she enjoyed it much, but I sure did. Like I said, she was kinda nuts. I was smart enough to leave it alone then, and things went back to our normal, friendly routine.

I had lost track of Berry by the end of summer. I always figured she had grown tired of her life and took off somewhere.

Berry showed up again at the end of '65. I learned she had gone off with an older man from the next town over, and they moved to Arizona close to where her dad was living at the time. Quickly growing tired of the dude, Berry ended up living with her dad, until she got the news her mom had died of a heart attack, leaving her the family house and some money. She still had the house.

Berry got me to take my first acid trip in the Southern California foothills above our hometown. I told her about the first time I smoked marijuana, and she laughed, smoking weed for some time herself and knowing how the first time could be.

She asked me if I knew about LSD, and I told her I had heard about it in the news, where it was said to be a major ingredient of the hippie lifestyle in San Francisco. Berry said she had some and was going to drop it with several friends. Did I want to try it? I asked her a few questions about what I might experience, and having taken several trips already, she explained the possibilities. She loved the unreal effects of the drug, the colors and distorted shapes, and the way it seemed to enhance her thought processes. I said I would give it a try, once. Yeah, right, just once.

Three days later, I connected with Berry and a couple of people I had also known in high school, one of whom, Dwayne, I had gotten blitzed with on beer after a home football game. How could you forget someone you had been bent over side by side with, losing all the beer you had both so happily consumed? The other person, Gail, I had only seen on campus.

We drove up to the base of the foothills in the evening, parked Berry's car, and hiked up about a half mile into this large field of rocks, sagebrush, and sand, where a bunch of flood-control pipes about five feet in diameter were stacked below an earthen dam. The moon was full and the shadows cast by it and the huge pile of pipes made the scene definitely eerie.

Berry handed each of us a white tablet, smaller than an aspirin, which we all swallowed at the same time, chasing it down with a swig of beer from the same bottle, adding a ritual feeling to the whole scene. She told us it took about twenty to thirty minutes to work. She was right.

A short while later, I was sitting on a large smooth rock when all of a sudden it felt like it was moving under me. I hopped off to look at it, and it seemed to be breathing. Instead of being freaked, I accepted it as being normal, and assumed I simply hadn't noticed it before, without the acid to help me see.

I started inspecting my surroundings. They almost looked like they did before I took the acid, but not quite. Everything appeared to be moving slightly, and I knew I was seeing the place as it truly was, conscious living energy, having a life force of its own, but all part of the same thing. I sat down again on the rock and continued to observe the changes.

I lifted my arm and looked at my hand, then placed it on the rock. It seemed to bond somehow with the surface of the boulder, as if it was made of the same stuff. All this time, a voice in the back of my mind was telling me it was all right, and nothing could harm me there.

I separated from the rock and walked toward the others. They were standing together at the end of one of the culvert pipes, hooting and whistling into them. The sounds were a trip, man. They seemed to echo away forever. I could feel and almost see the sound waves traveling through the air.

I believed my rock was a good place for me, but when I turned back to where it had been, I couldn't find it. At first I was disturbed, but decided it had just gone somewhere else.

I spent some time exploring the plants and rocks and other natural things around me. I saw a small lizard on a rock, probably looking for a night bug in the warm summer air. I moved slowly and got close to the lizard. It tilted its tiny head in my direction and I swear, it smiled at me. What a rush! I knew lizards didn't smile, but this one did. I had my hand on the rock it was perched upon. It skittered over to my hand and put the top of its head right against the tip of one of my fingers. In a flash, it was gone. Man, I had always loved the outdoors and animals, but this was like nothing I had experienced in the Boy Scouts!

I was standing still, a short while after the lizard episode, looking up at the incredible mountains beyond me. It was too much to take in, all the energy within them evident to me. But then something shifted, and I felt some concern creep into my mind.

I looked to my left, where the dirt access road to the dam was located, and there, maybe fifty yards away, right on the road, was this large black shape. It seemed almost animal-like, but not quite. It remained where it was a while, and then started slowly coming toward where we were, sort of floating along. I sensed it was a spirit from the desert, and it didn't seem friendly. I felt a power building inside of me, coming from a place I hadn't known before. I walked directly toward this thing, closing the distance by half. I stood facing it in what I thought was a strong stance. The spirit looked like a piece of the surroundings had been cut out, leaving a black void, which was the thing's body, but it also had real energy coming off of it. I aimed my thoughts at it, saying it could not pass this way; I would not allow it. I commanded it to leave us alone, and go back to where it came from. I stuck my right arm straight out, palm facing toward the thing. Though I didn't see anything come out of my hand, I felt energy shoot over from it to the thing. The spirit seemed to shimmer and shake, and it vanished quickly into the night sky.

Whoa! What had I experienced? Did it actually happen, or was I just loaded out of my mind? Could I get back to where I started, or would I be stuck in this strange place in my head? I suddenly realized I could do whatever I wanted, and then, though I still felt a little high, I returned to a normal state of mind.

My first trip was basically over, and I joined the others, who were still playing around. It was obvious to me they had no idea what heavy things I had experienced, and I felt their trips were for entertainment. I never told them about what I had seen and done.

We shared some beers, and by the time morning light was coming up I was settled in bed in my folks' home, though sleep was a while in coming. How could I sleep after having had such a far-out journey?

I have come to realize since my first acid trip and after the ones following, my connection and understanding of the natural world was expanded by them. I feel I can sense the life in all things around me more since going through those mind-opening trips.

I had never been given an operator's manual for making the best choices in life. I only knew my parents' life was not for me. There was obviously so much going on out there, I had to start someplace else. Besides, my mother had always told me I should think for myself, and my father was too busy to say much of anything to me except, "What trouble are you getting into now?"

The pre-induction physical I had left San Francisco for was a strange happening. I was processed like some piece of equipment, to see if I passed inspection. I was there with three other guys I had graduated with from high school. They were accepted into the military, but I wasn't. I had high blood pressure, and one flat foot, along with my extremely bad vision, 600/20 in both eyes. The blood pressure thing was natural, like with my old man and his before him, but I don't think the army believed it. I was given a 1-Y, meaning "unacceptable under present standards."

I was bummed out. Tad, Steve and Cliff were going, but I wasn't. As it turned out, only Cliff came home.

I tried to enlist six months later after losing twenty-five pounds, but the blood pressure thing was still there along with the other problems, and the 1-Y stuck. Two years later when I was already living the life in San Fran, totally separated from my old ways, a 4-F card was sent to my folks' place, which they forwarded to me.

I worked a job building truck trailers those six months between the pre-induction scene and when I tried to enlist, a gig my old man set up for me with a man he used to work with.

I continued to hang out with Berry and we got real close. I guess you could say she was my first real girlfriend, though I never felt I was deeply in love with her. We did a lot together, including several more acid trips and a bunch of marijuana.

We also shared some enjoyable sex together, once on acid, but things got way too strange. Right in the middle of it, we both felt we were melting into each other, so we had to back off and regroup.

Berry also introduced me to Red Mountain Wine, the worst grape product I've ever had in my life, but it was cheap and you could buy it by the gallon. You had to suck down a water glass full at first to be able to keep drinking it. If you started by sipping, you'd never keep going.

We had some good times, even taking a trip to Death Valley together in July, wanting to experience the place when it was going full bore. Man, it was way too hot!

When the army turned me down again in '66, I took the few grand I had saved up, packed some things, said some quick so longs to the folks, jumped in the '55 Chevy I had bought, and headed up to, you guessed it brother, San Francisco, the city which had already captured my mind and soul.

I'd been thinking about the place ever since I had left. I invited Berry to come with me, but she told me she was happy with her life the way it was. So, we spent a day and a night together and parted good friends, though I never saw her again.

After returning to San Francisco, I stayed with my brother until I got my own place, a single room with kitchen and bathroom privileges. A couple of days after settling into this groovy pad on Judah Street, I met Jerome.

Jerome was a trip and a half. He was a street mime and a hash freak. He smoked it all the time, but always seemed in control. For a mime, when he wasn't doing his gig, his mouth could run on and on, some high level stuff, too. Must have been, 'cause I didn't understand what he was yakking about half the time.

He lived in the pad on the floor below mine, and if he banged on the ceiling of his room a couple of times I'd go down and we'd puff and rap. He had an authentic old hookah from Turkey or Arabia or some faraway place, with four tubes and mouthpieces.

One time, when Jerome and I were loaded, we wrapped towels around our heads and pretended to be Turkish pashas. Some silly stuff, you know? We were cracking up over our funny routine when in walks his girlfriend whose name eludes me at the moment, and two other chicks, all of them feeling mellow themselves. They got off on seeing us doing our thing, got right into it with us, and we never missed a beat doing our act.

Right in the middle of this, with Jefferson Airplane on the stereo, Jerome, in an imperial voice, demanded the girls dance for us. Giggling, the girls stripped down to their scanties and pretended to be belly dancers. I forgot the part I was playing then, and just sat staring, especially since one of them wasn't wearing any undies anyways, but an elbow in the ribs from Jerome got me back on track, and then the night got interesting.

Never in my wildest dreams did I ever figure on anything like this! I don't think the word fun covers it, man, and the dancing soon turned into something else. In those days, heavy duty bummers like HIV and AIDS hadn't happened yet, and a dose of something more traditional could be cured with a shot or two. But, those were truly sweet young ladies enjoying life, so who was I to put a damper on things? Brother, the experience was a pure delight!

I got heavily into hash myself. In those days, it was cheap and plentiful. But, hash can dry out your mind, giving you brittle thoughts. I was smoking by myself most of the time. Jerome had gotten busy with his miming and other activities. I started getting into some real downer moods, feeling bummed out and sad. I wasn't even enjoying walking through Golden Gate Park any more, checking out all the cool people. I used to sit alone and stare at the sky. Maybe it was not having any direction, I don't know, but I kept on doing hash, and sinking lower. Jerome stopped asking me over, not wanting to get dragged out by the way I was acting.

I hadn't seen my brother in a while. He was working on an important paper for school, and didn't have time for anything else. Besides, the girl he had left behind in Southern Cal had enrolled in S.F. State, and had moved in with him, so I felt I'd be imposing anyways.

I was feeling totally alone and spaced out. After smoking the last chunk of hash I had one night, I took an old .38 pistol I had brought with me from home, one I had gotten for target practice, stuck it up to my temple and pulled the trigger. No thought first, no philosophical rap with myself on the emptiness of life, I just did it. And the darn thing misfired. I swear, it misfired. I sat there feeling totally numb and stupid. I opened the cylinder and set it up to fire the same round, aimed at the base of the wall, and pulled the trigger again. This time it fired, and sounded like a stick of TNT going off.

A few minutes later, the manager, who lived in one of the ground floor apartments, knocked on my door and asked if I knew what had made the loud noise. Like a dummy, I told him it was an accident with my gun. He told me the dope smell in the air wasn't an accident, and the next day I had to go looking for a new place.

The experience was enough of a wake-up call to get me right again. I cooled it with the hash immediately, and got rid of the pistol, too.

A week later, I moved into a two-room pad on Lyon Street right off Haight, across from the little park there, uh, Buena something Park.

I had been checking out the street scene on Haight for a while, and it was amazing. You never knew what was going to happen next, street performances of all kinds, music, dancing, freak-outs, drug deals, you name it. There were always large groups of young people hanging out around the head shops, being cool with each other, talking about all kinds of far-out ideas. You know, like how groovy life could be.

Sometimes when I was hungry, I'd go down to the lower end of Haight Street to Foghorn Fish & Chips, run by this head who sometimes traded fish and chips for a few joints. When he was loaded and in a good mood, you got maybe an extra piece of fish and some extra potatoes. If he was bummed out, you'd get the usual two pieces of cod and a so-so amount of chips. It all balanced out somewhere. The place had great atmosphere, including the smell of malt vinegar in the air. I could always find someone to rap with there.

Just down from Haight Street was the Panhandle section of Golden Gate Park. 'Course in those times, anywhere around there was a panhandle area. "Spare change, Man?" was the motto, and "Get lost," or "Why don't you get a job, you bum!" the usual reply. But a panhandler with charm, using a well-thought-out routine, could make some bucks, enough to eat on or to buy some tasty mind treat.

There was always some happening going on in the Panhandle, some improv music or dancing, chanting, drums, you name it. It was mellow, easy going, and joyful, a constant celebration.

The Haight district had been another small neighborhood unto itself, as a lot of the areas outside the main downtown section were, with all kinds of small businesses, clothing, food, bars, and movies. A person could probably live in one neighborhood without ever having to leave. The street scene was slow, steady, and peaceful.

Once the Hippie Movement started and the followers moved in, the population there exploded. There were so many people on the street, they were overflowing.

I knew one believer who I don't think ever rented a pad of his own in the time I knew him. He stayed one place or another, washed dishes, cleaned, or cooked for a place to crash. Sometimes he would just hang out, looking for a young lady to live with, in her place of course, at least for a while. He wasn't out to be a user, only going with the flow of the times, being Mr. Natural. I wonder what happened to him. . . .

I remember the rent on my digs at Lyon Street being one hundred bucks a month. But after moving in, I was left with only about two hundred bucks from the money I had brought with me. I needed to find steady work.

I was already getting out of the work mindset, you know, the nine-to-five routine. But I didn't want to be a complete street person, not having a place of my own, and maybe going hungry sometimes. It wasn't an especially healthy way to live, mixing with so many other people, sharing food, threads, living space and bodies.

It was a good thing when the Haight Free Clinic got set up and the anarchistic Diggers provided free food and clean discarded threads for those who needed them, especially as time went on and the scene turned bad.

No, I needed my own space, a den to go to and let the day's activities fade out. The energy on the street could be overwhelming at times. Sometimes I fell asleep in my pad still hearing the music and laughing voices and other street sounds I had been around all day.

I spent a few days drying out and cleaning up, and started checking out the employment ads. I saw an ad for an outpatient file clerk position at a big hospital, no experience needed, so I applied. Damned if I didn't get the job, too, there being no drug testing in those days. It didn't pay a whole lot to start, but it would cover my basic needs.

I was the only white guy in the file room, all the others being black. But I acted cool, going about my business, so it went okay. I took a bunch of jive from the brothers working there, but it was all right. It was a test to see if I was uptight or if I could get down with the scene there. I fit right in.

I ended up grooving with three of the brothers who worked there. They would go out and smoke some weed at lunchtime in a private spot. After a couple of weeks they invited me along, but told me I better be cool, or they'd take care of me. So I pulled out the fat doobie I had rolled to smoke at lunch by myself, and asked them if they wanted to try some of mine, and then it was cool all right. Trouble was, their dope and mine together got us bombed in a major way, and for the first hour after lunch, progress in finding and sending charts to their appropriate locations was a little slower than usual, but a lot more fun.

The only problem with the hospital job was having to dress neatly and act straight, because sometimes one of us file clerks would have to run mail up to the hospital offices. So, when I got home from work, I would happily slip into my street threads, my sandals, funky levis, and some colorful tie-dyed or nicely made Russian-type shirt tied with a sash in the middle, and go check out the street. It was like having to live two lives at once, and was hard on my mind sometimes. At least a tied-back ponytail was acceptable at work, which made it easier.

During a lunch break, after I had been working there a while, I wandered into an unused part of the hospital. Going through a set of double doors, I found myself in a small auditorium with a curtained stage. There were some things stored behind the curtain, including the only five-cent coke machine I ever saw. There were actually some tiny bottles still in it. The embossed price by the slot read five cents.

I was checking this out when a low, quiet voice behind me said this area wasn't supposed to be occupied.

I turned around to find an old black custodian I had seen several times before in the hallways. He had a graying goatee and was always neatly dressed, including a tie, which I thought was strange for a janitor, but was impressed with this man's dignified way.

He introduced himself as Carl. We got into an interesting conversation about things in general. We even talked about jazz.

As I was leaving to get back to work, he asked me if I'd like to come to his place for dinner. He told me his wife was a good cook and enjoyed having company.

I thought for a moment, and agreed. He gave me his address and I would go there the next evening.

The next night I went over to Carl's place as planned. His wife met me at the door. She smiled openly and welcomed me in.

Carl was sitting in his living room listening to Fats Waller on the record player. He had on a cardigan sweater, brown corduroy pants, and leather slippers. He waved me in without a word, and pointed to a comfortable old chair to sit in. His wife brought in a couple of beers.

When the Fats Waller record stopped, Carl said he loved Jelly Roll Morton's music. I asked him if he was going to play some next. Acting surprised, he said, "Oh, weren't we listening to him?" I told him I thought it sounded like Fats Waller.

He smiled and said, "Quite correct, young man, quite correct."

We sat back and relaxed, listening to some great sounds. A short while later, his wife came in with plates of hot dogs and beans, which wasn't what I had expected for dinner.

Funny how such a thing can make you notice other things, such as all the furniture being worn, as were Carl's slippers and sweater. I realized this was a groovy thing he had done, inviting me over, not worrying about me judging him and his life. The three of us sat eating our food in mellow silence, the music providing us with all the sounds we needed.

After we ate, a far-out thing happened. His wife came in and handed Carl something. It turned out to be his stash box, containing a small amount of weed and papers which he rolled into a thin, straight doobie.

I must have looked surprised, because Carl smiled at me and said, "I hope you aren't going to run a jive game on me about smoking this boo. It sure would put a damper on this copacetic time we're having. You see, my wife and I go down to this certain delicatessen on Haight Street every Saturday to buy some salami and cheese. We've been doing it for years. It's amazing who you might see down there. Why I could have sworn I even saw someone who looked exactly like you a time or two." After a brief silence, we both cracked up.

The rest of the night was groovy. We listened to more fine old tunes, rapped about all sorts of stuff and smoked some more weed.

I left around eleven, and told them it had been far out visiting with them, which made them both smile. Later, at work, I slipped Carl a couple of nice joints as a thank you.

Wanting to continue our friendship, a week later I invited Carl and his wife out for dinner. He gave me a long, sad look, and politely declined, saying it wouldn't work out, and then went back to his sweeping.

It was the last time we spoke. I didn't figure it out for a long time. But I eventually realized by asking him and his wife out, I was also asking them to step out of the comfort and security of their life, and the familiar paths they followed daily. I barely knew them, so I could only wonder what had happened in their lives to put them in such a place. I think Carl was disappointed I didn't understand. Sadly, the connection between us was broken, I guess because there was no place else to go with it.

A short while later, I changed positions at the hospital, becoming a mail runner, and even though I passed Carl in the halls while delivering mail, he'd only smile, nod, and continue on.

I used to call my folks about once a month in those days. They always asked me when I could come visit for a while. I figured they were worried about me, so I finally said I would.

I got up early on a Friday, called in sick, and headed down the road, my Chevy purring all the way. I picked up one guy hitching to Salinas, and took him all the way there on Highway 101. We shared some smoke and grooved on what a sweet road 101 was to cruise. Having somebody along to have a good rap with made the ride even better.

When I got to my folks' place they were both still at work, so I decided to shower up. My mother got home from her part-time job around three, and my decision to dress and look as normal as I could probably made it easier for us both. It was good to see her.

After we talked for a while, she gave me a glass of iced tea to drink while she freshened up from work. I was sitting in a chair on the patio, enjoying the back yard with the dwarf fruit trees and other plants in my mother's garden, when she came out of the house holding the plastic baggie of joints I had brought down with me to share with people or for a quick smoke late at night outside the house. I had forgotten my mother would, without a doubt, unpack my stuff. Dangling the baggie by two fingers in front of my face she said, "Is this what I think it is?"

"Yup, it's weed," I told her, "so please put it back in my pack."

"Do you know what this would do to your father if he found out?"

"Well, I'm not going to tell him, are you?"

"Son, if you want to visit here, you have to get rid of this stuff, please."

"All right mom," I answered, "if it'll make you feel better."

I went into the bathroom, stuffed the baggie in my pocket except for one joint, and pretended to flush the goods down the toilet. Then I came out of the bathroom with the joint in my mouth. I should tell you, my mother was always curious about new things. So, I figured what the heck, I'd see what would happen.

Mom was cleaning the kitchen counter. She asked me what I was doing with the marijuana cigarette in my mouth. I told her since I had gotten rid of the rest, I was gonna enjoy this one before Pop got home.

I lit it up and took a hit. Mom told me it had a funny smell to it. Then, she pulled it out of my hand and took a humongous drag, but blew it out again. At the time, she was smoking a pack of cigarettes a day.

I laughed and told her to hold the smoke in a while, so she took another toke. I watched as she bogarded the joint, sucking the smoke in like a pro. I only got one more hit out of it.

By the time Pop got home from work, tired and hungry as usual, Mom and I were sitting in the kitchen yukking it up about nothing at all, munching on the chocolate chip cookies she suddenly had a major craving to bake and eat. He came walking into the kitchen, and said, "Hi, how come there's nothing cooking?"

My mother jumped up holding her hand over her mouth to keep from laughing, and pushing past Pop to get through the kitchen doorway, ran to the bathroom and locked herself in.

Pop looked at me and at the look on my face, and said, "What's going on with your mother?"

"I don't know, Pop," I answered, "we were having a good time talking and we must have lost track of time."

His attitude the rest of the evening told me he didn't buy my excuse, though he never did figure it out. Mom had come out of the bathroom about twenty minutes later, seeming to be all together again, and started making dinner. Pop sat in front of the TV with a cigarette, waiting to eat.

At one point while cooking, she looked at me sitting at the kitchen table and said, "I bet these burgers are going to taste good, really, really good." She let out one more giggle for good measure.

This far-out scene never repeated itself, and we never talked about it, but I know neither of us ever forgot.

The rest of the visit went as expected with all kinds of questions about who, what, and where, and was I getting mixed up in what was happening in San Francisco with all those crazy kids, and didn't they know how worried their parents must be? But they were both satisfied I was okay once I told them about my job and apartment.

By Sunday morning, I needed to head home. I promised to call more often, got a sack of salami sandwiches, fruit, and cookies from my mom, and hit the road again.

Driving back to San Francisco, I decided I was not the innocent one anymore, and my parents were out of their element with me and my life, so I had to conceal a lot for their sake. But, I know now the wheel of life, as it turns, keeps throwing new and amazing things at you until you finally have to admit, if you're honest enough, none of us knows anything about anything. We're all innocent babes in the Universe.

Back in The City, I continued to live my life, meeting new people from all over. But the hippies I hung with, starting in '66, were from Ohio. Think it seems odd, hippies from Ohio? Robert Crumb, the grand master hippie cartoonist whose work is still in demand to this day, was one of this bunch. A number of his cartoon characters were based on some of the people I knew.

These people: Chet, Kurt, Bev, Burman, and several others had come out in late '65 from Cleveland to check things out, liked the way people were tripping, and stayed on. They were a straight-up group, and I liked them a lot. I also appreciated the way they didn't take crap from anybody. At their invite, I moved in with them where they lived on Eureka Street. We all clicked well together and a strong bond developed.

We all seemed to dig the same things. Rarely was any one of us alone, grooving on the life we were living. Each new day was an adventure for us. It seemed there was always something new happening. You could say our philosophy was, "Life's too mysterious; don't take it serious."

One thing we found amusing was after the hippie movement became known all through the country, the tourists coming to San Francisco started adding a visit to Haight Street to their list of things to see and do when in town.

Many of them came touring on the famous Gray Line Tour busses, driving through the Haight-Ashbury District like one of those funny shuttles rolling through a zoo for gawking at the animals. Some of them were brave enough to actually walk the street. They would often start out with smiles on their faces, checking out all the colorful people and places, but by time they made it all the way down the street, if they did, they looked uncomfortable and nervous. The street could be overwhelming to "straights," which is what we called people who lived a normal life. Panhandlers worked out on them, teasing and hassling them if they didn't come across.

One time, I saw a hippie child, maybe ten years old, stick a fire-cracker in a fresh pile of dog poop on the sidewalk. When a middle-aged straight couple walked by, already looking edgy and tightly holding hands, he lit the cracker, and slipped behind some other people. The couple was right next to the pile when the cracker went off. Several people yelled at the kid, but the deed was done. The two tourists stood there in disbelief, splatterings of dog poop covering them from their feet to their knees.

I heard the man say, "Martha, let's go home to Twin Falls!"

Mostly though, people on the street were very cool, putting out happy vibes, sharing food or whatever they had. Me, I loved all the colorful people there.

On Haight Street, people dressed in all kinds of trippy threads or costumes. Striped and multi-colored bellbottoms were common, and sandals, moccasins, or old-fashioned looking boots were basic footgear. Brown wingtips were out. Girls wore amazing dresses like rainbows gone crazy, and collarless Russian-style shirts were popular with the men. Several hippies used to wear top hats and tails with beat-up Levis, and tie-died T-shirts or no shirts at all. Afro hairdos, even on the white guys, flourished. What an amazing carnival of life it was. Tie-dyed clothing became an identifying symbol of the "Flower Children."

One beautiful morning, I made the walk from one end of Haight to the other. The street scene was going full blast. I stopped to share in some weed several times along the way, and drank from a bottle of juice laced, I decided later, with some mild psychedelic.

I was mid-way down the street, pleasantly tripping, when I saw a short school bus painted blue, with classic flowers and acid images painted all over it. As I walked by, happily buzzing, I saw the words "Jefferson Airplane" painted on the front fender. Without even thinking, I stepped into the bus and walked slowly through it and out the open back door, a few voices inside saying, "Who are you, man?" and "Hey, uncool!"

I thought it was very cool, even if Gracie Slick herself wasn't inside. But it did seem like a box of Cracker Jacks without the prize since she wasn't there.

In those times, being a vegetarian was in, many heads not wanting to harm our living fellow creatures. Me, I liked a good steak or some fried chicken, but didn't advertise the fact.

There were many ways people who were so inclined could openly express their religious or spiritual beliefs, preaching their philosophy right on the street to anybody who would listen, or by going to any of the churches in San Francisco accepting them, weird threads and all.

The wildest place you could go for spiritual expression was Glide Memorial Church. Its exact location eludes me now, and I don't even know if, at the time, it was actually a sanctified church. But if any of the religious upper crust ever got wind of what went on there, it would have freaked them out, and I'm sure they would have shut the place down for it.

At Glide, you could find any level or type of religious or spiritual activity to get into. You could be a died-in-the-wool Christian, a Buddhist, or a Hindu fakir, and you could get some satisfaction there. As I recall, in one of the lower-level floors of the church you might even find a group of people worshiping the dark power himself, upside-down crucifixes and all. In other words, what you prayed for was probably what you got. For me, one tour through the place and I was through. I'd stick to being out in nature as my church, a lot less interference from other people's ideas.

One spring morning in 1966, I was sitting on the second-story back porch of the Eureka Street pad I was sharing with the Ohio people. It was one of those groovy old Victorian houses converted into flats, one flat per floor. All the rooms had been changed into bedrooms except for the front room, bathroom, and kitchen. These old Victorian houses had groovy back porches too, on all but the ground floor, with wooden floorboards and solid, heavy, wooden railings.

Anyway, I was checking out a groovy conga drum I had picked up at a Fillmore Street pawnshop. The wooden body was painted mostly lime green, with gold and silver stars and moons, and palm trees, and grass shacks stenciled in silhouette. The skin was worn and had a gouge, but was still playable and had good tone, at least to my amateur ear.

I was pitty-patting away on it when this brown-skinned head sticks out over the third-floor back porch railing, with the most amazing hair I had ever seen. Dreadlocks are common now, even on pasty-faced, misplaced, middle-class white boys, but at the time they were something unusual in Frisco. The head said, "If you gwine to make dat drum talk, put your soul into it, or give it to somebody who will! Here's some inspiration, mon!"

A joint came dropping down like a miracle from the heavens, and after I had a good start on smoking it, the same head with body attached came walking out onto the porch from my kitchen. We never locked our doors in those days. I guess I still don't.

His name was Russell T., a tall, lean, island boy. He and I shared the rest of the number, and then we started getting down, me on my Conga, him on a small dark-bodied drum he said had been his papa's. The sounds we made seemed to have taken on a new aspect and resonance since we started smoking the good *ganja*. We got the vibes bouncing off the walls, man. I mean, I felt full of the sounds and some heavy emotional vibrations. It was such a high-level rush.

Later, when he had to leave to give his ninety-eight year old grandmamma, who lived with him, her evening meal, I asked him when we could work out with the drums again so he could teach me more rhythms.

He told me, "You don't need me no more now; it's inside you for permanent. You only has to talk to them and they'll be talkin' back."

One evening about three weeks after my drumming experience with Russell, I was mellowed out in the front room of our Eureka Street pad with three or four of my roommates. We were joyously tripping after having dropped some honest-for-true Owsley Acid. It was clear and pure, without a bad trip in the batch. I remember Chet, Burman, and Bev were there. The whole room was glowing with our complete connection. It was like it was Christmas, and we were the lit-up decorations, making the whole place bright with good cheer. The conversation was way beyond our usual mundane level, as if the LSD had dusted off all our unused brain cells and got them humming and dancing a jig together. It was a good thing going on.

Then, there was a tiny knocking at the door. We all stopped, not only physically, but totally stopped. I mean, visitors were a constant thing. We always had somebody dropping by, usually with something cool to talk about or try, but, why now? Didn't they know there was something outstanding going on? The cerebral beehive effect was put on hold momentarily. Being closest to the door, I got up and cautiously looked through the little window. I didn't see anything. Opening the door, I lowered my gaze and saw a strange gnome-like creature looking back at me.

I wasn't sure if this was an actual being making itself known, or something we had all somehow conjured up together. Whatever the reason, standing bent over in front of me was this wee little old lady, wrinkled beyond belief, of some unknown native origins. She had an amazing multi-colored bandana on her head, big gold hoop earrings, and a gnarly old cane to help support her ancient framework. I stood there open mouthed; she seemed so perfect in her own self.

Taking the cane in her other hand, she slowly brought her right hand, index finger extended, up to the level of my face, until the tip of her bony old finger actually touched the end of my nose, and I suddenly felt locked in place, frozen in time by the smallest of contacts with this tiny, ancient woman.

"I been listening to you peoples in my mind for a whiles now," she said, "and I'm telling you, you be goin' places you shouldn't be goin' and learnin' tings you shouldn't be knowin', and you better watch you doan fall in a place you can't get out from!"

Man, did I trip out! I stood there, my mind starting to spin, and I could feel myself beginning to lose it, and then Russell T. appeared and told his grandmamma it was time to go back up to bed and leave these nice people alone.

As he took her to his door, he turned his head, winked, and said, "My grandmamma, she knows tings sometimes without even being there, you see?"

I smiled and said, "I do now, man, I do now."

At times I have wondered what ever happened to the mellow island boy and his mystical grandma. After the incident at the front door, we never saw either of them again. But people in those days were always coming and going for no apparent reason. Even if you tried to pick up on the total scene going on around you, you could never keep up with it all.

Now, the acid we took was definitely some wondrous stuff, but without Grandmama putting in an appearance, things wouldn't have gotten as deep and as wide as they did man, no way. Our collective mindset soared after her visit, which had affected all of us, and after her mysterious moment, our trip knew no bounds. Our telepathic powers came on strong. We would answer unasked questions and complete sentences for each other. There was no anger or emotional distress, no matter what was said, or how.

By the time the light of morning snuck up on us, we were all at peace. I got up and went to my room. When I opened the door, there was a groovy poster of Einstein on the far wall. You know, the one with his hair sticking out all over the place? Right then, it looked as if it was dancing. Falling onto my bed, I slept like a baby. What did I dream then? I couldn't tell you man; I really couldn't.

You know, it's strange I never had a bad trip on LSD, and I've had my share of the amazing stuff. No flashbacks either, although if I think back hard, sometimes I can squeeze out a flutter of energy, know what I mean? Even the times I used to go off on my own, like to the redwood forest up the California coast, I never lost my grip on things, no matter what happened. I saw a few people who did though.

One night, a short while before I left the pad on Eureka Street, Chet woke me up in the wee hours, saying, "C'mon man, you gotta check out this freak tripping on the street."

We went out onto the front porch and saw a naked guy running up the street a short ways and back down again, muttering and mumbling to himself, waving his arms, being far gone and weird, like a lost and confused animal. Chet and I went out to try and calm this guy down. When we got closer, the look in his eyes yelled out BAD TRIP! to us. We couldn't get to him, you know, he was too messed up. Once I tried to grab his hand to make contact, and he jumped back and screeched something at me. So, Chet and I went back inside.

Sure enough, probably because some neighbor called in a complaint, a black and white came pulling up and the last thing we saw were these two cops chasing the guy up the street. Hope he got away, but we didn't watch any more. Considering what was stashed in our place, we sure as heck didn't want to bring the scene out there inside our pad.

I remember the last acid trip I ever took. It was after the time I lived on Eureka Street. I had hitchhiked up to Mt. Tamalpais over in Marin County and walked up to a heavily-forested section to do my thing. I had brought one hit of windowpane LSD with me, and some water to drink. I sat around a while in a secluded spot not usually frequented by other people, until I felt totally at ease, and then took the acid. Half an hour later, I was communing with nature. I watched the trees on the hillside across from me waving back and forth together. The sky was clear blue, and the day was warm and bright. It seemed a perfect time. I reached down and picked up a rock. I thought, "What a beautiful round rock."

A voice spoke in my mind: "Maybe it's not round; maybe it's square."

I froze. All the life around me seemed to pause, waiting for a response. I thought, "No, it's a round rock and will remain a round rock."

As soon as I made my declaration, I was in a normal state again. The trees stayed motionless, the rock was round, and my trip was over, truly over. I had decided to remain in the world I was used to, not wanting to go somewhere else. Later, back in my room on Eureka Street, I knew I had gone as far as I could on LSD, and I never took it again.

There's a theory which states: twenty minutes after you drop LSD and it starts working, the acid is out of your system, only being an agent to get areas of your brain which are normally sleeping to wake up. The way I was able to cause my last trip to suddenly stop, makes me think this is a true thing.

I was fortunate in being able to control my mind so I was not over-whelmed by the altering power of LSD. But, like the wild guy freaking in the street, some people couldn't maintain and had some bad trips. I never told anyone they should drop LSD, and never would.

Chet, Kurt, and I were visiting someone we knew a couple of blocks off of Haight Street for some tasty organic treats to enjoy later. Kurt went out to bring back some beer and wieners for lunch. A short while later, we heard some noise and scuffling going on outside, went out and saw two straight dudes hassling Kurt. Kurt stood only about five foot six, and though he was a spunky kid, two on one is rough. Judging from their haircuts, they were some new military guys, all juiced up and in The City for the weekend, when they saw a hippie to hassle.

Chet and I trotted outside, and suggested they back off and mellow out. The two of them smelled like stale beer, and they tried to start up with Chet and me, but their attempt to beat up some wimpy hippies soon came to a grinding halt. I might have been smoking weed regularly, but I hiked around a lot, ate healthy, was a lot younger than now and I weighed over two hundred pounds. Chet was no wimp either, so we got things settled down quickly.

Then we mellowed these two boys out, got them to understand we were not the enemy, and finally we all went into the pad and smoked the peace pipe. The two young soldiers told us they were on leave from boot camp, were in Frisco for several days, and had dropped acid the day before. There were three of them, but the third G.I. started freaking out. We asked them where he was. One of them said, "Oh, in the back of our van down the street, but it's okay, he's knocked out."

"Knocked out?" I asked.

"Yeah, we had to do it 'cause he was making a real scene. We gave him a bunch of reds, and he went to sleep like a baby. We tied him up to keep him safe." These two characters looked at each other and laughed.

"But what happens when he wakes up?"

"If he behaves himself, we'll let him loose to party some more. We're going overseas after our leave's up."

The brother, whose pad is was, got jittery when we all walked in, but as the pipe went around, he was cool with it. By time the army boys left we were all brothers, and they were surely wondering what destiny had in store for them. I hope they made it back home.

There were a lot of people who used to drift in and out of our scene on Eureka Street. It was a cool place to be, a mellow three-block section off Upper Market Street where a bunch of us hippies were living, but not flagrantly spewing forth the basic philosophy of love, peace, and let's get high for all the world to see and be emotionally disturbed by.

We were what you might call conservative hippies. Sounds wrong, I know. In those days, just having long hair and wearing colorful threads made people nervous.

One evening, we were playing Monopoly in the front room, when somebody says, "Hey, check it out, Dylan's getting out of a car full of black guys!"

No, not Bob Dylan, Stan Dylan, a late Ohio arrivee, a friend of Chet's. Stan was trying to fit in and be cool. He used the hippie lingo and got high, wore the right kind of threads, but he really didn't get it, know what I mean?

He was studying to be an accountant back in Cleveland when Chet wrote him about what a trip it was living in San Francisco, so he dropped out of classes and headed west. Dylan was a natural born straight, and we all knew it.

One thing you didn't do was buy your smoke from the black brothers. It just wasn't cool. Nine times out of ten they'd run a scam on the easy marks they figured hippies to be.

Anyways, Stan comes walking in with a paper-wrapped package looking for all the world like a key, you know, two-point-two pounds of hemp to smoke.

"Stan the Man!" says Chet. "Tell me you didn't buy weed from the brothers!"

"Hey," says Stan, thinking he had finally done something to get in our groovy graces, "it's cool, Chet. They were really mellow dudes. I had a taste and it's good smoke, and it only cost seventy-five bucks!"

Right away we knew it wasn't right. You could get a decent key for maybe one twenty-five then, sweet and a good high. So, we went into the kitchen, the bunch of us, cleared the table, covered it with newspaper, and prepared for the traditional ritual of Breaking-Down-the-Key, so we could each buy some depending on how much bread we had. Stan tore open the wrapping.

At first glance it looked okay, nicely pressed and smelling sweet. But then, when Stan tried to break it in half, there was some obstacle. He broke one end off, and then we saw it. Talk about a communal head shaking.

Kurt said, "At least you'll be able to make some cookies for munchies after smoking some of this wondrous weed." Right there, in the middle of the grass was a one pound bag of flour.

Stan was totally blown out, bummed and humiliated, and he never quite recovered from this one, maybe 'cause we never stopped reminding him of it. "Hey, Stan, bought any good weed lately?"

Not too long after this happened, Stan decided, with some help from Chet, the San Francisco scene was not for him. So back he went to Cleveland with our blessings.

By this time, late 1966, don't ask me what month, I had stopped working for the Hospital. I guess having to live in two worlds was getting heavy for me. My hair was crying out to be free, and the neatness thing was bugging me. So, I left the job.

About a week later, I was browsing through the Purple Heart Thrift Store downtown, when a flash of inspiration came over me. I usually frequented the second-hand stores to find groovy garments to wear on the street. Why not buy a bunch of stuff from the different thrift stores to sell instead of buying some things to use myself? There were always loads of unique, old, and far-out threads and other items in the thrift stores. I could set up something on Haight Street, and see how it went. People sold all kinds of stuff on the street, T-shirts, weird acid sketches, candles, incense and holders, you name it.

So, I took forty bucks and bought some threads I knew people in Haight-Ashbury would like. I went to Purple Heart, St. Vincent De Paul, Good Will, and Salvation Army trying to be choosey, and making deals. Amazing how much forty dollars would buy then. I mostly got shirts, dresses, a few hats, and even one pair of old ladies' high-button shoes. The thrift stores back then had some amazing stuff. Nowadays, most all thrift stores look alike, clothing all the same, junky kids toys, crappy furniture, and the like.

A few days later, I took my goods to Haight Street, laid an old blanket down, and neatly piled my stuff around me. I had a thermos of coffee, some peanut butter sandwiches, and a cushion to sit on. It felt very mellow sitting there.

A couple of hours later, all my items were gone, man, all gone, and I had about one hundred and twenty dollars in my pocket. What a rush! Some people had tried to trade me stuff, but I held out for cash.

These days, I guess I would be considered an entrepreneur. I figured I would see how far I could go with this, so I started hitting the thrift stores once or twice a week. Nobody else seemed to be doing the same thing at the time, so I acted like I was buying for myself and friends to keep my thing low key.

After about a month, my little business was going so good, I traded my '55 Chevy, which was a nice machine, for a '57, one-ton, International step van. This way, I could carry what I bought more easily and sell right out of the back, keeping things cool by putting coins in the parking meter. Then, storeowners couldn't hassle me for sitting in front of their place, like even the head-shop owners did, and the kids who tried to steal my stuff when I sat on the sidewalk couldn't ruin my day anymore.

Having the van also had some unexpected bonuses. Sometimes chicks would change into a top or skirt right there in the van to see if they fit. Yeah, those were some sweet days.

The old van was cool. It had lots of room, so I made it into a Gypsy wagon, with a fold-down plywood bed, a Coleman stove, and later, a tiny homemade wood stove for heating. On one side of the van were shelves and racks for my sellables. I could sit comfortably on the bed or on a folding chair in there with both back doors open, and people would look in and I'd invite them to check out the stuff, so I didn't even have to make it known outside what I was doing. This was a good thing, since I didn't have a business license and the cops would make random sweeps down Haight to hassle us street people, so I could say people were only visiting. If I had the parking meter paid up, it was cool.

Once my business became known, the flow was amazing. I didn't allow smoking weed or doing other drugs in the van, to avoid hassles while I was doin' business, but did do some bartering from time to time at the end of the day.

To make sure I got a chance at the good stuff in the thrift stores, I bribed the people working there to let me check out things before they were put out front for sale. One righteous brother, Art, was especially good about things. He worked at Purple Heart, I think. I'd give him twenty bucks a week, and sometimes he'd put good stuff aside for me.

One morning early, I went in and Art pulls me aside, saying, "I got something real interesting in back, but it's gonna cost you."

I had extra money by then, so I said, "You're on, Art, let's check it out."

In the back room, hidden under some old blankets and such, was one of those old round-top trunks, a scarce item even in those days, in great condition and locked. I had a gut feeling this might be a real treasure, and asked Art what he wanted for it, on the sly, of course. At first he wanted thirty-five, but only named his price after having me lift one end and heft it. It was heavy. I finally got Art down to twenty-five dollars, and the deal was done. He helped me load it up by the back door, and I took my treasure home.

Once I got the trunk into my place, I made a cup of coffee and sat, contemplating the problem of opening the lock without hurting the trunk. I knew it was old, maybe turn of the century, so no telling what lay within. I didn't want to break the latch, but had no key to fit it. Bit by bit, I pried and gently levered the latch side to side with a screwdriver until finally, after I gave it a sharp pull, SNAP! The latch came free. I lifted the lid of the trunk and sat for a few moments looking at what had been revealed.

There, right on top of the layers of threads in the trunk was this far-out, black sequined-and-beaded dress. It made me think of photos I had seen here and there of women in the 1920s, out partying and dancing. Under it was another dress, not as gaudy, but old, maybe one a woman would wear at home or shopping, a yellow dress with a white lace collar. I took out five or six different dresses, all in great condition.

Under the dresses were two pairs of shoes wrapped in paper, one pair red with sequined black bows, and one black shiny leather pair with tiny, gold-colored buckles. The leather wasn't cracked and dried, either. There was a man's wool tweed jacket, and white suit, made of linen, maybe.

There were not only other threads in the trunk, but also several old magazines from the early '20s, romance magazines. I figured maybe this was a trunk of threads that had been taken on a cruise, and I could envision some chick laying on a deck chair reading.

The last thing on the bottom was a costume, maybe for a Halloween party. It was wild, man. There was a pair of pointy-toed green and red slippers with bells on the curled-up toes, some green tights, a multi-colored velvet shirt, and a hat, if you could call it a hat. It had a round body, but four points came up from the base, one yellow, one red, one green and one black. These long floppy points had bells on them, too. I tried the hat on, and damned if it didn't fit! Okay, a little snug, but not too bad.

Brother, I had really lucked out! I didn't want to blow it with these treasures, so I went to an antique store on Fell Street and got this stuff appraised. The lady there was straight up with me about what the stuff was worth, and wanted to buy the sequined dress herself. I forget exactly what I got for it, but I know it more than paid for the whole trunk full, plus some. Righteous!

I loved the path I had picked for myself, living where I was, among the people I was with, in and around the Haight, and making my nut doing the old threads business. It was like being on a treasure hunt all the time. It fit right in with the street scene, too.

I decided to wear the crazy hat for laughs when I was selling from the van. Most people thought it was cool, and a few wanted to trade me out of it. Then, one girl told me it was the type of hat court jesters used to wear in the days of castles, knights, and wizards.

"I guess you must be a jester yourself," she said, and I liked the sound of it. I decided to make the hat part of my business scene.

The next day, we had a painting party on Eureka Street, and changed the looks of the van forever. It had originally been a seafood delivery van, and you could still see the faded crabs painted on each side. We bought some bright yellow paint, and with wide brushes painted the whole van, with the rub bars on each side painted red. But the entire flat front of the van was decorated with a smiley face, though some people later said it looked wild and scary as I drove it down the street, as if it wanted to chew them up. Of course, we were all loaded when we did it.

Kurt did a good job of painting **JESTER'S** on the lower middle of each side, with an image of the hat above it as I asked him to do, since he was the artistic one of the group. It looked good. I don't know if naming the business helped much, but it didn't hurt. I became an item on the street for a while. Later, I would paint the van much more subdued colors, and get rid of the face on front after it got busted up and looted outside Santa Cruz, though it happened after the life had started going sour anyways. But, ever after, I've been known as Jester, it being the name I give, and I guess, except for official business, it's how it will always be.

The powerful draw the scene in the Haight had on so many young people was amazing, man. There was an energy not to be denied. Once the news stations had been reporting on it for a while, young people were coming from all over the country, and eventually, people from all over the world were tripping on it. The Flower Power motto of "Peace and Love" fascinated them, and people started taking a different look at life, a radical one for most.

The idea of people living together in groups with no regularly scheduled activities including work, was too much for most normal citizens to accept, branding us lazy kids, irresponsible, and of no real use to society. The heavy drug use and easy sex freaked out straight people, and it created a real break between the generations.

Even though I loved the scene, I still had a need to make my own way and do my own thing. The communal lifestyle didn't suit me, though I enjoyed hanging out with all the people. Guess I couldn't totally give up on all the aspects of normal society, though so many others tried to. 'Course, I wasn't alone in this, or else the hippie store scene would not have happened as it did. Head shops thrived all up and down the street, selling threads, artwork, food, and drug accessories. I've heard there are still hippie stores on Haight Street even now, but I never go to S.F. anymore, so I'm not really sure.

Speaking of hippie power, one day someone unexpected showed up on our Eureka Street doorstep, in 1967, I think. It was Chet's brother Wilton, come out from Ohio to see how his younger brother was doing. Seems Chet's momma was worried about him, and since Chet hardly ever wrote, she convinced Wilton to fly out and see how things were.

Wil arrived dressed in a gray, three-piece, Brooks Brothers suit. He had a short haircut parted on the side, black plastic-framed glasses and brown wing-tipped shoes. He was a stockbroker, and looked the part. He was uncomfortable at first, as if he had walked into a pad full of crazies. But, by evening he had relaxed, taken off his jacket and tie, and was enjoying himself a bit. Then, Bev brought out the dish of brownies she had baked. Yeah, I know, we should have told him, but Chet said his brother Wil needed to loosen up, so . . . .

The brownies got us all tripping, including Wil, who was laughing and yakking it up with the rest of us. Being smart, he figured out the brownies were the reason relatively normal conversation seemed so funny. We admitted to the extra ingredient in them, and he confessed he had smoked once with friends at a party, but not enough to mess himself up.

The next day, Chet, being about the same size as Wil, loaned him some Levi's and a work shirt, and we all went down to Haight Street. We could see Wil taking it all in. He was amazed. I guess Ohio in the Sixties was still Heartland America, though Wil lived in cosmopolitan Cleveland. He completely fell in love with the place and what was going on. The first time we went to Foghorn Fish & Chips though, Wil wouldn't eat food from the place. He complained the tables and floor were dirty and there were dogs lying around under the tables. I told him I had never heard of anybody getting sick; at least I didn't think so.

After heading into the Park off of Stanyon Street at the end of Haight, we all sat down by Hippie Hill, and got loaded, including Wil. While we were there, he traded his wing tips for some funky old huaraches. The rest of us looked at each other and smiled.

Walking back up Haight later, Wil had a full-blown case of the munchies. He decided Foghorn Fish & Chips would be a great place to eat after all. We all started cracking up. Wil went in and came back out with a double batch. I guess the owner was high and happy.

A few blocks further up the street, this sweet-looking blonde girl, maybe eighteen or nineteen, comes up to Wil and asks if he wants to share his food. Wil went into a peace, love, what's your sign, your pad or mine trip with her, tells Chet he'll see him later, and floats away with this delightful young female. Then Chet tells us Wil had a real thing for the ladies, and always had a girlfriend around.

Kurt said, "He'll fit in, no problemo."

Hooking up with someone was almost too simple. Sometimes you didn't even have to say anything. If the two of you smiled the right way at each other, the next stop was some cozy private place and a wee bit of heaven! A typical line might be: "Peace, love, what's your sign? Scorpio? Far out, I love Scorpios. Want to go somewhere and do some groovy acid? Cool."

The Haight Street Free Clinic was always busy.

We didn't see Wil for two days, and when he showed up, he had a tie-dyed shirt, his old sandals, and a flower painted on one cheek. His glasses were gone, but luckily his sight wasn't too bad without 'em. A week later, he called the place he worked for back in Ohio, and got a leave of absence for a family emergency. But as far as I know, he never went back.

He proceeded to visit Haight Street daily, sampling the life, including any groovy chick he could connect with. He was like a kid in a candy store with a fistful of quarters. His hair and beard were growing out fast. Kurt had been right, He slid right into the scene, man.

But, a few weeks after he arrived, he bombed out. Seems he woke one morning scratching. Yup, you got it, crabs! Body lice, a common condition in those days. He took care of them with some lotion or other, but several days after, his urges kicked in again, and off he went, vowing to only groove with very clean young ladies. Right. Another dose of crabs, and Wil had his nickname, given to him by us all. Commodore Crab it would be. He shrugged, smiled and kept on doing his thing.

The money he had from his successful career back in Ohio made it possible for him to enjoy life without being concerned about the basics: food, shelter, and good drugs. He didn't mind sharing with us, so we didn't lack for much until he moved out to his own place, about two months after he'd arrived in the city.

About the time he left Eureka Street, he had started messing around with LSD, and had gotten heavily into Leary's philosophy of "Turn on, tune in, and drop out." His brother Chet was concerned about this, and told us he didn't think Wil would be able to cope with what acid could do. Chet said Wil had a very high-strung mind.

Many years later, while I was traveling in the vicinity of Nevada City, California, not far up the highway from San Francisco, I went to visit friends who were living in a commune up there, still going strong. I went to see my old friend Larry and his sweet wife Robin. We were having a good time walking around and rapping about the old Frisco days, but then I noticed someone I thought I knew sitting on the ground enjoying the day, so I went up to say hello and got shocked right outta my skin. There in front of me, clean and healthy looking was Wil, Chet's brother! I mean, this was around 1985, you dig? I squatted down in front of him and said, "Wil? Is it you, man? It's me, Jester. What's going on?"

With a distant look in his eyes, he said, "Yes, I knew a Jester. Are you the same Jester?"

"Yeah, man, it's me," I replied. "How are you?"

Wil said, "Hard to say, hard to say. All day I dream of things I used to know, but then I'm here, and the trees talk to me and tell me this is my place now."

"Cool, Wil. You're okay; this is your place," I told him.

I tried to talk to him some more, to see where life had taken him, but he drifted away somewhere in his mind, and sat staring out from wherever he was. I could only walk away. Larry told me Wil had come wandering up the road a few years before, dirty, barefoot and beat up. The commune took him in. "He does the chores we ask him to do so he can earn his keep and stay here, but sometimes his mind stops, and has to be jumpstarted again."

This left a sad knot in my belly, you know? He had been such a sharp-minded, together young man when I first met him! I have to say I felt guilty, as if I'd had a hand in what had happened to him.

The Haight scene might have been a blast for some people, and changed other people's lives for the better in some ways, but there were some like Wil, who got burnt up in the process, probably more than most know about. I hope he's still safe from harm on the commune.

There was a small group of kids who lived on our section of Eureka Street. They weren't choirboys, but were not nasty gun-toting punks like the gangbangers these days, either. They were just some neighborhood boys who hung together. They did get into some bad stuff though, no doubt about it.

The two I got to know best were brothers, Craig and Wallace McRae. They were only fifteen and thirteen, but savvy for their age. They knew the ways of the streets in their part of San Francisco.

Craig, the older McRae boy, loved to steal cars for joyrides, even after he did some juvenile time for it. The McRae brothers seemed to dig us hippie folk, meaning myself and the ones I was tight with on Eureka, because, as Wallace put it, "You ain't wimpy like some of the other freaks we've seen."

One time, several of us "hippie freaks" were sitting on the front porch, midmorning, sucking up some caffeine, when Craig drove up in a shiny, new-looking Lotus sports car. He asked if any of us wanted to go for a ride. Nobody took him up on his offer, and I told him he was nuts to keep doing the joyride thing, and whatever he was getting out of it wasn't worth the trouble he'd get into if he got caught again. He said, "They're not gonna catch me, Jester, I'm too quick for 'em!"

He flashed me a toothy grin, and roared off down the street. It was his nature I guess; the boy was being himself. He showed up later on foot, having avoided the heat one more time.

We let the street kids from our neighborhood use the basement room of our building, which was reached through the backyard, to hang out in. You could have called it a clubhouse, but not like Our Gang used to have. They got pretty frisky a few times, and we had to tell them to hold it down so a straight neighbor wouldn't put in a call to the cops, which wouldn't be cool for us in the pad. Sometimes, we'd catch a whiff of weed they were smoking, and we'd bang on the door and tell them to cool it. All we needed was for the heat to come snooping around, always having something in our place not technically legal.

Craig came to the front door one day. I was the only one there at the time. He told me if I liked to drink, I could come over to his place because his dad had brought a new batch of proof bottles home. His father, Angus McRae, worked for Hiram Walker in San Francisco, and Wallace had once told me he would bring proof bottles home. They never mentioned their mom, who must have been out of the picture for a while, but I never pushed for details.

Feeling the need for a change of pace, I said I would come up for a sip or two, even though I didn't care for the idea of his dad catching me with his young son drinking his booze in his pad.

We walked up the stairs to the second-story flat, and I sat in the kitchen while Craig brought in several small bottles from a back room. He cracked the seal on one of them, and poured us each a two-fingered shot. Man, what good booze, stronger than store whiskey, but smooth. Craig drank his down without a hitch. He told me Wallace was keeping watch for his dad, but he must have forgotten his assignment, because about half an hour into the sampling, who comes stomping up the stairs but Mr. Angus McRae himself. Angus and I had exchanged hellos a time or two, but it was obvious he was no great fan of us hippies. Mr. McRae was the classic, square Scotsman, being as wide as he was tall, and Craig told me he competed in the Highland Games when they were held in town.

"Craig," he says in a deep and stern voice, "how many times have I told ya not to be getting into my bottles, eh?" Then he reaches under the kitchen table with one hand, lifts it and tosses it aside, bottles, cups, and all flying every which way. He glares at me and says, "Be out of my home right now!"

Craig nods at me, and I split, figuring family was family. I could hear them getting into it as I hit the door. What a bummer.

A couple of days later, I saw Craig sitting on his front porch, sporting a shiner and a split lip. When I asked him how he was, he said, "I gave as good as I could, but my old man is still too strong to beat!"

The street kids were always trying to get us to share some weed with them, but we didn't want to lay any smoke on these minors. It wasn't our way. There were plenty of others who would have, but those were the same jerks who sometimes used to give a dose of LSD to cats and dogs, sometimes killing them. Speaking of which, someone visiting at the Eureka Street flat once got our housecat loaded.

The cat had come wandering in one day and decided to stay. He was a real alley cat, with one chewed up ear and the tip of his tail missing, so I guess living with us was his retirement plan. All in all, he was a mellow feline, as long as you didn't play too hard with him, 'cause he didn't know when to stop.

Anyway, we had a few people partying with us at the time, and one of them, we figured later, slipped the cat a little LSD. He started getting weird, hissing and running here and there, trying to get away from whatever was messing with his head. We didn't know who had done it, except it sure wasn't one of us, and figuring it was such a messed up thing to do, we shut the party down. The cat was out of it all night, moaning and running around.

By the next morning he was chilled out, but the poor guy couldn't get comfortable. He'd lie down for a while, then a minute later try another position. He'd sit a few minutes somewhere, then get up and go somewhere else. We got used to it, except nobody could safely pet him anymore, or sit too close to him on the couch, 'cause he'd give you a good nip, except for Bev, whose female vibes seemed to help him stay cool.

About three weeks after this happened, a few of us were perched on the front porch, and the cat came and sat near us on the top step. Up the street comes this shepherd-mix dog, happily trotting along, tongue hanging out. Just as he passes by the porch, the cat sees him, and with a low growl, leaps off the porch and jumps right onto the side of the dog and turns into this furry cyclone! With all four sets of claws and his jaws going, he starts working his way around this poor beast, who is taken totally unawares and starts running up the street going "Yii! Yii! Yii! Yii!," not knowing what was going on, only wanting it to stop. The cat continues to work his way around the dog's middle for at least half a block, then finally drops off, comes back to the porch, and sits down with this satisfied look on his face, wads of dog fur stuck in his mouth and claws.

After ravaging the dog, he was okay again. He must have decided the poor dog was the cause of all his discomfort, and now he had gotten even.

At any rate, all the people on Eureka Street, the hippies, the street kids, the regular folk were able to maintain a mellow level with each other, and no major problems ever came up.

As I said before, to most people on the outside looking in, the Eureka Street hippies seemed to be a strange, shiftless bunch, but we were actually a self reliant group. When it came to taking care of ourselves, we were like-minded. Clean-shaven Chet was working for the Post Office, Kurt was selling a lot of his drawings and paintings on Haight Street in the tourist section by the Marina, and Bev was actually a secretary downtown. The only one who quit working to trip out full time was Wil, who I told you about, but he had money to burn from his former straight life.

But once we were home, away from our chosen work, we really got into our free time. Me, I was lucky because what I did to survive, my van business, meant I could live the way I wanted all the time. There was no separation between my work and my life.

As far as drugs were concerned, none of us there on Eureka Street were what you would call addicts. None of us used smack or mainlined. We enjoyed getting ripped as more of a recreational scene, though there was a spiritual side, and we didn't make trouble for anyone.

A small old bus came rolling up in front of our Eureka pad one day, a Saturday as I recall. It was painted a dark green, like an old forestry vehicle, which, it turned out, it had been. Out steps Kurt and the owner of the bus, who was dressed more like a mountain man than a hippie from The City. He had on a deerskin shirt, striped old-fashioned pants, and tall, leather moccasins.

Kurt had met him on Haight, and invited him over to meet us. He was called "Captain Walt," and he was a trip. About six feet tall and lean, he had long hair held back with a leather band around his forehead and a long, droopy mustache, but no beard. He wore an amazing black leather belt with a large silver buckle beautifully formed in the shape of a snake's head.

The curtains he had hung on his twenty-passenger bus hid the groovy interior he had created. Attached to the ceiling was the traditional East Indian fabric hung in so many hippie pads with pictures of elephants, outrageous flowers, and dancing Indian statues. The walls in the back portion around the built-in bed were covered with thin wood shingles. There were old-time photos on the walls. One side of the bus had custom-built cabinets ceiling to floor, with a number of thin drawers. There was a fold-down worktable, and the other side had cabinets with lots of supplies and tools in them. In the roof there were two beautiful stained-glass sunroofs, which he had made.

Captain Walt was a jewelry maker, working mostly with silver and stones, but also some gold. He did rings, bracelets, and necklaces, along with some amazing castings and carvings, in miniature, of people and animals. The man was good. He was a bit older than us, in his early thirties. He was easy going, but I sensed he had real spine, too. I picked up on a calm steadiness to the man. You could see it in his eyes.

In rapping with Walt, we learned that he had spent many years in the wilds of Alaska, living with his uncle, a bona fide woodsman, as Walt put it. He told us about wild winters and wilder people, gold panning, plus a couple of run-ins with cranky bears, before he felt the need to travel and meet different people. He had been on the road ever since.

All of us enjoyed his cool, laid-back personality, along with his highly crafted and unique jewelry, which he displayed for us on a tour of his rolling workshop. So we invited him to stay a while. He took us up on our offer, and parked his bus in the back yard next to the Jester van, which he found to be highly whimsical, as he put it. While visiting, he made a couple of suggestions on how I could make better use of the insides of the van, which I appreciated.

Walt stayed at our place about a week. Even though all of us liked having him there, he and I developed a special connection during his stay. The two of us spent several evenings talking about our thoughts and feelings on life, which made it obvious Walt had some amazing experiences come his way.

On his last day with us, he gave Kurt, Chet, and me each a ring he had chosen from the drawers in his bus, which were filled with some mind-blowing examples of his craft. But, he gave Bev an amazing old Navajo necklace he had recently picked up. She had visited his bus several times by herself during his stay, spending quite a bit of time in there, so I suppose you could say they left a lasting impression on each other.

Captain Walt also left us a nice bag of peyote buttons. He had come up from a long stay in the Southwest, connecting with a number of Indian artists and craftsmen. He had shared some high-level mescaline experiences with some of them, taking part in some ceremonies.

We figured we might not see the Captain again. There was a lot of world out there to explore and be inspired by. As he warmed his bus up to leave, I told him I was sorry he had to go so soon.

Walt gave me a broad smile and said, "Don't worry, brother, we'll meet again." I had the feeling he was right.

I still have the silver and opal ring he gave me, part of a small, select bunch of things I've kept over the years from different times in my life.

A few days after his visit, we decided to make use of the peyote he had given us, remembering the things he had suggested "for a fulfilling journey," as he put it. Chet, Kurt, Bev and I went up on Mt. Tamalpias across the Bay in Marin County, "Mt. Tam" to locals, to take our trip. Our friend Ed, known as "Steady Eddie," came along to act as straight man, in case of a bad trip, and as driver.

Mt. Tam was a beautiful, peaceful area in spite of the large number of people who visited there. We had a place all picked out, almost all the way to the top. There was some facility there with a large parking area. But, if you hiked a ways further up, there were places where you could be all to yourself, with an amazing view of San Francisco across the bay.

We sat in a circle amongst some trees, and ate our peyote buttons, all of us with empty stomachs as Walt had told us to do. A short while later, Chet and Bev threw up, which can happen with the raspy peyote buttons. Kurt and I held ours down. Even if you tossed your buttons, you still got off.

About twenty minutes later, I felt what I can only describe as a "shift" in my surroundings, like when a scene is cut in a movie and you see a flicker in the film. The peyote had kicked in.

I interacted with the others for a while, but during the major part of my trip I was communing with all the natural things, the trees and rocks on Mt. Tam. I sensed their consciousness, their life energy, in ways I had before on other trips, but I never grew tired of being so aware.

I didn't pay much attention to the others, who didn't notice me doing my own thing anyway. When I was tripping, other people usually interfered with the process.

I wandered off a ways by myself so nothing could break my mindset. As I lay on the grass, I could feel the life beneath me. The earth seemed to be breathing, the trees whispering and dancing, and the boulders around me humming in low tones, but I wasn't afraid, and accepted what was happening. I became a part of it, and felt no one could see me as being separate from it all.

After a time I got up. I had heard someone calling my name. "Come and see the fog," the voice said. It was Bev; she was waving to me. I went down to where she and the others were, on the hillside overlooking the large parking lot which seemed like a wound on the land. As I sat there with them looking across at San Francisco, this huge thick blanket of fog rolled quickly in over the bay and the city, covering all but the tallest buildings and upper parts of the Golden Gate Bridge towers. It didn't take long for it to remove all signs of human activity from sight.

We all sat there completely silent in our own bodies, feeling humble and in awe. Bev started to cry from the overwhelming power and beauty of it. Man, I can still feel it, just by telling you what happened.

Then Kurt said, "Wow, wouldn't it be far out if the fog went away and the city was gone, man?"

We all sat there thinking about what he had said, trying to get our heads around such a freaky thing happening, until Bev said it was time to go home. The spell was broken, and we split.

It was a good thing we had brought Ed with us as a driver, a very good thing, as we were all too high to get back to Eureka Street. Who knows where we would have ended up! It was weird though, driving through the heavy fog, slowly cruising to our pad.

By the time we got home, most of the power of the peyote was gone. We ate a huge, heavy-duty salad Bev had made the night before. It was delicious. After we ate and evening had arrived, I took a walk to a favorite spot of mine a few blocks up Eureka.

It was where an old house had been torn down a long time ago, and was a grassy field now, with some parts of the low retaining walls left. I lay down in the grass, which hid me from people and cars going by. The fog had faded away, and the sky was clear and cloudless. I smoked a long roach. It seemed to bring back some of the peyote energy.

As I lay there, all the planets appeared before my eyes: Mars, Saturn, and Jupiter, like in science films I had seen in school. I was totally tuned into the amazing scene before me. After some time had gone by, I heard some soft, quick footsteps coming up to me, and lay there waiting to see what was making them. The footsteps stopped suddenly, as a dog's head appeared above mine. The dog, a Doberman I think, looked down and saw me looking up at it. It was held by my stare until I blew a puff of breath at its quivering nose. The dog's eyes seemed to flare open a moment, then it made a little yelping noise and an instant later it was gone, its running paw steps quickly fading away.

I've never told anybody about the dog scene before, and I know it may not sound as powerful to you as it felt to me. It was a rare and special moment. All I can do is try to tell it as it happened and hope some of it will connect with you. This way, at least, maybe some understanding of it will be shared, along with all the other things I tell you. It's all I can ask for. I'm gonna disappear someday, as the dog has by now, and as we all will. So, maybe something of me will be left behind, for what it's worth.

Kurt had a nice old Norton motorcycle. It was left chained up inside the garage behind the Eureka Street pad when he wasn't riding it. We had seen the kids checking it out, but reached a definite understanding with them about the consequences if it was messed with, especially with Craig, who seemed offended when we thought he would bother our stuff.

I had ridden bikes before coming to San Francisco, and Kurt was cool enough to let me ride the Norton a number of times. I enjoyed the rush it gave me when I cranked it on going down an open road. It handled well on the curves, too.

On one occasion, I had taken it across the Bay to Marin County, above the town of San Rafael. There were a lot of narrow, twisty roads in the foothills of Marin. The weather was beautiful, warm and clear.

I had stopped to take a leak by the side of the road, when several people on motorcycles stopped for the same reason I had. There was an old BMW and a couple of Hondas, I think. After taking care of our business, we all started rapping about what a great day it was for riding.

There were two single guys and one couple. After talking for a while, they told me they were on their way to a party, and invited me along. I was cool with it.

We wound our way up to a very nice pad near a hilltop. I had no idea whose place it was, and never did find out. It must have been a custom-built pad, blending in with the terrain, with lots of windows to catch the warm sun and a groovy open area in the middle of the place under a large skylight with a leafy tree growing there.

There was a mellow bunch of people there, most of them having ridden motorcycles to the place. Before I knew it, I had a glass of tasty wine in one hand and a half-smoked joint in the other. I wandered around, digging the company I was in, rapping with everybody. The pad was nicely furnished with lots of fine things, paintings, sculpture and old furniture, which I enjoyed checking out.

49

Then somebody suggested I reach into a large paper bag and grab some magic mushrooms. Go with the flow I always say, so I did. I munched on a bunch, followed by another glass of wine, and before long I was grinning from ear to ear. They gave me a lighthearted, humorous high.

On one side of the pad was a long redwood deck with a huge hot tub built right into one end. My joyfully tripping mind told me soaking in the hot tub would be the perfect thing to do. There were five or six people in it already, but I swear it could have held ten more. I stripped down and slid right in, with nobody objecting. Before long, I had the feeling that I was melting away, becoming part of the water in the tub, but then somebody laid their foot on my naked crotch. I didn't mind, but suddenly realized I didn't know whose foot was touching me, and it was a mixed group in the tub.

I abandoned my seat in the tub, picked up my threads, and tried to glide nonchalantly away. But I heard some quiet chuckling going on behind me. Maybe I should have found out whose foot it was.

I was out of it, the closest thing to a bad trip I ever experienced, feeling out of place and unsure of the scene. I decided I didn't know these people or all their ways of enjoying themselves, what my place was with them, or if I even had one. I wouldn't have minded making it with some friendly chick, but I had the feeling this scene might go past the point of where I was willing to wander. I got dressed, kicked the Norton's engine over, and headed out.

I was still tripping heavily, but the steady, solid beat of the engine helped me maintain control, and I ended up enjoying the ride. I wasn't sure of the way out of the hills and back to The City. As hard as I tried, I never seemed to get there. I must have ridden around for a couple of hours, trying to figure out the right direction of travel to get myself back to S.F.

There are a number of dams all through the Marin hills, changing the streams running through them into a number of finger lakes, part, I guess, of the water reservoir system there.

Riding along, I came to the end of one of these dams. I was alone, at night, no traffic anywhere on this two-lane, country road. I parked the Norton, and wandered on foot along the road where it crossed over the dam. About halfway across, there was a manhole cover off to one side. Blame it on the mushrooms or the full moon, but I lay down on the dam, right in the road, and put my ear to one of the holes in the manhole cover, wondering what sounds were inside of a dam. I found out.

At first, I could only hear what sounded like dripping water, but then, I heard a strange, high-pitched, pinging sound, like when somebody makes harmonic sounds on a guitar, way up the strings. Then I heard another, slightly off the tone of the first, then another. I was getting locked into listening to these eerie sounds. But something happened, chilling me all over. The sounds started getting louder, as if they were getting closer to my ear, like maybe they were zoned in on me tripping on them. I was getting edgy about this eerie thing happening. The sounds were definitely getting closer to my ear, and my mind.

With some real difficulty, I pushed myself up and away from the manhole cover. Standing there, I sucked in a few breaths, having forgotten to breathe for a minute. I was glad to be away from those sounds, and then, standing there I heard a loud ping! seeming to come from under the manhole cover. I ran to the Norton, almost falling over trying to kick-start it and get away. I finally got it together and rode back the way I had come, faster than was safe.

The further away I got from the dam, the better I felt, and I slowed down, figuring I had been lucky to get away from whatever it was. I finally wound my way out of the hills and back on the highway toward The City, Eureka Street, and home. I got back, chained up the bike, and went in. It was late, and I was the only one awake, which was okay with me.

I went into the kitchen to make coffee. I was looking in the fridge for some munchies, when I heard a tiny sound. It was coming from the sink, where the faucet always dripped. I went to the sink and stood to listen. The next time a drop of water left the faucet and hit the sink, I heard a quiet but definite ping! I ran out of the kitchen, into my room, and jumped into bed, threads and all, covered my head, and remained so 'til I fell asleep, thinking, "Man, those were some heavy duty mushrooms."

I never heard the pings again, and I never told Kurt about my mushroom ride on his Norton.

One day, I drove the Jester van down to the Great Highway, the coastal highway beginning at the ocean end of Golden Gate Park, near Playland Amusement Park. The highway heads south out of S.F. toward Half Moon Bay, then Santa Cruz and on down the line. I guess you could call it the headwaters of Highway 1.

Actually, where I was headed was on the "Lesser" Great Highway, which parallels the main one for a ways, only one step to the east of it, with a high grassy embankment separating them for several miles.

There are tunnels cut through the embankment as walkways to the beach and public restrooms normal people don't use. The Lesser Great Highway runs for a few miles from the base of Golden Gate Park off Lincoln Way down to the S.F. Zoo and Fleischaker's Pool, or where it used to be, and there it dead ends.

I had been invited to a party in one of the pads overlooking the sea, along the Lesser Highway. I parked the van and walked a couple of blocks to the party.

The place was owned by a straight couple trying to be hip, who had bought a few things from my van on the street. I figured they wanted to have a hippie over just so they could say they had. Maybe I was supposed to be the conversation piece. The other straight people at the party did ask me a lot of questions, and I laid the Flower Power rap on pretty thick, feeling used, you know? But, they had some good booze, food and some so-so weed, which they brought out like presenting the crown jewels. They asked if I would roll some to smoke. Yeah, I was the hippie at the party all right. Weird, man. They had all the current music, so I played the part for them, and got high on their weed, ate their food, drank their booze, and entertained their friends.

I woke up still in the straight pad. I must have passed out and slept all night in the comfortable chair I had been sitting in while I laid some bull on their friends. What a hangover! I wasn't much of a drinker, and the booze did me in. I woke up early, and the others were still asleep. What was left of the weed was on the kitchen table, so I rolled a couple of joints, took a can of soda from the fridge, and snuck out of the pad.

I was going to jump in the van and head back to my own place to clean up and crash for a while, but when I went outside, I freaked because it wasn't there. It was gone, man! Somebody had stolen my rig! The door didn't lock very firmly, but I never worried about it getting stolen. I looked up and down the street as far as I could see, and it wasn't there.

Finally, I went back to the party pad and used the phone to report it to the police. What else could I do? I gave them my location, and about twenty minutes later, two cops pull up in a black & white. In those days, the city cops were not what you see today. These were both beefy Irish-American boys, not surprising in S.F., with old-fashioned looking, blue-black uniforms, and hats like World War II pilots wore. They took one look at me, dragged out and hung over with my hippie street threads on, and gave each other a knowing look. But, they took the report, a full description of the van, with only a few snide remarks such as, "Are you sure you drove the vehicle here, or only thought you did?"

One of the cops summarized things: "So, what you're telling us is somebody stole a bright yellow one-ton van with a giant grinning face all over the front and a red raised stripe on each side. Correct."

When he put it like that, it did sound hard to believe, even to me. I kept my cool, suddenly remembering the two numbers in my pocket, and nodded politely,

I asked them if they might take me back up to the park so I could grab a bus to head home, which they did, remarking on the way it probably wasn't the first or last time I'd sit in the back of a police car, and didn't it seem odd to me anyone would want to steal a yellow van with a face on the front?

I told them I wanted to get home, please. They dropped me at the end of the park where the N Judah street car turns around, and I thanked them, saying I hoped they'd have a groovy day. I saw them both shaking their heads as they drove away.

I was getting on the next trolley about twenty minutes later, when I saw a police car to my right. It was the same two cops who had dropped me off, with the red lights flashing on their cruiser. The trolley stops, one of the cops sticks his head through the door and points at me, then tells me to get into the car again. They took me back to the same location where the party had been, but this time on the Great Highway itself, not the Lesser, on the other side of the high grassy embankment separating the two roads.

I had parked the van where I thought I had, only one street over, and in my booze and drug hung-over state had forgotten this one minor fact!

The cops didn't linger long, and said they could see why someone would steal such a lovely truck, it being so inconspicuous and all. Right.

There was a ticket under the wiper blade for parking illegally on the Great Highway overnight. I got in, started it up, and carefully drove home, where I showered, had a bite to eat, and stayed in my room snoozing for the rest of the day.

A week later, I drove the Jester van down to Half Moon Bay and then further south to Santa Cruz, figuring there were some thrift stores down there not too picked over to look through for some treasures for my business. I was mistaken about the stores, though. They weren't much, mostly carrying contemporary clothes and household items, though I found a few decent things, enough older garments to pay for the trip. Before heading back, I decided to go play at the Santa Cruz Boardwalk, and have some crab to eat.

I left the van in the corner of a parking lot, and headed down to the Boardwalk. I was gone about three hours, enjoying the seaside, the people and shops, and the good seafood I got there. I rapped with some people I had seen in the Haight who were down for some fun, too.

But, when I got back to the van, I saw someone had been at it. The door had been jimmied open, stuff was broken up inside and thrown around, the back door windows were broken, the windshield had a long crack on the passenger side, and a broken beer bottle was lying in front of the van. I didn't have many sellables in the back, but what I did have was either gone, or torn up. I noticed some jerk had peed in the back, too. My guts hurt to see what some uptight creeps had done. There was a lot of animosity toward hippies then, and I guess some straights had taken it out on my rig.

I got in, started it up, and headed for home. At least they hadn't flattened the tires, though I don't know why, except maybe they wanted me to be able to leave the area. After much thought, once I got home, I decided to repaint the front of the van and actually ended up painting the whole thing some drab, light-brown color, but with the Jester signs remaining on the sides. Truth to tell, I didn't miss the toothy face too much. It was one trip over the line, you know? I repaired or replaced what had been damaged, except the cracked windshield, and let the attack on my van fade away.

Okay, in 1967 the Be-In happened, the BIG Be-In. Call it a love-in if you want, it was all the same, a group of like-minded people getting together to tune into each other. It sounded like it would be a far-out happening, so I decided to go. I had been to a few love-ins before, usually with some rock group performing, people dancing in the crowd, making love, most of us stoned on one thing or another.

This grand organized event which had been heavily advertised with fliers and posters, was held at the Polo Grounds in Golden Gate Park, a large playing field surrounded by raised embankments of grass-covered earth. Lots of known people were there, including Dr. Timothy Leary, Allen Ginsburg, and even William S. Burroughs, I think. There was also an apprentice of Leary's, Richard Alpert, who later became known as Baba Ram Dass, who also preached the Turn On, Tune In, Drop Out acid philosophy Leary had been teaching.

I always figured Leary was on a huge, acidized ego trip, willing to tell other people this was the right way to be. It never seemed right to me to make LSD a way of life. Hey, it was an amazing, mind-altering drug, and lots of people got something out of it, but many others didn't, nothing good anyway.

There were a lot more people at the Be-In than had been expected. The several smaller love-ins I had been to had maybe a few hundred people, but this was the Be-In, and later estimates were between fifteen and sixty thousand people attended. I'd say at least twenty-five thousand to thirty thousand people were there. I saw many people I had known from Haight Street, but it was obvious there were a lot of people who had gotten wind of the happening and came to Frisco to be in on it. I had come with Chet and Kurt. We soon parted ways in the huge crowd, but it was cool.

The Be-In was surprisingly organized for a hippy get together. The platform where the celebrities would be was used for music, reading poetry, giving speeches, and preaching the acid philosophy. But I also saw the whole event as a power trip. It was still politics to me, a small number of people preaching "the right way to live" to a mass of people wanting something different and worthwhile to reach for. I wondered if this was what was originally planned during the early Hippie Movement.

I couldn't get my mind into the idea of using drugs as a permanent way of life. Some did, but I wondered how long the idea lasted with them. I now know most all of them eventually went back to a more normal life, working a steady job and having families and albums for their grandkids to check out. But I doubt many of these albums had photos from this time of life. Leary, as you probably know, went to jail for his acid preaching and drug dealings. He's gone from this world now, though I wonder where he ended up on the other side. There were an awful lot of young kids whose heads got fried trying to follow in his mindsteps.

Toward the end of the Be-In, a small airplane flew over, someone jumped out of it, and the chute that opened was colored like a rainbow. Only a few hundred feet up, the person in the chute started tossing little packets to the crowd below. Someone on stage spoke into the microphone, "It's Owsley, people, dropping some Clear Light for you to grow on," and it was Owsley Stanley, famed LSD maker, tossing tabs of acid down to the crowd.

When he drifted toward the far end of the field for an open place to land, the crowd surged toward him, as one single body it seemed, until he was totally surrounded by delighted heads and groovers of all sorts. As far as I know, nobody got hurt in this mass of moving people. I got myself several of the tossed tabs. I took one and saved one for later. Once the first tab hit me, I sat there with the rest of the population, grooving on all the mellow feelings being put out. I remember closing my eyes and being filled with the good energy there. It was incredible, like a gigantic psychic wave washing over. But then, the tide went out, and the Be-In came to an end. All the people drifted off to their assorted pads to let the moment fade out as it would. It was too much!

One thing showing the power of a united group of people like the ones at the Be-In, was the way the fabled horse-mounted S.F. police, stationed all along the top edges of the embankments, acted during the event. They resembled Cossacks awaiting their orders to charge into the milling crowd, but not one of them came down to oppose what was going on. I believe the energy coming off the thousands of tuned-in, together people kept them out.

Maybe the movie *Star Wars* was right, and there is a powerful force that flows through all life. It sure seemed like it that day! I went back there about a week later and I could still feel the energy from the Be-In coming off the Polo Grounds.

I started a new business soon after the Be-In, suggested to me by a wheeler-dealer, Sean Henry, who had come down from Portland, Oregon to see what was happening in the hippie scene. I met him while selling from the Jester van, and we hit it off right away. He liked the business I was doing, and my "mellow rap" as he put it.

He told me there was a fortune to be made in S.F. finding and selling old stuff, and one way to find nifty things was to do attic and basement cleaning which he did for a long time in Portland, Oregon.

I told him I thought nobody would want someone to come into their homes, especially a hippie. I was wrong. Sean knew what he was talking about. There were lots of older people who couldn't do it for themselves, but wanted to get rid of all the junk accumulated over the years, especially in the turn-of-the-century Victorian houses where they lived, some of them for their entire lives.

I put an ad in the San Francisco Examiner Classifieds advertising my clean-up business: "Jester's Hauling Service, removal of unwanted items from your attic, basement or yard," and my phone number. Three days later, I got my first call from a lady on Fell Street. She was a nice old lady in her seventies, who wasn't put off by my hair or threads. She wanted to get rid of a bunch of stuff gathering dust in her basement. This first job was what made me realize Sean Henry was right.

The job on Fell Street got me several cool old chairs, some beautiful old glass bowls and vases, some collectible bottles and a two-pound bag of frankincense, probably used for church incense burners in this heavily Catholic city.

I cut the lady a deal, only charging her half the amount I had quoted her, since I had gotten so much excellent old stuff. I knew I didn't have to, but it was my way. My easy-going style didn't hurt getting job referrals either, so it paid off in the long run.

It is amazing to me how much wonderful stuff people see as being worthless. Yeah, sure, I did have to haul away a lot of crap, but this was what I was getting paid for, and sometimes the people would trade me some of the items for the clean-up, or tell me to haul everything away. I got a lot of groovy old furniture, and all sorts of old household items, even some silver utensils, serving spoons and forks, and lots of old threads. I finally had so much stuff, I ended up renting one of the belowground garages under one of the Victorians on Eureka Street, across from my pad with the Ohio Hippies.

After several months of doing this work, I was getting steady gigs from my perpetual newspaper ad, and things were going good. I had a lot of stuff in my basement/garage storage space. I knew I was going to have to do something with it soon.

One afternoon, as I was unloading a desk I had traded for my whole clean-up fee, an old roll-top in good shape, a man walking by asked me where I had gotten the old desk and would I be interested in selling it? I fell into my trader mode and told him I had just bought it and wasn't sure if I wanted to sell it. But, after about ten minutes of rapping back and forth, he convinced me to let him have it for one hundred and fifty bucks, which was almost three times what I would have charged for the whole clean-up job where I had gotten it. I even loaded it up in my van and delivered it to where he lived.

As I was leaving after getting it unloaded, he told me I ought to have a garage sale on the weekends at my storage place and I wouldn't even need a business license for doing it.

I realized he was right, so I opened my underground store the next weekend, only I called it a garage sale as the guy had suggested, to avoid the intervention of local government wanting revenue from licenses and permits.

I paid Kurt to make a nice stand-up sign to put on the sidewalk, and in no time at all business grew, with help from another ad I put in the paper advertising my garage sale, and by word of mouth. Sometimes I even had people waiting for me to open the garage door on Saturday morning. I'd make a pot of coffee, and have cups with cream and sugar ready, sometimes even doughnuts, and it turned into a pleasant way to do business.

From my time hanging around the Haight, I had come to realize it was okay to work outside the system, on the fringe so to speak, and not be locked into the uptight world of licenses, permits, fees, taxes, and the life control such bureaucratic B.S. kept you under. I had found a way to do my thing, and make it all mine, nobody taking a piece of the pie just because they could. Hippie power, man, my own form of the concept, a very groovy gig.

The best find I made doing the clean-up gig was in an old pad on lower Divisadero Street, not a good neighborhood. The place was rundown, and the person living there for many years had passed away. The owner had called me to help clean up the place. He told me he had gone through the stuff in there and didn't want any of the remaining things, and I made a deal with him on the cost. Man, was there a load of crap, piles of newspapers and worthless magazines, musty old threads I didn't even want but would donate to one of my thrift stores, lots of chipped and cracked old kitchen goods, and such.

But, in one room I found, wrapped up in a piece of dirty old cotton cloth, buried under some old threads, a bundle of four animal hides, furs. Why the owner passed on them, I never could figure, unless he didn't spot them. But what mattered was they were waiting there for me. I didn't know what animals they were from, but the fur was thick and luxurious looking, mostly silver, gray, and black, and they were soft, not stiff, so I did know they had been properly prepared.

The other excellent find I discovered up in the top floor back room, were some hand-drawn plans for this same old Victorian house, the one I was clearing out. I made sure to get the furs and the four or five pages of house plans right out to the truck. I also found a groovy old radio in need of fixing up, especially its wooden cabinet.

That was the main bunch of worthwhile stuff I found, except for a couple of nice old oil lamps, a dented brass spittoon, and a small cardboard box full of old glass bottles, some of them still containing liquid.

The only bottle I thought might be of any value looked like an old scientist's glass stoppered bottle, full of a dark liquid, the stopper still sealed with what looked like wax.

The house plans I later took to an architectural company in downtown San Francisco. At first, the receptionist didn't want to let the top architect know I was there, until, using what charm I had, I got her to take one of the floor plans into his office. Two minutes later, he asked me to come in himself. After looking at all the floor plans, he made me out a nice check for them, saying they were extremely hard to find. Good enough.

The following Saturday, I opened my storage to the public, put my garage sale sign out, and sat down to wait. I had identified the furs with help from a brother I knew in the Haight who used to live in Canada, as being honest-to-gosh wolf hides. Boy, was I tripped out! I had them displayed hanging over the edge of a table in the garage, along with the two old lamps I had gotten with them, and the box of bottles.

Later, a woman pulled up to the curb in a new two-seater Mercedes convertible, and came to see what I had to sell, probably looking for antiques. She had on an expensive-looking business suit with her black hair pulled back tight. Not my usual type of chick, but she was looking good. When she saw the furs, she almost pounced on them, but got her cool back quickly and asked me how much I wanted for them. Before I could even answer, she offered me a hundred bucks apiece.

I never put price tags on my stuff, but I had planned on asking fifty for each one. I told her I was going to ask for one hundred twenty-five for them, but if she bought all four, then they were one hundred apiece. "I'll buy them all," was her answer. She took them right out and put them in the trunk of her Benz, then came back to see what else I had.

She ended up buying a number of old things, mostly old glassware, and also the table the furs had been lying on, a nice round oak table with carved animal feet, claws and all. I asked if she was an antiques dealer, but it turned out she was a lawyer who liked to collect nice things.

I arranged to deliver the table the next evening. As she was leaving, she told me she had looked at the stoppered bottle, and the liquid inside was rare and unique, but not her cup of tea. I immediately put the bottle away until I could find out what it was.

Her name was Denise, and she lived in a pad about three blocks from Coit Tower outside the upper end of China town. When I delivered the table, she was barefoot, and dressed in shorts and a T-shirt. She looked a lot more easy-going than she had in the business suit she was wearing when she bought the stuff.

After the table was safely inside, she offered me some coffee, and we hit it right off. She said she was fascinated with the whole hippie subculture thing going on, and we talked for quite a while about it, and life in general.

The afternoon was rolling on when she gave me a sly grin and said this was usually the time she relaxed. Would I care to share a joint with her?

Surprised, I said, "Cool, why not?" As if I was going to turn this down.

Denise was something when she was loaded, easy to be with, a clever, funny chick. Though she was somewhat older than me, she was a fine lady, all the way around.

While we were grooving together, she asked me if I had checked out the bottle she had mentioned to me. I said I had, but didn't know what it was, and would have to look it up somewhere. She told me there was no need to. The label on it was in Latin, *oilium Artemesium absinthium*, or, she told me, wormwood oil. Did I know about the drink absinthe? I had heard of it, and knew it got you loaded, and it was supposed to be why Van Gogh had cut his ear off, aside from his being a very disturbed man.

Denise told me wormwood oil was the stuff in absinthe making it what it was, a hallucinogenic, supposedly an aphrodisiac, and a real mind-bender if drunk regularly. "Careful what you do with the stuff," she added, "it's also very illegal."

I told her I'd be careful with it.

We ended up going out to China Town to the Ding Ho restaurant, a very old place known for its wonderful wonton soup. My brother had turned me on to it, and we had gone there together several times. The waiter was this skinny old Chinese man whose shirt was always hanging out, and who had a cigarette eternally stuck to his lower lip when he came to take the order. Why it never fell off when he talked, I'll never figure. Talk about a Zen character. Once when I went alone to eat there I asked him, "What is the meaning of life?" I was in a wiseass mood, I guess.

He looked at me for a moment and said, "Who gives a damn, you want the wonton or not?" Yeah, he was very cool.

Denise was tripping on the way the restaurant looked, with the old shellacked wooden partitions between the booths and the heavy round marble tabletops, soaked with over ninety years of oil from spilled food. She and I definitely got off on being there together, and afterward I stayed the night at her place, a hoped-for and righteously mellow end to the evening.

She got up early to go to her office, after putting on a professional pinstriped suit of armor. Watching her walk to her car to wage her daily battles, I was reminded of how lucky I was my work and my life were so free and easy compared to hers. I wasn't judging her for her life choices.

Denise obviously enjoyed her work and her life. But I was glad I would never have to live the life of suit and tie.

Denise and I hadn't talked about getting together again, but she'd come by my garage sales regularly, and always bought something. We hung out with each other a few more times.

Denise had gotten my curiosity up about the wormwood oil. I went to the San Francisco library and checked it out. The wormwood plant came mostly from Eastern Europe, and was used to make tea drunk a lot by older people, old Russian women, for example. But, when it was distilled down to produce its oil, it was a powerful herb indeed. What Denise had told me was true: the oil was the main draw to the drink absinthe, which had been outlawed by the Feds way back in the '20s. If the Feds outlawed it, it must be worth trying.

I took the bottle home with me to Eureka Street, and filled my housemates in on what I knew. I confessed I wasn't sure what the effects would be, but we could sample it if they wanted. Of course they all quickly agreed to sample this new turn-on.

Kurt went out and got a bottle of wine, and we put about an ounce of the stuff in it. We each had a full glass of the treated wine. Whoa! The oil was something else! It got you into a wildly physical high. It made you feel very organic, emphasizing your body instead of your brain. Chet and Bev starting tripping on each other, and we finally asked them to go to their room, please.

There were visual reactions, too, intensified colors and forms, perhaps the reason Van Gogh painted the way he did. The man was supposed to be heavily into drinking absinthe.

I called up Denise an hour later, and told her I had just tried the wormwood oil and it was out of sight. She invited me over. I think she was curious about how somebody would act on the stuff. The minute I got over there, I started getting physical with her. She got into it too, but I felt as if I could get it on with her all night, and she finally made me cool off. I think I overwhelmed her, and I know she liked to be in control of things. We parted on friendly terms, but I decided I shouldn't see her anymore if I was so loaded on anything. I only saw her once more, but only for dinner. I knew our lifestyles were far apart, and our thing faded out gracefully. It's always good when you have an unspoken understanding with someone and it stays good as long as it lasts and doesn't get messy at the end.

The wormwood oil was steadily being used up, shared with friends we knew would dig a strange turn-on. But then, something very freaky happened.

I was sitting with a glass of treated wine at my garage sale one weekend, having kept what was left in the bottle for myself. Luckily, there weren't any customers around. Out of thin air, a small black spot, like a strange flat ball, materialized in my mind, popped out of my head, bounced twice across the sidewalk, flipped off into the sky, and disappeared. Man, did it blow me away! No wonder Van Gogh did away with his ear.

Now I knew what Denise meant by it being a mind-bender, maybe a mind-breaker. I took the bottle to the storm drain by the curb and emptied the rest of it down into the grating. I even got rid of the bottle! For the next couple of weeks I kept an eye on myself, but nothing else so bizarre happened, thank goodness.

Robert Crumb, king of the hippie cartoonists, never came to visit us on Eureka Street, even though he knew all the Ohio people, being from Cleveland himself. But, we went over to his pad once in a while to check out his artwork. Man, it was amazing!

The hippie comics his drawing and the cartoons of others appeared in, had some really nasty titles, rude, sexy cartoons, and characters such as the Yummy of the Month, a caricature of a nubile young girl with exaggerated body parts, waiting to be ravaged by some hairy hippie freak! There were other weird characters like Mr. Natural, Flakey Foont, and the Furry Freak Brothers who were always getting loaded and in trouble. Oh, and there was also Captain Pissgums and his pervert pirates. That's all I'm going to say about them.

Crumb himself looked like some geeky caricature, tall and skinny with a large Adams apple, thick-lens glasses, and a large, beaked nose.

Now, I'm gonna tell you about what happened on one of these visits to Crumb's pad. We were in Crumb's living room, mellowed out behind some smoke, when there was a knock at the door. I got up to answer it since Crumb was busy with his work, and his wife Dana, a large girl, was changing their economy-sized baby.

Anyways, I opened the door, and there stood the queen herself, the singer of broken-hearted, gut-busting blues, Janis Joplin. As surprised and stoned as I was, all I could do was stand there and stare at her. I smelled the booze coming off her, and her threads were all rumpled as if she'd either done an all-nighter or slept in 'em, but she still looked amazing to me, like one of her own down-hearted songs.

Some fancy looking dude was with her, maybe Sam Andrews from Big Brother, but I didn't pay much attention to him. "Hey," Janis said, "Is Crumb here? We want to check out the album cover."

Though we didn't know it until then, Crumb was working on covering the back of her "Cheap Thrills" album with his cartoon characters. Turned out, it was so far out, it ended up becoming the front of the album.

Totally spacing what she had just asked, I looked at Janis a moment longer, then said, "Wow, this is so groovy!"

I still can't believe what I did next. I reached out my right hand and gently squeezed her left boob. She didn't even flinch, but said with a crooked smile, "Is that it?"

I suddenly felt my face getting hot, probably turning bright red. "Uh, yeah, I guess so." I went and sat back down and she walked in to see Crumb.

Feeling uncomfortable, I got up a minute later and walked back to Eureka Street. Chet and Kurt returned about an hour later. Chet looked at me and said, "Man, I can't believe what you did to Janice! You really have a set on you, you know?"

I sat there with what I know was a silly look on my face, not knowing what to say. Chet and Kurt started laughing and I had to do the same.

We didn't go to many movies. So much was going on all the time, we didn't usually need movies for entertainment. But, when an obviously groovy movie was showing we knew we would dig, such as *Yellow Submarine*, *Sergeant Pepper's Lonely Hearts Club Band*, the Beatle's *Magical Mystery Tour*, or *Hard Day's Night*, then we'd go.

When *2001 A Space Odyssey* came out, Chet, Kurt, our friend Gary, and I went to see it. Thing is, we dropped small doses of some good LSD before we went into a theater on Market Street in downtown San Francisco. Good thing we took a city bus to go see it, instead of driving. We sat in the first row, and by the time the promos were done and the movie came on, brother, were we ready for it!

We had all assumed the front-row slouch. The opening musical track with its long dramatic build-up blew our minds, man! We sat there for the next several hours unable to move, our eyes and ears glued to the screen, like babes in space.

When the last bit came on where Dave the astronaut was going through wild, colorful stuff, I think it was supposed to be a planet's atmosphere, the three of us must have repeated some deep remarks over and over, like, "Far out, man," or maybe "Wow!" a hundred times, until someone behind us told us to keep quiet, and we locked our jaws up.

We walked home after the show, going on and on about it. We felt we had actually been on the ship, you know? For days after, one of us would say, "Open the pod bay doors, Hal." And another of us would respond, "I'm sorry, Dave, I'm afraid I can't do that," then laugh our heads off.

When I went to see *Yellow Submarine*, I was so loaded on weed, I had to go back and see it again, I had spaced out so much of it the first time.

Meanwhile, my business was flowing along, and I actually made a chunk of money, but I didn't put it in a bank, keeping it in a safe hidey-hole in my Eureka Street bedroom instead. I felt rich, though I was far from it. It was so good to be making it on my own. Life, for a good long while, was sweet. I was only smoking weed, and hardly hitting the acid anymore, and I felt solid.

I met a sweet girl at the Foghorn one day, and we really connected. Her name was Gwen, or Lady Gwendolyn as I used to teasingly call her, and she made my life a lot brighter and tastier. Gwen was the most beautiful girl I had ever gotten close to, with naturally blonde hair, amazing green eyes, and glowing skin. She had a positive outlook on life, believing in the Flower Power philosophy a lot more than I did, and she always tried to get me to have more faith in it. She loved helping me with the garage sales, and I know she made them better by being there. I couldn't get her to hold the line on prices, but she had a good heart and such loving ways, I figured having her around out-weighed the few dollars I lost.

Gwen moved in with me, and we lived together on Eureka Street for about six months. The other people liked having her there. She made the whole place brighter. Bev was glad to finally have some female vibes around the place.

Gwen liked seeing foreign movies. We used to go down to the Surf Theatre at the end of Judah Street to see French, Italian, or Spanish movies, and then we would talk about them as we drove back up to Eureka Street where we'd spend the rest of the night being sweet to each other. She and Bev got along well in the kitchen, and the meals they made got better and better. The kitchen became more popular than it had been. We all liked to watch the girls doing their thing, and then consuming what they had created.

It's a bummer, but one of life's great lessons is: sooner or later all things come to an end, and the better things are, the harder it is to come to the ending. Gwen had to go back to Wisconsin because her father had become very ill. After she left, we communicated a lot by phone at first, but about a month later, during the call when she told me her dad was gone, she said she wouldn't be coming back for a long time because her mother needed a lot of help. I considered driving back east to be with her, but knew in my gut it wouldn't work out. Our contact faded away.

When things come full cycle, there isn't anything you can do to change it. Better to be glad for what you had and let things be, instead of pushing something already done and over. I missed Gwen and her light-filled eyes for a long time, and thought I always would.

By this time, in late '68, things in the Haight were getting rough. There were a lot of bad characters coming in to take advantage of what was going on there. People came from other parts of S.F., and as far away as Los Angeles. A lot of bad drugs were being sold, some girls had been beaten and raped, and even a few murders took place. Sexual disease cases increased. Theft and violent crime was "on the rise," as the six o'clock news would say.

There were runaway kids coming into the city too, believing every-thing was still all peace and love, instead of the rough scene it had turned into. It was sad. Some as young as ten or eleven were already experiencing more life than their confused and worried parents ever had. Imagine being a young girl or boy who had learned to survive any way they could on the streets, doing drugs, trading sex for food or a place to crash, and maybe they ran away from their parents' nice clean middle class home because they weren't allowed to stay out late.

Eventually places opened to help runaways get counseling, and to rejoin these kids with their folks, even though not all of them wanted to. I think Huckleberry House was the best of these places, and they had been open for quite a while. For some of the kids, it was too late, and they never got back to a normal, solid life. This was an unfortunate side effect of the Movement, or what was left of it.

Interestingly, most of the people who had started the Movement back in late '63 or early '64 had already split the scene by 1966, a lot of them going into the country further north in California, such as Humbolt County. Having planted the seed in San Francisco, they probably figured their job was done, or maybe they saw the hand-writing on the wall before it was even written. Like most things in life, the hippie scene couldn't stay good forever. Some people always seem to find a way to mess things up.

Section Two

In early '69 I took a bad turn, finally putting an end to my life in the city I had once found so amazing.

Our scene on Eureka Street had come undone. Chet and Bev had decided to move to Portland, Oregon, a mellow city in those days, without the gang and drug scene they have there now. Burman, always a wild man, had tripped out on LSD, driven his old Plymouth into a minor accident at the S.F. entrance to the Golden Gate Bridge and had split to parts unknown.

Kurt and I couldn't keep the place by ourselves. He moved to a small pad up on Hoffman Street, and I got a room just off Divisadero, with two people who had placed an ad in the paper for a roommate.

I was sorry to leave Eureka Street. Some great trips had gone down there. I would miss the people, but we all know the routine. I never did connect with them again, except a chance meeting with Kurt a few years later, and the unexpected meeting with Wil I already mentioned.

The two people on Divisadero, Eileen and her kinky boyfriend Billy, were into speed, crystal meth. They used to shoot up and party all night. Being open to new stuff, I tried snorting some. Even though it did a job on my nose, I got off on the rush it gave me. I'm not a speedy person by nature, so this was something new to me. I started getting high with them on a regular basis, and eventually I started shooting the speed straight up. Even now I find it hard to believe I tripped out so hard and fast on the evil stuff, which it most certainly is. I started losing weight, not eating much, staying wired, getting into the rush.

I fell into this pattern: I'd shoot up in the morning and go do whatever jobs had come my way. People were surprised at how fast I could clean things up. The meth caused some changes in the way I treated people. If I found some valuable item, instead of bringing it to my customer's attention I'd sometimes slip it amongst the trash and not even mention it to them. I became grouchy and impatient. This was not the usual me, but at the time I never gave it a second thought.

Sometimes I'd shoot up in the evening and go walking all over the city, often into areas I would normally avoid, places with a lot of shadows, getting into situations I'd rather not go into. Best those things stay buried in the past.

I did have to back myself out of several bad scenes with people I never would have encountered without doing speed and falling into the raspy mindset it gives you, feelings of invulnerability, power and aggressiveness, at least for me.

I got into a bad trip with one punk who pulled a knife on me while I was flying high. I was quicker than he was and took the blade away from him, but, here, see the two small scars on this forearm? Better we let the story end there, if you don't mind. At any rate, by the middle of '69 I was a mess.

I had given up selling out of the Jester van when the clean-up business took off and I opened my underground store. Now my clean-up business was going down the drain. I was so into the meth I was forgetting to go to jobs, or just wouldn't bother, and my garage-sale store was suffering too, since I lived a ways from there now and wasn't keeping it supplied.

When I did do the sale, my "new" personality didn't help business any. My raspiness put people off, so they left and didn't come back.

The meth had taken control over me to the point I didn't even think about paying my garage/store rent for several months. The owner of the garage finally got hold of me and told me I was out, and I could come get the rest of my stuff, which he had left in front of the garage door. I never even bothered to go back.

My business I had been so into, and had made me feel successful, had turned to dust. I had self-destructed. But it still took one more step for me to get free of the meth.

There was a place called the Crystal Palace on the outskirts of the Haight Ashbury District, a large old structure with many rooms. The whole building had turned into a speed freak hangout. I used to score there, until the day I went in and was pushed aside by a bunch of people headed for the door.

I probably should have headed back out with them, but I didn't. I hadn't seen any cops outside, or heard any sirens, so I went in further to see what had happened. I passed by an open door and stopped when I saw a couple of people leaning over a teenage girl lying on the floor, one of them checking for a pulse. Her eyes were wide open, but she wasn't looking at anything. Her arm was still tied off, the needle lying next to her.

Soon as I saw her, I knew she was already gone. The people in the room, seeing how it was with her, left the room and took off as the others had. I stood there for a few seconds, thinking how innocent and defenseless she looked, and then I left, completely bummed out. I had never seen a dead person before, not like this, and it shook me up. Man, what a waste. I can still see her lying there, all her choices and chances gone.

Now, I figured the handwriting was on the wall, a sign I better get my act together. I needed to get off the meth. I figured the best thing to do was leave town for a while. So, I called my folks, who I hadn't been in touch with for quite a long time, and asked if I could come visit for a while. It was okay with them, so I took enough money for the journey, threw some personals into a duffle, started up my old van, and headed down to Southern Cal.

Before leaving, I had stashed the rest of my savings in a safe hidey-hole in the Divisadero Street pad.

I drove down the newly-opened Highway 5, letting its long, straight stretches soothe my mind. The meth I had poisoned my body and mind with began to fade away. I kept drinking water and eating fruit. At one point, I stopped by the side of the road, got sick, and started crying tears of frustration and anger toward myself for letting this all happen.

The trip south was a start for getting cleaned up, but I must have been quite a sight to the folks, judging by the look I got when they opened the front door to greet me. My mother stood staring at me, my long shaggy beard and hair, my funky threads, and my leaned-out frame. A tear rolled down her cheek, while my father shook his head. They never would understand what had happened to their child, like so many parents all through those times.

Guess you can figure there were lots of questions, some I tried my best to answer so they'd understand, and some I wouldn't answer at all. I was able to stay about two weeks before the awkward interactions and tension of the visit finally made me feel the need for the open road.

But, my mom's cooking and the distance from the drug scene in S.F. helped get me healthy again.

I said my good-bys to the folks, thanking them for putting up with me and promising to stay in touch. Then I headed back north, the open windows letting in welcome fresh air as I considered what I would do next.

The last couple of weeks had been long enough to lose the urge for speed. I had stayed to myself at the folks' place, avoiding opportunities to get into more trouble. You know, when you are into drugs, you can somehow always find what you need, wherever you are. What I needed was a place to hide from it all, and I managed to find one.

My brother and I had lost contact, him being busy with school, and his continuing relationship with his girlfriend, now his wife. I had been to the wedding, and the folks had come up for the ceremony, but I had been stoned on weed, and things at the reception were uncomfortable.

I went to see my brother after my visit to the folks, and filled him in on what had been happening with me. He asked me if I needed some help, but I said his being there to talk to was help enough. He was a good brother.

In November of '69, he called me and asked if I could come over. His conscientious objector rating, which he felt so strongly about, and had worked hard to get, writing a paper on his personal beliefs, was taken back by the military. This was probably due to the escalated action in Nam and the need for more troops. His draft status was changed to 1-A and he had been sent an induction notice. He told me he had been in touch with some people he knew, and once he received his delinquent induction notice, since he was damned if he was giving up his beliefs, he was going to leave the country, but wouldn't say exactly where he'd go.

I was stunned, my own feelings about the war and my not being able to go, conflicting with my feelings toward my brother, after he told me this. I had to accept his decision, and several weeks later, his plans to leave became reality.

He asked me to mail him his packed-up books after he contacted me as to where to send them, and gave me a couple of one hundred dollar bills for the shipping, as there were a lot of boxed books. Then the three of us, my brother, his wife and I, went out for one last Chinese meal at the Ding Ho. I took them both to a motel down by the beach off the Great Highway on the night before they were to fly out, and we said some difficult good-byes. I was blown-out, and the suddenness of this happening didn't give me time to deal with it. My brother was gone, maybe forever. I felt alone, but sucked it up, and tried to get on with things.

About a month later, I got a letter from him, telling me they were in Sweden. He and his wife were okay, though getting acclimated to the country and the language was difficult. But they both hung in there and became teachers. They are both still in Sweden today, teaching in a university as tenured instructors.

Even though he had received a pardon some years later to come home after having dodged the draft, he preferred the academic atmosphere in Sweden, so he stayed on. It took years for my father, a World War II vet, to accept what he had done, and to start communicating with him again without difficulty.

I don't ask anybody to accept or condemn what my brother did. The simple fact is besides not believing in waging war, he was a scholar, and had wanted to be a teacher since he was six years old. I know in my heart he wouldn't have lasted five minutes in Nam, and the world would have lost another good mind.

I believe the politics happening in the Bay Area, especially Berkeley, had some influence on how the war eventually expired, because of the social pressure involved there. The energy put out by the Anti-War Movement, especially from the Spring Peace March must have had an effect on the whole country. It was a time of great conflict in the U.S, and I felt it strongly too.

I believed the desire for peace and an end to the war was a good thing, but I also hurt for our men over there and the hell and horror they were going through. I didn't want any more of my brothers to die, but wanted the conflict to end in such a way to save their dignity and honor their sacrifices. So the miserable, heartbreaking way they were treated coming home deeply hurt and angered me, man. This is all I'm going to say on the subject.

Since the Jester van had been so important to my life, I should tell you why and how I parted with it. In a way, my letting go of the van relates to what I was saying about the politics of the time. I was visiting some friends in Berkeley in late 1969, people I had known from the Haight who had become heavily political because of how Nam was going, and how they felt about the government in general. I never got into politics much, though as I said, I had my feelings about what was going on. I still enjoyed my Berkeley friends' company, in spite of their occasional rantings and ravings.

Anyways, I had parked my van where I thought it would be safe, and hung out with my people a few days. They talked me into going to several political meetings, which turned into flailing ego trips with people who supposedly believed in the same things not being able to agree on anything, and the arguments went round and round.

Three or four days later when it was time for me to head back to San Francisco, I got up early in the morning to leave. When I got to the van, the door was slightly open. I knew I had closed it up when I parked. I checked in the back, and everything looked okay. I got in the driver's seat and started warming up the old flathead engine. Glancing down, I saw some shiny bits on the floor mat. Curious, I picked up several metal chips, the curly kind made by a drill bit. Weird. I got a chill down my back. Looking around the insides of the truck, I didn't see anything else, and decided to let it pass.

But, as I put it in gear and started to roll, I hit the brakes. I had spotted two very small holes I knew hadn't been there before, drilled into the lower edge of the dash, to the right of the steering wheel. It tripped me out. I sure hadn't made the holes myself, and couldn't figure what it was all about. I drove home, went into my pad, lit up a doobie, and sat and ruminated for a while on this strange situation.

I finally decided it must have had something to do with me being in Berkeley with my political friends. Maybe somebody was going to plant a bug, and I had come back to the van before they could finish the job. I wasn't sure, but got righteously paranoid about the whole thing.

The next morning, after clearing all my personal stuff out of the van, I went down to one of the auto-wrecking yards in South San Francisco where I used to buy parts for the van, and sold it there. I think I got three hundred dollars and a ride back to my pad. The end of another era. I bought a solid old '52 Dodge pick-up truck for the three hundred a few days later.

By 1970, the hippie scene was an undeniable burnout, with all the wonderful high-level energy and enthusiasm of the Mid Sixties gone away. Too many had jumped on the bandwagon, and the concept of the original Flower Power people was washed away and faded out. It was sad to see. There were still some die-hard hippies there, but it was too late, and maybe it was just a part of the scene's natural progression.

I remember sitting in the park on the corner of Haight and Lyon streets enjoying some sunshine. A dude pulls up on Haight, in a new yellow Corvette, wearing a commercially-made leather hat and L.A. love beads and says, "Hey, man, know where I can score some good weed?"

I thought for a moment, then told him to continue on down the street for three blocks, then make a left, go another few blocks to a small corner store called Daddy's. I told him to ask for Jerome, and to tell the man behind the counter he wanted some of the good smoke.

He smiled and said, "Groovy, man, thanks," and drove off, headed right for the middle of the worst part of the Fillmore District. The store I told him about was notorious for giving hippies a hard time. As soon as he drove away, I went back to my pad to think things over. The episode with Mr. Corvette had bummed me out, and made me realize the scene was over for me.

I decided I needed a vacation. Eileen and her boyfriend had moved out of the Divisadero Street pad a few months before this, which was fine by me. When they found out I was off the meth they had packed up their stuff, along with some of mine, and disappeared. They were probably paranoid I might make trouble for them. Speed will affect to you in this way. I had a couple of grand still safely stashed, and decided to stay where I was, but without roommates. There was always some hassle coming up to spoil things, one way or another. They came by several times after moving, usually to try to borrow some money, and the visits were always short. I realized later they were actually checking to see if I was still around.

I was sitting in my pad, wondering where I would go for some R & R, when there was a knock on the front door. It was Ray, a bus driver I had become acquainted with on my jaunts downtown to catch a meal or a movie. It was easier, on those short trips, to leave my truck at home, avoiding downtown traffic and parking hassles. We had started talking together in those times, and I rode with him to the end of the line one night. We parked for a while, smoked a number, and got to be friends. I had gone to his place for dinner several times. His wife, Nadia, was a great cook. We used to smoke a joint after dinner, and watch creepy movies on TV, which was Ray's idea of a good time.

Anyways, Ray had come over to tell me he and his old lady were going down to Big Sur for a few days, and did I want to come along? Funny how things fall into place sometimes. I said it would be far out. I poked some cash in my pocket, grabbed my old sleeping bag, a change of threads, and a few personals, and after locking the Dodge up in the downstairs garage, went over with Ray to his place.

We left Friday morning early, heading south on Highway 1 in their fancy Chevy camper van, built at the factory. The first place we stopped was Kirk Creek Camp, a beautiful, tree-filled campground on the ocean side of the road in the heart of Big Sur.

I still love the area, and try to spend some time there during the summer, even now. But, it was less populated and built up than it is today. There was a wild feel to the place, especially at night when the traffic was down to nothing, and I lay in my sleeping bag under the stars and listened to the mind-calming sound of the waves below me slapping and whooshing on the beach, while Ray and his wife crashed out in their fancy van.

The second night we were there, I decided to chance slithering down the narrow, steep trail on the cliff side to the beach, around midnight. Nadia hadn't wanted to make the descent, and Ray decided to stay with her, so I went alone, which was okay with me. The moon was full, and cast a weird light over everything.

Big Sur is a place of mystery and magic to me, full of its own living energy.

When I reached the beach, the sea was calm. There was a driftwood log lying on the sand. I lay down with my back against it. It was an amazing scene. I forgot all about the fact that I had nothing going on, no work, no steady woman, and not a great reserve of cash. I completely gave myself up to the wondrous moment I was in, and communed with dear old Momma Nature, pure and beyond beautiful. The stars appeared as holes in a vast black background, with the brightest of light shining through. My mind became sharp and clear, heightening my own natural perceptions, making what was an amazing place even more incredible.

I was lying there grooving, when I caught a movement out of the corner of my eye. My senses were heightened and even though it had been a quick motion, I knew I had seen something. There it was again, a good-sized dark form running across the beach and then back down to the water's edge, but getting closer. Suddenly it hit me, this was sea otter territory. I knew it wasn't a seal because they couldn't move in such a way, but I also thought sea otters never left the water. Then I heard a chattering noise, a rare and unique sound to my ears, and I knew I was right.

I remained still and waited. After a while, the zigzag movement of the otter across the beach brought it close to me, and I couldn't resist. In as gentle and inoffensive a tone as I could, I called out, "Sea otter, oh sea otter. Where you goin', sea otter?"

The furry sea creature stopped in its tracks, in a sit-up-and-check-it-out position. It galumphed away a short distance, but then it came closer. I knew it was trying to see and sniff me out, so I lay still, not wanting to scare it.

I didn't expect my calling out to work, thinking the animal would never come close to a human being. But after calling to it several times more, it actually came to about ten feet in front of me. I softly said, "Hello there, furry one, having any luck with the clams?"

It rose up on its hind feet again, chattered something, and wriggled right up to my bare feet. It put one cold front paw on my right foot, and stared at me for a few seconds. It sniffed my other foot, and gave it a nip. They're good-sized critters, so it made me uneasy. I said "Hey!" and twitched my foot to the side. The otter jumped back, then headed straight to the water and safety, making all kinds of noises as it went. I lay there feeling full of amazement and joy. It was a magical rush!

Suddenly, in my heart, I knew things would work out for me. This experience had switched something on inside of me in a good place. I closed my eyes, and fell contentedly to sleep right where I was, thinking how great it would be if I could somehow live in Big Sur.

I awoke with daylight coming on. The tide had come in, and the sea was running cold saltwater up my pant legs. I scrabbled my way back up to the campground, where I lay on my sleeping bag, thoroughly dampened by the night mists of Big Sur.

When Ray and his wife woke up several hours later, I cooked us some Canadian bacon and eggs for breakfast, along with a pot of strong coffee.

As the morning wore on, we talked about finding another place to camp for a while, and decided to follow the dirt road climbing up into the hills, which began almost right across Highway 1 from Kirk Creek Camp. The sign read: Nacimiento-Ferguson Road.

While the van warmed up, I walked to the edge of the cliff and looked down to the beach where I had had such an amazing trip with the sea otter. It was beautiful, but revealed none of the magic I had experienced the night before. The moment had opened my mind and allowed me to see on a different level, but now the beach was just a beach once again. I had felt this way before while using psychedelic drugs, that where I was tripping was a stage set for what was playing out.

I thought maybe this whole scene with Ray and his wife was a means for me to change my typical reality, and break away from the burnt-out city life I was living. Again, I thought how cool it would be if I actually could live in Big Sur and make a life there. As far as I knew, even though it was great country, there was nothing there for me to do to survive. Walking back to the van, I got in and we headed up Nacimiento-Ferguson Road and whatever was to come next.

The road wound up and up for a number of miles. I enjoyed the scenic views and the oak trees flourishing there. We were only doing about five miles an hour when Ray was forced to hit the brakes. What must have been a wild pig and a pack of babies rushed across the road making all kinds of piggy grunts and snorts, tails straight up in the air. I didn't know there were wild boars in the area. Ray remembered reading somewhere there had been wealthy sportsmen's clubs in the general area of Monterey County, around the turn of the century, and wild pigs from Europe, along with other animals, had been imported to be hunted. I knew pigs breed quickly, so probably some of those pigs had gotten free and flourished in the heavy woods of the area, where there was plenty of natural food for them, such as acorns and roots.

We continued on up the road, and eventually it leveled out and turned into blacktop. A short way further on, we came to a typical California campground named Bonanza, with brown painted posts and railings, a blacktop parking area, carved wooden signs, and typical institutional outhouses. The whole enchilada for comfortable camping, middleclass style. We got out to look around.

Maybe I was being too heavy about it, but I always thought places like these actually removed you from nature, though I gotta say at my age, I prefer a little comfort over sticks and stones against my back in the morning.

I suggested we go further on down the road, to find a less civilized place to camp. I figured since they had the van to sleep in, it would be okay with Ray and his wife.

I was wrong, and the happy camping time started to change. Ray's wife didn't want to camp without an outhouse, having a hang-up about doing her thing au natural. Ray wanted to camp as I did, without a state-designated spot to break the unhindered natural view, as he said. They got into a real thing about it. I walked a short ways off 'til things were resolved. Finally Ray came over, red in the face, and said we would look further down the road. His wife sat stony faced as we continued to drive.

As we were slowly cruising along, I saw some crude little shelters, and then I spotted the first naked person, sitting beneath an oak tree, then another one walking along in the grassy meadow beyond. I counted five or six people altogether, all of them tan and young. I was somehow not too surprised, my earlier experience with the sea otter in some way setting the stage for this scene. It all seemed natural and mellow indeed.

I suggested Ray pull over to check out this unexpected happening. It was only then he saw what I had already noticed. He stopped the van and sat there staring and smiling.

Ray and I got out of the van, but his wife didn't budge, a funny look on her face, maybe nervous and unsure about this whole new scene.

Several of the young naked people had spotted us and came walking up to check us out. I felt as if we had stepped back in time, and were being approached by some native group of forest dwellers.

Two young men and one chick, completely naked, came to say hello and to ask if we had any food or drink to share and did we have any weed? Ray kept giving the girl a thorough eye examination, which was picked up on by his wife, not helping to brighten her mindset. The chick ignored Ray mentally groping her, and so, apparently, did the two guys with her.

As I was rolling a nice doobie to share while we rapped, another naked young man and woman walked past, hand in hand. He had a full head of hair and beard, and he was obviously well endowed. The girl had a smile on her face, so when they went inside one of the shelters, I guessed what they'd be doing.

This was the last straw for Ray's now thoroughly uptight old lady. She demanded Ray take us back to the campground with the outhouse. "Right now!"

Seeing me watch the couple walk by, the first girl said, "Those two are Jeff and Janey, and I'm Julie."

"Lots of jays around here," I said to her as a tease.

"Maybe, but not the kind we all like," she said, giving me a questioning look.

"I have the remedy," I told her, holding up the freshly-rolled joint. Julie gave me a smile causing my juices to begin bubbling. She told me she knew a nice quiet place we could go and share a smoke, if I wanted to.

If I wanted too? I wasn't about to pass up a perfect offer like this, so I rolled another number for the two guys who had come up with her, and they split with it.

After telling Ray I would catch up with them later, I let her take me by the hand and lead me to a small meadow about a quarter mile down a meandering creek running in the rocks and trees below us. In this meadow was the ancient gray trunk of a great fallen oak tree, which was at least four feet above the ground, even in its long-time resting place. Behind the trunk was a shelter made of canvas and plastic tarps, with three or four blankets laid out underneath, and a sleeping bag on top of the blankets. There were some threads rolled in one corner, a pair of sandals, and a gallon jug of water.

Except for a quick glance around at these things, there was only one thing I wanted to do: get close to Julie. I stripped down, and we lay together in this cozy nest behind the oak. We smoked a number together, and talked about different things, such as the city scene and what it had become, and how trippy it was to live in such a beautiful place as the Sur.

But, by then we were into each other, and the talking stopped, no more words being necessary. We had a sweet loving time of it. Julie had such an open way of giving herself, something I had never felt before, even with Gwen, and certainly not with Denise, who loved a good wrestle but always made it seem more of an athletic contest.

It was getting dark by time we had reached a point of mutual satisfaction. She said we should walk back to the main camp to meet Jeff and Janey, the leaders of the group, called J and J by the others. We both dressed against the cooling night air. She went down to the creek by herself for a few minutes, and then we headed back.

It was an uneven walk in the dark, but Julie knew the way, and we soon spotted the campfire in front of J and J's shelter. It was strange, I felt I was being led toward a native village, but outside normal time. I guess it was a tribe of sorts.

There had been some small Indian groups living here in older times, right in this area, before they were killed or run off and their time had faded out.

J and J and one of the young guys who had been with Julie when we first met, named Hawk, were sitting together, dressed, as we walked up. There were two other guys I hadn't seen before, but they seemed to be more in the background, not really taking part. They were Josh and his partner, who had been there a few weeks. Julie and I sat down, and a low-key conversation took place: where from, what doing, how's The City these days, and so on.

Jeff asked if I wanted to eat with them, saying they had scored from some campers who had left Bonanza Campground yesterday. I said it would be cool. Janey cooked up some Spam for sandwiches and a couple of cans of corn. We smoked while she cooked, with Janey reaching over for her share of hits. It seemed Jeff and Janey had hooked up a couple of years ago, though they didn't say where, and had been living in Big Sur for about nine months. They had decided to go basic as Jeff called it, to see how living was in these hills. Their money had run out a while back, but they managed with hand-outs from campers in the area, and from people coming in who decided to stay with them a while.

I figured if they stayed naked when it was daylight and warm, campers would be glad to give them some food so they would go away. Jeff said sometimes G.I.s from nearby Hunter-Liggett Army Reservation would come by with food and booze, but they were hoping to get laid, thinking hippie girls were easy.

They always put threads on when the G.I.s were spotted coming down the road, or would disappear until they left. The soldiers never got what they came for. He said these were "short time" soldiers who were leaving the army soon, maybe recently back from Nam, and sometimes the vibes around them were weird, and scary. But, the mountain hippies kept doing their thing, nothing bad had happened yet, and the food donations came in handy.

Janey then mentioned they had lost two of their steady people. A chick had become pregnant, and her boyfriend had taken her home to Southern California for proper care and feeding. "So, we're short on full-time people to help keep things going," said Jeff, giving me a look to indicate an offer was being made.

The winter had been rough, cold and rainy, but the four of them, Jeff, Janey, Julie, and Hawk, while out foraging, had come upon the home of an older rancher who had a small spread a few miles past Jolon. They offered to work in trade for a place to stay dry and warm, and being of good heart, he had let them stay in his barn in trade for doing chores.

He had eventually let them use an old bunkhouse during the coldness of mid winter. Julie and Janey did some cooking and cleaning for him, which didn't hurt the situation either. Seemed he had lost his wife several years before. He even let Jeff and Hawk wear some old threads he had, and gave the girls some of his wife's old dresses.

They had returned to their camp in early March, the weather finally warming up a bit, with some supplies and food the rancher had laid on them.

Their biggest problem had been with the Parks Department and BLM, who had come in several times once they were tipped off the group was "squatting" there. At first they were told they couldn't camp for more than several weeks at a time in the same area, so they moved their camp to keep it cool.

Once, when they were out exploring the hills, they came back to find their shelters torn down and their goods scattered. They figured the authorities had decided to run them out. It hadn't worked.

They moved their camp inland over one set of hills, 'til things cooled down, but had finally come back for the campers and the people who would come in off the road and hang with them for a while. They kept their camps cleaner than a lot of the common campers did, and were always amazed at the messes left there, and what was thrown away, making use of whatever good stuff they found.

By then, the fire had died down, and to my regret, Julie walked away with Hawk. J and J both smiled at me and went into their humble abode, so I said goodnight to the campfire and hiked back up the road to Bonanza Campground where Ray and his wife were parked.

They were down for the count, and my sleeping bag was lying rolled up outside the back of the van, along with a cooled-down skillet on the Coleman stove, with some cold fried potatoes and a hamburger patty in it.

As I lay there mellowed out by the star-filled night sky, I thought about the unspoken offer Jeff had made me to stay with them. I *was* looking for a way to leave The City, and this chance to stay in the Sur seemed pre-ordained. My pad on Divisadero was paid up for a full month, and I had enough cash on hand to hold me a while, especially if I lived the simple life out here. So I had nothing to lose by giving it a try.

The idea of getting into such a basic way of existing really grabbed me, and I felt if I did, there were going to be all sorts of adventures, though definitely not all carefree and full of joy, which appealed to me too.

This seemed clearly a cosmic offering to do what I wanted to do. It was almost too perfect, but who was I to argue with the Powers-That-Be. I slept on it.

Ray woke me up early in the morning to tell me he and his wife had decided to cut the trip short and head back to San Francisco. I guessed they had gotten into a bad scene about what had happened, and the trip had lost its fun atmosphere.

I told Ray I thought I would stay a while and check out the scene. He said he figured I would, and had put most of the food in a bag for me, and I rolled him a couple of numbers for the ride back.

His wife, after using the chemically-scented outhouse, got into the van and didn't say a word to me. Backing the van out of the campsite, they rolled down the road. I never saw them again.

Picking up my goods, I headed back down to the group's campsite. Jeff was sitting outside his shelter, soaking up some morning sun. I said if it was acceptable, I'd like to stay with the group, though I didn't know for how long.

"I was hoping you would," Jeff responded, "cause I figure you'd be good to have around."

I handed him my bag of assorted foodstuffs as an offering of good faith, I suppose you could say, as something to seal our agreement, and my decision to hang with them was settled.

So, another of my life adventures was set into motion. Each new experience, I figure, is a way to put the panorama of life in focus, a way to get a more complete overview as we go further around the wheel. Even at twenty-three, I already knew settling longtime into one way of living or working was not for me, and I would eventually start craving something new to get into, keeping things fresh. Never would I be a thirty-year man, retired from somewhere, with a gold watch as a symbol of my devotion to the company.

I never put these feelings into words at the time. It came later for me, when I had done enough and been enough to have a reserve of experiences to reflect on, as I am doing now. I think it's easier and probably more satisfying for most older people to answer the question, "What kind of work did you do?" by saying, "I was an engineer for twenty-five years," or "I was a mailman for twenty years," instead of saying "Oh, I did a little bit of everything, but mostly I wandered the highways and byways of America sampling life." Maybe not in those exact words, but you catch my drift, right? Cool.

So I could have my own place to stay, Jeff took me to the shelter by the downed oak tree, and together we moved it into the vicinity of the main camp. He told me, as we walked, to look for a spot I'd like for my own place.

As we passed a large, flat-topped granite boulder close by the creek, which was, it turned out, the Nacimiento River, I said I wanted to put my abode right next to the boulder. I took my time and made my forest pad as weatherproof and comfortable as I could. Jeff took the sleeping bag since I had my own, and one of the blankets, but there was still enough for a nice cushion, and I had picked the spot because it looked flat, and had been used before.

When I was done, I lay down beneath the tarp and absorbed the vibes. I decided it was a good place for me to be.

Feeling satisfied with my new home in the woods, I went over to J and J's place, but when I got there, I realized I was the only one not naked. I decided to fall right into the way of life they had evolved there, so I took off all my threads and laid them to the side.

Hawk looked at Jeff, smiled, and said, "Looks like a bear."

I gave Jeff a puzzled look, and he said, "You've got your camp name, man. We all have one. Your hairy bod gave you away."

"So, what's yours?" I asked.

Jeff gave me a flat look and said, "Has a Long Blade." Right. Janey was "Plays with Acorns," and Julie, "Makes Peace Girl." Hawk was Hawk, but the other two, Josh, and I forget the other one, only had their regular names because, as Jeff said, they are only temporary, which, it turned out, they were.

We ate a meal Janey and Julie had put together, a mixture of the hamburger I had donated, a can of beans, and some elbow macaroni.

We sat and smoked after the eats, day's end in the Big Sur hills. I finally got up and said, "Tomorrow." The others nodded, and I went down to my place by the boulder, feeling a sense of calmness all through me. I finished the roach I had carried back with me, and drifted off to dreams, snug in my nest.

I woke the next morning to some curious noises, low-level grunting and snorting. Pushing the edge of the tarp aside, I saw four or five pigs feeding on roots, only twenty-five or thirty feet from my shelter. At first I was nervous, and I lay quietly watching them. They must have caught my scent or a movement I made, because the one nearest me let out a loud squeal, his tail jerking straight up. In a flash, they took off, squealing and grunting until they were out of earshot. What a rush.

I went down to the creek and splashed my face with its cold, fresh-tasting wetness. Standing up again, I looked slowly around, making a steady three sixty, taking it all in. I had a feeling the place was checking me out, too, absorbing my vibes, as I was absorbing the sights, smells, and sounds around me. I could understand why the others had settled here, but maybe they didn't feel it as I did.

I went back to my shelter, and passing the other side of the low, wide, flat boulder, I saw a number of same-sized holes in its top. Looking closer, I saw they had been ground out, and didn't seem natural.

Looking around again, it hit me. Indians had lived here, probably used acorns for food, and maybe they had ground them up on this flat stone surface. How long it must have taken to wear these holes into it.

I got goose bumps all over. Turning to face the creek, I sensed this was a place where daily activities went on, preparing food and whatever. I wondered if this was why the spot had appealed to me, as if somehow I had picked up on its vibes.

Over the next few days I explored the area, hiking through the closest hills, while keeping an eye out for those pesky pigs, knowing they could be dangerous. Sometimes I went alone, which I liked best, but several times Jeff went with me, and Julie kept me company a few times, much to my enjoyment. There was a mellow connection in the camp, at least amongst the five of us, J and J, Julie, Hawk, and me. Josh and his buddy didn't seem to matter much. I had been accepted right away, almost as if I'd been there before and had returned.

There was a good-sized pool in the creek, below the large meadow where I had first seen the group. It was about twenty-five feet across, forty feet long, and five feet deep in the middle. It was our fun place, where we splashed and kidded around with each other. On the far side of the pool, there was a wall of fissured rock, with a ledge about ten feet up. We used it as a jumping-off spot, but as I said, the water was only about five feet deep there, and one day Josh jumped in the wrong way and hurt his ankle. He didn't break it, but made it very sore. Something about this event seemed to put him in a funky mood, which gradually became worse. He had a bad limp, and he got cranky, grumbling and complaining constantly. Finally, the last night he was there, it came to a head.

Food was getting low at this point. Very few campers had been coming to Bonanza Campground, and those that came didn't leave anything useable behind. We had gone up to one RV the day before, but when the man who was there with his wife saw us, he took a shotgun out of the RV, and we decided maybe we weren't so hungry after all.

Later, at the campfire, Josh came up from collecting wood, and threw a good-sized branch onto the fire, sending embers and sparks all over us. "This is a messed up scene!" he yelled.

Jeff and I took him aside, hoping to mellow him out, but he ignored our trying to be friendly. He suddenly took a swing at Jeff, only partly connecting. Even though Jeff may have been a lover, he wasn't any fighter. He buried his face between his upright forearms and backed up. I caught Josh a good one on the side of his face, and he went down.

He started crying and said, "You're all full of crap!"

Seeing Josh had no fight left in him, Jeff said, "I think it's time you moved on, Josh, right now."

Suddenly the whole thing caught up with Josh, and his bad attitude disappeared. Whatever had been gnawing at him was gone. He sat there, stunned. Jeff and I went back to the fire where Hawk was still sitting, a slight smile on his face.

Josh went over to his shelter, the one he shared with the other guy. A few minutes later, he and his buddy walked by, their arms full of stuff. "You're all gonna be sorry we're leaving. Up yours!"

We watched as they were enveloped by the darkness, headed in the direction of the road. We could hear them talking together for a while, walking in the direction of Bonanza, until they were out of earshot. It was instantly a lot cooler, with them gone.

But we never were sorry. What's done is done, and peace was restored to our family, at least for the time being. I guess I knew now Jeff was right. They needed me for backup. I hoped my protective services wouldn't be needed too often, but had a feeling they would be.

Staying where the Indians had once been was cool in some ways, being out in nature and living as a small tribe. Thinking back now, I know we had also accepted their fate, too, in our flawed and naïve way. We chose their path of life in so-called modern times, but nothing had actually changed. We had also chosen to become the ones who always got the short end of the stick.

The next day, Jeff and I talked about our food situation. Our supplies were getting low, and we had to do something about it. We hadn't had a complete meal in a couple of days. I told him I had about thirty dollars left from the money I had brought with me originally, and we could buy food with it. He said we should hike into the town of Jolon and get some groceries.

Jolon was some distance away, but we were up for it. It would only be Jeff, Janey, and me, since more people would attract too much attention. Janey had told me it was always interesting going to town because the local people would get nervous having a bunch of dirty hippies wandering around, looking for trouble, of course. Besides, somebody needed to watch our goods, so Hawk and Julie stayed behind. Maybe Josh and his buddy would come back if we were all gone and mess our stuff up out of spite. We weren't sure where they were right now.

The weather was clear and warm, so the walk through the woods along the county road toward Jolon was pleasant enough, but was also the road and direction taking us past Hunter-Liggett Army Reservation. Though the few interactions with the G.I.s hadn't been a real problem, they had always made the tribe edgy.

The way past the base went without a hitch, the guards at the front gate being the only people we saw as we went by. A while later, maybe a mile past the base, we were approached by a pick-up with two young farmer types going the other way. They stopped across from us on the road, and the country boy in the passenger seat leaned across the driver and said, "I sure hope you ain't gonna stop in town, 'cause it's trash day and you might get picked up by mistake!" They roared away up the road, probably impressed with their attempt at humor. No harm done, but it put an edge to my mood. Jeff and Janey brushed it off, probably having been through this kind of thing before. We kept on walking.

After several more miles, we got to the outskirts of Jolon. It was a small town with very few buildings. Jeff said we should stop outside the grocery store, figure what we want, let Janey go in and shop, and then head right back to camp. She had her normally wild-and-free hair neatly tied back, with a relatively clean and basic dress on, and some old sandals on her feet. As we headed to the store, I saw a tiny Mexican restaurant several buildings up from the market.

"I sure would love a good bowl of *menudo* or chile!" I said.

Jeff gave me a challenging look and said, "Since it's your idea, why don't you see what you can do."

I took on his challenge to see if I could provide for us, and we headed to the restaurant. But, instead of going in the front, I decided to go around back. It was instinct, I guess, 'cause I sure didn't have any real plan in mind. I knocked at the back screen door, the inner door being open to the kitchen. The smells coming out were almost overwhelming in the power of their deliciousness. We hadn't had a solid meal in about three days, munching on odds and ends. I actually felt queasy from the reaction of my stomach to the signals it was getting from my brain!

A middle-aged Mexican man came to the back door. He looked at us all, smiled this great toothy grin and said, "*Y que quieres, indios pobrecitos?*"

My three years of high school Spanish might finally have a realistic purpose. He had asked, in an amiable way, "What do you poor Indians want?"

"Okay, let's see where this goes," I thought. My Spanish was rusty, but I made the attempt. I told the man we hadn't had a real meal in about three days and asked him if we could trade some work, such as doing dishes, for some food.

Jeff and Janey stood there looking at me, obviously impressed with my command of the language, while I spoke in my stumbling Spanish.

The Mexican man opened the screen door and said in broken English, "Is okay, come in, come in, *no problemo*."

After we made introductions, we walked into the kitchen, and Mr. Calderon, the owner, led us to a table and told us to sit down.

"My daughter bring you some food. I must be cooking *ahorita*."

A few minutes later, this so-cute-it-hurts Mexican girl in her middle teens comes over with a shy smile, and asks us what we would like. Jeff got some enchiladas with rice and beans, and Janey got the same. But I politely asked if they had some *chile colorado*. she laughed, showing perfect white teeth and said *"El mejor,"* the best, and she was right.

I'm surprised the customers in the restaurant didn't hear our stomachs growling as we waited, but Mr. Calderon must have, because he said something to his daughter about the Indians with their *"estomigos pequenos."* I guess with our funky clothing, Jeff's headband, and our overall condition, Mr. Calderon saw us as poor Indians.

The food came, and man, it was incredible! We ate slowly but steadily, savoring each mouthful. At one point, Janey suggested we not mention this tasty meal to Julie and Hawk, so they wouldn't feel left out. Jeff and I both agreed it would be the fair thing to do. So saying, we all went back to work on our food.

Calderon's daughter came and sat beside me, wanting to know if I liked the chile.

I felt she was asking a lot more with those few words. Hey, I may not have been on top of the world, but I was clean, my hair and beard were in good shape, and I had leaned out already in the several weeks I had been in the trees. I was probably something unique to this sweet young thing. Maybe she was picking up on my energy. All I knew was I was getting off on sitting next to her, too, with her shiny black hair, pretty brown eyes, and her natural warmth. She also smelled wonderful, like some blossoming wildflower.

But, Mr. Calderon caught on to the cozy interaction between his daughter and me, and said something to her in quickly-spoken Spanish. After giving him a sharp look, and flashing one more heartbreaking smile at me, she took herself away to the front of the restaurant.

The *Senor* didn't act unfriendly, but we all figured it was time to finish up and see about paying for our meal in kitchen work.

But, he wouldn't hear of it, telling us to not worry about it. "Maybe you come back sometime, and you sit, *en el restaurante*, okay?"

I knew he meant it in a good way, like maybe our lives would get better, become more prosperous, and we could sit where we wanted. I praised his good cooking, and we went on our way. We never went back there together again, the way of things being what they are.

There are times when I don't know whether movies and books are taken from life, or if it's the other way around. The more I travel and experience things, the more I wonder about it. The memory of the way it went down in that kitchen sure gives me food for thought on the concept. The rest of the day after our meal was another whole trip, most definitely.

We headed over to the grocery store where Jeff and I sat on the bench outside, while Janey went in with the money and the mental list we had worked up beforehand.

She had been inside a few minutes, when a Cadillac sedan pulls up, and out steps a pot-bellied rancher type in a sharp, country-style suit and a pure white Stetson. He paused before he went into the store, and nodded in Jeff's direction, but not in a friendly way, more of a "What are you doing here again?" way.

After he went into the store, Jeff told me we ought to head out as soon as Janey came back with the food. I didn't ask what was up, but nodded my agreement.

A short while later, Janey came out carrying two full bags of groceries. Jeff and I each grabbed one and started moving away, back toward the county road we had come in on. We had gone about fifty yards, when Jeff told me to keep walking, but to take a quick look back.

A sheriff's car had pulled up outside the store, and the fat-bellied Stetson came out to talk to him. They looked in our direction, but for whatever reason, maybe because we were leaving and had paid with cash, they didn't hassle us, and we kept up a steady walk away from the pleasant town of Jolon.

Stopping to take a short break, setting the bags down on the edge of the road, I asked Jeff if he knew the man in the Stetson.

"You might say so," he said. "We had words last time I was at the store. He didn't like me asking him for spare change."

After telling me this, Jeff suggested we get back to camp. Picking up our bags, we headed back home. We made it past Hunter-Leggett Army Reservation, and just past it, I noticed some old, adobe-style buildings I hadn't seen for some reason when we came down the road. Janey told me it was the San Antonio Mission, and we might go there sometime to work in the garden, if they'd let us. She, Jeff, and Hawk had done it once and they were given a bag of homemade bread and some cooked meat to take with them.

About half way between Hunter-Liggett and our camp, we stepped to the side of the road when we heard a vehicle coming. It was a jeep from the base with two M.P.s in it. Jeff told us to keep to the side, but stay on the road.

The jeep pulled up close to us and the M.P.s got out. The larger of the two wanted to know what we were doing on base property and demanded to see some identification.

Jeff told them we were on the road, which was county property, and they had no right to ask us anything.

The big G.I. got pissed off and made a move toward Jeff. I don't know why, but I responded to this by crouching down and letting out a low growl. I do believe I would have jumped on the M.P. if he had connected with Jeff, even though he had a pistol on his belt.

He stopped dead, and the expression on his face told me he thought he was looking at a crazy man, and it seemed to take the wind out of his sails.

I stayed in this ready-to-leap position, not growling anymore, but glaring directly at him. Maybe he wasn't expecting such behavior from a hippie type, acting like a cornered animal. But I sure got his attention.

Backing away, he said something lame like, "Don't let us catch you around here again." They got back into their jeep, turned around, and disappeared. We all breathed easier then, and picked up our bags and continued walking. As we stepped along, Jeff smiled at me and said, "I knew you'd be good to have around. You did well."

Camp was as we'd left it. Hawk and Julie were down by the pool, lying in the sun. We all gathered by J and J's shelter and took stock of what we had gotten. Janey had chosen wisely, getting good basic foods, including a number of cans of the universal favorite, Spam. There were also canned vegetables, butter, bread, fresh carrots, and tomatoes. But, the best things she chose were several large, juicy, chuck steaks and a large bag of marshmallows. We cooked the steaks in the evening over an open fire on some camping grills gotten from Bonanza campground, and toasted the whole bag of marshmallows on pointed sticks we picked. Brother, what a childhood rush, roasting them over the campfire after dinner. It reminded me of the family picnics we used to have when I was a kid. I did what I did back then, getting a marshmallow burning, and blowing it out at the right time to create a tasty crunchy skin which I ate, after which I did the same thing to what was left, until it was all gone. Man, what a far-ago and long-away trip to remember.

I think what we went through to get this meal, and especially the marshmallows afterward, affected all of us the same way. We talked and laughed over things as a family might at a get-together.

I thought out loud, as we kicked back after dinner, when the marshmallows were all gone and the fire was crackling away as any self-respecting campfire should, saying it was too bad we didn't have any more weed to smoke. Julie smiled and produced half of a joint she had kept stashed away. We all murmured something about her great wisdom and foresight, then lit up and gratefully took a few hits each. It was enough to make a pleasant end to a groovy night, after a most amazing day of adventures in the lives of us "poor Indians."

We were careful with the food, but after a week, our supplies were getting lean again.

I was to have my first experience with a visit from some Hunter-Liggett G.I.s soon after that. One afternoon, less than a week past our run to Jolon, we heard a car driving up the county road. Julie was able to spot them as G.I.s they had met before, four of them. We all went to our shelters and got dressed. By the time we came out, they were standing next to their car, which had a large cardboard box sitting on its hood.

When they saw us, they waved, and came down to the camp with the box. These were army dudes in their early twenties, and they had nice friendly smiles on their faces, a little too friendly. Hawk had told me that what they wanted, when they came to visit with food and booze as they were doing now, was girls. They apparently figured hippie girls would do it with anybody in trade for some food or liquor.

These were bored and horny young men. Maybe they were back from Nam or somewhere else overseas, being reoriented to society, and needed some R & R. We kept it as light and friendly as we could, but we sure weren't going to let them mess with the girls, no way. Jeff whispered to me one of the chicks who was there briefly a few months before, had let a G.I. get into her skivvies, and they had been sniffing around ever since.

This particular time, the soldiers started laying some jive lines on the girls who politely listened, but were having none of it. The conversation got strained after a while, when the G.I.s talking to Janey and Julie picked up on the fact they weren't getting anywhere. The G.I.s were also obviously trying to ignore Jeff, Hawk, and me except for some cautious sideways glances.

Darkness had come on. The girls had drifted away, pretending to need to do something in another part of the camp. The box of food was sitting on the camp table we borrowed from Bonanza Campground a while back, half hidden behind an oak. Jeff nudged my arm, and nodded in its direction. Besides the chips, canned food, and sodas they had brought, there were two bottles of cheap whiskey. They had tried to get the girls to have some drinks, but had been turned down, and the bottles were still unopened.

The G.I.s had gone into a huddle, not sure what to do next. In a flash, Jeff and I had grabbed a bottle each and disappeared into the darkness away from the table. We were familiar with the area around our camp, but the G.I.s weren't. After yelling at us to bring the booze back, they ended up cursing at us for being dirty hippies, and a few other choice words. They took the box of food, flipped the table over and drove off.

After waiting about ten minutes to be sure they were gone, we all met up at Julie and Hawk's shelter. We didn't make a fire, but we did start hitting the whiskey. The girls had a taste, but Jeff and I and Hawk got deeply into the two fifths we had raided, and before long we were getting real dumb. The girls got disgusted, and went over to J and J's shelter, leaving us to our foolish goings on.

Jeff produced a small mouth harp and started playing. He had caught me off guard, but Hawk knew he could play. Jeff started putting out some blues noises, and Hawk and I started singing together. I'm sure we ran off any wildlife within a mile of camp with our less-than-perfect vocals. Our words finally turned into a drinking song Hawk knew, which I don't remember, drunk as I had been, it being such a momentous occasion.

If ever there was a song needing someone to actually be there to realize its full character and value, it was definitely this song, but we sang it over and over until Janey and Julie got up and dragged Hawk and Jeff away, which put an end to our raucous and hearty goings on. It was a good thing the G.I.s didn't come back looking for revenge over the captured booze at this point, because we couldn't have done a thing about it.

Our condition the next morning I'll leave to your imagination, but I woke up outside my shelter not having made it all the way in, and my mouth felt like a wild pig had sat in it. For all I knew, one could have.

The next few days were peaceful. There was nothing uptight going on. The soldiers hadn't returned, the weather was good, and we added a bit to our food supplies from a lone camper up at Bonanza campground, actually amused at our nakedness. Julie and Janey had spotted him, and I guess it was worth some chow to have them hang around a while in their tanned, lean, female altogether. They let him take a few pictures of them in the camp's natural surroundings.

Later in the day, Julie and Hawk became private, keeping to themselves, hidden amongst the oaks and granite boulders. They were definitely a solid item. Jeff & Janey decided to go hiking in a favorite area they liked, so I was left to myself.

I just took it easy, tripping out on how easy life felt. I got warmed up lying in the sun on the flat-topped boulder, to the point where I needed to cool off. I slid down to the sandy-bottomed pool on the other side of the boulder where my shelter was, and lay down in its coolness, resting my head on a low, flat, smooth rock sticking out from the bank.

I was feeling totally soothed, my mind drifting peacefully, letting the water calm me and take me far away, when I thought I heard some whispering. I lifted my head and looked around. Nobody was nearby. Laying my head back down, a moment later I heard it again. I listened as the sounds continued, more curious than startled. They sounded like a different language, but I couldn't identify it. Suddenly I had this vision in my mind of hands, or hand-shaped symbols, red, yellow, and green, moving up and down, up and down. I started hearing slapping sounds in time with the movement of the hand shapes, and then I heard giggling, so close it seemed to be right next to me. It was all a little too much.

I jumped up and stood there, water dripping off me. Going to a grassy spot up the bank, I sat still for a while, considering what had occurred. I had a realization: what I heard had happened a long time ago. I stood looking at the area of the pool and the smooth flat rock my head had rested on, and I suddenly knew it had been used for washing clothing, skins, and woven stuff.

I looked to my left at the boulder with the acorn-grinding holes in its flat top, and it all came so clear. My first feelings about this spot when I set up my shelter were right. I was in the middle of the long-gone Indian women's gathering place, where they came to do their daily chores, share gossip, and feel secure in their unity. I felt funny inside, as if I had been allowed to connect with something wonderful, and had somehow been accepted here. I felt the need to leave the pool though, sensing this amazing moment was done. I walked on down to the meadow by the fallen oak, and sat with my back against it to let the events at the pool roll around in my mind. The effects lasted the rest of the day.

I didn't tell anyone else about this. They'd probably think I was loaded on something, but I wasn't. I hadn't even smoked anything for days now. No, I figured this was a gift. I accepted it and placed it somewhere special in my mind.

This happening did something to me. Ever since then, I can always tell if the places I pick for camping are good for me or not, and if I will feel secure and out of harm's way there. Being out on the road, you have to be careful in new places. When I come to the Carson River, I always camp in this same spot, knowing it's right for me.

Next morning, Janey said she and Jeff were going down to Esalen Institute to enjoy the hot tubs there. I asked what Esalen Institute was, and she said it was one of those feel-good-about-yourself places, where people pay a lot of money to experts who teach them how to be all right. They must be experts, Janey said, since they were raking in the bread. I asked her if I could come along with them and she said sure.

So, we started hiking down Nacimiento-Ferguson road, and even though we saw several cars go by, nobody stopped to give us a ride. We reached Highway 1 a few hours later, and started walking the several miles north on the road to where Esalen Institute was.

There was no front gate, but Jeff told me to wait while he and Janey, who had been there before, checked out the situation. I wasn't sure what they meant, but I said I'd wait.

I sat down off the road and waited for what may have been an hour, and then decided to check things out myself. Walking down the entrance road, I skirted around the nearest building off to one side, not wanting to walk right through the grounds. Coming around the corner of the second concrete structure, I saw the back of it, the side facing the sea, was wide open, and it was actually a bath house with four or five hot tubs made out of concrete, but all tiled inside. There were several couples in two tubs, and one guy in another.

Thinking I could rap with the man about Esalen, I walked in, dropped my threads, and stepped into the tub where he sat. Brother, the steamy water sure felt good! The guy just sat on the other side of the tub, giving me an odd look.

"What's happening?" I asked, wanting to break the ice. But, he got right out of the tub, grabbed a towel, and walked away. I stayed where I was, enjoying the hot water.

A few minutes later, the same guy came back dressed, with two other men, all three of them looking unhappy. One of them asked me if I was a member of the Institute and I told him no, but I lived in Big Sur, so my being here should be cool. They didn't go for it, and had me get up and grab my threads, which I slowly put on, then walked me off the property.

Jeff and Janey were nowhere around, so I laid out under some bushes a little ways down from the road. The hot tub had done its job, and I dozed off, to be awakened a while later by J and J standing over me nudging me with their feet.

"What the heck did you do, Jester?" asked Jeff. Turns out, they knew one of the maintenance people working there, and they were going to hang out until the tubs were vacant later, then they would come and get me and we would have us a nice soak. Trouble was, during normal hours people would go down to the tubs to explore each other, if you catch my drift. So, when I got in the tub, the man got the wrong idea about why, and had gone for help. Jeff and Janey had to leave, the whole scene blown, and they were really unhappy with me.

We hiked on down the highway and back up Nacimiento-Ferguson road, not enjoying one step of the way and got back to the camp late, going to sleep without eating. Oh well, live and learn. Heck, it was only a tub of hot water anyways.

A couple of days later, two young hippies showed up in camp, down from San Francisco. They told us someone in the Haight who had stayed with the tribe for a week the past fall had told them about us, and these young brothers had come to check it out. Jeff thought he remembered the people they were talking about, probably because they had been generous to the tribe with food and other goodies.

Apparently our group had developed a reputation in The City. Jeff and I looked at each other and smiled.

The boys said they had brought some good eats in their van, and also some synthetic psilocybin, which was the latest high. So they were welcomed into the group as visitors. They didn't want to join our carefree band, but they would to be able to tell people they had stayed here with us. These two couldn't have been more than twenty, and were quite impressed with the stories we told about life in the mountains of Big Sur. After we had cooked the hamburgers, beans, and ears of corn they supplied, we took the psilocybin, put up in capsules.

This was fun stuff, called "sillycybin" by those who knew. It could make you grin 'til your jaws ached. We lay around enjoying ourselves, totally into the mellow atmosphere the stuff created.

Out of the blue, one of the new fellas started singing old mountain songs, which blew us away, this young man in hippie threads, singing songs right out of Appalachia. Turned out his people were all from Virginia. Jeff got out his mouth harp, and after a warm-up, joined right in, blending smoothly with the music the new guy was singing.

As the light started to fade, the sunset sky took on an opalescent sheen looking like mother of pearl. It was amazing. At first I was the only one who saw it, but once I started describing it, most of the others saw it too. Hooray for magic mushrooms, synthetic or otherwise!

The guy with the good voice sang one last song without Jeff playing the harmonica. It was an eerie song about love gone wrong, and ended with a man being hung for a crime he couldn't have committed because he had been with his lover. But, she was married, so being a gentleman, he didn't use her for an alibi. Ever after his execution, she walked the hills in sorrow. He sang it so well, when the song was done, we all said goodnight and quietly walked to our primitive dwellings.

The two mellow brothers hung around for a couple of days, and very kindly gave us a huge, heavy bud of weed when they left. It was a pleasant interlude for us all, leaving lots of lasting good vibes.

One morning, a little later, I told Jeff I needed to go back to San Francisco to put another month's rent on my pad, and get some more money so things could stay good in camp for a while. I said he was welcome to come along if he wanted. He told me he should, to make sure I'd come back. I realized he was only half kidding.

I asked "Don't you think I'm into the scene here enough to want to come back?"

"Maybe, but things happen, brother," Jeff answered. "Might not have anything to do with what you want."

So it was decided we would both go in a couple of days. As it turned out, it was good we didn't leave the same day.

Things had been peaceful for a while. Parks Department hadn't been around while I was there, and the G.I.s whose booze we stole still hadn't come back with a chip on their shoulder, and we figured they had either left the base, or just let it go. So, we weren't too concerned about leaving the girls and Hawk to mind camp for a couple of days. Hawk was good at dealing with things, but he was only one person, so we wouldn't stay away any longer than we had to. Later in the night though, the soldiers did come back.

The five of us were sitting around the campfire at J and J's shelter, when Hawk said quietly, "We've got company."

We all looked in the direction he was facing, and saw six soldiers in civilian clothes walking toward us. Two of them were of the four we had stolen the booze from, but the others we had never seen before and they were looking serious. There was one G.I. standing in front who was larger than the rest, and I figured him for the leader of the pack. He had a hard look in his eyes.

We were all on our feet by then, the girls having stepped behind us. After a brief pause, Jeff told the men they were welcome to share some food and coffee with us.

The guy in front said we must have thought we were real smart, ripping off boys who came to hang around.

Hawk said, "Since it seems you're set on doing something, let's forget the small talk. Those guys were trying to get at our women, which we can't allow. They must have the wrong idea about them, or they wouldn't have tried. They're our women and they won't be shared with anybody."

All the while he was saying this, I was wondering how badly we were gonna get our butts kicked, and if we could protect the girls, not knowing if these soldiers had brought any weapons with them, and what they had in mind.

The angry men started to move forward, and I knew they weren't going to be reasoned with. We readied ourselves for the trouble coming, and suddenly, there was Janey standing between them and us. Jeff, Hawk, Julie and I looked at each other, wondering what this was all about.

"Are you boys forgetting where you are?" asked Janey. The guys looked at each other, wondering what she meant, and so did we.

"What are you talking about?" asked the guy who was apparently the leader.

"This is the U.S.A.," said Janey, "which I thought you are supposed to defend, and we are not your enemy. You may not think much of us, but we're Americans too, and if you plan on doing what I think you are, then you'll be common criminals, instead of the brave wonderful boys I know you to be. We're all glad you're back home, and we're sorry about the booze we took."

"What do you know about it?" asked one of the others.

Janey quietly replied, "My brother was killed in Viet Nam three years ago. He'd only been there a few weeks."

When Janey said this, which none of us except Jeff knew about, it brought the whole thing to a halt. The man in front had lost the hard, cold look in his eyes. After searching for something to say, and not finding anything, he turned around, said, "We're done here; let's go."

Another guy said, "Okay, Sarge," and they slowly walked away.

A couple of minutes later, one of the men who had been there when the whiskey was stolen came back with a bottle of whiskey and handed it to Janey, then turned around and walked away again. We heard a car engine start up, then fade away into the distance. We were all looking at Janey, our heroine, and she just said, wiping tears from her eyes, "We've got some coffee left, anybody want some whiskey in theirs?"

Jeff and I headed out early in the morning, San Francisco bound. We figured there would be no more trouble with the G.I.s, so it was not a worry. He and I ended up walking all the way down Nacimiento-Ferguson Road, without seeing one car along the way. This road is known to locals as a back way to get to Highway 1, but nobody was using it at the time. It was a long hike, but we were feeling good and had a plastic bottle full of Nacimiento River water to drink. It was a beautiful walk, and downhill most all the way.

We saw some cat prints about half way down, but we weren't sure if they were bobcat or mountain lion, which most people don't know still live in those hills. We kept our eyes open watching for wildlife, but we only saw lots of birds. We reached the bottom of the road before noon, and seeing several camper vans across at Kirk Creek Camp, decided to see if we might get a bite to eat or drink.

At the first camper van, there was no one around, but the second one had an older couple in folding chairs relaxing, enjoying some quiet time. When they first saw us coming up to them, they looked concerned, but after talking with us a while, they became interested in what life was like living in the woods. So we told them about it, except for the parts we figured they would not get off on, such as drugs and nakedness.

Their name was Cummings, and Mrs. Cummings made us a couple of bologna sandwiches on Wonder Bread with mayonnaise. They tasted good, though the food value was minimal. We didn't complain, though.

Mr. Cummings was a World War II vet and a retired mechanic. His wife was a retired teacher, grammar school if I remember correctly. They were nice people, and didn't harbor any bad feelings toward us, not seeing us as dirty hippies when others would have.

We sat and talked, and when asked, I tried to explain what the hippie thing was all about. I told them it was basically all over with but the sorry stuff, and they both knew how good things could go bad, having lived long, full lives.

Mrs. Cummings asked me if I believed in what "that Leary person" was saying and I have to say she seemed pleased I didn't.

We finished our sandwiches and coffee, and said good-bye, telling them to head up Nacimiento-Ferguson Road if they wanted to see our camp, but they were headed south to visit their kids in L.A.

We didn't have any wild adventures on the rest of our journey. We got one ride after walking a few miles up Highway 1, sticking our thumbs out whenever we heard a vehicle coming up behind us as we headed north. It was with a head named Denny, in an old Caddy convertible. Man, was he buzzing! He'd left San Diego and had been driving all night, popping pills to stay awake. Denny later mentioned he was headed to S.F. to pick up some weed and LSD from some people he knew there, to take back down and sell in San Diego

Cruising up the highway, he asked us if we had any weed to smoke, since all the pills and coffee he had drunk had given him some rough edges, but, of course, we were without.

Denny had a good rap going. He was into Buckminster Fuller, who he called a futurist, the man who supposedly invented the Geodesic Dome. He said "Bucky" believed eventually there would be civilization all the way up and down the West Coast, nonstop. There would be people and buildings, homes and businesses everywhere. This certainly wasn't cool to hear, and bummed us out, so we told him we would believe it when we saw it. I now know he was not far off the mark there.

Denny got us as far as Santa Cruz, but after pulling into a McDonald's for some, as he put it, "burger trash" to eat, he told us he was starting to crash, and couldn't drive anymore. He was going to get a room in Santa Cruz to catch some zees.

We thanked him for getting us this far, and walked over to the road entrance to get us back onto Highway 1 heading north. We hadn't been thumbing there a few minutes when there goes Denny in his Caddy, headed toward S.F. He didn't look our way, but we didn't get bothered much by it, already burned out on his constant jawing.

Not even twenty minutes later, we got a lift from several fellow freaks in a VW van. After rapping with them about out our Big Sur home and sharing some potent weed they had, we settled into the back and cruised the rest of the way up, dozing off to some righteous tunes from Three Dog Night and The Grateful Dead.

They dropped us, in the evening, at my pad off Divisadero Street. I checked the padlock on the garage door where my truck was stored, and it looked good. But, finding the front door to the place unlocked put us on alert. Walking quietly up the stairs to my second-story pad showed the kitchen light to be on, and I sure hadn't left it on. The place smelled like dirty clothes. We reached the top of the stairs and turned left, walking into the living room area. Man, what a mess!

There was trash all over, snack bags and pizza boxes all around, empty beer and soda cans, plates, threads, you name it. On the couch was some loaded dude, zoned out, with a tie-off and needle lying on the floor next to the couch, and his cooking spoon and stuff on the trash-covered coffee table next to him.

I shook him awake, and he came to, startled and twitching. Angry, I asked him what he was doing in my pad. It came out he knew Eileen and her boyfriend, and they let him crash there for fifty bucks. They had given him the key they still had. I had thought about changing the front door lock after they had left with some of my goods, but had spaced it out.

I told the smackhead it was my place, and he had to get out.

He wanted to stay there, and tried to talk me into letting him, but I told him no way, he was a pig, and he was out of there.

The fool pulled out a pocketknife and threatened us. Jeff backed up a short way behind me, not wanting any part of a blade. I quick grabbed a funky leather jacket off a chair, and holding it in both hands, started hitting him with it as hard as I could. After four or five good hits, he dropped the knife and gave in.

I allowed him enough time to gather up the small amount of stuff he had there and made sure he found his way to the bottom of the stairs and out the door. Hey, I'm no hero; I was pissed off!

Going back up the stairs, I sat on a kitchen chair shaking my head. Jeff took the trashcan from the kitchen into the living room, and started cleaning up. I had no bad feelings toward him for not backing me up. He wasn't into violent action. Me, I didn't enjoy it either, but sometimes you have no choice in the matter.

A few minutes later, I started helping him, and soon enough, the place looked better. But, anything I had there of value was gone, including most of my threads. What a bummer, man! I felt ruined about this whole scene.

There was some edible bread in the kitchen, and some bacon in the fridge seemed good, so we had bacon sandwiches for eats. Suddenly I was pulled back to the main reason I had returned to the city and with a lump forming in my throat, thinking maybe what I had come back for was gone, I went into the bathroom and pulled away the floor molding behind the old radiator where I had stashed my money. It was still there! I had over eighteen hundred dollars left. I put it into my pants pocket and kept it there not wanting to lose contact with it.

After we ate, we went down to the garage through the lower back entrance, which was still locked. The truck was dusty from sitting there. Jeff went around and unlocked the garage door. I, meanwhile, had lifted the hood and reconnected the battery cables. It took a few tries, but she started and after a few minutes of warm-up was idling nicely. I shut it down, satisfied it was running okay.

By now it was late. Jeff and I were beat from our run up from Big Sur and the hassle once we got here, so we crashed out for the rest of the night.

Lying there in the dark, I decided it made no sense to keep renting the flat. I wasn't planning on living there anymore. The city seemed such a sad, nasty place to me now, noisy, dirty, and dangerous.

I considered for a moment how quickly I had changed my feelings about the "shining city" I had loved such a short time ago. We'd leave the apartment and head back to Big Sur as soon as we did some necessary business the next day. Once I made my decision, I felt better.

I also realized the truck would have no place in our lives in Big Sur. Yeah, it might be nice to drive down in our own rig, but then what? It would change things, having a vehicle there. The truck didn't fit into life in the woods. Talking to Jeff about it, he was of like mind. I would have to sell it, which would be no problem. I found it ironic to think something I had always felt was a necessity had become a burden.

As he was to do many times during the telling of his stories, Jester came back momentarily to the present, reflecting on how things had changed as he had aged, as his life rolled out before him.

These days, my friend, I don't know how I'd make it without some wheels. I'm too old to walk very far; my knees aren't so good anymore. Compromises for the sake of survival, man, is what it's about when you get older. There are times when I wish things were still simple and basic, like in my Big Sur days. But, there were problems then, too. Now I guess I've gotten my life down to as basic a process as I can and still be okay.

The next day, Jeff and I went out for some breakfast at the coffee shop on Duboce and Market. The place sure didn't feel the same. The old waitress wasn't there, and the customers looked normal, boring, so to speak.

Driving to Haight Street afterward, we went around to some of the stores and people on the street, looking to sell the truck. By the middle of the day, I had sold it to a fella in Fog Horn Fish & Chips, who jumped at the chance to buy such a groovy old truck. I got the three hundred back I originally paid for it. I had the title in my pocket, and it was all done five minutes after the guy had taken a test drive.

Jeff and I grabbed some take-out Chinese food on the way back to the pad, and made our plans for the next day. We'd head down to the Army-Navy store on lower Market Street and pick up some needed supplies, and leave for Sur the same day.

The Army-Navy store was cool, full of all kinds of surplus, and also newly-made goods. Jeff and I each got a pair of those tall, fringed "moccasins" popular then, even though the leather soles, if left as they were, didn't last long, being more for looks than wear. But, you could get some shoemaker's glue and add an extra piece of tough leather on the bottom for longer life, which we ended up doing. We also got Ka-Bar military-style knives for Jeff, me, and Hawk, along with a sharpening stone. We eventually picked out some other useful items for camp, wooden matches, two good-sized plastic tarps, and some cheap plastic ponchos. We bought two old military packs with wooden pack frames attached, to carry the supplies. We got out of there with all this stuff for a one hundred dollar bill.

Afterward, we went over to the Purple Heart Thrift Store some blocks up Market Street, but my old friend Art wasn't there anymore. We picked out several groovy dresses and blouses for the girls, and a nice pair of leather sandals Jeff said should fit Hawk.

We took a bus back to my old pad. There wasn't much to take from there, an old, light jacket of mine, a pair of pants, another shirt, and some socks. The rest of my goods had been stolen.

It was getting too late to start, so we went out for dinner, a pizza, and beer and called it a day, feeling pleased with our purchases.

I didn't mind putting out for the stuff from my money stash. These people had become like family and I was glad I could help out. Jeff didn't make all kinds of grateful noises, but I knew he appreciated the help. It wouldn't have been his way to say much anyways. I hadn't learned a lot about him or Janey. I would just have to accept what they volunteered, and learn about them from the way they acted around me. So far, I had come to like what I had seen. They weren't really family, of course, but they were more than friends, and I knew if I needed help, they would do whatever they could to give it. What more can you ask of somebody?

So, the next morning we headed back down to our home in the oak trees. We got stopped once by a cop, on the edge of the Great Highway below Golden Gate Park, who was going to give us a ticket for hitchhiking. Jeff started a mellow rap with him, convincing the officer since we were leaving San Francisco, it was worth letting us off to get rid of a couple of hippies from the area. The cop chuckled. Jeff had gotten to him, and he did let us off, telling us we better be leaving. No Problem. I had I.D., but Jeff didn't. I had a feeling Jeff having I.D. might have meant trouble for him.

On the way down, we got one ride from The City to Half Moon Bay, but got stuck there for a couple of hours, finally riding in the back of a pick-up truck all the way down to Kirk Creek Camp.

Neither one of us wanted to head all the way back up the road to our camp, since it was getting late already. There was no one at Kirk Creek Camp, and we spent an undisturbed evening by a small fire, using one of the plastic tarps we had bought to make a simple shelter.

We didn't talk much, though we did trade a few remarks about life. I told him about how I had traveled to S.F. and the visit with my brother, and how it had affected me.

Jeff actually volunteered he had come from a small town in Pennsylvania, and San Francisco had drawn him also.

Before I dropped off to sleep, I asked Jeff if he had ever been back to his hometown.

"Never have been and doubt I ever will," was all he said, and I never asked again.

Next morning, gnawing on some commercial beef jerky we had bought, we started back up the road. We rested several times along the way. When we had been in Half Moon Bay, we had stocked up on lots of canned goods, small bags of dried beans and such, and a few nice spices for cooking. We also bought a couple of loaves of dark shepherd's bread, locally baked in Half Moon bay. It didn't take long for us to feel the weight of our packs, walking on that long, long uphill road. Those old military pack frames weren't built for comfort.

When we finally got close to camp, we perked up a bit, happy to be home, but it didn't last long. Things looked bad.

No one was there to meet us, the shelters were all ripped up, and things were scattered all over. A fire had been used to burn a bunch of stuff like clothes and sleeping bags, judging from what remained in the ashes. One of Janey's cooking pots was in the firepit, too. We were freaked, and walked all over the place looking for Janey, Julie, and Hawk, our bellies knotted up with the bad thoughts we were having. We wanted to call out, but didn't know what the situation was, so we kept still.

Jeff and I ended up at my shelter down by the boulder, which had survived no better. After setting our packs down, we found my sleeping bag lying in the creek, but not ripped up much. My threads were torn up and scattered, though.

While we were sitting there trying to figure what to do next, we heard someone quietly crying. We went toward the sound, and found Janey and Julie sitting between two boulders overgrown with bushes. Julie was the one crying, but Janey had a terrible look on her face. They calmed down a little, after seeing we had returned. Janey ran up and grabbed onto Jeff, but Julie sat, quietly crying.

Janey said the day after we left, early in the morning, a park ranger came up with two county sheriffs and told them they had to leave. When they started packing things up, they were told to leave their things and go, or be arrested for squatting on state land. Hawk started arguing, telling them they were going to take their stuff.

After some verbal abuse between them, one of the sheriffs went to grab him, and Hawk resisted. The other sheriff came up and hit Hawk with his baton. Hawk managed to break away and took off, running across the creek and over the hill behind. Janey said she and Julie were backing away while this was going on, and had slipped off into the woods, too. The sheriffs and the Parks guy didn't chase them, but trashed and burned all our stuff before leaving.

Looking around, Jeff asked where Hawk was, and Julie started crying again.

"He's dead," said Janey.

"What? Hawk's dead? This is crazy, man! Where is he?"

"Back behind the hill straight across the creek."

Leaving the girls where they were, Jeff and I went to look.

A little while later we found him. He was dead all right, his body stone cold. It appeared Hawk had tripped while running away, smashing his head on the large rock it was still pressed up against. When we rolled him over on his back, his head dropped to one side at a strange angle. It was obvious he had broken his neck. The skin on his forehead was badly torn up.

We both stood there awhile, blankly staring at our friend. Oh, man, how weird it all felt! Reality had gotten all twisted up.

We closed his eyes, gathered him up, and carried him back to camp, not wanting to leave him there alone. Brother, I'm telling you, this was the heaviest thing I had ever experienced, or thought I would ever do again. My whole body felt strange, as if it wasn't even my own, my mind somewhere else. To have such a thing happen here, in this place? Tears ran out of my eyes as I helped carry him back to camp, but I didn't make a sound.

When we got back, the girls were sitting out in the open where my shelter had been. Julie stood up and came over to us, looked at Hawk, and started shaking. She had truly loved this boy. Hawk had really been her man. The sadness of this scene filled our minds with grief.

We laid him down on a grassy place, and put one of the torn blankets over him, but Julie asked us to leave his face exposed. His forehead was bloody where the rock had messed it up, so Janey and Julie went down to the creek with a piece of one of my shirts, wet it, and washed his head.

The way he was lying where we found him, he must have died instantly. Even though the sheriffs hadn't actually struck the killing blow, I felt they were responsible for his death.

After he was cleaned up, Julie said we could put him to rest.

Janey got a fire going, retrieved one of her pots from where it had been thrown, and made some coffee we had brought back. No one was hungry. We all sat there, sipping the coffee and talking about what should be done.

"There's nothing can be done," Jeff said quietly. "He's gone, and there's no way we're gonna bring him back. He's got no family except us; this is the end of his road."

We also knew we couldn't stay there with the sheriffs probably coming back to make sure we had left, especially with Hawk still lying there.

We knew there was only one thing to do, and after nightfall we took him down below the meadow where the fallen oak tree was, with only a partial moon to guide us. We buried him wrapped in the old blanket, along with the knife we had bought him, using our hands and a pot to dig the deep, loamy soil under an oak tree. It was hard, but we dug the hole deep enough to keep coyotes and other things out. We scattered oak leaves, sticks and acorns over the spot we had flattened and smoothed, then we each said something and stood silently awhile.

Afterward, we went down to the creek to wash off, and slowly walked back to our camp to rest as best we could, but nobody actually slept.

When morning light came, we gathered what usable items we could, including my wet sleeping bag, the two torn blankets, and our full packs. Going back down to where we placed Hawk, we went across the creek and behind a hill into a small glen, hidden from view, and settled in, using our new plastic tarps to make a shelter. We cautiously built a small fire and ate some food, more because we needed to than wanted to. We all felt listless.

Come nighttime, we all lay together for warmth and comfort, finally sleeping. No one had a word to say.

Next morning, Jeff and I slipped over to the old camp. It must have been about ten a.m. We spotted the park ranger alone, gathering up what debris was left, putting it all in plastic trash bags, and depositing them into the back of his truck. We figured he had assumed the camp was permanently deserted. We were angry, but figured it wisest to slip away to our new spot. Maybe no one would miss one hippie more or less, but a Parks Department man missing would be something else.

We stayed in our hiding place for several more days, there not being anything else to do. Julie went across to Hawk's resting place once a day, always tearful when she came back.

The four of us sat talking the third day after we had returned, when things had come crashing down on us. We couldn't stay there; our time for living in Big Sur was over.

Jeff suggested we go visit some people he knew on the Russian River, in Monte Rio, California. They were good people, and Jeff was sure they would let us hang out there awhile. It would give us time to let go of all this sadness, and to consider our next move. Janey was willing, of course, wanting to be wherever Jeff was, and so was I, but Julie had been thinking. She was going home to Oregon, to her folks' place for a while and get herself in order, as she put it.

So it was all decided. No one expressed their heavy feelings about what had happened. There was no need; we were all close enough more words weren't necessary.

During the night, with Julie lying close to me for comfort, I lay awake a long time, thinking how, in only a month, my life had been completely turned around. The cosmic forces sure have a heavy way sometimes, of putting you on another path to follow through life. But, I had some money, was in good health, and for some reason, as I drifted off to my last night of sleep in those blessed hills, I knew I was going to be okay.

Next morning, we started walking Nacimiento-Ferguson road, getting a lift from a couple of Mexican men in a stake-bed truck when we were part way down. They dropped us off at Highway 1. The four of us stood there a while, not speaking. We offered Julie one of the packs to take, but she just smiled, gave us each a long hug and started up the road north carrying her little wrapped-up bundle. As we watched her walk away, a sudden urge made me run up to where she was and put two hundred dollars in her hand.

"Take a bus, Julie, or whatever you want to do to get to Oregon, and be good to yourself," I told her.

She gave me a sweet kiss, and continued on up the road. I wanted to stop her and tell her to stay with us, not wanting to lose another sweet girl from my life, but knew it couldn't happen. When she was barely out of view, walking north up the road, a car stopped to give her a ride.

"She'll be all right," Janey said. "She's got an angel on her shoulder."

We knew she was right on.

Section Three

Monte Rio was a long way from Big Sur, north and then inland from Fort Ross on Hwy 116. We thought Julie would come along with us part way, but she needed to break away from the whole scene so she could shake her heavy sadness, which was why she had departed on her own so quickly.

Jeff, Janey, and I started hitching. We got several rides into the Bay Area, and I suggested since I had some money, we ought to take a bus the rest of the way to Monte Rio. The events of the last few days had really messed with our energy, so J and J agreed.

We hitchhiked our way north up the highway to the nearest Greyhound Bus depot, and waited a couple of hours for the right bus. We got the back seat to lie out on. There was a skinny young white guy dressed in shirt and tie sitting there, but Jeff and I stood staring at him until he got the point and moved to another seat.

The three of us snuggled side by side with Janey between us and slept like babies, beat down from our hitchhiking and Hawk's death. Early the next morning, we were in Monte Rio.

Jeff made a call to his friends, and about twenty minutes later, an old International Travelall pulls up, with a bushy-faced man driving. It was Jeff's friend Greg Brauer, who hopped out and gave Jeff a friendly bear hug. Greg was a bear himself, large, furry and happy to see Jeff and the rest of us.

"Let's get you pilgrims up to our place, scrape all the travel off you, and fill your bellies," said Greg.

So we went, finding it difficult to stay bummed around this positive and together guy. Jeff was right, this was what we needed.

Greg and his wife Marla lived in a homey, country-style pad surrounded by native pine trees. They had two sons, both of them mischievous rascals, but good kids, Evan and Todd. Greg was a leather smith, and made groovy hats, vests, belts, and the like, many of them hand embossed and carved. He made high quality leather goods, and had a real workshop for doing his leatherwork.

They also had a hot tub, and within an hour of arriving, we were sitting in the redwood tub, letting the bubbling water soak our woes away. By the time we were done, Marla had made a huge platter of breakfast, eggs mixed together with potatoes, onions, bell peppers, and ground venison. We also had homemade bread and jam. Man, what a tasty meal!

These were good-hearted people, and I was resolved to somehow do for them, as they were doing for us. It's hard to do anything for self-reliant people though. They did everything for themselves and asked for nothing in return. We stayed there for two weeks, hanging out and doing small chores around the place. I cleaned out the chicken coop, worked in their garden, and helped repair the shed roof.

I felt so good I had to remind myself it was temporary, not wanting to forget the fact. I tried to give them money for food, but they said no way; helping out like I had been doing was enough. I didn't know what the connection between Jeff and Greg was exactly, but they were tight.

One night, we sampled some of Greg's homemade beer. It tasted great, and was strong stuff, too! He told us the first batch he made didn't survive. He stored the fermenting bottles down in the basement of their pad, which he had built himself, but they never got to drink any. One evening, while they were relaxing in the living room, noises like muffled firecrackers began coming from the basement. The stuff had built up too much pressure, and all the bottles were blowing out.

Greg told us, "We didn't dare go down there for a few days, until things settled down. The next batch, my friends, we were much more careful about preparing!"

While the others were still enjoying the home brew, I decided to go crash in the tent they had set up in the backyard for me. Jeff and Janey had their own room.

I had been sleeping a while; it was maybe two or three in the morning. I woke up, because someone was slipping into bed with me. It was Janey. I was groggy, but came around quickly to this unexpected situation.

"It's cool, Jester," she said, "Jeff and I talked about it, and I wanted to come in and keep you company. It's all good, unless you object."

No, I was okay with it, but I had to lose some of the beer first. I slipped out and walked to the side yard fence. I was standing there communing with nature, when I noticed Jeff standing nearby in the same state. After a glance and a nod to each other, we finished and went our separate ways.

I went back to the tent and the woman waiting for me. Getting together with Janey was something I'd thought about before, and I knew Janey had too, checking me out once in a while at our old camp. So, we entered into the age-old wrestling match where hopefully nobody loses, and in this case, no one did. It was good, and sealed a final bond needing to be made.

As we lay there afterward snuggled up together, Janey told me she and Jeff were heading out in a few days, going back home for a while. Jeff had skipped out on a court case he was involved in sometime back. It's what started him on the road in the first place. Janey had met him near Santa Barbara over four years ago and they had been traveling together ever since. While we were at Greg's, he had made arrangements to go back and stand trial without any further charges being put on him. Whoever he had talked to had agreed, so they were going back.

Janey told me, "He's tired of this negative thing hanging over his head, waiting to get caught out here for some minor thing, identified, and sent back to worse charges. Besides, we've been out in it for a long time now, and need to settle down."

"It sure sounds like the right thing to do, the way you tell me. I hope you can trust them to hold up their end of the bargain."

"I know, Jester, I know." She gave me a one last kiss and slipped out of bed, the tent, and a few days later, out of my life, the two of them.

Later the same morning, Greg came up to talk, and asked me what I had planned.

"Nothing, really," I answered, "but I'll think of something. I don't want to overstay my welcome."

Greg smiled and told me I was far from being unwelcome. He told me his leather business was really growing, and he was thinking of taking someone on to help him. He asked me if I would be interested. I had made myself a belt, and was working on a vest during the time we'd been there. Greg said he was impressed with my work, thought I had a knack for it, and was not just trying to make me feel good by saying so. He asked me if I could take suggestions if they were for making things better. I told Greg I'd gladly take any help coming from him. He did excellent work, and I'd be a fool not to.

Greg told me I'd get a percentage of what we'd make selling the leather goods plus room and board in their pad until I got the cabin cleaned up enough to live in. When I asked him what cabin he was talking about, he drove me over there to show it to me.

Turned out Greg and Marla had a small piece of property about a half mile away, with an access road and a sweet-water well on it, along with a twelve-by-sixteen, one-room cabin needing some work. When I saw it, I knew right away it would suit me perfectly. My own hideaway. I wouldn't mind having a place alone, and even looked forward to it.

Greg told me, "The work you do fixing it up will be fair trade for you living there. I'm too busy to get to it, so it'll be good for us, too."

I told him I'd do it if he'd let me pay for materials, or it was no dice. With an understanding smile, he said it was fair enough. We shook hands and the deal was done.

When we got back to the pad, I told Jeff and Janey what had been arranged, and they were glad I had found a home. They hadn't felt good about leaving without knowing what was next for me. Two days later, they were gone. They woke me up early to say good-bye, before Greg took them to the bus station. I asked if they needed any money, but they said they were good. We did a heavy three-way hug, and then they were gone.

It's funny how you can know someone a short while and feel you've known them forever, but you can be around some people a long time indeed and never really connect with them. Jeff and Julie remain with me to this day, though we never met again. I hope their lives have turned out okay, but in this world, you never know, man, you just never know.

The cabin did need some work, the first thing being to put a new shingle roof on, and the roof framing needed some repairs too. I had never done this kind of work before, but it wasn't hard for me to figure out. I matched up the old boards with new ones. The shingles weren't too hard to do either. I walked around the neighborhood, looking at shingle roofs on other houses, and asked a few questions at the supply house. Greg let me use his old Travelall. What a great rig. It had over two hundred thousand miles, but was still running strong. Greg kept the body straight and the insides clean, too. He was righteously cool in my book.

I think the best way for me to describe people who are good and decent is to say they have a lot of heart. They're righteous, but not in a religious way, though it might play a part. It's how they live their daily lives: honest, up front, not judging anyone, willing to give a person a chance to "prove up," and show what they're made of. Greg and Marla were such people. They helped me get my trip together and find a good path for myself at a time when I wasn't sure what I would do.

I called the folks while I was staying with the Brauers, but my last visit had put them off, and the call was awkward. But I think I got them to understand I was doing okay.

Living in the Big Sur woods, even for such a short time, had broken some threads for me with so-called civilization. I had no desire to live in a real city again, for sure. A peaceful place to be, a few good friends, and something worthwhile to do to bring in some bucks was all I needed.

I wasn't looking for a steady chick. I needed to get my own thing together before sharing with someone else. If I felt lonely, I'd get into my leatherwork or do some more work on the cabin.

One day, when I was working on the cabin's interior walls, adding insulation and putting a layer of plastic sheeting on inside, I whacked my thumb with the hammer, then waited for the short painless moment to turn into a familiar, aching hurt. I turned toward the door, and there stood two guys I had never seen before, dressed in the style of most of this Northern California town's locals: long hair, baseball cap, torn plaid shirts, levis, and work boots. The local guys' hair might be long, and maybe they smoked some weed besides drinking beer, but they weren't hippies, a term, at the time, being applied to anybody wearing a headband and sandals.

One of them said, "Who are you and what are you doin' in this cabin?" My thumb was throbbing and I was in no mood.

"Why, you the cabin police?" I asked.

"We know who owns this place, but we don't know you," he answered.

The one not talking took a few steps forward, and I picked up my shingling hammer. "Close enough," I said, in my best John Wayne imitation. "This is Greg and Marla's cabin. I'm doing leatherwork for him, and he's letting me fix up the cabin and live here."

The one man had backed up and said to the other, trying to regain his edge, "I didn't know Greg knew any dumbass hippies."

I responded, getting into it, "I guess he knows at least two dumb rednecks."

The other one said, "I bet you smoke a lot of weed, too, dontcha?"

"All I can get hold of," I said, with attitude.

The one who hadn't moved smiled a snaggle-toothed grin and said, "I don't suppose you have any with you?"

It seemed I had made the right impression by not taking the crap they were putting out, so I broke out the one half-smoked number I had, and we lit up. I guess you could say we smoked the peace joint.

As they were leaving, pleasantly loaded and, I figured, satisfied I was okay to be there, I told them to drop in anytime. They did come back, a couple times a week, bringing a six-pack or a joint, and once some tasty venison jerky they had made.

They made suggestions on what to do to get the cabin right, and offered to help. I took their advice in a friendly way, but made it clear I wanted to work on it myself. It was a small cabin anyway. They were cool with it, and took no offense.

This was the way I came to meet the Lensel brothers, George and Avery, who had lived in Monte Rio by the Russian River all their lives, and did whatever they could to make a living, such as rough construction, and shade tree mechanic's work. They had met Greg when he and Marla had moved to the area about fifteen years before, and offered their services when Greg was building his house. In his usual giving way, Greg had paid them to help, and had been friends with them ever since.

They had their prejudices, but if you avoided certain subjects, you could get along. I have found in my travels, unless you meet people dead set against letting new people in, you can always get along by not pushing certain buttons.

I'll tell you what, though, if you ever wanted to meet a couple of boys who knew all the places to hunt and fish, or were willing to help out if you needed it, George and Avery Lensel were the ones, as I came to find out. They were alright by me.

I later learned Greg had already told them about me before they gave me a hard time at the cabin. A couple of real characters.

Greg was pleased I took to the leatherwork so quickly and easily, and cared enough to do quality work. At first I did make a few mistakes and ruined some leather, and I was strongly reminded of Greg's earlier question about me getting advice. But soon it got to the point where I wasn't making any mistakes. I developed my own style, and actually created several new hat designs, which Greg thought were groovy.

Marla sold their goods and consigned other people's craftwork in a tiny shop they had in downtown Monte Rio. I sat in a few times when they needed a break with the kids or had a show to do somewhere. I met some of the local people this way, and got along with most of them, accepting some teasing at first with more grace than I had with George and Avery.

Once I babysat the two boys, Evan and Todd for a weekend when their folks had a show to do. Greg and Marla did craft fairs and shows all over California, and made a good living from it. Greg told me to do what I needed to do to get them to mind me, but it was cool.

The two kids and I walked over to the cabin. I was doing some painting on the outside, and they helped. Man, I was glad I was using water-based paint, 'cause there was more on them than on the cabin by time we were done! They were fun to be with. I was glad, though, when they got tired and took a nap.

I lived with the Brauers in their home for about six weeks, until I finished getting the cabin ready. We never had a bad or awkward time. I helped with dishes and the garden, which I enjoyed, and I always kept my room clean.

One time, I had taken a good hot shower, and as I was stepping out, Marla accidentally walked in. After checking me out, She grinned and said, "Looks like Greg's in trouble now! Hey, Greg, looks like you've got some competition, mister!"

Greg peeked his head around the bathroom door and said, "You better be careful boy, or I'll unleash her on you, and then you'll be put to it!"

"Yes sir, Mr. Greg," I said, "I'll be most careful, sir."

We all chuckled about this for a while. We were so cool with each other, some friendly fooling around was taken without bad vibes messing things up.

When the cabin was ready, they threw me a moving-in party. Just some hot dogs, beer and chips, but it was nice.

The cabin was a mellow place for me, my sanctuary in the piney woods. I had it nicely stocked with what I needed to make a comfortable home. There was a foot trail going out behind the cabin. It ended about three miles away in the woods. I took a number of hikes on it when I needed time to think about things. It seemed to help.

I still went over to the Bauers' place often for dinner, and I worked with Greg at least four hours a day doing leatherwork. I was into it. I loved the smell and the feel of the leather, and how it came to life for me when I was working it. I learned lots of tricks to get the best results, thanks to Greg, who was a real master.

I had already made a few hundred bucks from work Greg had taken to some shows. He always sold a lot, had a name for himself, and people looked for him at the craft fairs and other events. I found out later he was giving me a percentage of the total sales, not just for my own work. As I said, he was a righteous man.

One Sunday, going through my old pack in the cabin, I came across several capsules of powdered psilocybin I had kept stashed through most of my time in Big Sur. I had actually forgotten I had it, so it was a pleasant surprise.

Since it was a perfect day, I decided to take the psilocybin and hike up the trail behind the cabin. As usual, walking through the woods was sweet. I had seen deer several times, and a raccoon. The coon had assumed a defensive position, so I gave him a wide birth.

I wasn't sure the capsules were still potent, but they turned out to be very good indeed. The trip started evolving in a familiar and comfortable way. Instead of the outrageous visuals some people get when they take psychedelics, I got into the heightened-senses trip I've mentioned before, the way I relate to the natural world around me. This trip was no different.

Walking a short way off the trail, I came to a small, natural spring flowing from under a grassy overhang of earth formed when a large tree fell a long time ago, its roots forming a dugout in the earth. I had tried the water when I first found the place. It had a wonderful taste and was ice cold. When I drank a handful this time, I could feel it spread to all the atoms in my body. I felt totally connected to my surroundings, the lush green forest I was in. I lay back against a small tree, and absorbed the wonder of it all. I closed my eyes, but I didn't know for how long. Could have been five minutes or twenty. It didn't matter. But, when I opened my eyes, I didn't recognize the place. I felt I was out on unknown land somewhere. It all looked the same. I wasn't scared, but I wondered where my mind and the psilocybin had taken me.

I thought of my last LSD trip, when I'd arrived at a place in my mind journeys where I needed to make a choice: to stay in the normal world I had always lived in or to perpetually wander in a state of awe and amazement, lost to the life I already knew. I had made the decision to stay put during the trip on Mt. Tamalpais, knowing it was the right thing to do.

As soon as I recalled making the decision, I was back in the woods where I was when I had closed my eyes. I was still high, but on a pleasant level. I spent another few hours grooving in the woods, appreciating all the natural beauty.

I walked back over to and down the trail to my cabin, made some coffee on my propane stove, lit my kerosene lantern, and zoned out the rest of the afternoon, blissful in my new-found release. I felt as if I had reached an important level in my life.

It was the last time I ever took psychedelics, knowing there was no reason for me to take any more of any kind, and it was cool. Guess it took a couple of times for me to finally get the message.

I had no running water at the cabin, so I filled several five-gallon water bottles at the well when needed. Rustic might be a good word here. Yeah, rustic, but I liked the way it felt, living the basics, more work, but so uncomplicated. No electricity either, but for light I had a kerosene lamp, and I liked the soft glow it gave at night. Living in such a simple way added to my peace of mind when I was in my cabin.

Sleeping on the pine board bed I had made for myself, a thick foam pad for a mattress under my old sleeping bag, I had a dream, or maybe a vision, I'm not sure. I was traveling across an open countryside. I couldn't tell if I was in some vehicle, or moving under my own steam. My sight in the dream was narrowed to straight ahead and a little to each side. I was gliding along smoothly and evenly.

Suddenly, there was a wolf pacing me to my right, turning its head toward me once in a while, with a wolfish grin, tongue hanging out. This seemed to go on for quite some time. I wasn't put off by this wild animal traveling along with me, because I sensed he was there for me, guarding me. In my dream, I thanked it for its protection, and right away, the wolf came at me and disappeared, almost as if it had gone right into me.

I woke up, full of thoughts and feelings about what I had experienced. I lay there for a while digesting what I had seen. I knew it had been a dream, but it felt very real. Finally I drifted off to sleep, waking up several hours later to a clear, bright morning.

I stayed to myself all day, enjoying the sights and smells inside and outside the cabin. I didn't think I was having any after effects from my trip in the woods, and never have had flashbacks from any of my trips. This one was a powerful learning experience, and my understanding of things on some levels have been greater ever since.

Later on in my life, I learned about Indian totems and animal guardians, and I know now I had received one in my dream, or I guess I'd have to say vision. I've wondered if my experience at the Big Sur campground, and my brief connection to the old Indian vibes in the pool had anything to do with it. I have always felt at home in the woods. I didn't know why these things happened, but I'm glad and the better for it.

Life moved along smoothly for several months. I was happy where I was, doing what I was doing. I had been developing my own style of leatherwork, using some patterns I had designed.

Greg once remarked that as good as I had become, I could go off on my own, "Outside my territory, of course." He said this in a friendly way, as he always did, but I figured he was letting me know I was free to go it on my own if I felt ready, no bad feelings on this score.

But I didn't want to. I was too content in the life I was leading to pull up roots at the time. I didn't want to give up this good circle of friends I had found. I kept contributing my work, and we did all right. Greg and Marla seemed happy to have me around, and I felt the same way about them.

I went with Greg to a popular crafts fair in Santa Rosa during this time. I had never been to a show with him, and it was exciting. We set up six tables in a rectangle, with a canvas roof overhead.

Once the tables and sunshade were set up and covers put on the tables, Greg suggested I put my stuff separately on one of the tables instead of mixing it up with the other goods as he usually did. Then he handed me a hand-printed sign, suggesting I stand it up in a visible location.

The sign, made by Marla, in nicely done calligraphy, said **LEATHERWORK BY JESTER**. I looked at Greg, and didn't know what to say. He smiled his wide bearded grin and winked at me.

I guess you could say I had been given my independence as a craftsman. It gave me a good feeling to be sitting there with my own leather goods for sale, waiting to see if people would enjoy what I had created.

When I sold my first belt at the show, I tried to hand Greg the money, but he said to keep it, and we'd see how it had gone by the end of the day.

I spent the rest of the day selling and rapping with people about the leather goods. It was a groovy day for me, reminding me of the times I'd had selling from the van and in my old basement garage store. I felt restored in some way.

In the quieter moments at the show, I'd sit and think about the recent past. Until then, I hadn't realized what a bad trip for my mind the sad ending in Big Sur had been. I had never lost someone the way I had lost Hawk, or been forced to leave a place I was living in, the way I had to split from Big Sur. Of course, there was a heck of a lot I hadn't yet experienced in my life. I did know I missed all the people I had lived with in Big Sur, and thought about them a lot. I wondered what they were doing and if they were okay, especially Jeff, with what he had to face, most probably jail time, though I never knew what he had done.

There were a lot of intimate moments with these special people I don't want to get into, but they made strong impressions on me. Again, I was aware of what a lot of good it did me to get connected to Greg,

114

Marla, and the others. Jeff and Janey must have talked a lot to Greg about me for him to take me in, giving me a chance to start over.

By the end of Saturday of the weekend crafts fair, I had taken in a goodly amount of money from my own stuff on the table and orders I had taken. I was going to do some custom work for people, and send it to them when finished. I was smart enough to give myself ample lead-time so I wouldn't have to rush it.

One customer asked me if I could make him some thick, leather-soled, moccasin-style footgear. After telling him I had never made such things, he said he was willing to work with me on it. So I agreed to do it, and he could send me what he thought they were worth after I sent them to him. We rapped about how he wanted them to look. I took outlines of his feet, got his address, and it was settled. When I mentioned to Greg about my payment agreement with the customer, he looked doubtful, but I told him I knew the man would be cool about it. Turned out I was right, and the man sent me a check right after getting the moccasins. Judging from the size of the check, and what he wrote in a little note, the moccasins were exactly the way he wanted them.

By the time the show was over on Sunday, I had made a lot more money than I expected to, not knowing how much people would groove on my work. On the way home, Greg and I sorted out what I owed him for table space and materials, which still left me way ahead.

Greg suggested we celebrate on the way home by eating at a Denny's. He liked Denny's. It made me think of eating in a movie set. Talk about a plastic coffee shop. Greg made me swear not to tell Marla, who would have been bummed about it. Apparently he always hit a Denny's while on the road alone doing shows. My lips were sealed.

Sunday night after we got back from the show, Marla told me to stick around and have dinner with them. Great! I always enjoyed eating at their place, no food to cook or dishes to wash.

What I didn't know was there was going to be someone else coming to dinner. Marla had a lot of lady friends in town. They did quilting, nee-dlepoint, and other crafts together. After I washed up for dinner, I came out of the bathroom to find Marla talking with a young woman I hadn't seen before. She seemed about my age, blonde, a little plump, but good to look at. But it was her eyes that caught me, not because they were an amazing green in color, but there was a special inner quality about them.

She came right up to me and said, "Hi, I'm Dawn, and Marla wants to set us up together." Marla yelled something at Dawn, and slipped quickly away to the kitchen. Looking at this sassy girl in front of me, I had to know more about her, and wondered what it would be like to get close to her. She may or may not have sensed my interest, 'cause I just stood there with a goofy smile on my face, no words coming out of my mouth. After a moment, she let out a little laugh, and taking my hand, led me to the table.

We didn't say much to each other at dinner, but we were watching and listening, feeling each other out. By the end of the meal, I felt comfortable with her. She had a sharp wit, and teased Greg a lot, which he obviously enjoyed, though she left him red-faced a couple of times. Dawn was not shy, and spoke her mind without hesitating.

At one point, I had a strong desire to make physical contact, touch her face, feel her cheek. While I was thinking this, she turned her head toward me and smiled, as if she had read my thoughts and didn't object.

From what Marla said, Dawn was good at doing homey crafts, old-timey stuff. She even did silhouettes, a lost art. She studied people's faces for a minute, then cut their profiles out of black paper by hand, using tiny scissors, then mounted them on heavy stock and matted them.

I told her it would be cool to see some of her work, and she replied, looking directly into my eyes, "there's a good chance you will."

I could feel the heat rise in my face after her comment, and it must have gotten red, cause the three of them got a laugh out of it. At a loss for words, I sat there with a goofy smile, again. This was one girl I had better be up front with, 'cause she pulled no punches, and I liked that.

Several days later I was working in my cabin, designing the moccasin-style footgear for the customer from the crafts show. At one point, I was at a loss on how to proceed. Sitting back in thought, drinking coffee, I heard a knock at the door. It was Dawn, with a woven basket covered in red-checked cloth, like something out of an old western movie.

She asked me if she could come in or was she invading my space? I told her she was welcome to visit anytime, and she came in. She wore an old-fashioned, blue-gingham dress with a lace collar, but somehow I found it sexy, even though it covered a lot more of her than most girls wore in those days.

Suddenly I got a whiff of the chicken in the basket. It smelled incredible. We talked quietly and comfortably together.

"So," I asked, "would you call this courting, like in the old days, Dawn?"

"If you want it be courting, then fine," she said, "or you don't have to call it anything at all."

"No, courting sounds good," I replied. "What say we munch up some of your chicken?" We did, and the biscuits, too. I made some fresh coffee.

I was getting off on the way this interesting girl presented herself. It was so different from anything I had experienced before. I wondered whether or not she was playing a part, but something told me this was the genuine Dawn, open and real. It made me feel warm all over. We had a very mellow time, eating and visiting with each other, lining up our feelings. What happened next blew me away.

We were sipping coffee and eating some cookies she had brought for dessert. For a moment she looked deeply into my eyes and said, "You've suffered a real loss recently, haven't you? Someone you knew was taken from you?"

"Uh, yeah, as a matter of fact," I told her.

She said, "You had to leave this person in a place few people know about."

At this point I got chills down my spine, and asked, "How do you know this, Dawn?" None of us, Jeff, Janey, or I had mentioned Hawk to Greg or Marla; this I knew. It was something none of us would ever talk about, even to close friends.

"Sometimes I know things," explained Dawn. "Hope I didn't make you uncomfortable."

"So, are you a psychic?" I asked with a smile, trying to lighten things up.

She answered, put off by my attempt at humor, "I'm not a Gypsy fortune teller, if that's what you mean."

I told her I didn't mean to sound as if I was putting her down, 'cause I wasn't.

She said she never tried to do it on purpose, it just happened, and she usually didn't say anything to the person she had a realization about, as she put it.

She added, "I have enough trouble with some of the things I say to people, without making them nervous about me knowing things I shouldn't know."

She gave me one of her beautiful smiles, which I had already come to love. She and I had strongly connected during the first dinner at Greg and Marla's. What we were doing now was beginning the long wonderful journey of getting to know each other on all the levels people falling in love do.

Finally, she had to leave, as it was getting late. I offered to walk with her, but she declined, saying she had been through these woods long before

I knew the place existed. Her family, she said, had lived here all their lives. Then, she came close and gave me a soft kiss, and started to walk away.

"So Dawn, what's your last name?"

"Lensel," she said, with mischief all over her face. "You probably ought to talk to Avery and George one of these days if we're going to be seeing each other."

Man, that blew me away. The brothers and I definitely needed to have a talk.

Dawn started seeing me regularly, including at Greg and Marla's home, showing up at the dinners I was invited to, but also during the day, when Greg and I were working in the shed on our leather goods. She didn't seem to mind me being busy, not paying attention to her, concentrating on the piece at hand. She truly seemed to enjoy being around me. I liked her being there and Greg ignored the whole thing, as long as work wasn't interfered with. Sometimes I would catch her scent as she stood close to me or walked by. To me, she smelled like cinnamon and nutmeg, which I found difficult to ignore.

I remember with such strong and sweet feelings the first time she came to me at the cabin late at night. She didn't knock before she came in. The light was out, and I was lying in bed, thinking. My thoughts were on her, how close and good I felt with her, and then the door opened. I spooked for a second, until I realized who it was. She moved close to where I lay, and I heard the soft sound of clothing falling to the floor. When she got into bed and pressed her body close to mine, an electric shiver run through me.

"Are you all right?" she asked.

"Dawn, I don't think I've ever been righter," I answered.

She had on some light, rose-scented perfume or oil. It got to me, and drew me right to her. By the end of our first time together, we were solidly connected, body and soul as they used to say. The moment she gave herself to me, I knew she was the one I was to be with, and I also knew she felt the same.

I figured after our night together, it was time to talk to Avery and George. I mentioned it to Dawn, and she said I should come to dinner at the family house.

I knew her dad had died when she was a little girl, killed because he lost control of his logging truck on one of the many narrow, steep logging roads in the area, when timber was still a going concern. But her mother Maxine would be there, along with the two brothers I hoped were real friends of mine. Dawn said her mother being there would make her brothers behave themselves in case they felt bothered by us being together, so they wouldn't go for their guns. Funny, very funny. Knowing Dawn's need to speak her mind, I could only wonder what she had said to her mom and two brothers.

Several nights later, I went over to the Lensels' for dinner, feeling shy. But, I should have mellowed out over it. I was pleasantly received by her family. This was not the usual get-together with the brothers over a beer or joint at the cabin, shooting the breeze with them. They were all cleaned up, too. At least their hair was combed and they were shaved, with clean plaid shirts on. Knowing them as I did, I knew they had made an effort.

Conversation went easily enough, Maxine asking me direct questions about things in general, how I was doing working with Greg, where I was from, and where my folks lived.

Toward the end of the meal, Maxine gave me a long, deep look, not saying anything. It made me uncomfortable, and I guess it showed, because Avery nudged my arm and said, "Momma used to stare at us like that when we were kids, if she wanted to know what we had been into. She could always tell."

Maxine said, "Enough out of you, Avery." I could sure tell who Dawn had gotten her direct ways from.

Maxine asked me if she was supposed to call me Jester. I told her it was the name I had taken for myself, but she could call me whatever she wanted.

Maxine stared at me again, then said, "A man has a right to be called whatever suits him, so Jester it'll be."

After Maxine's response, I felt I had been accepted, and I was glad. But then she said to me, right in front of the boys, "Have you taken my daughter to bed?"

I could feel George and Avery tense up. I thought they would pop right out of their chairs at her question. They sat there nervously looking from their mom to Dawn and then to me.

I paused to think this out. Feeling sure she already knew, I simply said, "Yes, Maxine, But you should know it was two people who care about each other making love."

She looked at me a moment longer, then nodded, apparently having accepted my honest response. She said it was an answer she could live with. Then she asked if anyone wanted dessert. "It's home-made apple pie." I could see the boys settling down again.

After dinner, George, Avery and I sat in the living room together, while Maxine and Dawn straightened up. We didn't say anything for a while until George quietly said, "Jester, I think I can say for Avery and me, we aren't overly pleased you've had your way with Dawn, but we know you to be a straight-up guy, especially for a hippie, and she wouldn't allow something to happen she didn't want, so we'll expect you to do right by her, for her sake and yours."

"Exactly what I plan to do, man," I said, "have no worries."

Avery said, with a twinkle in his eye, "Then, I guess you won't have to worry about ending up permanently quiet in your cabin some night."

Six weeks later, Dawn and I got married. I felt totally sure about it, and hopefully, I would stop getting looks from George and Avery during my regular dinners over there.

It was a groovy wedding, held out by my cabin in the little meadow in front, a grassy clearing perfect for this moment.

A local minister did the ceremony, and Dawn and I recited vows we had made up ourselves, independent of each other. It was sweet, man, I'm telling you.

Then, with all of us there, the Lensels, Greg and Marla Bauer, their boys, and about nine or ten locals I had also come to know, Greg revealed their communal wedding gift to us.

We were marched down to Greg's place, but before we walked into the back yard, he said, "Jester, remember the time you told me about Captain Walt, and the bus you liked so much?" I replied of course I did, starting to get a cool buzz off of what he was saying.

"Go look in the back yard, you and Dawn both," he said.

The two of us walked quickly down the driveway, and were completely blown away by what we saw. There, in all its banana-yellow glory, was a neat old school bus. We couldn't believe it. By then, all the others were there with us. Dawn had tears in her eyes, and I did too, amazed by the goodness in these people's hearts. We hugged everybody, and I mean everybody. "Man, wait until you see what we do with this sweetheart," I told Greg.

"I know you'll make a fine job of it," he said smiling.

Life felt perfect; life was perfect. I wish time could freeze itself at such moments, with nothing but mellow feelings happening. Since none of us ever know what each day will bring, why not pause it on a perfect day?

A guy named Harold who worked at the supply house where I got stuff for the cabin, and who had become a friend, handed me a bottle of champagne, and I christened the bus's bumper.

They had bought the bus from the local school district where it had spent its life carrying a bunch of yelling, rowdy kids between home and school. The bus had been properly maintained, and had a lot of miles left in it. Greg told me the engine had been rebuilt just before it was sold. We all decided to take a cruise around town, and when I turned the key, it started up instantly. It was a fine old vehicle, a better gift than we could ever have expected.

After dropping all my passengers off at Greg's again, Dawn and I drove up a back road to a clearing she knew about, and christened the bus properly.

Relaxing in the backseat, Dawn said, "You know, baby, we're going to travel far and wide in this mechanical beauty. I'm telling you, it's going to be great."

I knew without a doubt she was right, as usual.

Dawn and I settled into living in the cabin with no difficulties. Guess I don't have to say it was snug, but it was cozy. What a perfect time of life. She would sit and do her crocheting, quilting, and other projects and I would sketch new designs, or work on projects I brought home from Greg's shop.

I needed to finish another pair of "moccasin shoes," same as the ones I made for the customer from the Santa Rosa crafts fair. I had made an extra pair as a sample, and in the several shows Greg and I had done since, I got several more orders.

Dawn came with us to those shows, and she loved doing them with me. I think people picked up on our good vibes together, and it didn't hurt sales any. She put out a sign advertising her silhouettes with several examples, and did about a dozen during the show. It was amazing how quickly and accurately she could do them.

Greg's leather sales were always good, and he was pleased we were such a solid unit, working comfortably together.

Life went on in this way for quite a while. It was a busy time, too. There were a number of projects for me to do. I had the leatherwork, an addition to build onto the cabin, and conversion of the bus to a home-built RV with living quarters in the back, mainly a bed with shelves above and around it.

We took out eighteen seats, leaving the front two. We put in cabinets and a folding worktable, until the insides were the way we wanted them.

We glued some blue, low-pile carpeting on the ceiling and walls in back. Behind the metal back of the right front passenger seat, I installed a tiny, custom-made woodstove, made for us by a man in town in trade for a nice hat, vest, and belt. The stove was so small it might not have seemed efficient, but in the bus, it was. We painted the bus body a solid medium brown with a white top.

About a week after the bus was finished, Dawn told me she wanted to meet my folks. I said things had been strained between us for a while, which was why they had declined their invitation to the wedding.

She said, "All the more reason to go."

I already knew when Dawn put her mind to something, I might as well consider it done. So, I told Greg what we'd decided.

Greg said I ought to put together all the leatherwork I had finished and take it with me, and make a couple of signs I could hang on the sides of the bus. I thought it was a great idea. Marla made the signs, doing her usual excellent work. They read: **JESTER'S LEATHERWORKS, CUSTOM AND READYMADE.**

We got all set up, and headed for Southern California on the first visit I had made to my folks in a long spell. Those days, I dressed like Monte Rio people did, so I didn't look as funky as the last time my folks saw me. My hair and beard were neatly kept, and I had put some weight on, thanks to my yummy wife. I used to tell Dawn each time we made love I gained a few mores ounces because she was so delicious. It always got a sparkle out of her, and it became our private joke. Whenever one of us was in the mood, we'd ask the other if they wanted to gain some weight.

Dawn asked me if I would show her where I had camped in Big Sur while we were on this trip. I apologized, and said I would rather not. She said it was okay, but I would have to take her there sometime. I just nodded. I think Dawn felt she would learn more about me if we went there.

We didn't hurry on the journey, always stopping by mid-afternoon. The bus would easily cruise at fifty-five, but I usually kept her at fifty.

We hung out the signs on the bus wherever we'd stop for a meal, or just to stop for a while. We made a few sales, and took some special orders. Mostly, though, it was fun talking to people. Dawn had me get some business cards made up, which she designed. They were well done, and would certainly help future business.

We arrived at the folks' place three full days after we left Monte Rio. It was late afternoon, so both of them were home from work. I pulled the bus into their wide driveway, and honked the horn. I saw my mother look out the front window, and her mouth drop open. They both came out, looking older than I remembered.

Dawn went running over to my mother, who always took a while to warm up to strangers, especially other women, and gave her a hug. My mom stood there startled, then smiled and wrapped her arms around Dawn and hugged her in return. I was amazed. Then my father asked when he was going to get some, and Dawn hugged him, too.

So far, so good. I walked up to the front steps and shook my father's hand, and he even hugged me, something he didn't normally do. Same with mom, only she hugged me later in private in the kitchen where she was making pot roast, my favorite dish, and one of the few things she made well. It hadn't been offered the last time I had been there.

I sat and talked with dad while Dawn helped with the cooking, or watched my mother do it. Mom used to say there was room for only one cook in her kitchen.

I'm gonna sum the trip up as going better than I expected, but with a few tight moments which Dawn helped us through. She was such an amazing girl, wise beyond her years. It was a visit way overdue, and now I wish there had been a few more over the following years. Yeah I know, hindsight, but there you go.

There were large flea markets at various drive-in-movie lots in those days, and my folks suggested we all go together to one to sell my goods. It seemed a righteous thing to do. My folks were impressed by my work, but dad didn't think I could make a regular living at it. After we had finished the first day of the flea market, he had changed his mind. We did great, Dawn doing some silhouettes, and selling some crocheted hats and other items. I sold a lot of leather goods, even at the raised prices I had decided to try charging. I gave out a lot of business cards too.

We took the folks out to dinner after the flea market. Dad wore the special belt I had given him, and mom carried one of the sturdy handbags I had been making.

When we got back from dinner, Dawn brought out silhouettes she had done of the folks. They were cool, and you could immediately tell it was them. She even did one of my dad with a cigarette in his mouth, smoke curling up and all. He was a heavy smoker then, so this seemed appropriate. Dawn said if he ever quit smoking, he could cut the cigarette off the silhouette, since it wasn't glued on the backing. Dad laughed, and gave her a hug.

We stayed almost two weeks, and it was a sad parting when we left, which I guess you could say was a good thing. My folks had fallen in love with Dawn, no surprise to me. Taking my father to one side, I gave him some money to take mom out to dinner. At first he didn't want to take it, but he finally gave in, realizing what it meant to me. My mother made us sandwiches and snacks to take with us.

We hit the road again, heading back to Monte Rio. We were low on sellables, so we mostly just drove, making fewer stops. Our first night out, Dawn told me she really needed to see the Big Sur camp. After searching through my feelings, I told her the next morning we would go there. It had been over a year since I had left. We worked out our route to take Highway 1 and then go up Nacimiento-Ferguson Road.

I was feeling edgy, traveling up the old road. I didn't know how I would feel, being there again, or what I would find. But when we hit Bonanza Campground, my mood heightened and I suddenly wanted to get down to the camp and show it to Dawn. There were no people when we arrived, nor any signs a little tribe had once lived there. There was nothing to show that the "Indios Pobrecitos" had ever existed.

Dawn came down out of the bus and stood for a moment, then said, "This place has been used as a home for many people over a lot of time, and some of those times were full of sadness."

"Honey Girl, you speak true," I told her.

We took our time looking around, and when we got to where the grinding rock and pool were, she knew why I'd had my vision, which I had told her about. She waded barefoot into the pool, and then turned, facing me. She got this amazed smile on her face and all she could say was, "Wow!"

I went walking over to where my shelter had been, and tucked up against the boulder, partially hidden by some grasses was a piece of cotton cloth. I started to pick it up but froze, my hand a few inches from it. I could see some staining on the cloth, and knew it to be the one we used to wipe Hawk's face. I was stunned it was still there. I turned and walked away, old feelings rising up. Dawn approached me and asked if I was all right. I told her being there was very heavy for me.

I suggested we go into Jolon, 'cause I knew of a good Mexican restaurant, and she agreed, feeling my mood. But, as we headed down the road, up above the meadow with the fallen oak, Dawn asked me to please stop. I did, and she walked in a beeline for the meadow, with me right behind. She seemed in a heightened state as she stood looking at the meadow, the fallen tree and the area in general. She looked at me, and said, "Where is he, baby, we have to pay respects."

Even knowing her abilities, I was shocked at this whole thing, but knew I had to show her. I walked her over to the spot beneath the oak tree below the meadow, where we had laid Hawk to rest. The ground had been undisturbed as far as I could tell, covered with natural debris, but there was a slightly depressed area where he was buried.

Dawn kneeled down and gently put a hand on the grave. When she did that, I started crying quietly, my tears flowing.

Standing up a few moments later, she came over to me, gently took hold of my arms, and told me we had done the right thing, and it was a good place for someone to rest.

I turned and walked a short distance away, my back to her, letting my feelings run free, and she was wise enough to let me do so.

After a time, we headed back to the bus, and drove down the county road. We didn't pass anyone on the way to Jolon. We pulled up and parked right in front of the restaurant and walked in the front door, taking a table at a window. A minute later, up walks Mr. Calderon's daughter, looking grown up and definitely pregnant. She starts to ask us what we want to eat, but when she looks closer at me, her eyes open wide, and she runs in back, coming out a moment later with her father and a young man I took to be her husband.

"*Indio Pobrecito!*" said Mr. Calderon, recognizing me right away.

I replied, "*Y como esta, Senor* Calderon?"

He said, "I am good, good, and you, *Senor?*"

I answered, "I too am good. *Aqui esta mi esposa.*"

"*Con mucho gusto, Senora,*" he responded.

Dawn said hello. We talked a while, and then *Senor* Calderon urged us to order anything we wanted. I got chile colorado, of course, and several tasty tamales.

"You sit in front this time," he said, serving us himself.

"Yes, *Senor* Calderon, life has made it possible," I told him.

"*Si, si, gracias a Dios,*" he replied.

We ate our meal, talking to Mr. Calderon when he wasn't helping other customers. It lifted the sadness I had experienced at the old camp.

When we got ready to leave, he wouldn't hear of us paying, so, going out to the bus, I brought back the last vest I had, in a nice, natural, mottled-brown color. I gave it to him, and with great delight, he put it on. It fit him perfectly.

Seeing it was handmade, he asked, "You make this one?"

I told him yes, and he said he would be proud to wear such a beautiful thing.

We said our good-byes, and headed out on the road toward King City, and then north toward home. What a good first journey for us this had been. Dawn was right; it was only the first of many.

After we returned home, I got busy with the leatherwork I needed to catch up on to sell at shows with Greg. When Greg and I worked together, ideas flowed between us. It was a good working partnership. But, I also had some different ideas to work on for a special show Dawn had told me about.

In the past, she had been to a couple of Renaissance Pleasure Faires in Northern California. She had gone for fun, but had observed what went on there.

She told me it was a reproduction of a medieval market place, with actors and various entertainers, primitive games, rustic food and drink including British sausages called bangers, hand-baked breads, mead and mulled wine, and lots of other stuff.

Dawn was surprised I had never been to a Renaissance Faire before. I told her, "Different times and places, Honey Girl."

She said, " Your current work, like the belts and vests, are always good sellers, but if we could put our heads together and produce some period stuff: coin purses, soft leather pouches, special belts and hats, I bet we would do very well."

I would never knock any of Dawn's ideas. I had already found out how sharp she was. So, I said okay, as long as it didn't interfere with the work I did for Greg's business.

When I talked to Greg about it, he thought it was cool, but had no interest in doing the Faire himself, having enough to keep him busy. He told me I should order whatever leather, embossing tools, and buttons I would need to get my new projects done and we'd settle later. What a great guy he was.

Working together, Dawn and I designed a bunch of medieval-looking pieces. We found basic styles for them researching at the library. Dawn was also going to make some peasant blouses and women's cloth caps. She made arrangements with the Faire people for booth space. They wanted to see samples of what we would sell, so we sent some photos of the leather Robin Hood-type hats I had in mind, along with the coin purses and other items I had ready. They sent back a positive response, and we were all set.

Man, it was a hard row to hoe, getting ready for the Faire plus doing my regular work. There were a few sleepless nights. The next crafts show to be done was in Sacramento.

Greg knew I was burnt out trying to get ready for the Renaissance Faire and the show, so he insisted I stay home and finish up my projects for the Faire, and he and Marla would do the Sacramento show, taking Evan and Todd along this time. It was good having Greg for backup, and I always tried to return the help when I could.

Dawn had an old funky sewing machine, which wasn't up to what she wanted to do, but she still managed to get things done, often doing hand stitching out of necessity. So, I went down to the local Monte Rio hardware store, and ordered her a nice new machine capable of doing decorative stitching and all sorts of fancy work. When it came in, I replaced her old one with the new machine at her mom's pad where she had to work 'cause we had no electricity at the cabin. Nobody said anything to her about it. After she had gone to her mom's to struggle with the old machine and found the new one waiting for her, she came home to the cabin where I was waiting, with tears in her eyes. After she gave me a fierce hug, I asked her with a smile if she had cried all the way home.

"Nobody's ever done anything like this for me, Jester," she said. "I never had a doubt about us being together, Mr. Leather man, and you haven't proved me wrong yet. I will make you a shirt for the Faire you'll be proud to wear."

I'll tell you something: when Dawn and I were together, I came to realize there was truth in the old saying about there being a special someone for everyone, and the only thing needed was to be fortunate enough to find each other. Maybe this would take more than one lifetime, who could say? I did know I had found my special one, and many times over the years we were together, I was reminded and glad of it.

There was something special, too, about the whole time we were getting ready for the Renaissance Faire. It felt as though we were following the right path of action, the perfect thing for us to be doing. Maybe it was the magic of the two of us working together for the same purpose, or the love we shared growing while we were at our work, I don't know. Whatever it was, the things we made seemed to have something special to them. Some of the pieces I made were plain, with a small amount of decoration, but they seemed unique anyway.

The feelings I had at this time made my life so much better. I had stopped doing drugs completely. They didn't have any place in my life any more. Being with Dawn, I didn't need drugs any more. Dawn told me she had never even smoked weed. She told me it put her off balance inside.

It was about three days before we were to go to the Faire, when Dawn came up to me with something in her hands wrapped up in paper. "Here's your shirt, baby, I hope you like it," she said.

I took the package over to the table and opened it up. I was stunned. It was beautiful. Made of a deep maroon velvet, it had other, patterned fabric sewn onto it, on the front, back, and sleeves. It looked like a medieval shirt, and was beautifully done. I stood there, holding it up in front of me, until Dawn told me to put it on. It was perfect, a good fit, but loose and comfortable.

I turned to Dawn, and told her it was wonderful. She beamed, "I dreamed the pattern, and knew it was right."

"It is," I said. "But don't expect me to wear tights with it, no way."

Dawn said, "Oh, I think you will." As usual, she was right.

We drove our bus to the Faire, presented our paperwork, and found our booth space. While setting up, we were greeted by many far-out people working the Faire who were into this modern version of a medieval marketplace. Even though the Faire wasn't open yet, many of them wore their costumes. Our work was praised, and we found out we were the only ones with such leatherwork. Dawn's blouses and women's cloth hats were appreciated too.

The first afternoon there as we were going to the bus to call it quits for the day, a man dressed as a Norse barbarian invited us to attend a large "staff banquet" being held at a hand-built Viking longhouse up in the far corner of the Faire. When a side of beef being barbequed on a spit was mentioned, I smiled and said "Arrr, groovy."

The Viking house was amazing, man. It had taken a bunch of wild-looking guys several weeks to build. All the men and women staying there resembled Vikings. The leader was a man called Wolfgar the Vicious. Someone said he was a just and fair chieftain, the kind who would only punish a wrongdoer, but with Vikings, you never know, right?

There was half a beef over a major pit of coals, and the scene, especially after dark, could have been a thousand years ago. I liked the way it felt, the separation from modern civilization and all its complications.

The trouble started after the server had sliced off chunks of beef and handed them over along with a large mug of ale. I was talking to one of the Vikings about a hard leather helmet he wanted me to make, when I thought I heard Dawn's voice being firm with someone. I excused myself and walked in the direction I had heard her.

I saw her standing with some man who had a hand on her arm, and the look on her face told me she didn't appreciate his attention. Several other people were watching, but doing nothing. I went over and pulled his hand off my wife, and told him to back off. Dawn told me to take it easy, but when my head was turned toward her, he took a swing at me. I took the hit, then came back at him, putting him on the ground. The Vikings swarmed me, and I realized he was probably one of them. But, my blood was up, and I wasn't about to be put off by these primitive men.

The leader, Wolfgar, came striding up. He was a large sturdy fella with long blonde hair, a fierce face, and what appeared to be a Celtic Tattoo on each of his muscular arms. I hoped I wouldn't have to deal with him directly, though I didn't plan to back down. Nobody was going to mess with Dawn.

Wolfgar demanded to know what was going on. Dawn turned to face him while standing at my side, and told him what had happened. She told him if this creep was one of his, he better get him in line, get him sober, and tell him to keep his hands to himself. Wolfgar said he would make sure of it, but since I had tangled with the "tribesman" on "Viking ground," I would have to give him the right to combat. I was up for it.

So, here I was, already tripped out on adrenalin and red meat and protecting my mate, so of course I said, "No problem, brother, tell me where, and we'll get to it."

We were taken to where there was a circle marked on the ground about fifteen feet in diameter. This was to be the site of physical contests at the Viking ground during the Faire. I was told we were to wrestle with each other until one of us was put out of the circle, best out of three tries. It was after dark and the light from several campfires gave an eerie, ancient feel to the scene.

Facing my opponent, he didn't seem drunk, so his trying to put a hit on Dawn pissed me off even more. We stripped off our shirts, walked into the ring, and went at it. Maybe this was a Renaissance Faire, but it sure felt like real life, unchanged through the ages.

We wrestled. This Viking, I never did get his name, was strong, and I was hard put to move him. The first fall went to him. There was more than just wrestling going on, sneaky jabbing and elbows too. But losing the first fall jacked me up. I wasn't going to be bettered in front of my woman and this rowdy bunch. Going at it again, with great effort, I managed to walk him outside the line, which was considered a fall. Round two went to me.

The last round got rough. With the two of us hunched over, trying to put a lock on the other, he tried to give me a jab to my privates. It didn't land right, but really got me mad! I reached down and pulled his feet right out from under him as he stood up straight, putting him flat on his back, taking the wind out of his sails, but he had landed inside the circle. While he was trying to get himself together, I smiled and reached out a hand as if I was going to help him up. He went for it. But as soon as he was on his feet, I hooked him under one arm and lifted him onto my shoulders crosswise. Spinning around three or four times, I tossed him outside the ring. He landed hard, and lay there breathing heavily.

I thought I might get jumped by his tribesmen for beating him, but a loud cheer went up. Jeez, it was like something out of a primitive tribal scene. I was welcomed into the longhouse, Dawn at my side. I wasn't too badly damaged, except for a blood trickle out of my nose, but I was pooped, and covered with sweat and bits of debris from the ground.

The ale started flowing then. My adversary and I were made to shake hands, but we both knew it was an empty gesture.

Toward the end of the night, Wolfgar took me aside to a corner area, and asked me if I wanted a pick-me-up.

I said sure, not being in any state to refuse.

He opened a packet of white powder, and told me to snort some up my nose, but not too much.

I told him I didn't do speed, and he said, "It's not speed, my friend, it's cocaine."

Cocaine? I had never tried any. My inner voice warned me this might not be good, but I was still riding the physical high from fighting, and not thinking responsibly. Besides, who was I to turn down someone's hospitality?

Putting a pinch on the back of my hand, I took a hit. Oh man, what a rush! My senses were instantly heightened, and I felt larger than life. Thanking Wolfgar, I went to find Dawn and head back to our bus. She was not in a good mood from the earlier episode, and sensing a change in me, asked me what I had been doing.

I told her, and she stared long and hard at me. She said, "I don't want you to do it, Jester, it's bad stuff. Promise me you won't keep using it."

I promised her, but she didn't seem sure. After I washed up, we went to bed saying a quiet g'night to each other. Dawn went right to sleep, but it took me a while to settle down. What a day it had been!

The next morning I was dragged out, but Dawn was her usual jump-up-soon-as-you're-awake self, and she got me going with sweet kisses and some heavy coffee.

By the time the Faire officially opened, we were in the booth and ready. The sign Marla had made me for the Santa Rosa show worked great because it was in old-time calligraphy, and the name "Jester's Leatherworks" was perfect, too.

I had made myself a leather Jester-type headpiece, the one I originally had having been stolen from my Divisadero pad. The new one was not colorful, but it had the four long points and pointy crown in the middle with a small bell on each point. I was wearing the shirt Dawn had made me, and yes, black tights, too.

We were set up toward the back area of the Faire grounds, so it took a while for the tide of people to reach us, but when they did, boy did they buy.

By the end of the first day, we had sold a third of all our goods, Dawn's and mine, and I could see how I was gonna have some work to do to keep our booth stocked. But it sure felt good while it was happening. Lots of people came by in colorful costumes, putting out friendly vibes, and it sure did remind me of the Haight scene before it went bad. There were even some rent-a-cops walking a beat around the Faire, and they fitted in, too.

In the middle of the afternoon, who should come walking by but Kurt, my old Eureka Street brother. What a trip! The Faire grounds weren't far from the Bay Area, but I had had no idea what had become of him. I mean, here it was 1972, and he could have been anywhere. He walked by, looked right at me and started to walk away, then quickly spun around and yelled, "Holy cow, Jester! How the heck are you man? I haven't seen you in many a year, brother."

Smiling, I said hello back, but not quite so intensely. I pulled him into the booth and we started rapping about all he had been through since I had last seen him. He had been busted for weed and spent six months in county jail, but had stayed clean ever since.

"I don't use nothin' anymore, man," he said. "But my artwork is selling, and I have a line of T-shirts out, too. I got a groovy old lady I wish had come with me to meet ya. Fact is, I'm living a much cleaner life, and I'm feeling cool, Jester."

I introduced Kurt to Dawn. He put his hand on her shoulder and said hi. When he took his hand away, a shiver went through Dawn. Kurt and I looked at her and after a brief pause, she told him he had been very ill.

Kurt stared at her a moment, then looked at me and asked me if I had married a psychic.

I said "Actually, I did."

He got serious and told her she was right. He had contracted a major case of hepatitis, but was all better and wasn't contagious by any means. He said he had gotten it in jail from a dirty tattoo needle, then rolled up his sleeve to show us a crude "Doin' Time" on his arm.

Kurt said, "Jester, I am so glad I got my act straightened out. No, I didn't get religion, but I've seen the light, you dig?" I told him I understood.

Kurt sat with us for a while, before deciding it was time to wander the Faire grounds, saying twelve fifty was a high price to get in, so he ought to make use of it. I wrote him a note to give to the men at the Viking house, so he could get ale and a meat sandwich on homemade peasant bread for free. He said thanks, and we parted ways.

It was really good to see him. I was sorry he had been through some heavy times, but glad he had made it through and survived. It brought back memories, which I shared with Dawn late at night in the bus, since we were busy 'til the end of the day, and hadn't had time to talk.

I had taken numerous orders for custom and ready-made leather goods, and one was for a sturdy and functional carry bag for a lady. She called it a purse, but I never heard of a daily use bag as large as she wanted it to be. She wanted it made of buffalo hide for durability, and I told her so be it, but it would be spendy.

The Faire people had told me my prices needn't be too low, as the people coming to the Faire would be happy to pay what I charged. But being greedy isn't my way, so I charged fair prices for my work. Several people who bought some of the coin purses and small belt bags as I called them, as they had a loop to attach them to a belt, were pleased the prices were reasonable.

During our time at the Faire, we had several people come to buy "what a friend of theirs had bought the other day." It was flowing, man, the energy was good, and life was a groove. Every night I made as many items as I could in the bus, sitting at the worktable I had built from memory after Capt. Walt's set-up. Sometimes, I didn't get to sleep 'til the wee hours, but I had no choice if I wanted to keep selling and not run out of goods.

Something happened the next morning after the day Kurt had shown up. Now, I'm not saying I had developed psychic powers I didn't have before getting close to Dawn, but she had told me earlier, the powers I had within me, as all people have within themselves, might come out from being with her and becoming comfortable with the process.

Anyhow, I looked at her the next morning when I first woke up and she was already cooking us breakfast. For an instant, a darkness fell over her as she stood there, as if nighttime had formed itself around her, and I suddenly knew our time together was not going to be as long as we would wish. I just knew it. I got goose bumps all over me, man. She turned to look at me, and flashed her sunshine-morning smile, so I dropped the dark thoughts and smiled back, letting all the love I had for her come through. We went to our booth and had another bang-up day.

Life was here and now, and being in the present was what I had come to know as most important for being fully alive. The way I had been living since high school taught me this, and it has stayed strong in my mind.

The rest of the show was terrific for us. We actually ran out of a number of items, but we saved the last example of each piece, which I kept on display using them to take orders. On Sunday afternoon, Dawn made me take a break since she could handle whatever came along. She ran me out of the booth to explore a while.

The Faire was wonderful in the quality and quantity of the far-out crafts, performers, and displays. There was an accurate copy of the Globe Theatre, Shakespeare's theater, permanently constructed on the Faire grounds. Performances were given several times a day. There were wandering jugglers and minstrels, and comical characters too. There was lots of food, mostly basic meat and pastry kinds of stuff, and, of course, drinks all over the place.

I grabbed myself a cup of ale and a meat pasty as they called it, a small meat pie, and wandered around meeting people, getting complimented on my leather jester cap, belt and pouch, and the beautiful shirt Dawn had made me.

Eventually, I found myself in the Vikings' area. There were events going on, including wrestling in the circle. The Vikings were challenging people in the crowds to wrestle with them but were getting no takers. I chuckled to myself, figuring I could give them some pointers.

There was also something I had never seen before: the tossing of long heavy poles, called "tossing the caber." The contestants would be handed a pole, and they would grip the bottom end in two joined hands, and lean the pole against their shoulder. Once it was balanced, they would make a quick run forward, then toss the pole so the end they had been holding would flip up and forward, the other end hitting the ground, and the pole had to fall straight forward for a good score.

I was standing watching this event, when a firm hand was smacked down on my shoulder. Before I even turned, I knew it was Wolfgar. "Think you could toss the caber without embarrassing yourself?" He said it as a friendly challenge.

I smiled back and said there was only one way to find out. Removing my beautiful shirt, I got in the short line of contestants, and waited my turn. I carefully watched how the others handled this unusual event. The first two didn't manage to get the one hundred pound pole to flip forward enough to get a score, and the third lost control of the pole, and it fell backwards off his shoulder, almost center punching a wandering juggler, who was quick enough to get out of the way, though he did drop his balls.

Okay, now it was my turn. Wolfgar and one of his men held the pole off the ground until I got a grip on the end. It actually felt familiar and comfortable there.

"Remember, there's a flagon of honey mead for you if you succeed, and maybe a place in the long ship on our next raid," Wolfgar told me.

"And maybe another pick-me-up?" I said quietly to him.

"Hmmm, we shall see, we shall see," he responded.

The pole was released to me, and I took about five or six seconds to find my balance. I started my short run forward, maybe ten or twelve steps, paused for a second going into a crouch, and, using my whole body, legs, back, and arms, I flung it upward and forward as hard as I could, feeling my back stiffen as I did. The pole formed a perfect half circle and landed on the other end. For a second or two it remained standing on end, before falling forward in a perfect line away from me.

This was the second time I got a cheer from the crowd on Viking ground, and I loved it. I was also glad I had taken off the shirt Dawn made me before making the attempt, 'cause my right shoulder was roughed up. Better me than the shirt.

I was pleased at my toss, but before I could return to where Wolfgar was standing, here comes the guy I had wrestled before, and he yells out, "It was just luck, I know you couldn't do it twice in a row!" The crowd got quiet. I stood there thinking I should have expected this.

The man was definitely still feeling the sting of losing to me, and wanted payback. So, I said, louder than him, "Perhaps you'd care to put a wager on what your loud Viking mouth is saying. How about your Highland dagger against my hat, belt and purse, or do you lack the stomach for it?"

The crowd started laughing and yelling, getting into the mood. The Viking had no choice but to agree or lose face. He said, "Agreed, but this time the pole has to go forward with some energy, not like the last toss, barely falling the right way."

"Agreed, you filthy lout," says I, getting into the Faire character, "I'm ready!" There were more cheers and yells.

This time, as Wolfgar and his helper handed over the caber, Wolfgar said in a whisper, "This time, when you end your run, don't toss it as you make a step. Stop completely and toss it with both legs even. I tire of this fool myself."

I decided to trust his word, and when I ended my run this time, warmed up from the last, I did as he suggested. And not only did the caber swing up and around faster when it hit, it flung forward almost two feet from where it first landed! I was turned on by this one, a good shot in anybody's book. The crowd went wild, and I even got a full cup of ale tossed over my head as though I was a champion athlete. What a rush! My moment in the sun at the Faire!

The defeated Viking came up to me with blood in his eye, but begrudgingly handed me his dagger and sheath. It turned out to be a real Scottish dirk, and must have cost him a bundle. His dare had cost him, but I took it from him carefully, not wanting to seem spiteful.

As he was turning away, I said loudly, "Wait! I will give you the chance to regain your blade, Viking, if you do the toss as well as I just did. Are you game?"

"By Odin's breath, I'm ready!" he said, with a different look in his eye, a look of surprise for my giving him the chance. He took his place on the starting line, and when he had been given the pole and had its balance, he made a good run and let loose. The pole went flying forward and fell as neatly in line as mine had. The crowd cheered for his excellent attempt. I walked forward, and with a bow handed him back his valuable knife. I knew it meant something to him. He looked me in the eyes and bowed deeply, and then gave me a sweaty Viking bear hug!

So, our bad feelings toward each other were put aside, and afterward I savored several mugs of honey mead, with good feelings all around. As I was leaving to relieve my dear wife from working alone, Wolfgar came forward and shook my hand, leaving a small paper packet in it. "Use your strength and wisdom wisely, Sir Jester, and with moderation," he said.

"I will surely try, Brave Wolfgar," I replied.

On the way back to our booth, I slipped into one of the fragrant Porta-Potties located around the grounds. Opening up the packet Wolfgar gave me, I found there was another nose full of cocaine. I sniffed it up, and took a minute to let the initial rush fade out. Tossing the paper down the toilet, I stepped out into an energized beautiful scene. I took my time getting back to the booth, visiting with vendors and craftsmen along the way.

When I got back to our booth, Dawn looked happily busy, with five or six people who all wanted her attention at the same time. When we got a break, I told her what had happened at Viking ground. She gave me one of those looks I had come to know. She said, "You've been there before, and a long time ago."

"I know," I said to her, "I felt it too."

When our Faire weekend was over, I don't mind saying we were burned out, even though we'd had a great time all the way around. It had been a wonderful but intense experience. Even though we both enjoyed being around people, we needed to get home and be by ourselves again.

During the ride back to Monte Rio, she told me we might need a larger and better-equipped place soon. I thought she meant because our leather goods business was so successful. But, she patiently explained when a child comes on the scene, you need more room and supplies.

I pulled the bus over and asked her to please repeat what she had just said, and she did. I kept hugging and kissing her and saying, "Really? Are you sure? Really?" This was so totally unexpected. We had never talked about it; life was so busy as it was. But there we were, and I had no worries. I was just delighted, man! I felt warm all over, and started thinking of names as I drove, until Dawn finally told me to chill out, since we had eight months to decide.

I wish I could say I didn't start acting overly protective, trying to keep Dawn from straining herself. But more than once she got really mad at me and ran me out of the cabin when I overdid it. She finally sat me down and explained some things I apparently didn't know.

"I'm not a toy dolly, and I can deal with being pregnant a lot easier if you aren't driving me nuts. So, quit pestering me!"

I played it smart and chilled out, though I still worried on the inside.

Man, how far out this was, me going to be a papa. I resolved I would spend lots of time with the kid. Male or female, it wouldn't matter. Sitting outside the cabin one day on a bench I had made from three split pieces of a small pine log, I suddenly felt, for the first time, that I was firmly in place on the wheel of life, on a good path, and all would be cool.

I don't mean to make it sound so uneventful, but life went by smoothly for the rest of Dawn's pregnancy. Dawn and I did more shows, usually with Greg and Marla and their boys, working peacefully together. I was building a new, large addition onto the cabin, with Greg, George, and Avery helping. It would provide us with some much-needed extra space. One night after we announced the forthcoming kidling while at dinner with Greg and Marla, Greg made me an offer to sell me the cabin and land at a good price, to be paid each month as much as I could reasonably afford. At the price he quoted me, I could get it paid off quickly. Greg said to call it a Happy Baby deal. Wonderful people.

We had the baby at Greg and Marla's place with a local mid-wife a lot of people in town knew and whose services they had used. It was illegal at the time, but Dawn, along with many other locals, had been birthed by her, and Dawn insisted it was what she wanted. Turned out it couldn't have gone smoother, though I was concerned.

I was there when our boy was born, and helped bring him out, cut the cord, and gently bathe him. What a natural high! I thought new babies couldn't see, but I looked into his wide-open eyes and he looked right into mine. We knew each other, there was no doubt! We named him Nathan Buck, Buck being Dawn's father's name.

Dawn came through with flying colors. I was relieved for several reasons. First of all, for her well-being, but also because the last few months she was pregnant, she was a trip to be around. Never knew she could get so mean, but I kept in mind what was she was going through, and took plenty of solo walks to keep the peace.

About a month after Nathan was born, George and Avery came over to tell me they were going deer hunting, and did I want to come along? I thought about it. I knew how to shoot, but had only hunted once before as a teenager, unsuccessfully.

Dawn said she would love some fresh venison, which would be good for her and the baby. So I said sure, and when was opening day, so I could be sure to get a license in time?

They looked at each other, then smiled at me, saying, "Don't worry, we'll take care of it."

I figured they knew what they were doing, and left it to them to take care of things. I was going to use the boys' extra rifle, a 30-30 Winchester, which they said would be good for the quick shooting needed in the dense woods where we would be.

The next Saturday, I was sitting outside the cabin at about three a.m. when the boys drove up. At such an early hour, we just nodded to each other and I got in the truck. We drove up the highway headed north out of town. After about an hour, we turned off onto a dirt road I would never have spotted myself, overgrown as it was with willows and tall grass. We drove for about two miles, climbing slowly upward, finally pulling off in an open spot in the trees.

The three of us got out of the truck and took our guns from behind the seat. George told me not to make any noise closing the door. He said to me in a low voice, "From here on we've got to be very, very quiet."

The dark morning air, about an hour before light, had incredible smells to it, natural and organic. The three of us walked quietly up the dirt road, with me close behind to keep track of the brothers, who had begun hunting here with their dad before they hit high school age. Once in a while we'd hear noises, as something moved away from us in the woods. Each time, we stopped until the sounds had faded before moving again. When there was almost enough light to see, we turned off on a trail heading slightly downhill. We had been steadily climbing as we walked the road.

About a quarter mile in, George whispered to me and pointed to a stand directly on my right, at a tree with a patch of blue surveyor's tape nailed to it. He said I should get onto the stand and wait there quietly for a deer to slip by, and get some meat. I didn't even know what he meant by "a stand," but I nodded, and walked away to my right. About twenty yards in, I spotted the patch of blue surveyor's ribbon. I stood there dumbly looking around for this "stand," and couldn't see anything, so I decided being next to the tree was being in the stand.

It was full light now, and I saw heavy spikes sticking out of the tree. I realized they formed steps on either side of the trunk. Looking higher, I saw something in the tree at least fifteen feet up.

Slinging the rifle on my back, I started carefully climbing, and soon came to a small, sturdy, platform to stand on. I was concerned about being so high up, but saw a nylon belt with a latching belt buckle on it. In fact, it was a car seat belt attached to the tree trunk. I worked my way onto the platform, and carefully got the belt around me. And there I stood, ready for whatever would happen next.

I slung the rifle in front of me, and slowly worked a cartridge into the chamber as George had shown me when he checked me out on the rifle. After telling me how to aim with this particular gun's sights, he told me not to worry about making a precise target-type shot, as the deer would be close when I shot it, if I did.

I found I could aim the gun through an opening in the branches and leaves which had been carefully trimmed to conceal a person, but allow a clear shot. I stood there for quite a while, hopefully blending in. I found that with some effort, I could keep very still.

I'd had a little practice learning to be quiet in Big Sur on my solo hikes into the hills behind our camp. I watched deer and pig several times, and when I did, I found myself becoming silent inside, as if I wasn't there. Unless the air moved so they got my scent, I could watch to my heart's content.

But this was different. I wasn't merely watching, I was intentionally putting myself in a place on the natural food chain.

I was standing still, but moving my eyes and head, carefully looking for deer, and all of a sudden, there was a doe about fifty feet in front of the stand. Then there was another one, but no buck. I got a chill all over seeing them there, unaware of me.

When we first left in early morning, the boys told me we weren't supposed to be here hunting, but we were going after meat to eat, not trophies, and would only take one deer. Besides, the herds had gotten way too large under the present wildlife management plan, with road-killed deer occurring more and more. I had been given the choice of whether to come or not, but somehow, paying for a hunting license didn't seem to have anything to do with what we were about.

I'm not saying hunting out of season is an acceptable thing, but this didn't seem like poaching, with George and Avery belonging here just as the deer did, having known these woods all their lives. I told them I was okay with it.

A buck had suddenly materialized behind the second doe. He didn't have large antlers, but it didn't matter to me. Instinctively, I raised the rifle a bit each time the deer lowered his head to feed, and stopped when he lifted it up. After some long minutes, I had the rifle to my shoulder and was aiming carefully, so I could put the deer down quickly with one good shot. I cocked the hammer back, and it made A VERY LOUD CLICK, because I had forgotten to hold the trigger back while cocking it as I had been instructed.

All three deer snapped their heads up and looked right at the sound, which was right at me. The two does took off running to my left, their pure white tails straight up like flags as they went. But the buck stood there, looking at me. I was aiming at him, but he didn't move, except to drop his head and start browsing again.

At first I thought he hadn't seen me, but had only heard the noise. But when the does took off, he should have run right after them. Don't ask me how, but I knew the deer was allowing me the shot. He was accepting his fate, and giving himself to me. It sounds far out, man, but I know it was true. I took a breath, held it, and pulled the trigger.

The noise of the gun going off in the silent woods sounded like the end of the world, and I guess, for the deer, it was. The 30-30 at such close range knocked him right down. He struggled to get up and then lay still. I stood there on the stand watching him, and waited until I was sure he was dead. Then I unbelted myself, and climbed down to the forest floor.

I went up to the deer, and squatting down, put my hand on his side. His scent was strong but sweet. He smelled like the woods after a rain. I touched my finger to the bullet hole, and without thinking why, I touched my forehead with the finger I had dipped in the deer's blood, leaving a spot there, and said thank you to the deer. It seemed the proper thing to do.

I had been sitting there tripping on this whole magical, almost holy event, when George and Avery came trotting through the woods toward me. They stopped, seeing me sitting there quietly, and understood what I was feeling. After allowing a moment to pass, letting me finish my appreciation of the whole scene, George said, "Okay, Jester, time to dress the deer out and get on up the trail. You did good, brother-in-law."

George handed me a heavily-used hunting knife and a shoelace, and took me step by step through the process of field-dressing the deer, which was an essential part of the hunt. He showed me how to open the deer and remove its organs in a specific order. This had to be done so the deer's meat could cool down quickly and not spoil. The shoelace was used for tying off the end of the deer's intestines so deer poop wouldn't taint the meat. We saved some of the organs to eat later, and left the rest for the forest animals. When we were done, I handed Avery the rifle and hoisted the deer onto my shoulders.

As we walked along, taking turns carrying the deer, we quietly talked about being in the woods, hunting, fishing, and camping. It was obvious to me these boys had been living this life as long as they could remember, and I felt good knowing they trusted me enough to take me with them. But I wondered if I would ever be a regular hunter. I was grateful for the experience, but my life was not the same as theirs.

The Lensels weren't poor, but getting fresh meat was a boon to their lives. I felt it had been an honest happening. A food gathering out in these woods seemed more real than buying packaged food from the store. But I didn't think it would ever be a normal part of my life. I will say, though, something inside me had been fulfilled, and it gave me food for thought.

When we got to the truck, we put the deer under some tarps, and made it look like a pile of equipment. The rifles went behind the seat. We drove on out of the hills, and back down the highway finally coming to the cabin, where they dropped me off.

George said, "We're going to hang the deer a while in our shed to age the meat, and we'll skin it out, salt the hide, and put it in the freezer along with the meat, where it will keep 'til you want to tan it, Jester."

I told the brothers I wanted them to have it for letting me go with them.

They gave me the deer's heart, hunter's breakfast as they called it. Dawn loved fried deer heart, they told me.

"Thanks, boys, it's been a very special thing for me," I said.

"It always is, you know," said George. We shook hands, and they headed home.

I went into the cabin, and Dawn was asleep in the easy chair we had gotten at the thrift store a while back, with Nathan, a tiny sleeping angel, in her arms. Life was perfectly groovy. I lay down on the bed and dozed right off.

When I woke up, I could smell something cooking, and it smelled different. Dawn was in front of our small propane range, cooking the deer heart, sliced, with onions. "Is my mighty hunter awake and hungry?" she asked.

I sat down at the table with little Nathan peacefully sleeping in his cradle, an old Lensel family piece. He looked blissful and without a care in the world.

Dawn and I ate together at the table. The heart was strong but delicious, perfect with the onions.

While we were eating, we talked about finishing the addition to the cabin, maybe getting electricity and a phone, which seemed a good idea since we had Nathan now. We also agreed not to do any major road trips until Nathan was at least two years old, to be on the safe side.

I told Dawn I had been thinking of a tour of the Southwest in the future, selling at the many shows held there. We could take our time and plan carefully. It sounded as if it could be a profitable and fun adventure. I wanted to have a lot of ready-made things to sell, and a good supply of materials for custom items, special designs. Dawn was all for it.

Neither of us had been to the Southwest, Arizona and New Mexico, and it felt good to consider going there. The scenery would be groovy, lots of beautiful desert scenes, sunrises and sunsets, and hopefully we'd meet some far-out people, maybe doing the same thing we would be doing, living life on the road. But, we would still have a solid home to come back to whenever we wanted.

So, we slowly but surely gathered information and created lots of goods to sell, and when it was right, we would head out. We definitely had plenty to do to get ready. Dawn and I always seemed to be busy, and we loved doing our life together. If you had asked me several years before, when my life was on such a different path, I would never have believed how things could change so much. But, life is changes, and I don't think anyone without a lot of gall could say they know what will come next. Yeah, a lot of gall.

I submerged myself for the next couple of years in the blissful life I had been given. We got the addition done, building it in the same style as the old cabin, as if the whole thing was an original structure. I bought a whole mess of old shingles, and did the outside walls so it all looked the same. We found some nice old windows, and hung a solid-wood door. I got a great deal on a wood-burning stove for heating the place, and put some hand-wrought iron railings around it, so Nathan wouldn't singe his fingers.

We had the county hook us up with electricity. It cost us a bit, but we were able to arrange payments with them. Finally, we had the phone company set us up with a phone line for staying in touch with the outside world. I never did like having a phone, the way it would ring when I was into working the leather or just sitting back, relaxing. But, at night, the electric lights were nice to have, easier on our eyes than the kerosene lamps when Dawn and I were busy doing projects.

The old saw about kids growing up fast proved to be true. Seemed like every time I turned around, Nathan had either grown some more, or gotten into something else. He was a busy boy, and he learned quickly. He began talking early, and never stopped chattering away. He could get serious at times, but had a cool sense of humor, right from the get-go. I really loved him.

Sometimes, if I was sitting reading or relaxing, he would come and tuck up alongside me, and once he was settled in, he'd let out a sigh, never failing to put a happy lump in my throat. There were many times when he'd do something cute, and I wanted to laugh, but held back, not wanting to offend his sense of dignity. He was truly a blessing.

He was also a bright spot for everyone else. Even Greg would stop working if Nathan was around, and do things to make Nathan laugh, tickling him or playing some childish game with him as he had probably done when his own boys were younger. It was funny and sweet, seeing this old bear of a man on his hands and knees being silly with my boy.

In 1975, one of those unhappy surprises life too often lays on us made sure Nathan wouldn't have a lot more fun time with our good-natured friend. Greg was diagnosed with cancer of the pancreas. He hadn't been his usual, hearty self for a while. At first, the doctor in the town, a great GP, had treated him for diabetes, but soon it became obvious Greg's illness was worse. Greg had to go through all kinds of hell trying to beat it, but it was apparently a hard kind of cancer to put a stop to. We all did all we could to help out. I worked with him a lot, getting the leather goods done, and by myself when he couldn't do good work anymore. I did the shows with him as usual, and then by myself.

But, no matter what was done to or for him, we knew the time was coming. About nine months after he was diagnosed, Greg couldn't take anymore. The cancer had spread and overwhelmed his body too much to defeat it. He had refused the major doses of painkillers at the end, wanting to spend as much time with his family and friends as he could. Even though he was bedridden, and in and out of consciousness, we knew somehow he was aware of us, and we continued to talk and be with him. It hurt so much to watch him go. It seemed life itself was letting go of him, instead of the other way around.

Marla was a real trooper all the way through, but Dawn spent a lot of time alone with her. Since they were close like sisters, she gave her a lot of support when she needed it the most.

The Lensel brothers and I were left to deal with it as best we could.

When Greg finally left us, we buried him in the town cemetery right next to Maxine's husband. I ached all over from the loss I was feeling.

During the ceremony, I thought of Hawk for a moment, the sudden way he had gone, probably with no pain, and thought to him, "You were lucky your end came so quickly, brother. It could have been worse, much worse." I left early from the reception at the Brauer home. It was too hard for me. Marla had come out to me where I sat alone in Greg's workshop, and told me to go home and rest. After we held each other a while, sharing the pain, I headed back to the cabin.

Home alone later, I decided, even though friends and family pass away, they're not gone from us forever; they're just somewhere else. I felt the truth of this in my heart, my gut, and my mind. A few days later, I called my folks to let them know Greg was gone. I had mentioned him and the others to them a number of times by phone and letter, and at one point, my mother wrote to say she was glad I had met such good people. She was sincerely sorry when I gave her the news.

My father, who had been in World War II and saw many men he knew die, and whose own family had dwindled, took the phone. After I explained the situation to him he was quiet for a moment, before mumbling something to me about having to learn to accept this sort of thing, as it was a definite part of life. He gave the phone back to mom.

About a week later, Marla and her sons came over to the cabin to visit. I have to say she was doing all right. Dawn told me Marla had said she didn't feel Greg was really gone, not his spirit, only his physical presence, and knowing this had made it easier. Their boys were having a rough time, but we all surrounded them with our love to help ease the pain.

Marla wanted to know if I would be interested in buying out Greg's leatherworking goods, materials and tools. I hadn't thought about such a possibility, and even if I had, I wouldn't have asked Marla about it, at least not yet. I told her I would be glad to take his supplies and tools over, especially if the money would help her, but I might not have enough all at once, since Greg had a lot of stuff.

Marla said money was no problem at all. Apparently, when their second son, Todd was born, Greg had taken out a substantial life insurance policy, and Marla was in good shape financially. It was no surprise to anyone that Greg had provided well for his family.

As far as buying the leatherworks, Marla made me a one-time offer amounting to about ten cents on the dollar of its real value. She told me she didn't want to hear any arguments about this, and she knew Greg would have wanted me to take over and have his goods to use, So I should just say okay.

Tears were rolling down her cheeks, so I said, "Okay, Marla," and gave her a long hug. Todd and Evan came up and joined us. Seeing what was happening, Dawn joined us, too. It was a bittersweet moment, one I'll never let go of. I could feel Marla's heart beating, and knew there would always be a big hollow space where Greg used to be.

Dawn, Nathan, and I moved into the cabin addition completely. I had so many leatherworking tools and supplies, I needed to use the entire old cabin for a workshop.

I felt rich in a number of ways, having such a wonderful selection of materials to use and a lot of good tools to work with, including some custom ones Greg had bought or made. When I used the tools, I often felt as if Greg was working right beside me. If Marla came to visit with Dawn, Evan and Todd would hang out with me while I worked. I never turned them away, even when I was deep in thought on a new design. I knew it made them feel close to their dad to be there with his stuff, and we enjoyed each other's company.

I had set aside a good basic set of leatherworking tools, enough for both boys to use when they were a little older, if they wanted to follow in Greg's footsteps. It was something I had to do.

The boys loved to play with Nathan, and were gentle with him. I would give Evan some half and half, half coffee, half milk, if Marla wasn't watching. It made him feel grown up. Todd said he wanted some too, but we gave him the "maybe next year" bit, and he begrudgingly accepted the fate of being the younger brother.

The time finally came when our preparations for heading to the Southwest were complete. Nathan was old enough, and "it was a go," as the NASA space techs might say. The bus was in great shape, and I had added on a wooden storage unit I had built to the back of the bus, to house materials for leatherworking.

With a small, quiet generator in place on the bottom shelf of this unit to supply juice for the lights in the bus, Dawn's sewing machine, and several other small electric tools, I figured we were properly set up. I had added storage under our bed, too, and a bunk for our boy. Yeah, we were ready to rock and roll.

We had gotten a lot of information on shows and fairs we could do, and had a schedule all set up. We had already paid for table space at half a dozen events, so business should be good. We didn't want to leave our home vacant for what might be an extended period, so we let the daughter of one of Marla's lady friends house sit.

Dawn and I were given a great going-away party. Maxine and Marla did all the cooking, so there was lots of tasty food. At one point, the boys went out to their truck and came back with the rifle I had used to take my deer, and presented it to me with a box of shells. George said it might come in handy as we traveled all over heck and gone. Avery nodded his approval. I thanked them sincerely, then I handed George and Avery what I had made for them: two leather vests with their names applied in different-color leather on the lower back. I had made one of them from the hide of my deer which they had tanned for me. The other one was cut from high-quality, soft, steer hide leather, dyed black. I made sure the vests each had two good-sized lower pockets and one upper one, since the brothers were always carrying a bunch of small stuff. This was not lost on them as they admired the vests. George and Avery were speechless, for once.

Dawn had made Maxine and Marla peasant blouses, beautifully done. Marla's boys got wallets with their names stamped on them, lots of hand-done floral designs, laced with real gut lacing for strength. They were thrilled, and stood holding them as if they were gold bars.

Sometimes you can tell how a journey is going to be, generally speaking, by the way it starts. The amazing thing was, we didn't forget anything, not personal goods, materials, or tools. Everything we planned to bring, we brought.

The bus started right up, and sat there idling steadily, waiting to stretch its mechanical legs. One thing I had installed, thinking it would be cool, was a round Plexiglas dome in the roof. It was about two feet in diameter and two feet high in the center. Not only was it an unusual skylight, but you could also step on the bed and look through it like an observation port. Nathan loved it when his mama would hold him up to look through it, but he was a chunky boy, and her arms would tire long before he got bored with the view. I got the dome at the only junkyard in Monte Rio, which was actually someone's big backyard, totally covered with piles of stuff. I doubted if the owner had a license for his business.

The dome looked like something from an old plane, but I had no idea where it had actually come from, and neither did the fellow who sold it to me. I made sure the dome was properly sealed and secured in the bus roof. Leaky roofs irritate me, no matter where they are.

Dawn would work on her garments while I drove, and I would do leatherwork while she drove. Working while in motion depended on the road, of course. During our journey, we encountered some rough

146

roads which made working impossible, but those times allowed us to kick back and observe the land.

I had ultimately removed all but the front left bus seat and installed one comfortable chair, bolted down to the floor behind the vertical metal panel between the front seat area and the door off the front-door area. Nathan's bunk was positioned right behind the left front seat, with raised sides to keep the active sleeper my son was from rolling off the bed at night or on bumpy roads. His bed could also serve as a small table, with the bedding removed.

Our first stop to sell was at a huge flea market we didn't know about until we saw it as we were driving along. It was outside Santa Barbara, California, set up right on the bluffs overlooking the ocean. We checked in and paid our fee, which included parking the bus right behind our space. Displaying our items on Pendleton blankets laid over folding tables, we waited for customers. It made me think of my early days selling on Haight Street before I got the van, except now I had the luxury of tables.

Dawn and I settled down on our folding chairs, but Nathan was antsy to go exploring, so Dawn took him around to see the other vendors. Sales were nonexistent in the morning, so Dawn wasn't needed yet. This was Sunday, and Sundays can be like that.

After twelve noon, people showed up in big numbers, and I began to make some sales, and in a couple of hours had earned enough to make selling there worthwhile. We were hoping we could at least pay for the trip with what we made on the road, in between scheduled shows. A lot of people I wouldn't expect to see at a flea market showed up, upper-middle class, I guess you could say. But, there were a lot of vendors selling good quality things, like pottery, hand-made soaps and candles, and unique clothing, more crafts fair things instead of typical flea market goods. My hard and soft pouches, whose styles I had designed for the Renaissance Faire, sold quickly. I also sold several leather handbags, but my belts seemed to be of most interest.

The Jester sign on the bus made people curious, so I finally put my leather jester hat on. Some showmanship never hurt. Dawn had come back with Nathan around two, having gotten into long worthwhile raps with some crafts people who also did the road circuit selling their wares. She put Nathan down for a nap in his bunk. Business had slowed, so I took a break.

Walking around, talking to the vendors, I got the idea this journey of ours was going to be a wonderful adventure. There's nothing like meeting a lot of like-minded, good-hearted people. Makes you feel like the world is a mellow place.

When I got back to our space, Dawn was upset. She told me she had noticed several of our belts were gone after she had sold a vest to a customer. It had only been about fifteen minutes ago. There was always something to put a dent in things. I told her I'd be right back, and let her hang onto Nathan.

I wandered around the grounds acting casual, looking all around. While I stood checking out some pottery, I saw a boy, maybe twelve, behind the pottery stand, admiring two leather belts, obviously the ones taken. I asked the person running the pottery stand if he knew the kid in back. He told me he was the son of the food concession owner, who was there each weekend.

Rather than confront the boy, I went over to the snack stand and talked to the father about what was happening.

He didn't even deny or get upset about it, but said, "My boy has some problems, and I'll bring you back the belts soon, okay?"

I said "Okay, and we can keep it between ourselves."

I went back and told Dawn what was up. An hour later, here comes the father with his son, both belts in his hand. The son came up, head hanging down, told me he was sorry, and handed back the belts.

It was then I noticed the large red mark on the kid's right cheek. I looked at the father, and he must have seen me looking at his son's face, because he turned his head away frowning when I looked at him. Reaching down, I picked up a small, soft leather belt pouch with a silver concho button on it. "Here," I said to the kid, "for being honest and owning up to what you did."

The kid just stared at me in disbelief, took the pouch, mumbled something, then turned and ran away.

The father apologized, telling me it had been rough since his wife left.

"Rougher for the kid than for you, apparently," I said, angry at this abusive man. "I wonder why his mom left."

The dad got mad, and took a step forward, putting his hand in his right pocket at the same time. But, as with most bullies, he stopped short before reaching me, as I was now on my feet, and he saw I was standing my ground. Dawn put a hand on my arm, but I stood looking him in the eyes, until he finally turned and walked away.

Hey, maybe I did overreact, but I figured the mark on his cheek wasn't the first thing the boy had suffered at his old man's hand.

"I think it's time we packed up, baby," Dawn said.

I agreed, and a short while later, we were heading south down the highway, a sour taste still in my mouth.

Dawn came up behind me and put her hand on my neck as I drove.

"I sure am glad it's you doing the driving, and not somebody else," she said.

"My sweet girl," I replied, "there are some things you and Nathan will never have to worry about, my sacred oath on it."

We kept on driving, the Los Angeles area our destination, to visit my folks and let them see their grandson. They had come up for a long weekend once, after Nathan was born, and we all had a good time, once my folks got used to the unique personalities surrounding them.

This visit with my folks turned out good, but my mother's health was not at its best. She was always a heavy eater, lots of meat and potatoes. She was only about four foot eleven, but she was plump, quite a chubby lady, to tell the truth. She was being treated for diabetes, and some mild heart trouble. She needed to lose weight, but no one was about to tell her she couldn't eat what she enjoyed, no sir.

They loved Nathan, and he loved them back. He took to both of them right away, and they perked up. One day while visiting there, I asked them if they would watch him while Dawn and I took a drive. My dad insisted we take his Plymouth sedan, instead of the bus.

I took Dawn to all my old haunts, including my high school, which I hadn't seen in a long time. We had lunch at the coffee shop in the middle of town, one of my favorite hangouts as a teenager. We had chili dogs and fries, which were as good as I remembered. Then, we went down to the old section of town. It was not the best neighborhood, but had lots of interesting old buildings.

We were driving past a large, strangely-designed building, the oldest in town, when Dawn asked me to please stop. We parked by the building's side and got out. "What is this place?" she asked. It was called the Harrelson Building, built in the late 1880s by Mr. Harrelson, one of the founding fathers of the town. I asked Dawn why she wanted to stop there.

"Because it has a strong presence to it, very strong."

"You mean as in haunted?" I asked.

"I don't know, but it's definitely putting out a lot of weird energy."

I told her, "When I was going to high school, people used to say it was haunted. Want to take a look inside?"

"Yes, I do," she said.

Okay, so we went to the front door and walked in. The building covered the whole length of a short city block. Most of the shops were shut down and deserted, but there had been a small bank, a barbershop, and a dry goods store. The second floor had been a gambling hall, saloon, and whorehouse, so I had been told. The architecture was odd. There were lots of turrets, overhanging balconies, and other unique features.

The only part still being used was a combination thrift and antique store in the lower front of the building. The old guy sitting there smoking his pipe nodded to us as we came in. I asked him if we could go upstairs. He nodded and smiled, as if he knew why we wanted to go up to the second floor.

"Small, tight stairway in back to your left," he said.

We thanked him and found the snug half-twisting stairway leading to the second floor. Giving each other a look and a smile, we climbed the stairs.

Stepping onto the second floor, we immediately knew this was a different kind of place. The light filtering through the dirty, old-fashioned narrow windows created an atmosphere perfect for an old building like this. You could see lots of dust particles floating in the air. The pine flooring was so old and dry you could scuff away bits of the surface with the toe of your shoe.

There were a number of small, round depressions in the floor. Dawn and I figured they were from heavy gaming tables sitting there for many years. It was easy to see the place had been a saloon, because of the beat-up bar, with a mirror still behind it coated with years of dust and grunge.

Dawn decided to explore the back rooms where the whorehouse had probably been. I decided to check out the large room off the side of the saloon, which was directly above the thrift store below. It had been reached from the saloon through a pair of sliding doors, but the doors themselves were long gone.

Immediately after Dawn left, I got the old "I-know-I'm-being-watched" feeling, but stronger than I'd ever felt before. I wandered through the front room looking at all the piles of old stuff. Considering the layer of dust that lay on everything, it appeared nothing had been disturbed for a long time. There were old books, bottles, threads, and kitchen stuff, all of it coated with a heavy layer of dust. It was all creepy looking, but what gave me a real chill was when I looked up from an old book I was checking out and thought I saw a shadow drift away from the opposite wall. The hairs on my neck tingled, and I became uncomfortable being there.

A short while later, Dawn called my name and I walked out to the saloon. She said she was all done exploring, and I told her I was too. We walked to the head of the steep, narrow stairs, turning around for one more look at the place.

"Nothing here out of the ordinary," I said.

Dawn didn't say anything, but only nodded. As soon as she did, something happened I will never forget. It felt as though someone put a hand on my chest and pushed. Turned out Dawn felt the same thing. We both involuntarily took a step back, down to the next stair. We looked at each other for a brief moment, and moved down the stairs as quickly as we could and still stay upright. We found ourselves back in the front room shop, and the old guy was at his desk, smiling knowingly at us.

He said, "Not very friendly, are they? Probably miss all the fun they used to have. I sometimes hear them walking around up there."

Dawn and I just smiled at him and got the heck out of the freaky old place. The further we drove from the building, the better I felt. Finally I pulled over and asked Dawn what she had experienced.

"There sure was a lot of living done there," she said, "but I think it has been quiet a long time. I saw rooms full of stored stuff of all kinds. One room had bed frames; another had, believe it or not, a whole bunch of toilets stashed there.

"But when I started walking back toward the front room, I heard a door click shut. I looked back and the furthest-back room door was closed, and it had been open before. When you and I were at the head of the stairs, it felt as if someone had pushed me backwards, and I heard a voice say, so softly I barely heard it, 'Go away.'"

I looked at her a moment, knowing if she said it happened, then it did. I pulled back out onto the street and we drove the Plymouth Fury to my folks' place.

When we got back, Nathan came running up and yelled the word "Together!" at us, which was his way of saying he wanted a three-way hug. The folks looked happy but pooped out, which didn't surprise me. My boy could burn up the energy. He probably ran them ragged, having fun, of course.

We had chicken for dinner, the worst thing my mother cooked. We made the best of it, but there isn't much you can do to make boiled chicken enjoyable.

During dinner, Dawn told my folks about Harrelson's, and what had happened to us there. I swear my mom's face turned pure white. When I asked her what was up, she told us:

"A few years ago I went there more out of curiosity than for any other reason, but thought there might be some interesting old books. The man in the shop said there were plenty of old books upstairs. So, I went upstairs, and while looking through the books, I thought I heard some whispering. After looking around to see who was there and finding no one, I went back to looking at books. Suddenly, one fell from an upper shelf and hit me on the shoulder. It really scared me, but then another book popped off a shelf right in front of me, and I got out of there as fast as my shaky legs could carry me."

A shiver went through my mom after she finished the story.

"You never told me about this," dad said.

"You would have just pooh-poohed the whole thing if I had," mom replied.

My father became uncomfortable then, but Nathan broke up the mood by accidentally flipping a spoonful of pudding onto his forehead. Instead of crying, he started giggling, which broke us all up.

This visit broke down any remaining bad feelings between the folks and me, since it was easy for them to see my life was groovy again. How could it be otherwise with such a sweet little family?

I had found time during our stay to work on some leather goods. My father sat in the bus with me several times while I cut, stitched, and stamped the leather. He was apparently impressed with my ability to turn raw leather into useful objects. Before we left, I gave him the belt I had made him, a sturdy, black harness-leather belt with a heavy brass buckle and nice stamped border on both edges. He liked it, and put it on right away.

Early in the morning several days later, we left to continue our journey. From L.A., we hit Highway 10 and headed east for Arizona. We stopped after dark in Blythe, California, at a KOA campsite. It was one of the few times I can remember staying at a civilized campground, if you could actually call it a campground. It was more of a remote parking lot with facilities.

The next day, we headed across the Arizona border and drove all the way to Phoenix and our first show, which was a western-and-collectibles event. It ran Friday, Saturday, and Sunday, and was a classy affair. During the show, Dawn wore her blue gingham dress, and I had on one of the leather vests I had made over a calico shirt Dawn had made for me.

We knew this was the real Old West, and I had made a lot of sturdy western-style belts, with doubled and stitched leather and an additional piece of leather for hooking into the buckle. I also had a dozen basic vests of black and brown leather, similar to the ones I had made for George and Avery, a workingman's vest.

Surprisingly, the belt pouches from the Renaissance Faire proved popular, and I took a number of orders and worked out a half-dozen new designs. I got one request for a leather western-style hat like a modified Stetson, which I agreed to make. But I told the man I'd need time to make it, and would have to mail it to him. He sketched a picture of what he'd like. I had made several small hats modeled after Civil War kepis, except made of leather, with a hard-leather brim. I sold the three I had, and took orders for several more. I had gotten into the habit of taking photos of all my designs, at Dawn's urging, so I would have something to show if an item sold out.

There was a ton of people at this show, and maybe a thousand vendor tables. Dawn did a lot of silhouettes and sold some blouses too, but mostly helped me sell leather goods. As always, she was a great help.

The most unusual idea I got was when one cowboy asked me if I could make a small leather holder for a can of snoose, to fit on a belt. I told him I was sure I could, and he gave me an empty snoose can for size. I had fun making the piece, and sent it to him free of charge, thanking him for the idea.

I was sorry when the show ended. I had talked with several other leather workers, sharing ideas with them. We talked leather for hours, in the evenings after the show had closed for the day.

When we left after the show was over, we were way ahead profit wise, even after expenses. This journey was a good thing for us already. I had been given some useful information on where to get leather and supplies right there in Phoenix, and the Monday after the show was done, I picked up a lot of good material to keep things going.

Our next show wasn't until the following weekend in Flagstaff, so we took the highway north, and stopped several times along the way to enjoy the journey and the beautiful country around us. The breaks gave us time to do more leather work for the shows, too. We left the signs out on the sides of the bus wherever we stopped.

Even though we only made a few sales at those times, we did meet some groovy people, including half a dozen local bikers who turned out to be pretty cool. They bought a couple of belts, and had some good smoke to share, though Dawn declined politely and took Nathan for a walk.

They were classic bikers, the way they dressed and acted, right out of some old movie. Funky and dirty, they appeared to have been on the road with their choppers forever, a side effect of the life they had chosen to live. 'Course, I never would speak badly about rebellious people. It would definitely be hypocritical of me, now wouldn't it. They had heart, though, without a doubt.

The two women in the group descended on Dawn and Nathan when they came back. They loved Nathan, who took it all in stride, clowning around for them, and giving hugs, raspy looking though the biker chicks were.

One of the men wanted my leather jester hat, but I didn't want to let go of it. I offered to make him one of his own, but he wanted this one. He tried to haggle with me, and at one point got angry, but I teased him about it and he cooled off.

I smoked one more doobie with them before they left. Two of them had visited and stayed in the Haight in the Sixties, as a lot of bikers did, and we had some laughs discussing those times before they finally thundered their way down the road.

Just as they were leaving, headed who knows where, I had them wait a minute, went into the bus and came out with the jester hat, which I gave to the biker who had wanted it so badly. He smiled and showed as many gaps as teeth. He shook my hand and said, simply, "Thanks, brother." But those two words spoke volumes. Roaring down the road on their choppers, they were gone.

Dawn came up to me and gave me a tight hug. She said, "No wonder I love you."

We got a lot done on the way to Flagstaff. Nathan got to go for a walk in the desert with his mom who was careful to watch for ornery reptiles, while I worked on the western-style hat for the customer from the Phoenix show. I even added a smooth leather sweatband. I felt sure the man would like it.

We arrived in Flagstaff a few days later, on Friday, the set-up day for the show. After reaching the fairgrounds, I pulled up in the vendor parking area and walked over to confirm our reservations and table space at the show, while Dawn started making our evening meal.

On the way back, another bus in the parking lot caught my eye. It sure looked familiar. I went over, and couldn't believe it. There, sitting under an awning attached to the side of this forest-green bus, was none other than Captain Walt! He looked a bit older, and had a longer ponytail, but otherwise looked much the same as he had on Eureka Street. He was wearing a nice deerskin jacket with lots of beadwork on it. I walked up to say hello, but before I could say a word, he looked up, smiled and said, "Hello, Jester, I told you we'd meet again."

I said hello back, glad to be shaking his hand. It was amazing and good to see him. We talked a few minutes before I went over to get Dawn and Nathan to meet him. I had mentioned Captain Walt to Dawn several times, telling her about his excellent jewelry, and how cool he was.

When I returned, he had a lovely young black chick by his side, about half his age, I'd say. He introduced her as Emerald, "the finest jewel in the world," at which she rolled her eyes, smiled a beautific smile, slung her arm around Walt, and said hello.

Dawn and Nathan said hello back, and then Nathan blew my mind by saying to Walt, "You know my daddy a long time."

Neither Dawn nor I had said anything to Nathan about him. He was definitely Dawn's child.

After we all visited a while, Captain Walt asked me what I was going to be selling at the show. When I told him about my leatherwork, he immediately wanted to see it. I knew my work was good, but Captain Walt made some amazing jewelry. I had always considered him a high-level craftsman, and I didn't see my work as being in the same league.

After seeing and praising our bus and admiring the Plexiglas dome, Walt looked at my different leather pieces, and he seemed to truly admire my work, which was definitely praise coming from him. He asked me what space I had at the show. When I told him, he said we should see if we could get spaces right next to each other. We went back to the sign-in area, and after some good-natured pleading and whining, we scored and would be set up side by side.

Walt said, "You ought to have a small work area to show how you do your leatherwork, stamping designs. People love to watch." As usual, his idea sounded good to me.

After the show, and our dinner with Walt and Emerald, Dawn and I were lying in bed talking, and we agreed being around them was a good thing for us all, and all the good energy would help draw people in. Dawn said, "Whatever he suggests will be good for us. This won't be the last we see of them." It was food for thought, as we dropped off to sleep.

I spent a while early on Saturday morning setting up a small leatherworking area in our space, as Captain Walt had suggested. Walt was right, people enjoyed watching me work the leather, and it became a regular part of my show set-up.

Captain Walt worked on jewelry during the show. He made some really fine beaten, silver-and-gold earrings and necklaces, and the tapping of his metal working hammer and the hiss of his miniature torch drew people in like some magical music.

Walt had a good line of talk, being the easy-going, intelligent man he was. Having Emerald there didn't hurt either, just as Dawn being at the shows helped sales. Motherhood had caused Dawn to bloom, as is the case with some women, and she looked prettier than ever. She had lost most of the plumpness she had when I first met her, but was still a nice handful, as I often told her. So, we had two beautiful women to catch the customer's eye.

We all ate together on Friday and Saturday night, and talked about what had happened to us since Walt and I had met in San Francisco so long ago. On Sunday night, after the show was over and we had packed up our goods, we went to a good steakhouse Walt knew about. I told him over dinner about the far-out peyote trip we had taken up on Mt. Tamalpais after his visit, with the buttons he had given us.

When I told him about my own experience, becoming part of the land, he said we should talk after dinner about some things he was considering. Dawn gently nudged my foot with hers.

Sitting with Walt in his bus later while Dawn and Emerald were in ours, chatting away as if they'd known each other for years, Nathan sleeping in his bunk, I discussed future plans with him. He suggested we travel together to the shows we were both planning to do. He said, "I think it would be good for all of us to combine our talents to help sales, and besides, it would be good to have some friends along on the road."

I agreed, and told him we should join forces. He asked me if I wanted to talk to Dawn about it first, but I told him it was already cool with her. He smiled, we shook hands, and it was done.

Walt had been producing some cast silver buckles the last few months, and my showing up was definitely not coincidence as far as he was concerned. Neither of us believed in coincidence anyway. He wanted me to make the belts for the buckles, since it wasn't one of his talents, but was most definitely mine.

To make it short, the bunch of us traveled through the Southwest doing shows and camping out together. Walt was doing all the shows I was signed up for, plus a few more I had no trouble getting into. Some of them were on the funky side, being more a social event for people living out on the road making a living in many different ways so they could keep on rolling.

I did belts whenever I could for Walt's buckles, which were beautifully done, of course. They were of many different designs, mostly freeform shapes, some with small, semi-precious stones set in them. I had a good supply of top-quality leather, including several rolls of harness leather, very tough stuff. I would make a different belt for each individual buckle. I'd hold the buckle, looking it over, and after a short while I'd get a good idea what the belt should be like. Walt was always satisfied with the way the belts and buckles worked together.

After the Flagstaff show, we had another week to kill before the next show. Walt asked me if I was up for some spiritual exploration. I said I would be if he told me more about it. He told me to trust in his perception. I told him I already did.

Next morning, we headed east from Flagstaff and drove on out to Winslow, Arizona. Dawn drove our bus with Emerald and Nathan on board, while I kicked back with Captain Walt in his. The vibes on Walt's bus are hard to describe. It was as though all his experiences, and the people he had met, of which there were many with special qualities, had somehow left their essence. Dawn would probably have called it a presence, but a good one.

As I slowly looked around his bus, Walt seemed to have read my mind, because he smiled and said there had been "many a high-level trip taken on the bus," his "Heavenly Road Warrior," as he called it. He told me we were going to see a friend of his, Gregorio by name, to do a cleansing and an inner journey. "Gregorio follows the Road."

"What do you mean, follows the Road, Walt?" I asked.

"The Peyote Road, Jester, the Peyote Road," said Walt. "He may or may not invite us to travel with him, it depends on how the sweat goes."

I asked him what a sweat was and he said, "Man, you do have some things to learn. Just have faith and go with it, okay?"

"Sure, I can dig it," I told him.

"Cool, oh Mighty Hippie Out of Big Tree Country, traveling in the desert wonderland." Walt walked away, chuckling over his own joke.

The next day we were passing through Winslow, headed south. About ten miles further on, Walt pulled over on a gravel turnout where there were several old easy chairs by the side of the road. It was obviously a place where people sat and waited.

"We'll wait here a while," said Walt, and went to lie down on his bed.

I slipped off the bus to see how Dawn and Nathan were doing. I passed Emerald going the other way, and she gave me a kiss on the cheek, saying, "You have a sweet family there, Jester. You're a lucky man."

Dawn was relaxing with Nathan. She said she had enjoyed the driving and the female company, but was glad to see me. The three of us laid out on our cozy bed and took a siesta.

It must have been several hours later when I woke up to see an Indian man standing in front of me. He was about five foot six and lean, with a sharp, brown face, a thick-wrapped headband of many colorful stripes, a white cotton shirt, Levis, and a type of moccasin I'd never seen before. "Come on," he said, "it's time to go."

I got up and nodded my agreement, drowsy, not knowing what to say to him. So, when he walked over to Captain Walt's bus and got in and it started moving, I started up our bus and followed along. Dawn asked me where we were going, and I said her guess was as good as mine, but I was sure it was okay.

We headed a few miles further south, before turning east onto a dusty dirt road. We proceeded slowly along this road for what seemed many miles, but in reality it was only five or six. Somehow, the nature of the country made time stretch out, as we traveled through it. There was lots of cactus and sagebrush, and once the elevation rose a bit, some pinion pines started showing up. There was a large, classic mesa coming up ahead of us.

Finally, we came to what I figured was Gregorio's place. After we parked the buses and got out, I saw there was a small, flat-roofed house, a larger outbuilding, and a small, low, round structure covered with skins or tarps. There was an old Dodge pick-up truck in the side yard next to the shed, with its hood up.

Walt came over to me with the Indian man I woke up to in my bus, and introduced him as Gregorio. When Walt introduced me as Jester, Gregorio got a funny look in his eye, nodded knowingly, and said, "Of course." I just stood there looking at him, not knowing what to say.

Gregorio motioned us all into his home. There was a woman inside making bread, probably his wife, and she never said a word although she smiled in greeting. I was following Walt's lead, and Dawn and Nathan followed mine.

We all sat on some beautiful Indian rugs on the dirt floor. Nathan was being very still, though he normally started looking around at everything in a new place. Gregorio walked over to where he was sitting. Putting his hands under Nathan's arms, he lifted him up to face level. Nathan stared at him for a few seconds, until Gregorio made a funny cross-eyed face at him, and Nathan laughed his funny little boy laugh.

Gregorio's woman brought us sweet breads to eat and coffee to drink. The coffee was rich and strong, made the old-fashioned way in an old beat-up percolator. Gregorio and Nathan were sitting close together now, playing strange games with their fingers.

After we sat quietly drinking and eating a while, Gregorio looked at Walt and said, "Damned truck is acting up again. I can't get it to start. Maybe I'll run it into the river, and forget the thing once and for all."

I asked him if I could take a look at it.

"If you think you won't blow it up, go right ahead," Gregorio said in reply. "There are some tools in the shed."

I said, "I've got my own tools in back of the bus, but thanks."

I went and got my toolbox and timing light, and walked over to the truck. It had a flathead six cylinder engine just like my old step van's motor. I checked the plugs and wires, and the distributor cap and rotor. The contact posts on the cap and the rotor were badly fouled, so I carefully cleaned them. I also cleaned up the ignition points.

The key was in the ignition, so I turned it and stepped on the starter button. After a half dozen cranks, the engine started but was idling roughly. Shutting the engine off, I got out and removed the fuel jets in the carb, cleaned some gunk out of them, put them back, then fiddled with the old single-barrel carb until the idle seemed better. I checked the timing and adjusted it. I reset the carb, and she smoothed right out. I revved the engine, and shut it off. I closed the hood, and when I turned around, there were Walt and Gregorio nodding their approval. "She hasn't sounded so good since I first got her," Gregorio said.

"When did you get her?"

"'Bout ten years ago, as I recall. Yeah, Jaime Rodriguez gave it to me in payment for a ceremony."

"Nice old truck. Got a good heart," I said, and I meant it.

"You think trucks have heart?" Gregorio asked.

"Sure," I said, "just as everything else on this earth has a heart and a soul."

Gregorio nodded his agreement. We went back into the house, where we had lamb stew and homemade bread for dinner and more tasty coffee.

Gregorio went into the back room after dinner, and came out with a trippy-looking bracelet. He handed it to me. "For fixing the truck," he said. It was a beautiful piece: hand cast silver in a curving X shape inside a rectangular frame, all as one piece, mounted on a leather band with laces to wrap around the wrist.

"This is a good piece. Thank you," I said.

Gregorio explained the piece he had given me: "It's Navajo work, called a *ketoh*, styled after an arm protector when using a bow. We Apaches haven't always gotten on with the Navajo. In the old days, they kicked our asses a few times. Now we deal peacefully with each other for the most part. I'm gonna turn in. We got things to do tomorrow to prepare the sweat."

We said our goodnights, and went off to our wheeled homes.

Next morning, I awoke to the smell of freshly-brewed coffee. When we left the bus, Walt was already up, and nodded a good morning to me. There was a small wooden table with three chairs outside. Dawn and Nathan went into the house. Gregorio came out with three mugs of coffee, and we sat at the chairs sipping the hot, potent brew.

"Today we will go collect wood to heat the stones for a sweat," said Gregorio, "then we will do the sweat and cleanse ourselves of any bad thoughts and feelings, leaving our hearts clean. Jester, what goes on in the sweat stays there. Whatever we purge from our spirits goes out with the sweat and steam, understand?"

"Yes, I do," I said.

So, we spent time collecting dry hard wood while Gregorio gathered the stones to be heated. The stones were placed in the fire Gregorio had made, until they were extremely hot. They looked like volcanic rock, pumice stone, full of pits and pockets.

When the stones were ready, we started the sweat. Gregorio told me if I felt dizzy or thought I was gonna pass out, I should go outside for a while, then come back in.

The sweat lodge had room to hold six or eight people, and was dark inside. Gregorio had prepared the heated stones in a hole in the center of the lodge, which was made of canvas squares draped in heavy layers over a willow-stick frame, the structure I had seen when we arrived.

The lodge was already hot, so I was glad I had to strip down to do the sweat. After a short while, I was sweating hard. Gregorio poured ladles of water from a bucket onto the stones, softly chanting.

After about fifteen minutes inside, I had to go out for a few moments, and when the outside air hit me, I revived quickly. There were several buckets of cold water outside, and I poured some over my head. A few minutes later, cooled down, I went back inside and took my place again.

Gregorio was still chanting quietly, and Walt was silently sitting and slowly rocking forward and back. I must have been back in the sweat about twenty minutes, when I felt a pressure in my chest, and then I started crying, hard. Gregorio said I should look to the source of my sorrow and let it go, set it free. When he spoke, I saw Hawk's face clearly in front of me.

"Who is this one?" Gregorio asked. He could obviously see or sense him.

"A friend I lost, not long ago," I replied.

Gregorio was silent a while, as if in deep thought. "His death was not your fault. It was his time to die. We all have our time planned ahead of us. You did right for him after his death."

When he said it, I knew it was true. I closed my eyes, and felt a rush of cool air go past me. Opening my eyes again, I could swear I saw the flap covering the sweat lodge door move as though pushed aside. Hawk's face was gone, and I felt a weight had been lifted from inside of me.

I started rapping about the resentment and anger I had inside from bad experiences I'd had with people and their hurtful ways. I wished I could be rid of it. I asked forgiveness for any bad deeds I had done. I talked on a while, and then fell silent, feeling I had poured out a bucket of emotional waste and was now empty, cleaned out.

I reached for the ladle, and poured some water on the stones, after which I sat still, finally silent. I felt totally refreshed.

Gregorio spoke: "Sometimes we hold onto people we lose, so their spirits cannot leave. You have released your friend's spirit so he is free now. Your sweat is over, so go outside, wash yourself, and sit in the sun a while."

I had done my first sweat, and it was a wonderful cleansing experience. As Gregorio suggested, I went outside and poured a bucket of water over me. The chill of it invigorated me in a wonderful way. I felt as if all my cells were renewed. I felt completely calm, something different for me. A towel was hanging outside and I wrapped it around me, then sat on one of the chairs.

All my senses were heightened, as I had often felt on LSD, but this was better, a natural thing from inside. I had been touched with something special, and I sat there feeling totally mellowed out. Dawn brought out a pitcher of cold water and two glasses. She placed them on the table, and went back inside. The water was sweet and cold. I learned it came from a deep well behind the house. It was wonderful.

About ten minutes later, Walt came out, doused himself with water as I had, took the other towel, and sat down next to me. He drank some of the water from the pitcher, and made a loud sound of satisfaction. "It's been too long since my last sweat. Wonderful, isn't it?"

"Walt, it was a far-out experience, like nothing I've ever done before," I told him.

Gregorio came out a few minutes later. He took the last towel, but instead of sitting with us, he went behind the house for a while, remaining silent.

We spent the rest of the morning and early afternoon enjoying the peacefulness we felt. I was amazed such a simple act had caused such a wonderful change, but knew there was more going on than I could get my head around at the time. I have since come to know the power of spiritual healing in the company of healers such as Gregorio. I learned sometimes the intent is more important than the act itself to bring about inner peace. Remembering this would help me to keep body and soul together in later times.

I had changed into some clean threads. Walt called me over to his bus, and asked me to choose one of the three belts he had lying on his worktable, the special silver buckled belts we had worked on together. I chose the middle one. The buckle resembled a snake's head in shape, with two green stones for eyes. It was a beautiful piece, with the pin of the buckle resembling a snake's tongue. Walt told me it was the one he had chosen to give Gregorio for the sweat, and my choosing it confirmed its rightness.

We walked over to the house. There were a bunch of singing birds in a tree behind it. They didn't fly away when we walked over. Gregorio was sitting under the tree, lost in what seemed a meditative trance.

He came around in a few minutes. Walt handed the belt to him. "For the sweat," he said.

Gregorio nodded and rolled it up. Holding it in his hand, he said, "It will last, I think."

We had dinner as we had the night before, but I ate very little, not wanting to change the light, clear way I was feeling by loading up on food, a real change for me. After dinner, Gregorio spoke to us about something else:

"Jester, you went into the sweat with an open heart, which is why you were able to release the burdens you have been carrying. There is much for you to learn in this life, and I hope you have the clarity to do so. I know you will only be here with us a short time; however, I have an offer to make you if you are interested and would be willing to remain here several more days to take part. Are you interested?"

"Yes, Gregorio, very much so," I said. "The sweat has released me from a lot of burdens, and I thank you for showing me the way. I would gladly join you in whatever you have in mind."

"Good," he said. "I will take part in a peyote ceremony soon for the purpose of raising spiritual levels. Would this touch your heart? Have you partaken of this sacrament?"

"I have taken peyote before," I told him, "not with any real purpose, just for the experience of feeling its effects, but I would be honored to take part."

He said, "The peyote ceremony I am offering to let you take part in is for sharing and advancing our religious beliefs. If you join us in our next ceremony, it will be as a guest, and you will not be expected to participate beyond your ability. I will speak with the others and let you know our decision. Tomorrow morning early, however, I have a thing for you to do to prepare for the possibility of joining us, so get some rest now."

Man, it was hard to believe what an amazing trip this visit had become. I felt I had been received into a special, inner society. I have come to know this tiny planet we live on is covered with these societies, whose realities are hidden to most people, a world covered with inner circles.

The next morning, before the sun was up, Gregorio gently shook me awake. I never felt intruded upon by him, when normally I would be bummed by someone coming into my home and taking me out of a pleasant sleep, which I value highly. I knew he meant me and mine no harm. He only wanted to take me to a higher place of understanding.

After I got dressed, he took me over to his shed and we went in. It seemed at first, by the light from the lantern he carried, to be a typical storage shed, filled with all sorts of tools and implements. I noticed there were also many artifacts made out of natural things such as bone, feathers, gourds, and fur. The shed had an unusual feel to it, a different vibration or energy.

Gregorio took a small, heavy blanket with many colored stripes and handed it to me. He also gave me a rattle made from a gourd, highly decorated with paint, attached to the end of a stick. "Come," he said, and walked out of the shed carrying the kerosene lantern. He took me to a trail leading away from the back of the shed, which seemed to go in the direction of the mesa beyond.

"Walk this trail now," he instructed, "and when you get to the base of the mesa, find a suitable large rock, put the horse blanket down, and sit on it. You should stay there until you know your time is complete. Once you sit on the rock, do not get up until it is time for you to leave.

"Whenever you feel it is right, rattle the gourd and try to pray. The prayer is to be your own. It will be as a little song. You understand all this, Jester?"

"Yes, I do," I said.

I turned to the trail which was dimly lit by the lantern, and started walking. There was barely any light to see by, but I walked slowly, and when my eyes adjusted I could make out the trail enough to stay on it. I walked for quite a ways, and the morning light was coming on by the time I reached the base of the mesa. I marveled at being here and doing this, and knew this could only be good for me.

Man, what a far cry from my childhood and life in the concrete suburbs of Southern California. But, I realized before "civilization" came along, the people originally there probably did similar things, being one with nature, a pure perfect part of it. I also felt sure my living in the Big Sur camp had somehow helped prepare me for this.

I stood looking around at the many large rocks, until I saw one with a small depression in its top, about the right height to sit on. I placed the horse blanket on it and sat down, wriggling around until things felt good. So, there I was, not knowing how to feel, until I decided not to feel anything, but to simply be there doing as I had been told. I rattled the gourd. It had a nice sound to it. I rattled it again, and the sound seemed to increase in volume on its own. I was startled, but I did it again. Suddenly, I flashed on Russell, back at the old Eureka Street pad, and how he had told me I had the drum inside me now. I related his words to being here with the gourd rattle, as if it, like the drum and the sounds it made, were a natural part of things, and connected.

I sat quietly for a while absorbing this new awareness, but soon I started rattling in a slow rhythm which I increased steadily in speed until it felt right. After a time, I found myself wanting to sing along with the rattle, and words started forming, matching the rattle's rhythm. I will not go into what these words were, as this is a private thing, but the song developed its own meaning as time went on. I found myself singing this over and over, with my eyes closed. Suddenly, in my mind's eye, I was in company with my wolf guide again, only this time I could see us both, as from a distance, running among the trees of an unfamiliar forest. This continued for some time. The wolf again rushed sidelong at me, and went inside me as before.

I stopped rattling and opened my eyes. Some distance from me, a crow was sitting on a rock watching me. For some reason, this black bird made me uneasy. I felt it knew more than a bird should. "I hope you liked my prayer, Mr. Crow," I said. The bird spread its wings, cawed several times, and flew away. The trippy thing was I could hear his wings flapping for a long time after I couldn't see him anymore. A chill ran down my back. I knew it was time to go, and picking up the blanket I started back up the trail.

It took me about an hour to return to Gregorio's home, and along the way I saw lizards, rabbits, and even a coyote, as it slipped away behind a rock only to peek out again a moment later. It seemed I was being welcomed. Maybe that wasn't really the way it was, but it sure felt like it.

When I had returned and placed the lantern, blanket, and rattle in the shed, I went over to the house, to be greeted by Dawn outside the door. She gave one of her deep looks, smiled and said, "You have been to a faraway place, haven't you, my love?"

"Yes, my dear wife, I have," I told her, "and it was amazing. I am also very thirsty."

We went inside and were soon eating and drinking together, all of us. A while after the meal, I walked outside with Gregorio and Walt. We went behind the house under the singing-bird tree and sat down. I related what had happened, except for singing my prayer for them, which was mine alone. Gregorio and Walt looked at each other, with something like surprise on their faces. "What?" I asked.

"Jester," Walt said, "I had to go on a quest four times before I found my prayer, and here you go and do it right away. I guess you are more than you appear to be, to most people and to yourself."

"I'm just beginning to learn about myself, Walt," I said.

Gregorio smiled, and said we would take part in the peyote ceremony in two days if it felt right for me. I told him I was honored, then gathered up Dawn and Nathan and went to the bus for a good sleep. Dreams came and went all night, but all were good and peaceful, and none hard to accept.

Now, I know you want to hear all about the ceremony, but I know if I described it to you, I would be breaking a sacred trust.

There are others who have written about the ceremonies in great detail, but I will remain silent on my own experiences. I will tell you I took part in the peyote sacrament with Gregorio and four other men, and what happened there will forever remain as one of the great lessons I have learned in this life. My eyes, mind, and heart were opened by the sincere and powerful beliefs of these men, and the powerful magic of the peyote itself when used properly by anyone who follows the Peyote Road, as they call it. It is a wonderful and complete way, as I see it, to reach out to higher energy, to God, and be a part of what I see as the real way of things in the natural world.

I have since taken part in several more ceremonies, but I have never taken Peyote for lesser reasons since then. How could I? It would be like wasting life itself. The whole wonderful adventure with Gregorio, Walt, and the others will remain special to me always.

A few days before we were to do the last big show of the season, in Albuquerque, we were at a small flea market on the outskirts of Taos, New Mexico. Lots of unusual people in amazing road homes were there. One vehicle, originally a flatbed truck, had this far-out, shingled home on its back, with a roof shaped like one an old cottage might have. It even had a small bay window on the front. It was whimsical, and looked like a place where elves or gnomes would live. The guy who lived in it was named Dudley, and he actually was a little person, about five feet tall, with pointy ears, though not like Mr. Spock. He did some juggling and miming. He was a lively character, and full of mischief. Walt suggested we watch our stuff when Dudley was around, and I intended to do so.

The weather at Taos was fine, with the kind of deep blue sky existing only in the Southwest. Later, caught up in an impossible sunset, I had even asked Dawn if she would like to live there someday. She told me she couldn't even consider it, though she was loving the journey. I understood. I loved the Monte Rio area too, with its beautiful, mysterious woods, and Dawn had her whole family and history there. Wherever Dawn wanted to live, we would live there.

We didn't sell much at Taos. As I said, it was as much a social event as anything else. But, it was good to see others who were on the road, picking up stories and ideas to make traveling full time better and easier.

These folks would probably be called hippies by some. The term had become old and misused, but, they were living and working outside the Establishment, as we used to say, and they dressed as they pleased. So, there were some earmarks of hippieness involved. Heck, I guess they were hippies. I know my experiences during the Flower Power era have molded the way I live my life, even now as I'm telling you this. It's as if the essence, the purest part of the philosophy has left its influence on me. I don't mean the externals, such as clothing or decorated vehicles. It's the living free of government restraints, except maybe registering the bus and other minimal things. I do know I could never work in an office as an accountant or retail store manager. No, I don't think so, man.

We had been on the road about a dozen weeks doing shows, meeting folks, and enjoying life. I continued to make belts for Walt's buckles. I wanted to only charge Walt cost for my materials, but he insisted on paying me for my labor, also.

"Whatever you do is of value, and you should be willing to ask what your time is worth, man."

After the show we did during our last weekend in Albuquerque, Dawn told me she needed to get back home, and I was more than ready myself. I told Walt we were gonna head back to Monte Rio. He said they might come to visit in about a month. I told him we would love it if they did.

So, on Monday morning after the show, we headed back home. We would just drive on through, only stopping to eat and sleep and enjoy the ride. Truth to tell, we were weary of the selling, and had done better than expected, so going home was right on. It would be good to see how everybody was doing. We would stop to see my folks on the way back, for a day, just to check in.

Not doing any selling on the way home made it a real vacation for the three of us. Nathan was a good traveler, too. He never seemed to get bored, always finding a way to keep himself busy. For a kidling his age, he sure had a grasp of abstract ideas. Dawn and I had always talked to him as a small, but whole person, which he was, same as most children. I used to recite the alphabet and sing to him, and tell him stories when he was an infant, while I was holding him. He used to stare intently at my mouth when I did these things, absorbing it all like a sponge.

We had gotten back to my folks' place, and Nathan ran from the bus, yelling, "Grandma and Grandpa, Grandma and Grandpa!!" When he reached them, he held hands with them both and beamed up at them. Nathan sure had developed a bond with them on the last visit. The folks were glad to see us too, and we had a nice, two-day visit with them, which wasn't enough, of course, but we needed to get home.

While we were there, Dad took me aside and told me Mom was in ill health. Her diabetes was under control, but she had a congestive heart condition. It was being treated with medicine, but unless she lost a lot of weight, it wasn't going to get better. He was worried, as you might expect. I told him I'd talk to mom.

My mother had always been a compulsive eater. Eating was one of her real pleasures in life. I talked to her when a chance arose, and even though she knew what I told her was right and true, I realized she wasn't going to ease up much in the munching department. I believe you can't change someone's destiny. You might think you can, but that's not how it works.

After several days of visiting, we headed north to Monte Rio. On the way up, we stopped at Kirk Creek Camp, but didn't head up to the old campsite along the Nacimiento River. I knew I would see it again sometime, but what Gregorio had told me during the sweat had released me from concern about Hawk being where he was. I knew now he was properly laid to rest and at peace.

We got home to Monte Rio several evenings later. We stopped at Maxine's house first, so Dawn could check in on her mom and brothers. They were all fine, and glad to see us. Maxine made us some food while we sat back in their cozy living room, still feeling as if we were traveling down the highway. We told them about most of the happenings along the road, and they were fascinated when I described meeting up with Captain Walt, who I had mentioned to them before. I said they might get to meet him in a month, if he could make it up this way. When Avery asked me if he was as cool a guy as I had said, I told him he was even cooler than I had remembered.

It sure was groovy to get back home. Nathan was fast asleep, so we laid him on his bed, just taking his little red tennis shoes off. Dawn made us some tea, and we sat quietly, feeling the miles fall away. We often sat together without saying much at all, being so comfortable with each other.

Dawn asked me, "Okay baby, what's next?" I walked over to where she was sitting, took her by the hand, and showed her what was next. Tomorrow was a ways off yet, and the night was just right. After reaffirming our deep love for each other, we slept the sleep of contented babies.

The next few years moved along like a peaceful, slow-moving river, gentle but steady. We did our California shows, a couple in Oregon, and one in Reno, Nevada, which was a huge gun and western collectibles show. This show had about twenty-five hundred tables, and was held in the convention center of a large hotel-casino. The promoter I made reservations with said people came from all over the country to this one, and some from overseas, Australia, England and Germany.

I figured I'd better get busy. I made up lots of my standard stuff, but decided to make some bandoleers for shotgun shells and rifle cartridges, as they used to use in the Old West. I also made up some decorated leather gauntlets as cowboys used to wear, which laced up with leather thongs, some with traditional floral patterns on them and some with my own designs. They looked good. I styled them after ones I had seen in photos I found in library books. I also made some copies

168

of leather cartridge boxes from the Civil War Era. It took about two months for me to make all the items I wanted to for this show. It was good I made a bunch.

When the time came for the show, Nathan got chicken pox. He got a bad case and was miserable, the poor little guy. I was going to cancel doing the show, but Dawn insisted I go it alone, since I had worked so long and hard to prepare. The cowboy things were designed for this show after all. So, reluctantly, I agreed.

It was good I went, because this was one far-out show! I had developed an interest in guns, the way they are made, the way the metal and wood are fitted together, though they're such opposing materials. When a good gunsmith makes a custom rifle, the wood and metal are so closely fitted they look as if they grew together.

I had walked through several of the shows we had done on our Southwest road trip where guns were being sold, mostly old collectibles, but new ones too, and they did fascinate me. I hadn't bought one, though. A lot of the guns and exhibits at this show were amazing, with incredible engraving, inlay, and perfect stock work. I could only check them out before the show, though, because without Dawn I had my hands full keeping up with the customers and their demands.

It was a three-day show, with set up on Thursday, and the show days ran from 9:00 a.m. to 6:00 p.m. Friday, Saturday, and Sunday. Brother, did I sell! By the end of Saturday, I had virtually nothing left. I couldn't even keep things as samples to show, though I had put together the photo album of pieces I had made.

There were a bunch of folks there who called themselves Cowboy Shooters. They would dress up in vintage Old West style clothing, and do a shooting competition with a cowboy atmosphere. They were interested in the cartridge belts I made. These things were already available from commercial companies, but they were plain, and not as nicely made as mine. My leather gauntlets sold right out, the whole dozen sets I had. I took a lot of orders, too. By the end of the show I was burned out, but my pockets were full.

I had walked around looking at guns Sunday morning before the show opened, and an 1886 Winchester lever action had caught my eye. It fired the 45-70, a classic old cartridge with plenty of power for hunting. It shot a large bullet, had seen much military service, and had accounted for many head of wild game. Funny thing, calling them game animals. Not a game for them, for sure.

Anyways, the gun was only in fair condition appearance wise, which is bad for a collectible. But, the inside of the barrel was in great shape, and mechanically it was excellent. After about half an hour of bartering with the seller, I got it for a fair price, including some leather goods I would make him: two leather rifle scabbards of a design he sketched out, and two cartridge bandoleers. The man told me never to have the outside of the gun refinished, even if it didn't look so great, because its antique value would decrease if I changed it.

I walked back to my table proud as a peacock with this old Winchester, a real piece of American history. I couldn't wait to see George and Avery's faces when they saw it.

It took a full day to get home, but man, I was still buzzing over the show! I had already paid in advance for the next one I would do in six months, to make sure I had table space. Dawn was amazed at how much I had sold. She was also happy when she took the money from the sales down to the bank. I was right about the old Winchester, too, when I showed it to the boys. I finally had to take it away from them before they wore the action out, as they couldn't get over the tight, smooth way this seventy-five year old gun operated.

The next visit I had with Jester was very different, and at least partly explained why he was down by the river where I found him, still on the road and alone. When I went to see him, the sky was overcast and it was drizzling rain, as it had been for several days. Summer had already turned into fall, but even so, rain in this area is normally scarce. I drove down to the canyon as usual, but Jester was not visible at his campsite, which had some things lying around outside unprotected from the rain.

I parked, walked up to Jester's truck camper, and knocked at the back door. No answer. I knocked again, and he opened the door, looking old and tired, the spark he usually emanated seeming to be extinguished. "Come in out of the rain, son," he said. So I did, and once we were settled at the table in the camper with coffee and cigarettes going, the rain drumming steadily on the sheet metal roof of the camper, he started talking to me, but not as before.

"This is a special day today," he began. "I don't really feel like talking, but I guess you should know the hard stuff along with the good. Wouldn't be honest otherwise. This is the anniversary of my wife and son's death in 1978. It's part of my life, so I guess it's part of the stories I'm telling you, too."

Jester became silent, and seemed to go inside himself, head down and shoulders sagging. It took a few minutes, but he gathered himself together, and I had a feeling it wasn't the first time he'd had to pick himself up and continue on. He told me he wanted to be alone on this day, but I was tight enough with him, especially with my recording his words, I could hang with him for a while, and learn what had happened. He cleared his throat and began quietly talking.

We were heading down to Bakersfield to do a small show, one we had done once before. It was late September, as it is now, and we were getting some real rain along the way. The bus handled the wet road okay, so I wasn't too concerned, having driven it through a lot of bad weather already.

We were about a mile from the off ramp we needed to take. Ahead of us, I saw something very wrong. There was a diesel rig out of control having come across the center section, ending up going the wrong way on our side of the road heading right toward us. It seemed to last forever, as I watched the truck coming our way, its trailer sliding first to the right and then the left, tires wailing on the damp road. I was in the second lane from the right, and tried to pull over to the slow lane, but there was a car right next to me.

Dawn and Nathan were on the bed playing some game. I remember hearing Nathan giggling.

When the front of the semi hit us, the bus was flipped up and over on its right side, hitting the car in the slow lane, pivoting the bus up in the air. The bus rolled twice more, and I remembered nothing more 'til I woke up in the hospital.

When I did wake up, I was alone in a hospital room, a cast on my left arm and my ribs taped, an I.V. tube in me and some wires hooked up to my chest. I found out later I had three cracked ribs, my left arm was broken, I had a gash on my scalp and a bad concussion, and nothing else.

I managed to find the button to call the nurse, and when she came in I asked her how my wife and child were, if they were all right. She said she'd get the doctor, and walked out. A few minutes later, the doctor came in, but I already knew what he was going to say. I knew, but tried to deny it inside.

"I'm sorry to have to tell you this," he said, "but your wife and child were killed in the accident. I'm terribly sorry."

When he said those words to me, I went numb, man, completely numb. The pain of my injuries was overcome by the total emptiness I immediately felt. I just lay there, not hearing what the doctor was saying to me.

Holding up my good arm and pointing at him, I said I wanted to see them, but he suggested I get some rest first. I told him he didn't have a choice in the matter, unless he wanted me to cause him more grief than he could handle. After again voicing his opinion, the doctor had the nurse free me of the wires, and they took me downstairs in a wheelchair to where Dawn and Nathan were.

The doc was right. The accident had not been kind to either of them. When they allowed me to view my whole life lying there in such terrible condition, I heard a horrible noise coming from somewhere far away. Then I knew it was me screaming, my heart tearing apart. I was on my knees on the floor, and they helped me into the chair again, then took me to my room and mercifully knocked me out on sedatives. I don't know how long I was out, at least a day. But when I came to, there were George, Avery, and Maxine sitting in my room.

All I could say was, "They're gone. It's impossible, impossible. Please forgive me."

The brothers came over to me, and hugged me as best they could. We cried together, but found no comfort in it. A few minutes later, Maxine came over to me and silently held my hand, tears streaming out of her eyes. All I could do was repeat what I had said to the boys. My tears flowed as if they would never end, and I'll tell you this, they may not show, but my tears have never stopped.

I was released two days later. The Lensels had made arrangements for bringing Dawn and Nathan home, and we drove back in Maxine's Buick. I don't think any of us said a word all the way home. We got some coffee to go, but I just held mine, until Avery took it from me, cold, and tossed it out the window.

When we got to Monte Rio, I stayed at the Lensel home, Maxine insisting I shouldn't be alone yet. Those wonderful, loving people took care of what needed doing. Man, I couldn't have done anything anyhow. They made arrangements to have Dawn and Nathan buried together. During the funeral, when the first handful of dirt was tossed on the coffin, I felt as if a mountain had fallen on me, and I passed out. My folks had come up to be with me, but after several days they had to leave. My mother was ill, and the grieving was too much for her.

A week after the funeral, I went back home to the cabin. I didn't know how I would feel being there alone. All their stuff was around me, and I felt they were actually there, but I just couldn't see them. I drifted around, looking at and touching all the things they would never use again. I cried on and off, and sometimes I walked down the trail into the woods, but I found no comfort there. It was all I could do to keep from just running off into the trees until I couldn't run anymore and fall down somewhere to never get up. I felt I didn't have any reason for anything anymore.

Eventually, the insurance people came around. Dawn had always insisted we have at least minimum insurance on the bus, to keep things right.

Maxine knocked on the cabin door, and came in with these two suited men, who said they were from the insurance company covering the firm whose truck had hit us, a major shipping company. They gave me some quick sympathies before getting into their rap about what they were willing to offer me. I wanted to tell them to take their money and get out, but didn't have it in me. It was a lot of money they offered, but at the time, it simply didn't matter.

I asked them to step outside for a minute, and then told Maxine I wasn't able to deal with this. Maxine handled her sorrow differently, though I knew her pain was as great as mine. She said, "I have a lawyer downtown who handled the situation when Buck died. I'll send these boys away and get in touch with him. I'm sure he'll handle it for you."

I said if it wasn't too much for her, I would be grateful.

Maxine told me probably the only way I could get back at those bastards was to hit them in the wallet.

Maxine's lawyer handled the whole thing. He found out, according to hospital reports there was evidence of drugs in the truck driver's system, when he was treated for his relatively minor injuries. The lawyer made the insurance company one offer for an out-of-court settlement, or as he put it to Maxine, "I told them I would cut the trucking company a new one if they didn't accept."

They settled. I won't tell you how much it was, but it insured I would never need to work again. It wouldn't bring my dear family back, but, as Maxine had said, at least I hurt them financially.

For the next week, I floated around in my head, trying to get myself aligned with my new world. I was grateful for the love my people in Monte Rio gave me, and I tried to return it to them. We were all in this grievous state together. Marla was especially kind, seeming to know what to do and say at the right time, but then, she had suffered the same way and understood everything.

Once I was able to function again, I bought an old Toyota pickup, and drove down to where the bus was being stored outside Bakersfield. George went with me for backup, since driving was still hard on me. We found the yard where the bus was being stored. The man running the place took us over to where it was lying. It was bad, man: a real twisted wreck. There was a lot of stuff all jumbled up inside. We took all the tools out, along with the personal effects still there. After looking around for a while, we went over to his office, and I told him firmly, "I want what was in the drawer under the bed."

The guy looked at me and started to say something, but both George and I were looking him right in the eyes, and he dropped the B.S. he was going to put out, went over to the closet in his office, took the Winchester out and handed it over. Except for a fresh small scratch on the stock, it seemed fine. I told the man at the yard he could have the bus for scrap, which he said was fine, and I signed it over to him.

On the way home, George asked me if I was going to keep the leather business going, and I told him no. It was part of my life with Dawn and Nathan, and I just couldn't carry on.

When we got back, I went home to the cabin, got in bed and slept until late the next morning.

Two days later, with George and Avery's help, I went over to Marla's place and gave her back Greg's old tools, telling her what I told George about the business, saying maybe the boys could use them, or she could just have them for sentimental reasons. She accepted my offer, telling me I could have them back any time I wanted to start up again.

After living in the cabin for another month, I couldn't take it anymore. I felt I was stuck in time, and needed to break away. I knew Dawn and Nathan were inside of me, and the outside stuff didn't matter. I decided I would move back to the Bay Area and see how it would go. I know now why I wanted to do this, but hid from the truth at the time.

I loaded up the Toyota with only what I needed. I left the Winchester with the brothers for safekeeping. Somehow, the old piece of iron had come to mean something special to me, though I don't know why to this day, but it did and does. I also gave the 30-30, which had been in the cabin, back to the boys.

I transferred a bunch of money from one of my new accounts to a bank in San Francisco. The next day I was there, having said my good-byes the day before, promising to let them know where I settled.

I found a place near Clement Street in San Francisco, a neighbor-hood reminiscent of the old Haight-Ashbury, the way it must have been before the Hippie Movement. It was a mellow street, and I got a one-bedroom apartment. It was a nice pad, clean and convenient. It would do. I spent the first several weeks furnishing it. It was hard getting used to having more money than I probably ever would need. I still wanted to live simply, but things have been known to change. In my first food shopping, I bought a bottle of wine. It didn't last the night. I also got a TV and stereo system, and one of them was on all the time, even when I wasn't there.

I developed a daily routine. I would go down each day to Clement Street for lunch at one of the many ethnic restaurants, and then a streetside coffee house, where you could buy some java, sit at an outdoor table and read, or simply watch it all go by. A lot of people made friendly noises, which I usually returned, but I wasn't looking to do a lot of socializing. I visited the several bookstores on Clement, and started reading all kinds of stuff, science fiction, books about all kinds of different places, from Alaska to Fiji, anything catching my interest. But no matter what I did during the day, I would always end up at the Irish bar toward the upper end of the street by nightfall, if not sooner. It was called The Plough and The Stars, and it was as close to an Irish pub as you could get. It even had a Belfast Children's Fund jar on the bar.

I'd start off with a pint of half and half, but as the night rolled on, I would be drinking straight Irish whiskey, until I could barely walk home, but I always managed. Then one day, trouble reached out and tapped me on the shoulder.

One of the drinkers I had become acquainted with at the pub during the six months I had lived in the area, came into the men's room right after I had gone in. "My friend," he said, "care for some toot to resurrect your senses?"

I told him sure, why not, and did a couple of lines. I hadn't had any since the Renaissance Faire, but it seemed now was as good a time as any for getting reacquainted.

Before we headed back out, I asked him if he could get me some.

He said no problem, how much did I want?

Enough to last a while was what I told him, and gave him the cash he requested.

So, a few evenings later, he catches my attention at the bar, we go to a table in a dark corner, and he hands me a fat paper envelope, an "eight ball," he called it, and I was set.

I loved the stuff, man; it kept me from getting down. I felt energized and thought my depression had lifted. Yeah, sure, as long as I had the powder. Whenever I ran low, my "friend" could supply me with more. As I think about it, it is amazing how quickly I got into coke, doing it all the time. It was always available. I needed to feel up, and the cocaine did it, as long as I kept refreshing myself. It's a good thing I had ample money, or I would have hit bottom real fast and kept going.

I used to do some lines, and then go down to Clement street. But instead of eating, I'd go to the Plough as soon as it was open and drink my fill, adjourning to the can once in a while to snort up and regain my momentary high feelings. Before long, it was all I was doing, and I didn't care.

I started messing around with a couple of chicks who frequented Churchill's, the other bar I started hanging in, a few blocks down Clement. A different sort of place, it gave me another level to experience, so I wouldn't get bored. Mostly a low-key singles bar, I went there one night with my coke dealer from the Plough.

We were hanging loose when a girl he knew came over, and after a few minutes they went off together. A chick sitting alone at a small table gave me a smile, and without considering anything, I went over, sat down, and started rapping with her. She was attractive and alone, and I needed something to do.

After a while, she suggested we go to her place, so I agreed, and we walked the few blocks to where she lived. We messed around for a while. She was quite frisky. After we had spent each other's energy, she asked me if I had done cocaine before, I nodded, and she produced a small silver box with what must have been three or four grams in it, and we both had some. Cocaine can certainly get you going sexually, and keep you there, too.

But after another hour, she told me I had to leave. I didn't want to, and told her I would rather spend the night. Since it was Saturday, I could take her out to breakfast, maybe spend some time together. She got upset and told me firmly to go. I finally saw the wisdom in splitting, and didn't even say thanks for the good time.

I walked the few blocks to my own place, my mind racing. The evening hadn't been very fulfilling. I didn't get off on just getting laid. I'd had a full life with Dawn, and this hadn't even come near the satisfaction I needed. I ended up getting bummed, and would have loved to crash, just close my eyes and sleep, but I couldn't with all the coke I had in me. So, I went to the liquor store down the street and bought a pint of bourbon. I got all messed up, but the coke in my system still wouldn't let me crash. What a rough night. I must have been making a lot of noise. The neighbor downstairs kept banging on his ceiling with something 'til I screamed something at him and he cooled it. I decided I should do the same.

I went back to the Plough the very next night, and got into a brawl with what I thought was one troublemaker and turned out to be two. There was a man in his late sixties named O'Grady, who was a feisty old Irishman with a sharp wit. He was a regular at The Plough & The Stars, adding a bit of the Old Country to the place's atmosphere.

One evening while I was sitting nearby, he remarked to a much younger fellow the way he was playing pool, he might want to take up another hobby. The guy had lost some bucks on the table. He took offense, and when O'Grady went to walk away, he shoved the old man, who lost his balance and fell down. He wasn't hurt much, but I hate a bully, and went over to the young punk and told him what an a-hole he was, roughing up an old man. He shrugged and took a swing at me, but telegraphed his punch. I blocked it and gave him a shot to the gut. But, the other man who was standing by the pool table watching all this was a friend of the fella I'd just hit, and he sucker punched me on the side of the jaw, jolting me. By this time, the other one had recovered enough to give me a couple of shots too.

I ended up taking a real beating. I got in a few good licks of my own, but lost two upper teeth in the process.

I guess you could say my lifestyle took a real dump compared to the way I had been living in Monte Rio, but as I said, without Dawn and Nathan I didn't feel I had any reason to live a good life. Maybe I somehow felt guilty, too, because I hadn't been able to save them, though Lord knows what I could have done.

I wish I could tell you I came to my senses in time to save myself a lot of grief, but I'd be lying. I got into a crash with the Toyota one night and had some coke on me, of course. No one was hurt, but the cops busted me. I ended up getting ninety days in county jail after pleading no contest, plus a stiff fine and three years probation.

After I got out, feeling rough, I started getting right back into the toot. One morning I woke up in my apartment and blood was all over my pillow and the side of my face, coming from my nose. After washing up, I sat myself down to consider my situation. I thought to myself, "Is this what Dawn and Nathan would expect from me? Was it?"

I contacted a major rehab center, and voluntarily put myself into their program. It turned out to be the break I needed. I had some individual counseling and group sessions that got pretty heavy. I talked with the other people who were there who had stories as bad, if not worse, than my own, and I started coming around. After four weeks of this, I was told I had a choice. I seemed to have made a good recovery in a short time, and I could remain a few more weeks if I felt the need, or try it on the outside again. I was ready to leave.

After I got back to my pad, I decided a road trip would be just the thing I needed. I wondered where Captain Walt was, wishing I had some way to get in touch. Then I had a brainstorm. I would buy a good vehicle for the journey and look for Walt. I mean, why not? What else did I have to do? Being in The City had turned out to be a bummer.

One night, I dreamed of Dawn, which I hadn't done for quite a while. It was a simple dream, but it told me what I needed to know. There she was, as wonderful as ever, standing by the side of a long straight road looking as if it went on forever. Dawn smiled at me and lifting her left arm straight in front of her, moved it out to the left, as if to say, "There it is, baby, what are you waiting for, the road is yours," before she simply shimmered away. I woke right up, and it was settled. A road trip it would be.

Jester took a deep breath, and asked me if I could come back the next day. He said he was tired and wanted to sleep. I told him it would be fine, and I hoped tomorrow would be better. I saw such great sadness in his eyes. This normally cheerful man had seen and been through a lot, and it showed. I told him I would be back the next morning and he nodded and shut his camper door. I hesitated to leave him but knew he would be okay. When I went back the next morning he was more his usual self. I found him sitting in his camp chair smoking and drinking coffee. The drizzling rain had finally stopped, and the sun was warming things up. After handing me a mug of hot coffee, he asked me to remind him where he had left off, and when I told him, he took a moment to get his mind up to speed, then continued his story.

I considered my decision to find Walt. Something about being around him helped me to sort out reality, to realize the size of my life at the time, and to develop new perspectives. It was amazing how strongly connected we were from the get-go, especially since we had actually only known each other for a couple of months. I figured going to see him could only be a good thing. He hadn't gotten up to Monte Rio, so he wasn't aware of the major changes to my life. Yeah, finding him would be a good thing.

The first thing I needed for my journey was a solid vehicle, not too big, but one able to handle all kinds of roads. I decided to get a

Jeep Wrangler with a hardtop, a brand new one. I had never had a new vehicle. I went to the dealer in Oakland, and went through all the typical bull with the salesperson, unavoidable when looking for a new car or truck. Even if you tell the salesman exactly what you want and how much you can or will pay, it still takes a lot of shifting around and tap dancing to get it done. But, I finally made a deal with the guy for a nice rig, a demo with only a few hundred miles on it. I even had him throw in a better set of tires in case I did some traveling off the main road.

Driving my new ride home, I considered where I would go to try and find Captain Walt. The only place I could think of was Gregorio's. I knew I would be welcome there, and it would be good to see them both. I figured if anyone knew where Captain Walt would be, it was Gregorio. After purchasing food and other basic supplies and packing what personal stuff I figured I would need, I left my pad as it was and took off, heading to the Southwest.

It was mid-April, and the weather was great. I headed south down the highway, but didn't plan on visiting the folks this time. It would have been too rough on me being there alone. I did call them before I left my apartment, to let them know I was okay.

I drove and drove, playing the radio in the jeep when the mood struck, or running along in silence with only the deep hum of the new engine and the whine of the knobby tires, music of the open road.

I doglegged down California's main highways and secondary roads, until I hit Highway 15. I took Highway 15 east until it connected with Highway 40, and took it into Arizona through Needles, California. My first stop was Kingman, Arizona.

I wasn't interested in meeting anybody. My desire to make acquaintances hadn't picked up at this point. I suppose you could say I was on a quest to find Captain Walt, and I wanted to avoid any distractions from my goal.

I know now I probably missed a lot of interesting times, wearing blinders, but didn't have much choice. I felt driven, and I think the constant motion of being on the road was therapy for my heart and mind, you dig?

I had chosen my vehicle wisely. The jeep had a good heart, and proved to be a loyal rig, taking me wherever I needed to go without complaint. 'Course I had no idea at the time how far it would actually have to take me. Truth to tell, if I had realized beforehand how many miles and days of searching would be laid down before I found Walt, I might not have considered starting the trip in the first place. But, in my state of mind, I never thought about it. Man, I just put it in gear and rolled!

Driving through Arizona, I stopped several times to camp along the way, taking a long walk in the desert each time I stopped. I found I had missed the desert's way of being, its hidden life and magical essence.

I continued my journey until Winslow came into view once again, and I turned off south as before. My thoughts grew heavy as I followed this last part of the journey to Gregorio's home. Feelings and memories resurfacing were disturbing, and making the trip now, without Dawn and Nathan along, gave me cause to think this was a foolish thing I was doing, trying to find a way home again. For this what I think I was truly attempting to do. But, I kept on my way. Maybe I hoped to find something to help me regain my desire to live life fully again.

I came to the pull-off where we had all waited for Gregorio to show up. I didn't think it would happen again, believing it had probably been planned, and my waiting this time would come up empty. But, I decided to try it anyway. Shutting off the jeep's engine, I sat and waited, still hearing the engine and tires singing their song in the back of my mind.

I must have dozed off, because I woke up to the sound of an engine running alongside me. Far out! It was Gregorio in his old Dodge pick-up! I was blown away. I got out of the jeep and went over to where Gregorio was now standing outside his truck. "Gregorio, how did you know I was waiting for you?" I asked.

"I didn't," he said. "How would I know? I was on my way to Winslow to get some supplies, and saw you parked here sleeping in your nice, shiny jeep. It is good to see you, but what are you doing here?"

"There's a lot to tell. Can I go with you to Winslow?"

"Sure, we'll take your jeep, save me some gas money."

So Gregorio and I headed up to Winslow. We stopped at a local diner and we sat there drinking coffee, Gregorio eating vanilla ice cream. I filled him in on all the events having occurred since I had last seen him and Walt. I babbled on until I had nothing left to tell.

Gregorio had stopped eating, and sat listening, not saying a word, letting me rid myself of all the things plaguing me. Finally, he spoke:

"My heart is filled with great sadness for your loss, Jester. Perhaps you can find some comfort in knowing they are always with you, no matter what, but it is up to you to keep them alive. Cast off your sorrow. Always remember their love and goodness. Keep it with you always."

Gregorio paused a moment, closing his eyes for a few moments before continuing. "I haven't seen Walter for some time because he headed north shortly after you were with us. After you found your song, he decided to look for one himself, and this time he was given a strong vision, one which told him to go as far north as he could to find his destiny. So, you will not find him here. But, I see you need a cleansing, and you are welcome to come back with me and do another sweat. You missed taking part in another peyote ceremony by less than a week, which is unfortunate, because it is obvious you need spiritual healing and understanding. There will be others."

I told Gregorio I'd found much good in doing a sweat, and would be happy to see his home again.

"We need to buy fresh coffee if we can get our butts going," he said. "Let's get out of here."

We did the small amount of shopping Gregorio needed to do before we headed back to his place. Stopping to get his truck, we headed down the dirt road to his home. It surprised me how familiar it all looked, as though my mind had found it an important thing to keep in memory. I got a real buzz the way the land revealed itself as we drove along. I felt welcome, as though the land was glad to have me here again.

I spent the rest of the day visiting with Gregorio, his lovely wife making sure we kept our coffee cups and bellies full. He and I walked in the desert, and he told me many things about this wonderful place where he had lived his entire life. He seemed to know every rock, animal, and bush. Once, we walked past a rabbit which was only a couple of feet away from Gregorio, and it never even stopped chewing on the plant it held in its front paws. When I made a comment about this, Gregorio told me he had made a "deal" with the animals around his home. If they didn't bother his garden or the chickens he kept for eggs, he wouldn't bother them, and I could tell the bargain had never been broken. I took this thing he told me in stride, knowing Gregorio had deep understandings of many things.

The next morning, we started the preparation for the sweat like we had done for my first sweat. Just before everything was ready, there appeared, coming down the dirt road, the figure of a man, and he shimmered as he approached from the distance, probably from the heat waves coming off the desert sand. When I turned to tell Gregorio about this, he was already looking up the road, but when I turned to look back again, there wasn't anyone.

I started to say something to Gregorio, but was startled to see how his face had changed. His eyes were totally black, as if the pupils had opened enormously, and his whole face has a strange tension in it, as though his entire being was focusing on something. I figured it was the now-missing figure on the road. I waited 'til he was finally relaxed again. His eyes had suddenly gone back to normal. Gregorio said, "Let's go into the house for now, until I know he is gone."

We walked over to his home, went in and shut the door. "I'll be right back," Gregorio said, and went into the back room.

His wife surprised me by speaking for the first time. "He has been having trouble with a man who lives to the east of us. But he will make it right."

"What trouble, if I may ask? Can I help in any way?"

She smiled and slowly shook her head in the negative. "Best to just wait for him to return," was all she said.

About half an hour later, Gregorio came back in through the front door. He told me things were all right now. "I think it is okay to do the sweat, if you wish."

We went out to the fire heating the stones. They were plenty hot, so Gregorio had me lift them with a scorched wooden scoop into a bucket and take them into the sweat. After three trips, it was ready. Everything was in place, so we stripped down, and carrying the water bucket and ladle, we went into this now-familiar shelter.

After the first twenty minutes, as in my first sweat, I had to leave the lodge, douse my head with water, and cool down for a few minutes before going back inside. When I did, I was immediately immersed in the scent of sage, a wonderful herb, full of healing, as Gregorio had told me. I breathed in the smell. Gregorio started his chanting again. I felt myself start rocking slowly back and forth, but I can't say for how long. The sweat dripping off my body felt good, 'cause I knew this was cleaning me out physically and spiritually. Then I heard something.

It sounded as if another voice was singing along with Gregorio. I opened my eyes and looked around in the darkness of the sweat lodge. I heard nothing. This startled me, but I sat and allowed whatever was happening to continue.

I could sense Gregorio looking at me. "Look into your heart and tell me what you see."

I closed my eyes again and let my mind go blank. In an instant, a flash of light lit up my mind. It so startled me, I opened my eyes, and sat up straight. After a short while, I relaxed again. I closed my eyes and tried to get back to the place where I had seen the light, but it was gone.

I heard a whispering in my right ear. Keeping my eyes closed this time, I just listened. The voice suddenly got louder, and it was Dawn's voice, saying "I am with you wherever you go and whatever you do," and then it was over.

I opened my eyes, and feeling a lightness in my heart I hadn't felt for a long time, I started singing my prayer song. I hadn't sung it since my time at the mesa, but I remembered it all. I sang it over and over, louder and louder, until I knew I was done. Leaving the darkness of the lodge, I saw Gregorio was already outside, grinning from ear to ear. "Why are you smiling?" I asked.

"Because I know you are all right," he said, "and your life may continue on now. What was dead inside you is alive again."

He was right. I felt a lightness where the familiar heaviness had been. Dawn's coming to me and telling me I would never be without her helped me find the right place to put my loving feelings for her and Nathan. I don't know how it had all come around in the sweat, and won't even try to explain it, but things were righter than they had been since I lost them. I still get sad when this time of year comes around, as you now know, but it is more because my time to rejoin them hasn't come yet, and it's been a long while now.

Anyway, I poured the water bucket over my head and chilled myself nicely. I was going to sit at the table as before, but Gregorio beckoned me to follow him, and we both walked to the spot where Walt and I had found him after the last sweat, behind the house under the bird tree. There was a rug on the ground, and we sat down and let ourselves cool off. Birds weren't singing in the tree when we arrived, but after a few minutes they started showing up, and soon the tree was full of them, all singing together. It was wonderful, man. I wanted to sit there forever, but life had other plans for me.

A number of times during Jester's story telling over the weeks I was with him, I wondered about some of the amazing stories he told. Considering the amount and variety of drugs he had gotten involved with, especially during his hippie days, I thought perhaps his mind might cross back and forth over the line between truth and fantasy. I guess I'll never know for sure, but I also knew Jester spoke from the heart, without guile, and decided to accept what he said as his truth. I do know a lot of astounding things happen in this world, and Jester certainly had his share. I kept in mind my earlier impressions of the understanding and acceptance of life's wonders Jester had. I saw him as a fascinating man, willing to put his life on display for me, no matter how I would react. In his words, he was "really a trip!"

The next morning over breakfast, Gregorio and I discussed where I might look for Walt. "The way Walter told me his vision went, he is going to be going north as far as he can go," he said.

"I guess I'll be heading up to Alaska, Walt's old home."

"Might not be a bad idea, if you're prepared to do it," Gregorio said. "When Walter sets his mind to something, he usually doesn't stop 'til he has got it done. If the vision said to go far north, it is probably what he is doing. I wish I could help you find the way. He has a long head start on you."

I knew Gregorio was right, so it seemed I would be making a run all the way up to Alaska. I had the feeling it would be another interesting journey.

Gregorio's wife gave me a large bag full of those Indian sweet breads I liked, and some dried meat to gnaw on as I drove. As I went to leave, I looked at Gregorio and asked him how old he was. Putting on a serious look, he said, "Wouldn't you like to know."

"Sometimes he acts like a young man again after a good sweat," his wife said.

Gregorio gave her a look. "Jester doesn't have to know such a thing, but we'll talk about it soon as he's gone." His wife flashed a big grin. I waved at them, got into my jeep, and started up the dirt road.

I drove all the way to Kingman, stopping only once. Sitting in the cafe I picked to eat in, I came to the conclusion I needed to go back to Monte Rio for a while, to regroup. I wanted to sit in my cabin again, and reflect on things. After I had received my settlement, I had fully paid Marla for the place. I knew George and Avery would check on it from time to time. Yeah, Monte Rio was a good plan. Besides, if I did have to go all the way to Alaska, I wanted the old Winchester along, as it might come in handy. So, I drove west to the ocean, before heading north up the coast again.

As I had hoped, things in Monte Rio hadn't changed since the last time I had been there. Everybody was fine, which was a relief. We had a nice dinner my first night back at the Lensels. I won't say there weren't a few sad moments while I was there; I expected it. But, time had passed, and the wounds were healing.

Maxine had blown up several pictures of Dawn and Nathan, hanging them in the hallway. I went all soft inside as I stood there looking at them. Maxine came over and put her arm around me. "We were all lucky to have had them in our lives, Jester. I think of it that way, and it helps."

I nodded my agreement, and we walked out to their front porch to sit and enjoy the warm night air.

Next morning, George, Avery, and I took the old Winchester to their target-shooting area a few miles out of town. They had never shot it, even though I told them they could if they wanted. They had kept it clean and oiled, though. We took some empty cans to shoot at. When I first cut loose on one of them, we were amused to see how hard the old cartridge hit them, and how far they bounced and rolled. We took turns plinking away, until we were out of ammunition.

On the way back, we stopped at the hardware/gun store in town and got several more boxes of the heavy cartridges. The storeowner wanted to see the rifle, and after bringing it in and letting him admire it, he made me an offer on it if I ever wanted to sell. I wouldn't, of course, but what he offered me was beyond the price I had paid, including the leatherwork I had given in trade. Apparently, the man I got it from had been square with me regarding its value. After getting back to the Lensel house, I decided it was time to go to the cabin.

The cabin had been kept clean and in good shape all around. No animals had gotten in to mess things up. I spent several nights there, and it was okay. After the sweat with Gregorio, I felt things differently, and was glad to spend time in the little home the three of us had shared in such a loving way. I thought about whether or not I might ever find someone to help fill the void in my life. I figured trying to find someone wasn't the way. It would just have to happen, and if it didn't, I guess I'd already had my one true family, and it would have to be enough.

The first night, before falling asleep in my own bed, our bed, I asked God to watch over my wife and child, and to help me in my search, since I felt there was something right and necessary to my doing it. Maybe my destiny was on the road north, tied up with Walt's. All I knew was I had to go, and go I would.

It was hard for me to leave Monte Rio and my people. I had gotten comfortable there in the week since I had returned. It felt more like home than any other place I had been. I was told, as I was leaving in my tightly-packed jeep, I would always be welcome, and my cabin would be safe. I knew it was true. I set off on my quest for the invisible Captain Walt, wherever he might be.

I figured if Walt had headed to Alaska, he would probably be easier to find there, since roads and people were fewer, or so I thought. The weather was good, and the jeep was running strong. I had bought some extra parts and fluids for it in Monte Rio, and other things I thought might come in handy, such as radiator hoses and fan belts. Amazing what you can pile in a jeep if you do it right. The Winchester was there, too.

I had studied some maps starting from Gregorio's area, and I had a handle on what route Walt might have taken. I knew Highway 5 up through California and the Northwest was probably the highway he would have chosen, then up the Alcan Highway through Canada and on into Alaska. It sure seemed like a lot of road, but highways had been a regular part of my life for a long time. The major experiences in my life had been connected by journeys, so why not do one now, when the time seemed right for it? I didn't plan my trip north, regarding the whens and wheres. I would take it as it came along. This would definitely be a grand adventure, whether I found Walt or not.

There is an awful lot of beautiful country heading north from California, not including the stripped mountain sides once you get into Oregon, the trees being totally gone in places. I caught some heavy rain on the evening I made my way through Coos Bay, Oregon, and had to pull my jeep over and shut it down until the rain let up. It kept on for quite a while, and the sound of it on the metal roof lulled me into a sound sleep.

Early in the morning, I awoke to one of the most wonderful scenes I had ever experienced. I had parked by the side of a slough, with lots of trees on the far side. There was a mist over the water, which gave the early-morning light a magical quality. I opened the passenger side door, and listened to the chorus of frogs croaking away. I also heard a loon calling, which added a sweetness to the scene. A small boat came slowly up the slough headed to I don't know where, its outboard motor burbling quietly, as if it didn't want to intrude on the peaceful scene. Stepping outside the jeep, I waved to the solitary figure in the boat, and got waved to in return. The boat slowly glided out of sight.

I regretted having to start the engine, but I needed to get along, find a place to wash up, eat, and fuel up for the day on the road ahead of me.

There was something about the way Jester sometimes closed his eyes when he told his stories. I could feel him going back to wherever or whoever he was talking about. It amazed me how I was pulled into his remembrances. I sometimes felt I was actually there with him, sharing in what was happening. It was difficult not to get involved, because he told his sto-

ries so vividly. Once or twice, he stopped and opened his eyes and apologized for rambling on. I was glad I had my tape recorder going, because I would have forgotten to write down the bulk of his stories. I was too busy living them with him at the time.

The weather was definitely colder down by the Carson River. The last time I was there, Jester's camp was all packed up, and he was inside his camper with the propane heater breaking the morning chill.

He said, "The weather has become less than hospitable, my friend, so I am going down to visit my friend in Temecula, as I told you I would."

I said I hoped it wasn't the last I would see of him.

"No, I don't think it will be. It's been a real pleasure telling you my life's stories, and I think we will need to continue on with it soon."

I gave Jester my phone number and address, and offered to take him out for a breakfast before he left.

He then said the strangest thing. "No, our visits should be at the river. I know it is the proper place for us to hang out together, whether I'm telling you stories or not."

I couldn't understand at first why he said that, but later figured it was something he had learned from Gregorio. He certainly was a man who had a great love and connection to nature, so perhaps it wasn't so strange after all. I only hoped it wouldn't be too long before he got in touch again.

It was almost six months later when Jester made contact with me, but not as he had before. In late April, I came home from work to find a UPS package on my front porch. When I opened it up there was a thick stack of handwritten pages inside, with a note on the front. It went: "Brother, I am sorry I can't share time with you as I had, sitting and talking your ear off. Life has put me in a situation making that impossible. But I have put to paper the other things I think are important for you to know and, considering my handwriting, to translate. I hope we will be able to visit in person another time, but for now, this will have to do. Take care, Jester."

I didn't know what to make of this turn of events. I had to accept what Jester wrote in his note, and resigned myself to the situation, there being nothing else to do. I did hope I would see Jester again, but apparently, I couldn't count on it. I spent most of the night reading his roughly written words, and I couldn't stop reading until I began nodding off and had to sleep. So, what will be written from this point on is from Jester's hand and not his voice. I have had to do a lot of cleaning up of his language and time-lines, as with the earlier stories. Reading his words, I realized his search for Captain Walt had put Jester on another path, so to speak, in his life, but it did nothing to lessen his proclivity for finding adventure wherever he went.

Section Four

I've been in Temecula for the last six months, staying with the friend I told you I would go see when weather at the Carson River got funky.

After staying with Frank about a month, I decided I would start writing the stories I hadn't told you yet. I wasn't sure how long I would be here, or what I would be doing at whatever time I would leave, so writing would be one way to make sure you would know the rest of the stories, in case something should happen to me. You never know. I have never written my history before, so I simply accepted it as another adventure, but covering inside distances, instead of outside ones.

I am writing about my experiences with Frank before continuing with my stories of earlier times. Maybe this is doing things out of order, but it seems the right thing for me to do, so I hope it's okay.

Frank was someone I met while on the road, about ten years ago. He was a retired mechanic who helped me fix my truck, the one I still have, when it was broken down on the side of the road outside Provo, Utah. There are better places to be stuck in, I can tell you. I got a lot of blank stares from people driving by, but no offers to help until Frank came along. He got my truck running again. Since he was traveling for his own enjoyment, having recently retired, he suggested we cruise a while together. He seemed a cool guy, so I took him up on his offer, ending up a few weeks later at his place in Temecula, California.

Frank was always straight-up with me, a quality getting harder to find in people. We remained friends all these years, making it a point to see each other at least once a year since we'd met.

After I said my good-byes to you and left the Carson River, I headed right on down there and found him at home, but not in good shape. He'd been real sick for a while, suffering several heart attacks since I'd last seen him. Frank had been a heavy smoker and drinker all the time I had known him, so I felt sure it had something to do with his heart trouble. He had been told he needed bypass surgery after his first heart attack, but had put it off. The second one made him change his mind.

Frank was bad off when I arrived, and he asked me, if I wasn't too busy, maybe I could stay with him a while and help with things. The fact he was asking for help at all made me realize how bad off he was, so I agreed to stay and help him.

We both made adjustments and compromises so we would be able to settle in with each other. We did a lot of card playing, sitting outside on the patio under the awning, or watching the tube, and generally living the easy life. I made sure he took his medications, and kept his smoking and drinking to as low a level as I could, but his condition worsened.

He'd had triple bypass surgery about three months before I'd come down, and developed complications right after the operation. Pneumonia had scarred his lungs. He hadn't gone back to the doctor right away when he started feeling bad after the surgery, so the pneumonia had a chance to hurt him. He finally called for help, and had been taken to the hospital to get better, until he could come home again.

I'm glad I was able to spend time with him, partly because his family was all on the East Coast and didn't seem to be too interested in doing anything for him. They didn't even call much, except his youngest, who lives with her family in Philadelphia.

We'd settled in together easily, even though we had different routines. Frank usually went to bed early, and since I'm a real night owl, I needed to find a way to keep from getting too restless and waking him up. I took a lot of walks in the area around his place, even after I started writing, which was always after Frank went to bed and I could concentrate.

It is real desert country. There was a dirt road behind Frank's pad, and I would walk a couple of miles down it some nights, to work off the energy built up sitting around the house. One night, I had an unusual experience during my walk.

It must have been around eleven in the evening, and I was about half a mile from Frank's. It was a stretch of road I was familiar with by then. I carried a small flashlight with me, in order to see my way. But there was a full moon that cast a mysterious glow on the land the way only moonlight can in rural areas where there isn't much man-made illumination.

I was slowly walking along, when I had to come to a sudden stop. There, about twenty-five feet in front of me, was a coyote with a wise-ass look on its face wily coyotes do so perfectly when they catch you by surprise. I quietly said, "Hello there Mr. Trickster, how is it with you this far-out evening? I'm a Jester, too."

When I spoke, he did exactly the opposite of what I expected he'd do hearing a human voice. Instead of instantly disappearing into the sagebrush, he sat down on the road in front of me! So, I followed my instincts and carefully sat down too, waiting to see what would happen next. He lay down in sphinx pose, with both his legs stretched out in front of him. We sat there looking at each other. I hoped I was not looking at him in an aggressive way. I did what I do when looking at cats: I looked at his ear instead of directly into his eyes. When I did, he opened his mouth, tongue out, in what was obviously a smile, almost as if he acknowledged my attempts to be cool. We sat there about two minutes, which seemed a long time to be so close to a wild coyote. All of a sudden I let out a gasp and jumped up, which made the coyote leap up and disappear into the brush.

Something had sniffed the back of my neck, scaring the hell out of me. Turning on my flashlight, I looked at the area behind me. At first I saw nothing, until I caught two glowing eyes in the light about ten yards away in the sage. At first I thought it was the same coyote I had been connecting with, but looking at the surface of the dirt road, I saw fresh coyote tracks made over my footprints. What a trip! I decided it must have been the coyote's mate, sneaking up on me for a sniff. At this point, I figured I had done my walk for the night and headed back to Frank's place. He was up when I got home, getting himself a drink from the kitchen sink.

"Having fun out there?" he asked.

"Yeah, visiting with the coyotes," I told him.

"Right, Jester, tell me another one," he said, "I'm going back to bed."

I went to bed too, and slept soundly.

Frank was a good man, but he got cranky while I was staying with him. I'd heard after people have heart surgery, they sometimes have personality changes. I chalked up his orneriness to this, since he had always been easy going around me in the past. I accepted his moods as part of his suffering, and was able to deal with them. I figured he might not be around a lot longer, so tolerance was a good thing for me to practice.

The only time his attitude would bum me out was when I would cook us a meal and he would complain about the food. I found a way to chill him out, though. One time, he made unhappy noises about a meatloaf I had conjured up, so I reached over, grabbed his plate and took it over to the sink.

"What the heck you doin' Jester?"

"Frank," I said, "if you don't like it, I'll dump it in the disposal, and you can make yourself a bologna sandwich."

Frank snapped, "Oh, don't be a fool! Bring my dinner back and quit foolin' around!"

I set Frank's plate down in front of him again, and we both started eating in silence. After a while, Frank quietly said, "This meatloaf ain't so bad. Better than the craploaf my ex used to make."

Toward the end of our dinner, Frank gave me a sheepish look and asked me if I would have thrown out his dinner.

"Frank," I said, "I figured it was either pitch it or lock you outside with the coyotes, but I thought the coyotes might toss you back in after listening to you grumbling about things."

Frank and I just looked at each other, before we both broke out in grins. Frank grunted, told me I was probably right, and took another mouthful of meatloaf. He never gave me a hard time about meals again.

After I had been in Temecula about five months, in the wee hours one morning I heard a loud crash. Getting up, I saw the bathroom door was almost shut with the light on. I couldn't get the door all the way open to find out what had happened, as Frank's body was blocking it, but I was able to reach his wrist and feel for a pulse. I couldn't find one. After calling his name a few times, I called the paramedics. They came and got him out of the bathroom, before pronouncing him dead. Personally, I think Frank's heart gave out, having taken enough abuse from its owner.

He was gone, and since he had his will written up with me named executor, I took care of his estate, as Frank had asked. I knew where his money was. He told me whatever was left over, I should send it to his youngest daughter, since, as he put it, "I wouldn't give the rest of them a pot full of poop, but at least my daughter still gets in touch once in a while."

Frank had been a marine, and he was a veteran of the Korean War and Nam. I had him buried in the military cemetery in San Diego. I had an estate sale for all his possessions, as he had asked me to, and gave what was left to the Salvation Army, except for a small toolbox full of useful hand tools, which I still have in my truck. His old house, which he had built himself, was in decent repair. He had told me to give it over to the local Lutheran Church, having already signed the papers to avoid any problems, for them to sell and use the money. I never knew Frank was at all religious, though he used the Lord's name often enough.

The only member of his family I contacted was his youngest daughter. She was able to get there in time to attend the burial ceremonies. We visited the day before she left. She knew I had been there for Frank, so when I gave her the sizeable amount of cash left, she wanted me to have some of it for helping. But, I told her I was in good shape and Frank had wanted her to have it. When she was leaving, she handed me a large envelope with something weighty in it, saying, "This was in the box of stuff my dad had put aside for me. I think you should have it. I don't care for the things, but you might. Maybe he brought it home from Korea or Nam."

So saying, she gave me a kiss on the cheek, got in her rent-a-car, and drove off. I opened the envelope, and pulled out a cloth-covered bundle. It was a Colt .45 semi-auto pistol, clean and oiled, with "U.S. Property" stamped on the side. Frank's daughter had figured right about where it probably came from. The magazine was loaded. I stashed it away in the camper.

My time in Temecula was over, and now I had someone else to miss in my life. Losing friends and family was getting old you know, even if, at this point, I understood it was part of getting older.

I think I better get on with my remembrances, and I hope my absence will not make them any less worth knowing. I hope they will be of value, and I will come see you again in the future. I'll mail them out when I get them finished up, which should be soon.

I paused in my reading to consider how the time with his friend Frank was for Jester. I had, at this point, realized how important it was for Jester to keep things fresh by traveling around, seeing new places, meeting new people, and getting into more situations and adventures. Even when he was married, he kept the wheels turning. As much as he was obviously friends with Frank, it must have still put some pressure on him to stay as long as he did. At least I assumed so. But, I also knew what friends and loyalty meant to him, and it must have taken precedence over his itchy feet and vast curiosity about what was around the next bend in the road. Then I got back to the words Jester had written down. I did wish his handwriting was more legible.

During my journey looking for Captain Walt, I had many wonderful times camping out in the Northwest. The country through

Western Oregon and Washington is incredibly green in spring. Washington State has some dense forestland. I camped out as often as possible, rather than moteling it all the way. I did plan to use a motel once in a while, to shower up and kick back on a cozy bed I wouldn't have to make up in the morning. I'm glad I had chosen to get a jeep with a hardtop, so I wouldn't have to keep moving the goods in and out of it when staying somewhere overnight, to keep things from getting ripped off. But the old Winchester always went inside with me.

I stopped my northward direction to head east when I hit the Columbia River, the border between Oregon and Washington. What a magnificent piece of water. Even when the surface is smooth, if you let your mind connect to it, you can feel the powerful pull of the water flowing between its banks. I don't think it's a river you'd want to casually go swimming in, or be on it in an underpowered boat. I drove the highway running along the north side of the river, heading east for a long ways. Starting at Vancouver, I drove past places with strange names such as Camas, Washougal, and Skamania. Skamania was a mere spot on the north side of the road with a store, two gas pumps, and a tiny cafe with the best cinnamon rolls I'd ever tasted.

Surprisingly, my interest in making the journey for its own sake was becoming almost as important as finding Walt, even though it would be groovy to see him again. Maybe Walt's vision to go north was part of my destiny too. Funny how things work, because a short while after I had decided this, I got my first lead on Walt's travels.

I drove along the Lower Columbia River, absorbing all the beauty around me until I felt my northern quest calling me again, and I headed back west and then north along Highway 5 toward Seattle.

A short way south of Seattle, I pulled off the side of the road to stop and eat at a local coffee shop. Most of the time, I only ordered breakfast at places I hadn't eaten in before, figuring breakfasts would be harder to mess up.

As I pulled into the parking lot, I saw there was a small native arts store near it. This gave me a mind buzz, and I had an urge to check it out. After parking, I walked over to the store. I was surprised at the amount and quality of the goods inside. There was clothing made of deer hide: jackets, moccasins, and gloves. There were beautiful drums and pipes, and lots of native jewelry. But also, in a glass-topped case were several belt buckles whose style looked familiar to me. I knew it was some of Walt's work.

I said hello to the native man sitting behind the counter. He nodded, not saying anything. I made small talk with him to break the ice. I praised the quality of the goods in the store, and he told me he made the pipes himself.

Something relaxed in his face, and he told me his name was Charlie. And, when I told him I was called Jester, he stared at me for a moment, then said, "I've heard your name before."

I asked him if he'd heard it from the man who had made the belt buckles in the case.

He answered, "Yup, he told me somebody named Jester had made some fine belts for the buckles he'd made before."

"Yeah, Jester is me," I replied.

Charley said, "Walt's a good man. He has a good heart. Told me you did too."

"I try to live a decent life," I said. "About how long ago did you see him?"

"Oh, must have been maybe four or five months ago," Charlie answered.

I said, "Yeah, sounds about right."

Charlie asked, "You looking for him?"

"Yeah, I am, but it may be a difficult search," I said.

"You still friends with him?" asked Charlie.

"Sure," I answered, "you could say Walt and I are brothers."

"I can tell you he's working his way up to Alaska," said Charlie, "some place called Homer, south of Anchorage. Told me he had decided he wanted to go there to fish for halibut. Something about a thing he was told to do."

I said, "Yeah, in his vision, I think."

Charlie sat looking at me for a few moments, and then asked if I knew about visions. I told him I did, and if he'd be there a while longer, I would be glad to talk to him some more, but I needed to go get a bite to eat first. Charlie said he knew a better place to eat, if I liked home-cooked food. I told him I always preferred good home cooking.

Charlie said, "It's been slow today, so why don't I shut 'er down and we'll go get something to eat, O.K.?"

I told him it was cool with me.

While Charlie closed down the store, I thought about how easy it was talking to him, as if talking to a good friend I had never met before. As with other native people I've met over the years, for whatever reason, I felt at ease with him. Of course, I hadn't met Charlie's brother-in-law Ralph, yet.

So, Charlie shut the shop down, and I followed behind his funky old Chevy truck. It must have been a cool hot rod at one time, but time and miles had done their work on it. We drove south down the road a short way and turned off onto a hard-packed dirt road winding its way into the trees.

After about half a mile, we came to an old log house, nicely built and fitted. There were three or four old cars in the side yard, and some chickens in a fenced-in coop off to the right of the driveway. Smoke was coming from a metal chimney pipe, with the sweet smell of burning cedar.

As soon as we parked, four kids came running over to Charlie's truck, jumping up and down all around him, glad to see him from what I could tell. He called me over, and when the kids saw me, they got quiet and wrapped themselves tightly around Charlie's legs. Charlie said, "These are my offspring, my mischief makers."

I knelt down and said "Hi, Charlie's kids!" They giggled and squirmed around. The youngest, a girl around two, came over, and looked at me a moment. She held her arms wide open in the universal kids language for "Hold me!" I picked her up and smiled at her round-cheeked, happy dirty face.

My heart twinged as I was holding her, the first child I'd held since Nathan. My face must have shown how I felt, 'cause I saw Charlie giving me a questioning look.

He said, "C'mon Jester, let's go in and meet the wife. She takes getting used to."

We walked over to the house, and Charlie opened the door and called. "Molly, we got company. Are you decent?"

A low booming voice said, "If we got company, Charlie Paul, they better be decent!" Charlie smiled and pushed me in ahead of him. There before me stood a large woman, tall as I was, with plenty of meat on her bones. She wasn't smiling, but the twinkle in her eye told me her tough front covered up a soft heart.

"Afternoon, Mrs. Paul," I said, "my name is Jester."

She said, "What the heck kind of name is, wait a minute, you know Walt?"

"Yup, I do," I told her.

"Come on in, set your butt down in a chair and call me Molly," she said. "Want some coffee?"

Charlie and I both sat down. The toddler wriggled out of my arms and toddled over to her mama, who patted her on the head, and put her in an old high chair, giving her a piece of home-made bread to chew on and play with.

What a happy, warm home. Charlie and Molly Paul were mellow people. We talked about Walt and Emerald, who was with him, about how I met him in S.F. and reunited with him on the show road years later. Molly asked where my wife was now, and I told her she and my child were gone. They saddened at this, giving me their sympathies from the heart. I thanked them, and said I knew they were still with me, always, and I kept their memories alive so it would stay that way. They nodded, understanding what I meant. Charlie asked me if I talked to them, and when I told him I did, he replied it was a good thing to do.

Molly told us, a while later, food was going to be served real quick, so we better grab a seat while we could. Charlie went outside and called loudly for someone named Ralph. When I asked who Ralph was, Charlie told me he was Molly's brother.

A few minutes later, in walks one of the largest people I had ever seen. Not much fat, just really big. Ralph had to bend his head down a bit and turn slightly to walk in the door. If he wasn't seven feet tall, he wasn't off by much. He had on deerskin pants, a calico shirt, and a headband. When he came in, he gave me a hard look.

"He's okay," Charlie said, "He's Jester, a friend of Walt's."

"Yeah. I've heard the name," Ralph said. "You're already here and it's dinner time, so I guess you're welcome." He walked to the back of the room and went into another room off to the side.

Charlie said, "Ralph doesn't take to white people, but he'll get used to you. Just don't sit in the blue chair at the table. It's his."

I said I would be sure not to.

Dinner was enjoyable, even though Ralph made it a point to ignore me. The Pauls were Christian people, so we said grace first. I'm not religious, but I find something "right" in it. Molly asked me, as their guest, to say grace. I didn't let on it wasn't something I usually did. But I kept it simple, and it came out all right.

We had some veggies from their garden, including some small, but tasty potatoes Molly was proud of. "Never grew them before," she said. "Different from lettuce or tomatoes, for sure."

"Kinda puny, though," Ralph said, teasing Molly.

"I don't see it stopping you from eating 'em," she said. "Maybe eating my puny potatoes will stop you from growing any more, which would be a blessing, Ralph."

196

Ralph smiled, but didn't answer, having done what he wanted to do, push one of Molly's buttons. When he glanced over at me, though, he put on a serious face again.

The vegetables went with a delicious roast. It had a mild flavor, and was tender. When I complimented Molly on such a good beef roast she told me it wasn't beef, but black bear, a spring bear Charlie had taken.

"Far out," I said. "It's delicious."

"Far out?" said Ralph. "What are you, some hippie?" This got me hoping this was not the beginning of something bad. Even the kids watched us both, waiting, except the littlest. She was busy munching up her veggies.

"Yes, Ralph," I said, "I'm a retired hippie. I hope it doesn't throw your appetite off."

Molly responded, saying, "Not likely, 'cept maybe if a bolt of lightning hits him."

Everybody chuckled, except Ralph and me. But Molly's joke had chilled the situation. A few minutes later, his plate empty, Ralph excused himself, after thanking Molly for the meal.

"Sorry, Jester," Charlie said.

"For what, Charlie," I asked, "I've had a good meal and a pleasant time here with all of you tonight, and I thank you."

Molly and Charlie grinned. "Good enough, Jester," Molly said.

Sitting a while in their living room after dinner, I asked Charlie if he wanted to see my old Winchester. He perked up, and said he sure would. I brought it in from the jeep. Charlie and Molly both admired it, and Charlie told me he thought his grandpa had a model '86 like this, only with a longer barrel in a different caliber.

"Long gone, now, probably pawned it to get booze money," Charlie said. "Grandpa's been gone for a long time now."

It was getting late, so I excused myself because I had to get a room in town to wash off the road grime. They wouldn't hear of it, and insisted I stay the night. These were decent people, open and hospitable, but I don't think I'd want to get on their bad side, though it wouldn't happen on my account.

Charlie showed me to the bathroom, which had an oversized shower in it, probably because of Ralph, and gave me a fresh towel, telling me to have at it. Afterward, Charlie showed me to the loft above the shop. There were two small sleeping rooms, one at each end of the loft, and Charlie showed me one of them. He said, "If you get up in the night to go out and take a leak, remember which room is yours, 'cause the other one is Ralph's, and I won't be responsible for what could happen." Charlie's smile spread from ear to ear.

I couldn't help but smile with him. "Oh, don't worry, I'll be careful," I said. It had been a long day though, so I slept through the night.

Next morning early, I awoke to sounds below me in the shop. I got up, went downstairs and out behind a pine tree not visible from the house, to relieve myself. There's something satisfying about doing your thing outdoors, a funny moment of freedom.

On the way back in, I paused at the shop door, where I saw Ralph inside, working on some deerskin garment at an old Singer sewing machine. I walked up quietly, stopping at a good point where I could watch him work without disturbing him.

For such a big man, with really large hands, Ralph had a fine touch. I noticed a lot of nicely done deerskin garments around. They all looked good. "These are some nicely done pieces, Ralph," I said.

Ralph didn't look my way and just grunted.

Trying again, I said, "I almost always worked in heavier leather, except for my vests and some pouches I used to make."

After a minute, he asked if I was still doing my work. I told him I stopped after I lost my wife and child.

He nodded, and said, "My pop taught me how to work with deer skin when I was a kid: the whole process, from taking the deer, to tanning the hides, and making clothes. Been doing it ever since. I make a decent living at it."

I told him I had done okay too. I asked if his mom had made clothing too.

Ralph stopped sewing, turned the machine off, and sat there, his back to me, as if in deep thought. He turned around, and looked me straight in the eye. I could see he was struggling with something.

I told him, "Ralph, if you want to tell me something, it won't go any further."

Ralph took a deep breath and began, "About eight years ago, my mom was coming out of a store one evening, and was grabbed by some drunken loggers coming out of the bar next door. They carried her back into the trees behind the buildings. When they got done using her, they beat her to death. They were all white men. At the trial, the young, green attorney we were appointed screwed up big-time. He wanted the loggers tried together, and the defense attorney manipulated things so it couldn't be proved who had raped or beaten her to death. They all got off. End of story."

I was silent for a few minutes, absorbing this horrible story. Then I told him what happened to Dawn and Nathan, finishing by telling him the driver of the truck got off with minor charges for negligent driving. The accident was caused by the weather, according to the driver's lawyers. Something about working for a rich company, I guessed. The only thing making it at all okay was the judge awarding me a large financial settlement, so at least it hurt the trucking people in the pocketbook.

Ralph, after nodding his head, dropped the subject and started talking leatherwork with me. It turned into a pleasant enough morning, and I felt good he had opened up to me. We had some things in common, unpleasant as those things were. It created a bond allowing him to put his anger aside.

We went into the house later, after Charlie yelled out, "Breakfast is ready!" The morning meal was filling, with more of the puny potatoes sliced up and fried with some onions and bacon, venison sausage and eggs.

After breakfast, I went out to the jeep and got several of the leather pieces I had brought with me, leftovers from my business. I gave Molly and Charlie soft leather pouches, and I gave Ralph a belt luckily able to fit around him, since I hadn't trimmed the end or punched all the holes yet. It had a nice solid brass buckle.

Ralph looked at me and said he didn't deserve such a nice belt, so I kiddingly reached out and said I'd take it back. Big as he was, he was quick too, and, grabbed my wrist, giving me a fierce look. "Hey," he said, "you don't want to be known as an Indian giver, do you?" and flashed a grin, which made him look like a different person.

I relaxed, after tensing up when he grabbed me, and said, "No, man, I certainly wouldn't." I smiled back at him. He released my hand and patted me on the shoulder.

I thanked them for their kindness and hospitality, and said I had a lot of miles to go, so I had better continue on my way. They all walked me out, and I warmed my jeep up. Just before I took off, Ralph brought out a beautiful buckskin jacket, no beadwork on it, but beautifully stitched, with fringe on the arms and all. He casually tossed it in the open window of the jeep, saying it might come in handy some time. I said, "You're a good man, Ralph, I'm glad I met you."

He smiled and nodded. "Likewise," was all he said.

I smiled, shook his hand, and waved good-by to all the Pauls, backed out the driveway, and headed out to the road, sorry to see them getting smaller in my rear view mirror. The warm feelings I got from being with them lasted for a lot of miles. I felt fortunate to have met them.

After Charlie Paul had told me what he knew about Captain Walt's destination, all I wanted to do was head north. I figured if I did connect with him, he would be surprised and maybe even amazed I had found him. I knew Walt might have already been in Alaska for a while, with such a long head start on me. For all I knew, he had found what he had set out to discover and was headed back down to the Lower Forty-Eight already. Only time would tell, so putting miles under my tires seemed a good thing.

I continued north up Highway 5 through Seattle after leaving the Pauls. I didn't stop there, as I no longer had any love for cities. I know there are a lot of interesting things to do, places to go, and things to see in cities, but I think they are also traps for the unwary. You get sucked into a maze of people, places, and things distracting you, in my opinion, from the basic priorities of life, making them less clear to the mind. I find plenty to do in smaller towns, and have come to appreciate people more in less populated places. For me, keeping things of real value in mind is easier too.

I was about five miles south of Bellingham, Washington, when I passed a hitchhiker on my side of the road. Even at my speed, I saw it was a young guy with a large pack lying next to him. He seemed dressed for the outdoors. I drove on past, not normally picking up hikers.

As I kept driving, I thought having someone on the trip with me might not be a bad idea if they were cool and could give me a break from the steady driving. So, I turned around at the next off ramp, and headed back the other way, figuring if he was still there, I would pick him up. I spotted him as I drove to the next off ramp south of him, and finally returned on the right side to pick him up. I pulled off the shoulder onto a gravel pad and shut the engine off. The young man had grabbed his pack soon as he saw me slowing down. He came up to the jeep, where I sat waiting.

"Thanks for stopping; I've been here a few hours," he said.

"No problem, man," I said, "but let's rap first, okay? Where you headed? He said, "I'm headed to Fairbanks, Alaska. How about you?"

"I'm going to Alaska too, to locate a friend, maybe in a place called Homer," I told him.

He said, "If you're headed anywhere in Alaska you could get me a whole lot closer to it than I am now."

"I guess we're cool then," I said. "Do you have a driver's license I could see, and can you drive this rig safely?"

"Of course. I've got a jeep too, but it needs a new engine, so it's sitting in my garage at home."

I told him we had to be in good shape at the border to avoid any hassles and if he had any goodies, even one joint, he had to get rid of it; and if he had any handguns, he couldn't take them across. I watched his eyes as I talked to him and thought I saw a flicker in them. He said it would be fine; he had no guns.

Reaching down, he rummaged through his pack and brought a baggie out with about a quarter ounce of weed in it, walked over to the barbed wire fence several yards further off the road, and shook it all out, finally letting the empty baggie drop out of his hand to blow away in the breeze.

I could tell he wasn't happy, and said, "Better than getting nailed at the border, my friend."

He nodded his agreement, though with little enthusiasm. He said, "My name's Cary, Cary Taylor."

"Yeah, so your license said. You can call me Jester," I told him.

"Jester? Really?" he asked.

"Yea, really. Let's get rolling."

We traveled up into what I would call the Washington Waterways, Puget Sound, and the Straits of San Juan De Fuca. Highway 5 takes you along this way on up past Bellingham and up to the British Columbian border at Sumas. I could have crossed at Blaine but I didn't, wanting to stay on the more central route through Canada.

At the border crossing, we didn't have much of a problem. I left the old Winchester in plain sight. I had the ammo for it locked in the glove box. I was questioned about it, and had to show it to the guards at the U.S. side and sign a form showing I had it before I entered Canada. I showed the gun and form to the Canadian guards, who looked it over as the U.S. guards had, which seemed to me to be for their personal interest as much as in their official capacity. The Canadian guard I was checked out by asked me if I thought I could kill a grizzly bear with it. I told him yes, but I had no plans to do so unless my life was in real danger, and even then I hoped it wouldn't be necessary. I told him I was going to Alaska, and might do some hunting there, but not in Canada.

The guard asked Cary if he had any weapons, and Cary said he only had a hunting knife in his pack. The guard actually asked to check his pack, but found nothing of consequence. Cary gave me a quick glance as the guard checked his pack.

The Canadian asked if I had sufficient funds, and I said I had about a grand in U.S. dollars, and more readily available from my accounts. He asked if we were both going the same place, and before Cary could say anything, I said we were making the whole trip together. He seemed satisfied and let us go, passing us through after wishing me a good trip through Canada.

I had never been out of the Lower Forty-Eight States, and this was exciting for me. Cary said he had been into Canada several years before, but had been rousted by some dudes at Watson Lake and had decided to drive back home. I told him it was better to travel with someone else, and he nodded his agreement.

We stopped at the small town of Kamloops to eat, and Cary offered to pay and I accepted. We had stopped at a store earlier for coffee and doughnuts, and they had a money-exchange counter there, so we both changed some of our U.S. paper for Canadian, to get more for our money on food and gas. Cary was a smoker, and was stunned by what cigarettes cost at the store.

At the coffee shop, we enjoyed our meal as best we could. We had ordered cheeseburgers, fries, and coffee, but the burgers had no flavor and the fries were greasy. Even this would have been a easier to deal with if the people at the café weren't giving us funny looks, especially after they picked up on our American accents. They weren't being hostile, but not friendly either. I never experienced this before, even as a poor Indian in Big Sur. We were either liked or disliked, with no in between. So, we didn't enjoy our food, but kept chewing until it was gone, paid the check, and left.

After getting back on the road, we discussed the next section of our route and decided to head further up Highway 5 to a place with the sweet name Tete Jaune Cache, just below where Highway 5 joins Highway 16, then head west toward Prince George. After hitting Highway 16, we drove on west 'til we found a campground where we could set up our tents, have dinner, and crash for the night.

We sat for a while after munching down a pot of franks and beans with bread, which I had brought up with me from the States, not knowing what I might find north of the border.

We had talked while driving, though not nonstop, pausing in our conversation to quietly admire the terrific scenery all around us. So far, Cary had proved to be a good driving partner, and he had driven from Kamloops to Highway 16 and on to the campground. I wasn't comfortable enough to actually sleep while he drove, but he did get us up the road safe and sound.

We talked about our plans while we were traveling. He said he had an uncle in Fairbanks who was glad to have him coming up to sample life in Alaska. The uncle had a sporting goods store, and would put him to work for the remainder of the summer. Cary was twenty-four, and wasn't settled into a particular lifestyle. He told me he had a groovy girlfriend, but he couldn't get her to quit her job and come with him on this trip. Too bad in more ways than one, he had told me, since she had a Chevy Blazer in great shape.

I explained to him about my journey in search of Captain Walt. I told what I felt was okay to tell, but left some details out. Cary said he thought it was a cool thing to do, and that he hoped I'd find Captain Walt. He asked me if I'd been a hippie, since he recognized some of the terms I used as coming from the Sixties. I said yeah, I had been, and those times became the topic of conversation for quite a few miles. He seemed genuinely curious, so I told him some of the stories I have told you.

It was the first time I realized the next generation might be interested in what happened back then. I was in my late thirties at this time, and was already feeling like a social dinosaur, or maybe a white elephant. Talking with Cary as we cruised down the road, made me feel different, as if what I had been involved in did have real social consequences. It was good to think my experiences back then were of interest and value to someone now.

At the end of the day, when we finally crashed in our separate tents, I felt we had made a strong connection. As I said, I didn't pick up hitchhikers much, having had several bad experiences not worth talking about. Minor bummers happen a lot, and aren't always worth spending extra energy on.

I could sense a change in Jester as I read what he had written. Perhaps he was just getting older, or losing his wife and child had taught him to be easier in the way he treated life, I'm not sure. Though I was glad he had put things to paper, I sure missed him sitting across the camp table and talking to me. I was glad to accept what I got, though, and planned on making his words clearer, but still his, as I had been all along.

The next morning early, Cary and I came out of our tents at the same time. Seeing him stick his head out, I got such a flashback from the Big Sur days, greeting each other in the mornings, and he must have seen something in my face, 'cause he asked me if I was okay. I told him I was good, just not awake yet.

There was a high breeze blowing, moving through the tops of the trees, not down at ground level. It made shussing sounds as it rustled the leaves, and I had fallen fast asleep listening to it.

But now it was a new day, and there were miles of unknown road ahead of us. I looked forward to what today would bring. Cary had taken a camera out of his pack, and snapped a few shots of our simple camp. He tried to take a picture of me, but I turned my head away.

"Not up for getting your photo taken?" he asked.

"I guess not," was all I said.

We decided to wait on breakfast until we reached McBride, further west on Highway 16, figuring we'd have an appetite by time we got there. Cary sure was tripping on the country we were traveling through, and I stopped several times to let him take some more photographs.

We were about twenty-five miles from where we had camped, when I brought the jeep to a sudden stop and pointed out a bear I had spotted, quietly grazing about one hundred yards off the left side of the road in a large meadow. Cary got all excited about it, and before I could say anything, slipped out of the jeep and started working his way toward the bear. He didn't have a long lens, and wanted a better shot, I guess. I started feeling edgy about the whole thing, knowing this was not a good idea, but Cary was young and quick, and he was away before I could say anything. I thought if I yelled at him, it might spook the bear and maybe send it running in the wrong direction, putting Cary in real danger.

It was similar to watching a wildlife movie, sitting in the jeep, seeing the whole scene unwind. Cary was about forty yards from the bear, when I spotted a cub standing up from where it had been hidden. It was closer to its mother, but between Cary and the adult bear. I don't know why it had stood up; maybe it caught Cary's scent. Anyway, it let out a bawl I could hear from the jeep. I knew this was going to get bad quickly.

Cary had already caught sight of the cub, which the mother bear started woofing at, sending it running away from Cary, past the mother, and into the trees behind her. I lost sight of it, but figured it had gone up a tree.

The mother bear started running around in circles, finally stopping with her nose pointed in Cary's direction. What Cary did next blew my mind. Instead of heading for the nearest tree, he started snapping photos. I couldn't hear the camera, but figured the bear had, because a second later, she charged straight at him. Cary saw her heading toward him. I'm sure he was scared, with adrenalin already pumping, 'cause even though the bear covered ground like you wouldn't believe, Cary was quicker, dropping his camera and shinnying up a medium-sized evergreen tree at record speed. The bear got to the tree, and stretched up, trying to grab his foot or leg. Luckily, she missed.

I did something I probably wouldn't have done if I had thought about it beforehand. I turned off the road and started driving toward the bear honking my horn on and off all the way. I kept the jeep in low gear, and the engine was growling away, making plenty of noise. Luckily, the ground was firm, and I had no trouble heading in. I was about thirty yards from the bear before she broke away from the tree. But, instead of running away from the sound and sight of the jeep, she ran right for it. All I could think was, "Oh, swell, now she's gonna tear up the jeep, and me too."

When the bear was almost to me, I brought the jeep to a stop, not wanting to hit her, though I figured she'd more than likely cause more damage to me and the jeep than we might to her. Even as she headed toward me, I thought, "What a beautiful bear." Closing with the rig, she took a swipe at the front corner. I heard glass break and some scraping, metallic sounds. I was still honking the horn, and the next thing she did was break off the passenger-side mirror. So, I quit honking and shut the engine off. I know it sounds silly, saying it now, but I hoped she might think she had hurt or killed the jeep, and leave. I may have been right, because after hitting the right front fender hard enough to shake the whole jeep, she ran off in the opposite direction, and disappeared into the woods about where her cub had gone.

I breathed a sigh of relief, until I saw the passenger side window had been open all this time. "Far out," was all I could think, or maybe I said it out loud, who knows which. I had a lump in my throat and in my gut, which I figured was from my *cojones* creeping up to my belly button for protection.

After several minutes, I started the engine again, and slowly drove it almost all the way to Cary's hidey-tree. I stuck my head out the window, and called quietly to him to come on down and get inside. He did, and once he hit the ground, he swooped the camera up from where he had dropped it, and reached the jeep in a couple of long jumps.

"Let's get out of here, man!" he yelled. No problem. We turned around, and headed back to the road. I got on the blacktop and drove a couple of miles, before pulling off on a turnout and shutting the engine off. We sat there in silence a minute or two, absorbing what had happened.

"Do me a favor, Cary," I said. "Next town we come to, buy a tele-photo lens, okay?"

"No problem, Jester. But from now on I'll stick to deer and moose."

"Forget the moose, man, stick to deer and rodents, okay?"

Letting out a sheepish laugh, he agreed to my suggestion.

After checking out the bear damage to the jeep, we continued to Prince George, with no more life-threatening events along the way. When we got there, we looked for a place to get the jeep's headlight and side mirror fixed up. We found a garage willing do the work, given a couple of hours. The mechanic suggested a shop in town to fix the body damage, but I told him I liked the three, deep, parallel scrapes where the bear's claws had raked the front corner of the fender after destroying the headlight and its frame. I told the man to go ahead and fix the headlight and mirror.

Cary and I walked down the street to find a coffee shop. We both hoped the food would be better than the last meal we had eaten in a Canadian restaurant.

We were glad when our food came and it was freshly made and delicious. We found, on the rest of the trip, eating at Canadian restau-rants was a crapshoot. We did much better when we picked up food at a store and either made simple sandwiches or cooked our food for dinner at a campsite.

It was funny, Canada seemed almost the same as the U.S. but not quite. The attitude of the people we came in contact with was never friendly with a few exceptions, but not openly hostile either. Cary and I talked about it and decided it was as much us being Americans and strangers as it might have been anything personal, which made sense since they had never met us before. "We're just passing through, Cary," I said, "so it isn't important. If we have any trouble, we'll deal with it as easily as we can." It turned out we had a peaceful trip the rest of the way.

We went back to the garage and the jeep was ready, except the mirror the man had installed was chrome, while the original one on the left side was black. When I mentioned it to him, he told me it was the only one he had. I knew getting into hassle with him about it would have been useless, and so I paid him what he asked, which seemed a reasonable amount. Cary thought I should have given him a hard time, but Cary was young. I told him it wouldn't have helped, and at least this way we had two side view mirrors.

We had some good talks about life as we drove along. Cary was a smart guy. We found we shared the same points of view about a lot of things. Our long-winded conversations made the miles roll by quickly. I did stop several times to let Cary take more photos, but not of anything large and furry.

The jeep moved along without a burp or a stumble. I know even new vehicles can have problems, but having one with low mileage you know has been properly maintained, since you were the one who has taken care of things, sure reduces the chance of getting broken down out in the middle of nowhere, and brother, was there a lot of nowhere around here, beautiful or not.

Several times, I thought about how much Dawn and Nathan would have loved being on a journey such as this, and figured maybe they were, in their own way.

When we left Prince George, we had decided to head further west and hook up to Highway 37 at Kitwanga, which is a small place I'm sure few people know about. Cary had suggested this route, heading north on 37, the Cassiar Highway, because it was supposed to go through some lush, beautiful country along a series of wild rivers between the Skeena and the Coastal Mountains. Turned out it was true, and I think, driving along the Cassiar, we went through some of the most beautiful country I had ever seen.

We saw a lot of black bears along the highway. It seemed like all the time we drove, a bear was either running across the road ahead of us, or running away off to either side. We must have seen forty black bears in the several days we traveled through. Now I'm usually comfortable out on the land, but the idea of camping out in this area didn't sit right, with all the bruin activity. It didn't seem safe; we would be asking for trouble. Cary agreed with me, not surprising after his recent hair-raising bear episode.

We stayed at one lodge, a real old-fashioned place off the highway near Dease Lake. There were little log cabins to stay in, with wood stoves for heat. The central lodge building was a nicely made log affair.

The Fitzgeralds, an older couple who owned the place, were cool. We were the only ones staying there, and they invited us to eat dinner with them in their picturesque dining room. There were old snowshoes, mounts of moose, deer, and even a caribou on the wall. There was also a huge grizzly bear hide covering a large portion of one end wall.

Mr. Fitzgerald told us, "It's actually a brown bear hide, from a bear I took on Kodiak Island in Alaska back in '59. He was a massive fellow, as you can see, and I hit him right in the heart with a heavy bullet from a 30-06. He ran off into some alders, roaring and snapping off three-inch trunks as if they were matchsticks. My guide told me to be ready, and sure enough, the bear heads back right at us. I don't mind telling you boys I was scared crapless, pardon my language, dear."

Mr. Fitzgerald's wife gave him a long-suffering look, as though she had heard this tale a hundred times already, if not more. But it was new to us.

He said, "The guide had an old Winchester .348, which was not the best round for back-up, but was better than nothing by far, I tell you. The guide and I both had our rifles at the ready, and when the bear emerged running from the alders, maybe fifty feet away, we both cut loose, almost simultaneously. The bear dropped down on his belly as if a switch was shut off inside him, and slid to a stop about five feet away from us.

"We had both worked another round into the chamber, but didn't need to fire again. However, the guide walked carefully around to the side of the bear, and pumped another into his boiler room for good measure. He told me, 'Never hurts to be sure. Sometimes they wake up when you don't expect it.' Now I have him proudly displayed on my wall, and I still have great respect for him. He was such a majestic creature."

Mrs. Fitzgerald spoke up. "If we can now lay the poor beast to rest, gentlemen, perhaps some moose stew and homemade bread might be in order."

It was, and what a delicious meal, with sweet potatoes and green beans too. I ate more than I should have, but Mrs. Fitzgerald would have been insulted if I hadn't, so I felt it was my duty. During dinner, we mentioned the large number of black bears we had seen along the road, and wondered if it was normal.

Mr. Fitzgerald gave his wife an obvious "I told you so," look, and remarked he had seen a lot of bears the last several weeks himself, around the lodge and up the road. "Don't know why, but once in a while, their population seems to explode."

We talked with them for a while longer over coffee and a delicious apple cobbler Mrs. Fitzgerald had made, but the miles had taken their toll, and soon after the heavy meal we said our goodnights and hit the sack. I don't remember much after laying my head on the down pillow, until morning came.

We were awakened at seven by Mr. Fitzgerald, who apologized for the early hour, but told us if we were late for Mrs. Fitzgerald's breakfast, he wouldn't have any peace the rest of the day. The morning meal was as tasty, in its own right, as the dinner the night before, and we thoroughly enjoyed ourselves, especially since there was real maple syrup at the table to go with genuine sourdough flapjacks. Visiting with these good folks afterward was a real treat.

Mr. Fitzgerald had come from Scotland when he was twenty years old, wanting to follow in the footsteps of his grandfather, who had come to this area of Canada when he was a young man. Mr. Fitzgerald was about seventy years old when Cary and I met him, so his grandfather definitely came here in wilder days.

We finally had to say our good-byes, but not before Mrs. Fitzgerald brought us a jar of something wrapped up in a piece of what seemed to be cotton cloth. It was sourdough starter, which she said no one who traveled the North Country should be without. She said, "Just keep it cool when you're not using it, and feed it some water and sugar once in a while. It could last you a lifetime if you care for and feed it properly."

Tripping on this far-out gift, I felt I had arrived at a milepost in my quest, this sourdough being a confirmation I was on the right path. I knew about sourdough being a real staple in the North, and sourdoughs, the name given to old veteran Alaskans, and people in the Yukon too, was because it supposedly took sourdough a year to mature, and if someone made it a full year in the North and survived, they were called a sourdough. In my childhood, I had read Jack London books, and now I felt close to the source of his stories. It was a rush, knowing such things still existed. I felt a sudden urge to get into the Yukon and on up to Alaska.

We thanked the Fitzgeralds for their kindness and hospitality, packed up, and continued north. I had thought about staying longer, but sometimes you just know when something has come full cycle and it's time to leave.

After staying with the Fitzgeralds at their lodge, I realized the franks and beans I brought up with me weren't the great necessity I thought.

But, not having been to Canada before, I wanted to be sure I had a supply of familiar food. Now I wished I had gotten a batch of moose stew from Mrs. Fitzgerald for the rest of our journey.

Cary and I were both hot to get into the Yukon. He had read stories of the area too, and so we had the same basic desire to see the country. When we got to the Yukon border we had a difference of opinion, of wants, actually, almost causing us to part ways.

It turned out Cary wanted to go west on Highway 1, the Alaska Highway, but then turn north onto Highway 2 after hitting Whitehorse, in order to go past Lake Laberge. The Yukon poet, Robert Service, had mentioned Lake Laberge in his wild-and-woolly poem, "The Cremation of Sam Magee," a funny yet grisly tale of the frozen north. Service had called it Lake Lebarge though. I wanted to continue on Highway 1 into Alaska, a shorter route. Cary argued we could continue on up Highway 2 and still get into Alaska in several days. I held my ground. Even though I was enjoying our trip together, I needed to get into Alaska as soon as possible, sensing it was necessary to my finding Walt, though I wasn't sure why a day or two more or less would matter.

After telling Cary I had my mind made up, he suggested we split up, and he'd hitchhike up the road by himself. It was up to him what he wanted to do, but I told him it wasn't a good idea, being risky at best. I said to him, "Didn't the run-in with the bear teach you anything, man?"

"Such as?" he asked.

I didn't want to put him off, and told him right out, "You're not ready for this, to be alone here on the road. This country could eat you up if it wanted to."

At first my remark pissed Cary off, his face getting red, and his youthful pride taking hold. But, a moment later, he deflated, and said in an unhappy voice, "Maybe you're right, but I'll see this country sometime when I don't have anyone else to deal with."

"I imagine you will, Cary; let's get going." We drove on in silence for a while, and the rest of the trip I did the driving, it being understood I wasn't going to ask him to drive someplace he didn't want to go.

South of Whitehorse, we stopped at a roadhouse for a bite to eat. I ordered the fried chicken, and Cary did the same. What a disappointment! When the food came it looked and tasted like a TV dinner that had been heated and put on a plate to be served. You can't miss the flavor of veggies from a TV meal, or the way the batter on the chicken tastes. It wasn't cheap either. The franks and beans had redeemed themselves again in my mind. If the quality of the food was so inconsistent up here, better safe than sorry.

When we reached Whitehorse, we were excited to be checking out this historic place we had both heard about. Sorry to say, it was less than expected. Funny how you can build up illusions about things when the reality is so much grimier. Whitehorse seemed a dirty, poorly-run town, at least the area we were in. When we pulled into a store parking lot, we had to work our way around drunks standing by the entrance, fighting and bumming money to buy booze. Sad to say, they were mostly Indians. We bought some snacks to have on the way, along with our faithful wieners and baked beans, before slipping out of there.

We did stop further up the highway at a native crafts store full of beautiful clothing and other traditional goods. I was tempted to buy a pair of newly-made moccasins, beautifully done, covered with bead and porcupine-quill decorations. I got off on the moccasins' appearance and the quality of their construction.

While I was looking at them, an older Indian woman came up and told me if I tried them on and they fit, they were meant for me. She asked if they called out to me. I had to admit to her they did.

Okay, so I tried them on, and they were snug, which meant they would stretch out to a perfect fit. "I guess I have a new pair of moccasins," I said.

"I told you so," said the Indian lady, "I'll put them in a bag for you."

I asked the lady what style they were.

"Cree, just like me," she said.

Cary, who had been watching the whole thing, had an amused smile on his face.

"They do fit perfectly," I said to him.

"Of course they do, Jester," Cary said, his smile widening a little more.

The moment in the store lightened the mood between us, which was a good thing. Driving along with somebody when there are bad feelings is a real bummer, and makes the miles definitely grow longer. We fired up the jeep, and after a stop to fill the gas tank and check the oil, we continued on our way.

Soon enough, we reached the area of Kluane Lake, a large body of water the highway ran along for quite a ways. It was a beautiful lake with some far-out views. We stopped several times so Cary could take some photos. At one point, we pulled to the side of the road, and Cary walked down a short dirt bank through some willows and onto the gravel at the lake's shore, disappearing from sight. He hadn't been gone long when he came scooting up the bank, hopped into the truck suggesting we get going. When I asked him what was up, he said there was a large bear a ways up the shore, making the one he had tangled with earlier resemble a cub. I told him, no problem, I'd just start honking the horn. Cary told me not to be an jerk. I laughed and we headed up the road again. At least he had learned the ins and outs of surviving outdoor photography!

Soon, we came to the Blue Lake Lodge, a great-looking structure made of massive logs with typical crisscross joints. Under the front eaves of the overhanging front roof, was mounted a large pair of moose antlers. They stood out, wide and high.

There were some cabins in the back for travelers such as us, and I was ready for a hot shower and a warm bed. We got out of the now-silent jeep, stretched our stiff limbs and went in. We had decided to take a chance on the food there.

There were four or five people inside, including one middle-aged dude in a black Stetson-style hat, a silky-looking shirt, and a heavy gold necklace. The whole package looked out of place there, even to my stranger's eyes. When the waiter, who turned out to be the owner, Joseph Beauchamp, or simply Joe, as he told us to call him, came to take our order, I ordered something called the Blue Lake Lodge burger and a bowl of homemade vegetable soup. I was hungry! Cary ordered some salmon chowder and a turkey sandwich.

I didn't realize when Joe said the burger was very special he meant it was huge. It was. As I recall, it had two burger patties, some bacon, eggs, a sausage sliced flat, topped with cheese, onion, tomato, and lettuce. The bowl of soup was large too, with one of those tasty miniature loaves of bread you sometimes see in a home-style restaurant. Joe served the food, with an enthusiastic *"Bon appetit!"*

I was sitting there trying to figure out the best way to start this rig going down, when Mr. Silk shirt said in a boisterous voice, "Friend, I think you bit off more than you can chew this time."

The other people there turned and looked from him to me and smiled.

"Oh, I think I'll be fine," I said.

"I'll bet you five dollars Canadian you won't be able to finish," Silk Shirt said.

I smiled, and told him I'd take the bet. I knew my ability to pack it away when in the right frame of mind and body. I proceeded to begin chewing away at the edges of the burger while spooning up the soup once in a while, too. I didn't hurry. Cary shook his head several times, watching me devour the burger, the soup, and the mini bread loaf. It took me a while, but I finally finished the incredible grilled construction, the soup, and of course the bread. The cocky dude watched me, his concern deepening as he realized he was going to be out the five bucks.

I held the last bit of the bread loaf in my hand, with a dab of butter on it, and chatted with Joe about the area.

"You gonna finish or not?!" said Silk Shirt, upset, because he knew I was rubbing it in.

"Oh, yeah," I said, and downed the last bit. The two other people who had been there from the start applauded. Silk Shirt begrudgingly came over and tossed the money on the table, then went back to his seat looking unhappy. I got up slowly, and walked over to where the cook was working.

"Did you make the giant burger I just finished?" I asked.

"Yes I did," he said.

I handed him the five bucks, and thanked him for the good meal. He looked at me, then at Silk Shirt and caught the whole point of it.

"Why, you are most welcome," he responded in a loud voice, and made an exaggerated motion to put it in his pocket. Silk Shirt mumbled something and stomped out of the place.

I went over to pay Joe, and he said, "Nope, it's on the house. I've been wishing someone would put loudmouth in his place for quite a while, and it was worth the meal to see it happen. But, you can pay for breakfast in the morning. I figure you'll be wanting to spend the night and let the burger digest."

"Maybe, Joe, but I don't even want to discuss breakfast right now, if you don't mind," I said.

He chuckled, and I went with him to the reservation desk and paid for a night's lodging. But Cary came up before I could finish, and said he wanted to get a room to himself for the evening, and it was okay with me, since we'd been together for a while now.

I went to my cabin, took off my shoes and pants, turned on the TV to the one station I could get clearly, and laid out on the bed letting my packed belly slowly settle down. What a trip!

We did go in for breakfast the next morning, but I only had a cup of coffee, a sweet roll, and a small bowl of peaches. We said our good-byes, and after thoroughly checking out the jeep, we headed out on the road to Alaska, which was getting close.

Further up the road, we stopped near Beaver Creek, and munched on cold hot dogs and chips for lunch. We didn't say much, but things seemed good again between us.

"Did you know Jack London wasn't up in this country a full year?" Cary asked.

"Yeah, so I heard," I answered, "but I think the North filled him up, and he had a natural connection, a feel for the country and what went on here with the people and life in general. Everything in the north seems special and larger than life."

Cary told me he thought even the air up here seemed to have a special energy all its own, and I replied I'd thought several times I'd be happy to lose myself somewhere in this great country.

Cary said, "What would stop you?"

I knew what would stop me, and told him: "Loneliness."

Cary thought for a bit, then nodded his agreement.

Several hours later, we crossed the border into Alaska at Port Alcan without a hitch. A few questions were asked, no search was made, and then we were told "Welcome to Alaska!" I felt I had arrived, even though I still had a ways to go. It wouldn't be much longer before we arrived in Tok Junction, where we would part ways. Cary gave me the phone number and address of his uncle's store in Fairbanks.

"Believe it or not," Cary said, "I had a great time traveling with you, Jester. I hope we see each other again."

"Yeah, I'd like it, Cary," I said, "and I hope you enjoy Fairbanks. I have a feeling you may be staying for a while, and it won't be too long before you'll be a dyed-in-the-wool sourdough."

Cary smiled, shook my hand, and went over to stand on the right corner to hitch a ride up to Fairbanks. Me, I got back in my trusty jeep and headed down Highway 1 toward Anchorage, and whatever waited for me.

I did enjoy the part of the trip with Cary along, in spite of our falling out. But most of the time I dug cruising alone, having time to myself, and thinking my own thoughts without interference. Even when Dawn was traveling with me, which was always a sweet time, I sometimes got lost in my own thoughts about life, doing my work, planning stuff, and whatever.

The run from Tok Junction down the road toward Anchorage was good for me. It was interesting country, but without the rich greenness of British Columbia. It was impressive land, but the trees weren't very large, and there was more open country. At one point, about sixty miles below Tok, I had to stop while a small herd of caribou crossed the road. They were groovy animals, similar to reindeer, but larger. Their summer coats were a beautiful combination of brown, gray, and white. The curve of their antlers and their whole shape was perfect. Some of their racks seemed oversized, but they carried them upright without any trouble.

There was a roadhouse further on, north of a place called Sheep Mountain, although I didn't see any of its namesakes when I later went by. I had a burger and fries with coffee at the place, and it was a tasty meal.

I got into a conversation with the owner. Turned out he remembered Captain Walt when he had come through.

"It was a few months back, though," he said. "He came in here with a pretty young lady. They seemed a happy pair. They drew you right into their happy ways. Look at this." So saying, he lifted his flannel shirt and showed me one of Walt's buckles attached to one of my belts.

The cafe owner said when he asked Walt what he did, Walt took him out to his old bus and showed him his handmade jewelry. "I couldn't resist getting something from him," he said. "Actually, I traded them a good meal apiece and some cash for this belt, and a beautiful silver pendant for the wife. He liked to trade things for his work, he told me.

"I let him stay in our back parking lot in his bus a few days. Told me he'd been doing a lot of driving and was getting a bit weary of it. I suggested he settle down here and open a shop of his own, but I know this area is too remote, and he needed a place with more people. I suggested Anchorage, since it has more people than anywhere else in Alaska. Doesn't make it nice, mind you, but it's the best place for business. The local joke is Anchorage is only forty-five minutes from Alaska. You'll know what I mean when you get there."

I thanked him for the information and the good burger. I told him it had a richer taste than most burgers.

He said, "It's because it isn't beef; it's ground caribou meat. All natural, no hormones." Interesting.

Anchorage wasn't far now, maybe one hundred miles. I was driving along the road a ways south of Sheep Mountain, and could look down into river valleys similar to ones I had seen in films about the Alaskan outdoors. Someone had told me Alaska would get to you one way or another. Some loved it and some hated it. Me, I really dug it. The more I drove through it, the more it seemed to fill me up. Taking it all in, its major scenery gave me one surprise after another.

I finally came to the northern outskirts of Anchorage, actually an area called the Matanuska Valley, with the small towns of Palmer and Wasilla being distant suburbs of Anchorage. Real civilization. Anchorage was about forty miles further south, but I could sense a change. There were large open swampy areas south of Wasilla, before I passed over a bridge spanning a twisty river, called the Knik, which I guessed must be a native name.

But the closer I got to Anchorage, there were more buildings, houses, and businesses. Then I started hitting the edges of Anchorage proper, and was I blown away. It was not at all what I expected. I could have been driving into the outskirts of a funky part of L.A. man, truly. The same run-down buildings, same trashy streets. I couldn't believe it. It was a letdown. My romantic illusions of how it would be died fast and hard.

I got lost as I went deeper into the city, finally coming to a stop on a one-way street facing a strange piece of water, Cook Inlet. It was unfriendly looking, with ugly gray mudflats exposed by the low tide. I went around the block and drove the other way, finally coming to Fourth or Fifth Street. I drove slowly along, watching the people on the sidewalks. I saw a JC Penney store, lots of tourist shops, a surplus store, and a bunch of bars with stumbling sidewalk drunks all around. Alaska was forty-five minutes from downtown Anchorage, as the burger man on Sheep Mountain had told me, and it wasn't a joke.

I decided to drive through the city to the south, just to do it. I drove down one street and pulled into a place called "Gwenny's, a True Alaskan Restaurant."

There were a lot of people there, so I figured it must be a good place to eat. They served breakfast twenty-four hours a day, which sounded good to me. So I ordered a heavy breakfast, including some caribou sausage slices. Listening to the conversations going on all around me, they sounded the same as small talk anywhere. I had hoped for more colorful rapping.

Still, the food was good and there was lots of it, so I left satisfied. It was nice to not get odd stares while I was eating, as I did in Canada.

I found a motel to clean up in and spend the night. All the driving had taken its toll of me. It cost me almost one hundred bucks for the room 'cause it was tourist season, but I needed someplace to set. The desk clerk was a young lady who had moved out from Wisconsin a few months before. When I asked her what she thought of the place, she told me it wasn't quite what she expected, but she was moving to

Juneau soon. She had been offered a job there, and it was supposed to be a lot more "Alaskan" in flavor. I wished her luck before heading to my generic motel room, where, once inside, I could have been in any city in the country. At least it was clean and had plenty of hot water for a good shower, which I definitely needed.

Lying there before dropping off into the sweet oblivion of sleep, I felt Walt couldn't have settled in this town. It wasn't his style. No, he would have looked for a smaller, less complicated place to light. I decided to continue south in my search.

The next morning, I had another breakfast at Gwenny's, and headed south on the Seward Highway, which runs along the edge of another part of Cook Inlet called Turnagain Arm. I stopped along the way, about ten miles south of Anchorage, to watch some mountain sheep hanging out on the cliff side above the road in plain view. Being early summer, the snow was mostly melted off, so the sheep with their pure white color, stood out clearly.

The condition of the road was better than I expected it to be, a smooth, civilized highway. The scenery along the way was a strange mixture of raw green wilderness and out-of-place human structures: buildings, signs, and business displays. I got the impression if you strayed one hundred yards off the road, you might as well be a hundred miles away from anything. It seemed like people had only intruded upon the edges of this incredible land. I toyed with the idea of settling down somewhere in Alaska. It certainly would be a daily adventure, for sure. Nowhere else I'd been could compare with Alaska's lush wilderness. For now, I would check things out while looking for Walt, wherever he might be. I was soon to find out.

I was about one hundred miles south of Anchorage, near a place called Cooper's Landing, when I whipped my jeep over to the left side of the road by a bunch of cabins and a store. There, by the side of the store, was, without a doubt, Captain Walt's bus! What a trip! After all the plans and travels and things along the way, all of a sudden it was over. Or was it? The bus seemed empty, though I couldn't see inside it. I walked closer to it, and saw it really was empty. Oh, all the custom "furniture" was there, the narrow drawers, workbench, and the bed in back. But, there was nothing else there, no goods, and no personal items.

A man with a flannel shirt and suspenders came over to me, and asked if I was interested, because it was for sale. I told him actually I was looking for the owner, an old friend of mine. He gave me a funny look and asked me the owner's name. I told him his name was Walt, Captain Walt, and his woman's name was Emerald.

After a little thought, he said, "They're in Seward. The turnoff is a few more miles down the road."

"Seward?" I asked.

"Yeah," he said, "when they stopped here to eat, a few months back, he told me he had opened a jewelry shop there. He asked me if I knew anybody who might want to trade the bus for a good pick-up. I had an older Dodge Power Wagon in good shape, and we worked out a deal. The bus has lots of miles on her, but runs great and doesn't use any oil."

I told him Walt took primo care of his bus. I needed to adjust to the fact it wasn't Walt's anymore. It just didn't seem right.

"He's probably still down in Seward so if you want to see him, you'll need to go there." he said. "He'll probably be glad to see ya."

I told him I would, and jumping back into the jeep, I headed on down to Seward, Alaska, and another reunion with Walt.

As I drove, I considered how Walt and I didn't stay in touch regularly. Instead, we kept connecting all over the place, San Francisco, Arizona, and now Alaska. It was an unusual friendship, but a solid one. We didn't share in the more common connections. Ours seemed a union of the spirits. I was going to be glad to see him, to see them both.

I took the turn-off, and Seward wasn't far beyond. When I got there, it amazed me how it resembled a postcard picture. Seward was built into the land and cliffs around a nice, natural inlet, a snug harbor. It sure matched my idea of a classic coastal town in Alaska. There were a number of original old buildings, but a lot of touristy places too. Before I looked for Walt and Emerald's shop, which I was sure I could find, I picked an old funky looking bar, of which there were several, and went in to have a beer and relax a bit.

This was an old fashioned saloon, with a rough wooden floor and a great old bar with a brass rail to rest a weary foot on. The bartender had a bushy salt and pepper beard and a sparkle in his eye. I ordered a draft, and when it came, asked him how long he had lived in Seward. He told me about twelve years ago he had retired from fishing, and started tending bar there. He was a partner in the place now. "A lot safer than crabbing, I can tell you, except for Friday nights, at which time it comes close."

I sat there and sipped my beer, soaking up the feelings in the place. It being a weekday, there were only a few people there, and they were all dressed in similar threads: Carhartt pants, flannel shirts, suspenders, and some work boots. It reminded me of how local men in Monte Rio dressed, except for Levis instead of Carhartts.

I had settled down from all my driving, and felt pleasantly relaxed. I called the bartender over, and asked him if he knew of a jewelry store recently opened.

"Yeah, a fella named Walt and his old lady opened one up a while back. You go out the door, turn left, and go up a few stores. You can't miss it."

"I wouldn't miss it for the world," I told him, which made him give me a curious look. I followed his simple directions, and soon came to Walt's shop. On the front window of this narrow two-story building was written in old-timey letters "WALT & EMERALD," and down below it said, "CUSTOM MADE JEWELRY." I walked in.

Walt was working in the back of the narrow room, tapping away with his jeweler's hammer, as I had heard him do before at the shows. Without looking up, he said, "Be with you in a moment."

"You better be!"

"Well I'll be. Hello, brother Jester. This is unexpected."

"It's far out to find you here, Walt."

"What brings you to Alaska and Seward?"

"You, man, you."

"You came all the way up here to see me?"

"Of course I did. Figured it was time to make contact again. Gregorio told me about your vision, and he figured if you were to go north, you'd go as far north as Alaska, so here I am. The only real clue I got was in Washington State, where I saw some of your stuff at a native shop."

"Oh, yeah, Charlie Paul's place. Did you meet his family?"

"Yeah, and they are something special, especially Ralph. But we ended up friends. He gave me a far-out deerskin jacket."

Just then, Emerald came in the door with some lunch for them, some sandwiches, but when she saw me, she actually dropped the bag, ran over, and gave me a hug. "It's amazing to see you, Jester. I'm glad you're here." I saw Walt tilt his head down and give it slow sad shake. I would have to ask him why later.

Emerald said, "Will you be able to stay with us for a while?"

"I sure hope so," I said.

"We've got plenty of room, brother," Walt told me.

"Groovy."

"So, where are Dawn and Nathan? Did they come with you?"

Oh man, I had forgotten in my gladness at seeing Walt and Emerald they didn't know what had happened. I had to do it all over again. So, I asked if I could see their place. Emerald gave Walt a look, then took me upstairs to show me where they lived. It was an old place, built maybe seventy years ago. The building looked original but solid. It had sheet-metal ceiling decorations, tin panels, painted white, the kind I often saw in S.F. The two lights in the front room looked like gaslights converted to electricity. There was comfortable old stuffed furniture all over. Emerald took me to the spare room, showing me where I could stay, after which we went into the kitchen where we had coffee and talked. Walt came up a short while later, and we all sat and jawed.

Taking a deep breath, I told them about Dawn and Nathan. I didn't want to put a downer on the day, but it was necessary. I was surprised I was able to tell the tale without losing it. I guess the old saw about time healing all wounds is true. But, this was fresh sadness for Walt and Emerald, and she shed some tears and came over and held me around the shoulders for a while. It got to me.

Emerald told me she'd had a miscarriage, and was not going to be able to have children because of complications. This was a rough thing to hear. I told her, "I guess we have to share sad times too. I wish it could be different."

"I'm just glad we can spend time together," Walt said to me. "So, you'll stay a while?"

"Walt, I'd like nothing better," I told him.

I told Walt later, over a delicious salmon dinner, how strange it was seeing the bus up the road.

"Yeah, it was hard parting with her, but you know, I've been on the road a long time. When we got to Alaska, even the first day coming into Tok Junction, I knew this was the place my vision told me to find. But, where I used to live years ago is much further north, rough country, and really cold in the winters, so I wanted to travel further south.

"When we got to Seward, after turning away from the same urban crap one sees in Anchorage, and rejecting Homer after a stay there, I knew this particular place was for us. I just knew. I know you can understand the way I mean it, Jester. My soul swelled inside me, out of joy I think. So, we checked around, found this place for a fair price and bought it."

"You mean you own the building?"

"Yup, Jester, it's all ours. You know, I'm a frugal cat who likes to live simply, so I have saved a lot of cash over the years. I had enough to buy the place and set it up my own way. We will only have a lot of business in the summer, with the tourists coming in, but I'll still do enough work off-season to be okay."

"With the beautiful stuff you make, I'm not surprised, man."

"I already have a contract with several shops in Anchorage to make Alaska-related stuff for them. Set it up while I was there. I do small castings of bears, wolves and other Alaskan animals, and mount them on pieces of quartz with some gold in them the shops send me. It's satisfying work, and pays well. They wanted to pay me after the pieces sold, but I told them, 'I make them and get paid for them. The sales are up to you.' They weren't too pleased, but agreed. So, I think we'll be okay here. I bet if you checked around you could find something to do if you wanted to stay a while."

I told Walt the settlement from our accident had made it possible for me to do as I wished, including nothing if I preferred.

"Aren't you doing your leatherwork anymore?"

"No, the accident ended it."

"I understand, Jester, but it would be hard to believe you don't want to do anything."

"If I decide to stay for a long time, I'll get something going. Maybe I'll go crab fishing."

Though I was half kidding, Walt reacted more strongly than I expected. "What, are you nuts? It's a young man's game, and more dangerous than you would believe! The waters these fishermen go crabbing in regularly have thirty-foot waves up in the Bering Sea, and boats ice up and flip over in a heartbeat."

"I wasn't serious, Walt."

"I'm glad to hear it."

I was surprised to see there was a chink in Walt's general mellowness. He had an edge I wasn't used to. Still, life can put a kink in anybody's tail. But what was coming next I didn't expect.

I woke up early the next morning to yelling coming from outside my door. I lay there listening. It was Walt and Emerald having a blow out. I couldn't hear the words, but figured something must have finally come to a head. When things had settled down, after one of them stomped down the stairs and slammed the door, I waited about ten minutes, then came out to go to the can. I passed Emerald sitting crying at the kitchen table. I went into the bathroom to relieve myself and wake up. Washing my face, the cold water was very cold. I took a breath and walked out. Emerald was cooking something.

"I'm making breakfast; sit down."

"Oh, you don't have to go to the trouble."

She turned and gave me a look, and I sat. Emerald slid eggs and sausages onto the plate and handed it to me. I took a thick slice of toasted homemade bread, buttered it, and busied myself eating.

I was almost done when she told me, "I'm leaving soon."

I looked up at her, in surprise.

"Things haven't been good for a while, Jester, and I need some space."

I told her I was sorry to hear it, and asked when she might be coming back. Wrong question. She started crying, and ran out of the kitchen. I just sat there, even though I wanted to go give her a hug. Sometimes it's better to let things be, you know?

A minute later, she came back in. "I don't know," she said. "I'm going to spend time with my folks in Denver, and will just have to see. I'm glad I got to see you again." Emerald smiled, and tried real hard to seem okay, but she couldn't pull it off. I tried to do likewise and came out about the same.

It's funny, Walt and Emerald were special people to me, but they were only people after all, with their share of baggage, but I never figured they would ever break up. I guess I wanted them to be a beacon to me, showing life could be good and stay good. Since losing Dawn and Nathan, I needed a reason for hope, 'cause in the back of my mind, most of the time, was the thought I'd never have it right again. So, finding these two righteous people had lost their way with each other was difficult to handle.

Emerald was gone two days later. I came into their shop after taking an early morning walk, and Walt was sitting on his stool behind the counter, staring at the coffee in the mug he was holding. This was a Walt I had never seen before. I asked him how he was doing. He slowly lifted his head and there was a dullness in his eyes I had never seen. "I blew it, man. I didn't pay attention to the signs and didn't give enough. Now, I've lost the best woman I'll ever have."

"Oh, I don't know, Walt. I bet she'll miss you soon. I know she really loves you."

"Did, Jester, did. I let too much go for too long without attention. I shut her out too many times. It's over. We both know it, so I guess you need to accept it too."

"Okay, Walt, I'll let it be."

"Thanks, man. I'm glad you're here, and you're welcome to stay as long as you want. This is your home too, now. But, think you could go exploring for a few days? I need to work some stuff out. Maybe you could head down the road, check out Homer for a while maybe. Okay with you?"

"Sure, brother, it would be cool. I was thinking about it, anyway."

A few hours later, I had packed some things in my jeep, including the old Winchester, and was heading down toward Homer, a town at the end of the road on the Kenai Peninsula, where, if you wanted to go any further, you'd need a boat or an airplane with floats.

Homer was only a few hours ride from Seward, but I took my time, enjoying the road and the incredible greenery around me. I had never seen such dense country as Alaska grew. Funny thing was, I thought I'd see moose and maybe even a bear, but all I saw was more birds than I expected. Guess all the road noise kept the animals away during the day.

I soon passed through the town of Sterling, scattered buildings along the road: cafes, tourist shops, and taxidermy, but soon I started seeing larger buildings and stores. I had come to the town of Soldotna, and was surprised at its size. It had all the things any small town had, anywhere. Guess I was losing a few of the illusions I had about the Great Northland. I figured Jack London was rolling around in his grave over "progress." I stopped at the local Safeway and got coffee and a ready-made sandwich, which I ate and drank while sitting in the parking lot watching it all go by.

I heard a loud "clunk," and scratching sounds on the roof of the jeep, and a raven jumped onto the hood. He peered at me through the windshield, and I peered back. Something connected. I got the feeling I shouldn't judge Alaska by what I was seeing right then. I slowly reached my hand out the window with a nice chunk of sandwich in it, and held it for the raven to take. It did one of those twisted-head looks birds do, and made a few tentative steps toward the offering. With a quick thrust of its neck, the raven had the piece in its beak and was instantly flapping away with the prize, somehow managing to make a few squawks without losing its grip on the food.

I cranked up the jeep and headed down to Homer, about sixty miles to the south. Adventures seemed to keep coming my way. It would be difficult to be bored in Alaska, I figured.

The rest of the drive toward Homer was through forested areas with swampy meadows scattered on the left side of the road, and the coast kept coming in and out of view on the right. This wasn't the coast of the Northern Pacific, though. This was the coast of Cook Inlet. The ocean was past the Inlet, through a passage beyond the Alaskan Peninsula.

I passed through places like Clam Gulch, Ninilchik, and Anchor Point before I came to Homer, at the end of the Kenai Peninsula. All these places were small, with only a few stores and maybe one restaurant. They all had charter fishing businesses, though. Homer, by comparison, was large.

I came up and over a rise and there was Homer below me. What a far-out view! There was what is called the Homer Spit, an arm of land stretching what seemed half way across the bottom of Kachemak Bay, which started on the left side of the Spit. To the right was the wide water of Cook Inlet, the end of it flanked with amazing and mysterious black mountains, with giant snowcaps and glaciers all over the place! The scene was so rich to my eyes, man. It was hard at first to take it all in. I had pulled over to the viewpoint at the top of the hill. There were several motor homes, "Tunabagos," as I call them, with touristy people out with their camcorders and two typical small doggies yapping at nothing in particular. I figured tourism was probably worth a lot of revenue to Homer and the other places up the road. I was right. Turned out Homer was a real tourist draw, with the majority of people coming to fish for salmon, halibut, and even cod.

I cranked up the jeep again, and headed down the hill into Homer. A sign said, "Welcome to Homer - population 3,800."

I drove along the bottom edge of the town on the same road, going around a curve to the right, over a low roadway seeming to double as a dam across the end of a body of water, with an outlet for a stream of water running down to the Inlet again. Found out it was called Beluga Slough. Quaint, as the rest of Homer seemed to be. I continued across, following the road finally leading me to the Homer Spit, which extended maybe three miles out across the water.

Lots of tents, RVs, and campers were parked or set up all over the spit. There were also colonies of crude shelters, some quite unique, with plywood sides or windbreaks and plastic tarp roofs, making me think of the shelters in Big Sur.

There was an official visitor center, and I stopped to get a map. The only other person there was the clerk. She was a fine young woman named Annie who was working at the center for the summer. She had long, sun-bleached hair, deep blue eyes, and a tempting mouth.

Talking to her, I learned she and her boyfriend had come out from Massachusetts about a month ago to see Alaska. Her boyfriend had been scared by a moose when they were out hiking, and he decided to go back home. She had stayed, having become quickly attached to the place.

I got a map from her, and a business directory. I turned to leave, but something made me turn around again and ask her if she wanted to share a meal with me later. I Don't know why I did it, not having such things in mind those days. Besides, I was probably fifteen years older than she was. She took a long look into my eyes and said, "O.K."

"Yeah?"

"Yeah."

"Cool." I told her I'd pick her up around seven, and we'd go from there.

"Have you been to the Salty Dawg yet?" she asked.

"Nope, just now got here."

Smiling, she said, "you work fast."

"Not usually."

"I'll see you at seven. What's your name?"

"Jester."

"Jester?"

"A long story, which I shall unfold for you over whatever we'll have to eat and drink."

"I look forward to it." She smiled this gut-warming smile, full of straight, naturally white teeth.

"Okay, Annie."

I went out to my jeep and sat there, surprised at my own behavior. It had been a long time since I had desired female company. As I split, I noticed her watching me through the window. I drove out the spit to see the sights, the tourist shops, charter boats, and the fish-processing plant. The Homer harbor was full of interesting boats, commercial and privately owned. All in all, a colorful place.

I also passed the Salty Dawg bar, which looked like a short lighthouse. I stopped at one place, and bought fish and chips made with local halibut, which was tasty, especially with the dark ale I had with it.

After eating, I walked around and below the place, which was built on tall pilings, and stood on the beach checking out the water. Those magical glaciered mountains were all around, it seemed. I looked up and saw two bald eagles circling above, probably looking for fish on the surface. Sure enough, one of them made a quick dive and snatched something in its claws, before soaring up again and spiraling away somewhere with the other majestic bird, to munch on what it had taken from the sea. It was a simple act for them, but I was overwhelmed by its perfection.

I felt something surge up in me. I loved this place, not just Homer, but Alaska in general. What a miracle it seemed, with all the high-tech, instant progress going on elsewhere. I suddenly wanted to stop here, to stay and become part of this place. I had to consider this, take some time, and see a lot more before I made any definite plans. Man, I sure had changed. There was a time when I would have gone for it, working it out as I went, but not now.

I looked for a motel room for the evening, wanting to clean up for my date. My date? What a rush! Still, she was a sweet young lady. Yeah, it had been a while. I found a room at the Ocean View Motel, which was funky but had atmosphere. The owners were proud of the place, judging by what they charged. Turned out it was the cheapest place in town during tourist season. The manager, Dave Christensen, said without the summer season, Homer, same as small coastal towns anywhere, wouldn't make it. "You got to have two or three things you can do to make money, depending on the season. Otherwise, it can get real hard. Unless, of course, you're independently wealthy!"

I went to my motel room and settled down after a much-needed hot shower. Lying on the bed mellowing out, letting the day slip away, I thought about many things, such as how quickly the whole Alaska journey had gone by, even with all the adventures I'd experienced along the way. It's funny how time can stretch at one point and shrink at another. It seemed as if only a few days had passed since I had left Monte Rio. When I thought of Monte Rio I felt a stab of longing, and decided when this trip was over, I'd head back and spend more time there. No matter where else I traveled, Monte Rio would always be the constant in my life, the one place I knew I could always find love and contentment. Guess I just didn't know what I would do from there.

I also looked deep into my feelings to know if hooking up with this young lady, Annie, was okay, or whether I was breaking a trust I had made to the one woman who had been meant for me.

I talked to Dawn as I had so many times since she had been taken from me in this life. She never responded with real words, but I always knew when she was there.

I decided this "date" was okay. I was still a vital human being with a lot more life to live and Dawn would want me to be okay. The life force within me needed release in a healthy way. If this girl Annie wasn't a healthy way to feel alive, then nothing was. I felt calm right in the middle of my gut about her, which was a good thing. It seemed as though I was at a time in my life when I should feel easy about whatever life provided me. I had been around the wheel a few times.

Time came to go meet Annie, so I dressed and went out to my stalwart jeep, which was covered with the grime of many different places, and headed out the Homer Spit again. I pulled up in front of the Visitor Center and waited for Annie to come out, which she did a few minutes later. She was wearing a brilliant smile. It was as if a light was beaming out of her through it. Sliding in beside me, Annie gave me a sweet little kiss. She thanked me for coming to get her as I had said I would. Feeling warm all over, I told her it was good to see her again.

It may sound to you as if things were happening quickly, but it felt completely natural, and I meant what I told her. She asked me if I'd care for some good seafood for dinner, and I said definitely. "Land's End has good food, but it's kind of expensive." she said.

I told her it wasn't a problem, and I'd enjoy going somewhere nice with her.

She said Land's End was at the far end of the spit and we headed out there. We parked and walked in, and I suddenly realized we were holding hands, something I hadn't done much in the past, not even with Dawn.

We ordered the Dungeness crab, caught locally, and a bottle of wine, which I thought would be cool. While we waited for the food, Annie reminded me I was to tell her the story of how I got my name, so I did, holding nothing back. I had to weave the whole tale of the Haight to put my naming in proper order, and when I stopped to ask her if I was boring her, she said absolutely not, and to keep going, so I did.

By the time the dinner and the bottle of wine was over, we had told each other a lot, and I was surprised to learn she was twenty-eight, not twenty-two as I had assumed. She had been married, but her old man had just boogied one day for no reason, and she had divorced him a year ago. She had really been into this fool, as I figured he'd have to be a fool to dump such a fine girl. So, we had both lost someone we loved without having a choice.

After dinner, we took a walk along the shore behind the restaurant, which was also the end of the spit, and there was water all around us, and those eerie magical mountains across the bay, even more mysterious in the summer dimness of evening. Annie came up close and wrapped her arms around me and buried her face in my beard. My heart actually jumped then. I felt something hard melt inside me, and realized I had carried an emotional knot since Dawn, and now it was gone. It was overwhelming, but I maintained, enjoying this sweet, warm moment.

Our coming together was no coincidence, not at all. 'Course, I didn't believe in coincidence any more, anyways.

I lifted her face, and we kissed long, slow and deep. There was such a strong feeling in that kiss, we separated and stood looking at each other. We smiled together, knowing what this was. I suggested we go back to my motel room. She smiled and said she'd rather take me to her shelter on the spit, and I agreed without hesitation.

When we got to her wood-framed, plastic-tarp tent, right behind the visitor center, it seemed so familiar, being similar to the Big Sur shelters, only sturdier, and with all sorts of beach stuff around the inner edges, shells and bits of strangely shaped driftwood. There was a thick, dense foam pad, with doubled sleeping bags on top.

Annie and I took off our shoes and lay down together. We lay there looking at each other, totally enjoying being together. We spoke quietly about life and love and favorite places. After a time, we pulled the sleeping bags over us, held each other close and closed our eyes to sleep the sleep of angels.

In the morning, we woke up and made love, as if we'd been together for years.

Too soon, Annie had to go to work. She suggested I hang out in the area, but I wanted to do some exploring, promising to be back before the end of day. As she was bent over, leaving the shelter, I gave her a nip on the backside making her yelp. She got red in the face, since there were several other spit dwellers, locally called "Spit Rats," outside. Leaning back in, she said with a smile, "I can see I'll have to watch out for you, Jester."

"Count on it," I said.

I spent most of the day checking out Homer. I took a drive up East End Road, which heads east out of Homer along the northern side of Kachemak Bay. I drove out the first ten miles on blacktop, before the road turned to dirt. I felt the road climbing, and had to stop a number of times to stand in awe of this incredible country. Seeing the bay below me and the glaciered mountains across the way as far as I could see was a major rush, and took my breath away.

I had a brochure and identified Portlock, Dixon, and Gruening Glacier, which seemed the grandest of the three. From where I stood, I could see up to the head of Kachemak Bay, with several braided rivers flowing down into it. Though the mountains across the bay still looked black, the land on my side, all around me, was very green. I thought Washington State was green, but Alaska had it beat for sure.

I headed back to town after the road ended at a village, with a steep-looking road dropping down, probably to the shore of the upper bay. Turned out it was a village of people called Old Believer Russians, who had sought religious asylum, leaving Russia at the turn of the century, to settle in China, then South America, then Oregon, and finally ending up in Alaska. They apparently had their own society, not always coinciding with everyone else's, and they kept to themselves. They were hard-working people, fishermen mostly.

I got back to the spit around four to reconnect with Annie. She was in the visitor's booth, telling some travelers about Homer. She gave them several brochures, and sent them out to have fun. Looking around, she leaned over the counter, and gave me a delicious kiss. "Please! We've only just met!" I told her in a mock serious manner.

"Oh, we'll get to know each other soon enough." We laughed more out of happiness to be together again than at the humor of it. I told her I'd be waiting in her beach pad, and napped until she got back and woke me.

We spent another evening tripping on each other. On her Coleman camp stove, Annie made a pot of beans with cut-up hot dogs in them, and put some melted cheese on top. It reminded me of my trip north with Carey, well, sort of.

After dinner, we walked down the beach, talking and laughing. There was plenty of light in spite of the late hour, it being summer in Alaska. We stopped to watch some eagles wheeling around each other way up high, playing or courting, I didn't know which, but they were beautiful.

Back at her shelter, I stopped and put my fingers to her lips, asking for silence. There was some young dude with his head in the open door of the jeep. I motioned for Annie to stay where she was. Sneaking up quietly, I gave him a good swift kick in the ass. He jumped so hard he cracked his head on the doorframe, and fell backwards onto his butt. Before he could get up, I put a boot on his chest, holding him down, and asked him what he thought he was doing, messing with my jeep. Annie came up and asked me not to hurt him, saying he was somebody she knew.

Turned out this boy had come up to work in the fish processing plant on the spit, hadn't lasted there, and couldn't get another steady job. He'd had a number of short-time jobs, but was hurting, money wise. "I was just looking for some food, is all."

"Next time you might consider asking. A lot better than stealing."

I moved my boot and held out a hand. He took it and I pulled him up. I took out my wallet, and gave him a one hundred dollar bill. He stood there, a blank look on his face, so I stuffed the bill in his shirt pocket. After talking a while, I learned he still had his return ticket home, so I told him he ought to head back and come up again next year after securing a job he could handle first. He still couldn't believe I gave him the money, and thanked me too much.

"Just get squared away, brother. Best advice I can give you."

He said thanks again, and walked away. Annie looked at me strangely. I asked if she was okay.

"Very much so," she said. "The more I learn about you, the more I like what I learn."

"Oh, you'll probably get tired of me soon enough," I told her.

"I seriously doubt it."

Annie asked me if giving her friend money was going to put a pinch in my resources. I thought for a second, and then told her I was okay financially, so no problem. She told me it didn't matter to her if I had a lot of money.

"Sure makes things easier though," I answered, smiling.

Annie had the next several days off, and I asked her if she'd like to take a ride with me to meet the man I had come to Alaska to find. She was more than up for it, so the next morning we headed north. Before leaving, I checked the old Winchester where it was wrapped up and buried under the other stuff in the jeep. Annie was fascinated by it, recognizing its quality and age. She said she didn't care for guns much, but knew this was a special one. This girl had heart, no doubt about it. I told her she could shoot it sometime, and she said she'd like me to teach her.

We headed up the road toward Seward and, as usual, having someone good to talk to made the miles go by quickly. We got to Seward about three hours later, and soon we were parked in front of Walt and Emerald's shop. I knew they were split up, but couldn't help thinking of it as both of theirs. When we walked up to the door, there was a note taped to the inside of the glass: "Jester, go see the bartender down the block. Your brother, Walt."

So, we went down to the bar I had sat in when I arrived in Seward, and asked the bartender if there was anything for me from Walt. After asking me my name, he handed me a note.

"Jester, I'm gone to Colorado to fix things up with Emerald. I know there's not much chance of it happening, but I have to try. I gave all my valuables to the bartender, who is honest as the day is long, to keep for me in his safe. Don't know when I'll be back, but you can stay in our place long as you want. Be of good heart, brother. I hope to see you soon. Walt." Below that was an address in Denver, Colorado.

I asked the bartender for the key to their pad, and he willingly gave it over.

Annie and I went back to the shop and walked upstairs. I checked in the fridge, and it was empty except for two Coronas. I laughed to myself, as this was definitely a Walt thing. I had told Annie about Walt and Emerald, so his going to Colorado was not a puzzle to her.

"See how true love is," she said. "It is impossible to be whole without it."

How well I knew this fact. "I miss the feeling, Annie, but I'm lately being reminded of how it can be."

Damned if she didn't give me a melting look, and one large tear left her eye and rolled down her sweet cheek. I kissed it away. We went out to get something to eat and decide what to do next.

As we walked to the restaurant across the street, I pondered on how incredible life can be, the way it moves you from one place or person to the next, showing you all the signs along the way to remind you of what is worthwhile. I was glad I had been paying attention. I suddenly realized: while you can hold tight to things which were precious to you in the past, you have to put them in their proper place to keep them from coloring life in the future. You can't stop living in the present; you have to move on and not get stuck, 'cause life will walk past you in a heartbeat, brother.

While Annie and I ate, I got lost in my thoughts over what move I needed to make next. She was looking at me, and asked what I was thinking. Taking a breath, I laid it all out.

"Without Walt here, as beautiful as Alaska is, it doesn't have a hold on me, because he's the reason I came up. Walt and I have a strong connection; we're true brothers. I have the feeling he'll be gone for quite a while. It took a long time for things to unravel for him and Emerald, and may take longer to heal. I feel the need to head back down to Monte Rio, California, the place I told you about. The people there are dear to me, and I need to spend time with them."

Annie slumped in the chair she was sitting in and said, "So, it's over already? You're saying good-by?"

"I do feel the need to head back, Annie, but I don't want to leave you behind. I know we're new to each other, even though it doesn't feel that way to me. I want to know if you'll go with me and see where we can take this. If you can't, then we'll have to do something else."

Annie sat looking at me a moment, before saying, "Jester, I'd love to go with you, if I wouldn't be intruding. But, how do you think your people would react to me? You know what I mean."

"Annie, my wife has been gone for quite a while now. If they can't accept you as being who I want to be with, we'll have to leave, as much as it might hurt, and it would be their loss. I'll give them a call before we get there to let them know, so they can adjust. We can spend time on the trip down learning more about each other."

She smiled. When she asked me if I meant it, I told her I absolutely did. Annie suggested we spend the night in Seward, then head back to Homer to get the belongings she had there, and she could tell the Visitor Center people she was leaving. And so we did.

Lying in bed later, Annie sleeping and me thinking, I wondered if I had truly found a kindred spirit. She was as up for traveling as I was, and really seemed to want to be with me. I hoped it would last, but as they say, only time would tell. I decided to simply enjoy us and not worry about the future. Having made a decision, I drifted off into a contented sleep, snuggled close to this sweet girl beside me. Sometimes keeping life simple was the best, no, the only way, to live it fully.

We shut down Walt and Emerald's place the next morning, left an explanatory note for Walt on the kitchen table, returned the key to the bartender, and went back to Homer. We actually spent several days there, getting the jeep tuned up, and collecting some needed supplies for the long journey south to Monte Rio.

We headed out, following in reverse the same route Cary and I had taken coming up, but first we did a detour to Fairbanks to see the place, and find out how he was doing. But when we got to his uncle's store, it turned out Cary had gone to Anchorage to find other work.

"He was more interested in hiking and taking photos than working in my store, so I gave him an ultimatum, which he declined, not very graciously." His Uncle obviously got less than he expected from his nephew.

So, back on the road we went, Canada ahead of us.

We stopped at the same places Cary and I had stopped on our way up. Joe at the Blue Lake Lodge commented I had definitely traded Cary in on a much better model. He asked with a challenging look if I was going to have the Blue Lake Lodge burger for dinner, and Annie asked what it was. When Joe told her, not having to exaggerate to make an impression, Annie said she wanted to try one. Joe looked at me and I shrugged. I had the halibut and fries, and Annie had the burger, and darned if she had no trouble finishing it. 'Course, she didn't have the soup and bread. She had a tight round little tummy when she was through, but seemed content and pleased with herself. Joe treated us to pie and coffee for dessert. Annie said no thanks, she didn't have any room left. I had a piece though, and it was quite tasty.

I woke up the next morning early, before Annie had opened her eyes. I lay there looking at her face. She looked like an innocent sleeping there, not a wrinkle on her forehead, with a peaceful look on her face. I realized the look might have something to do with us. I had a moment of unsteadiness about it. I was glad she slept while I went through my mental twitching. I told myself this was all cool, no concerns. Still, there was a nagging doubt and I did the only thing I could do: I leaned over and gave her sweet mouth a kiss. The mouth smiled, asking for more. What could I do? I gave it more, lots more.

It was more enjoyable traveling down the road with Annie instead of Cary, for sure. We stopped at the same Indian crafts store, where I treated her to a woman's pair of moccasins made by the same Cree lady. She was so excited about them she held and looked at the mocs for a long time as we drove on down the road.

We cruised along enjoying the country around us, with its lushness and grandeur, which it had in major amounts. At the places we stopped, the people seemed friendlier than when I had traveled through with Cary. I decided it was because of Annie, and because we were so obviously having a great time together. It just rubbed off on other people.

We stopped at the Fitzgerald's lodge on the Cassiar Highway. They were glad to see me, but looked a bit put off when they saw I was with a young lady. They were an older couple, so maybe they weren't approving of us being together, you know? But, when we were all settled in, they did invite us to dinner. There were other people there this time: a retirement-age couple who were driving an RV from Peoria, Illinois to Fairbanks, Alaska. They had decided the lodge looked so quaint they would stay there for an evening. I saw Mr. Fitzgerald wince when the woman described his place as "quaint."

Dinner was good, with a tasty beef pie, a salad of fresh, natural greens, which the RV couple found too strong, more sweet potatoes, and a wonderful peach cobbler. The RV lady asked if they were locally-grown peaches, and Mrs. Fitzgerald said, with a funny smile, they were canned, because they didn't grow peaches there. I had two servings.

By the end of dinner, the Fitzgeralds were completely won over by Annie's groovy personality. She asked if Mr. Fitzgerald had shot the bear whose hide was on the wall.

Mr. Fitzgerald looked at me with a pretend angry look on his face, asking me why I hadn't told her the story of how the courageous hunter and his guide had stood their ground in the face of this wounded raging beast.

Annie looked at him and said, judging from the skin, it would have to be a brave hunter who brought him down, but she'd love to hear the story. She had won Mr. Fitzgerald over.

Mrs. Fitzgerald smiled, and asked Mr. Fitzgerald to "Please tell her the tale, dear," which Mr. Fitzgerald was only too happy to do.

When he was done with the story, the RV lady said she didn't think her husband would have been able to do it.

Mr. Fitzgerald, on hearing the sting her husband must have felt, responded by saying, "You never know what you can do until you're put to it, and your husband would probably do the same." Saying this, Mr. Fitzgerald got an appreciating look from the put-upon RV husband.

When I heard the RV lady make her remark, I thought to myself Dawn would never put me down in front of anybody. I turned and saw Annie sitting there, not Dawn. I felt a knot form in my gut. Annie gave me a curious look, as if she had seen something in my expression.

I paused in my reading of this unexpected portion of Jester's tale. I was happy for him, but surprised, too. His love for Dawn and Nathan had seemed so perfect, as if it was the real love of his life. I wondered if he was going to be able to maintain this relationship, even though he obviously enjoyed Annie's company. I questioned though, his decision to take her with him to Monte Rio, wondering why he wanted to. Maybe it was an unconscious desire to lay things to rest. It made me think about my own relationship with my wife. Ours was a good marriage, though we hadn't had any children. The depth of feeling, though, wasn't the same as Jester's connection with Dawn. I have to admit I felt some envy for the life they'd had together. I continued reading.

The next morning, Annie and I got up early and drove off, heading south. The moist air carried all the rich, natural smells of the land. It was pure magic for us. As we drove, I soon saw there were far fewer bears than I had seen on the way up. Annie even asked me where all the bears were I had mentioned. "Beats me," I told her. "Things change." She seemed disappointed, but about five miles farther down the road, we saw a large black bear feeding about fifty yards off the road on the right side. I pulled slowly to a stop and shut off the engine. Annie was thrilled, taking at least a dozen photos of the bear. But when she started to get out of the jeep, I quickly grabbed her left arm and told her strongly not to leave the jeep.

She gave me a look, but said, "Okay, Jester."

A minute later, the bear suddenly stood on its hind legs, looked in our general direction and took off into the trees.

"Sorry, Annie, but these are definitely wild bears and you shouldn't take chances with 'em. They can be real trouble if provoked."

She smiled at me, kissed me on the cheek and said, "Okay, Mister."

I wasn't sure how this made me feel, so I just started up the jeep and headed on down the road.

The rest of our journey south flowed smoothly without any hassles. Each road has its own rhythm, and this one was no different. Sometimes, sitting quietly together side by side with Annie enjoying the feel of it all, I slipped into perfect balance with the highway, its feel and rhythm, so it was as though we were floating.

Crossing the border couldn't have been easier. I actually forgot to mention the Winchester, and it didn't even make any difference. We were waved on through with smiles all around.

Once we made it south of Oregon and into Northern California, the country took on a new energy. We stopped at Eureka for a night, eating at the Samoa Cookhouse, a place I had gone to with my folks when I was a kid. It had been a cookhouse in the early days for the sailing ship crews bringing supplies and picking up logs from the area to haul elsewhere for processing. They still serve meals the way they did for the crews. If you order a turkey or roast beef dinner, you are brought an entire platter of meat, full bowls of potatoes and peas, a large schooner of gravy, and a complete loaf of fresh-baked bread. For dessert, if you have any room left, you could ask for maybe apple or pumpkin pie and get a whole pie and a bowl of whipped cream. Man, what a spread.

After dinner, Annie told me she'd have a permanent round belly if she stayed with me a long time, then gave me a questioning look. I smiled at her and winked. She smiled back, but I thought she wasn't completely satisfied with my response. Later, in bed, she asked me to please just hold her and I did, until she drifted off to sleep. It was an awkward time, the first real one since we had been together, but we hadn't been together long, and in spite of our obvious connection, we were still new to each other. I wondered, before dozing off, how things would go over the next few days.

It only took another partial day's drive to reach Monte Rio. I had called the Lensels from Eureka to let them know I was coming in and Annie was with me. Mother Lensel paused for a moment, then told me whoever I brought would be welcome. Maxine really was the best.

When we pulled into the Lenzels' driveway, Maxine, George, and Avery came out onto the front porch together, followed by Marla a moment later. Her boys came running out right behind her, ran up to the jeep on my side, and stood there with grins on their faces, glad to see me. They had grown since I'd last seen them. Annie got out and walked around to where I now stood by the jeep. They all came down the porch stairs, and we went into a group hug, Annie included. All the tension building in Annie and me about this moment simply melted away.

"It sure is good to see you, Jester, and it's about time, too!" George tried to fake a frown, but was too glad to see me and couldn't pull it off.

"You must be Annie," Maxine said. "It's a pleasure to meet you. Come on in, and we'll put together a tray of munchies."

"Munchies, Maxine? Have you got the munchies?" I asked.

"Yes, munchies, Jester. The boys and I have been sharing a lot lately. Is it a problem?"

"'Course not Mom, you just caught me off guard."

"Dawn told me it wasn't hard to do," she said, to tease me, and then realized she shouldn't have said it. Maxine looked apologetically at Annie.

"It's alright Mrs. Lensel, I'm okay."

Maxine kissed Annie on the cheek and told her to call her Maxine. "Shall we get those snacks made up then?" Annie smiled and they walked into the house with Marla.

George, Avery, and I walked up and sat on the porch. We filled each other in on what had been going on, and it seemed life in Monte Rio hadn't changed much, which is what I loved about the place.

I told George and Avery they ought to go check out Alaska, it being such an amazing place. George replied he figured there was enough right there in Monte Rio to keep them busy and satisfied. Avery came back onto the porch after having gone to the back yard shed. He held in his hands an absolutely huge set of antlers.

"Far out, Avery, did you take this?"

"No, George did, with a running shot at about seventy-five yards. I know they would be a record, but, the time of year we took this

236

buck would make it a dumb thing to turn them in to the officials for scoring." He showed his snaggle-toothed grin.

"I should have known, man. But at least you have your memory of the event."

"We do, Jester, for sure."

The girls came out onto the porch with several dishes full of sandwiches, chips, and other treats. There was also a jug of iced tea, and we had a fine time sitting, talking, and laughing together. Annie was made a part of it, and I was grateful. While she was talking to Marla, I saw Maxine studying her, after which she cast me a glance, smiled, and winked at me. I got a real lump in my throat.

Maxine told me my folks called every few months for news of me. They always mentioned my brother was still in Sweden, teaching and giving lectures. Maxine told me I should give Mom and Pop a call while I was there. It had been a long time since I had made contact. I told her I'd be sure to get in touch.

After a couple of hours, I suggested Annie and I go over to my cabin to kick back a while.

"Your place is fine, Jester. We've kept the electricity going there." George smiled at me, as if to tell me he knew I'd be coming back.

Annie and I drove to the cabin. She thought it was sweet-looking. I unlocked the door and we stepped in. The atmosphere hit me like a ton of bricks. All the old vibes were there, as if Dawn and Nathan were still around. Annie walked in, looked around, and asked me if it was hard coming back.

"I haven't been here in a while. I just need a minute to adjust."

"I could go sit outside a while if you want, Jester."

"No, no, this is okay."

But, to tell the truth, it was barely okay. I tried real hard to clear the air for Annie. I opened the window, and turned on the radio. Checking in the fridge, I found a nice assortment of things to eat and drink. The Lensels must have stocked the fridge after I called them, in case we stayed at the cabin. But, we were both more tired from our journey than anything else. We went into the new part of the cabin and made use of the shower I had put in. It felt good, putting us in the mood for a nap, after which we dozed off in each other's arms. I awoke because Annie was shaking me hard. I sat up and asked what was wrong. It was dark by then.

"There's someone here, Jester, but I can't see anybody. I'm scared." Turning on the lamp by the bed, I told her not to be, there wasn't anything there to cause either of us any harm.

Immediately after I said that, a breeze came through the open window, seemed to travel around the room, and was gone. Then, a finch landed on the windowsill, chirped a few times, and flew away. We both stayed propped up in bed, feeling the energy which had filled the room.

Annie asked me what I thought had happened. I told her I thought we had just been welcomed into the place; everything was okay.

She had trouble digesting that. Annie and I had never discussed spiritual happenings. When we talked, she said she had never experienced such things before, but was open minded about it. "I could say a breeze came through and a bird landed and then flew away, Jester, but it sure felt like more than that. Do you think Dawn was just here?"

"I'm not positive, Annie, but it is likely. Dawn was a sensitive person, a psychic, so anything is possible, but I can't say for sure."

When I said this, a teacup Dawn loved fell off the shelf over the sink and broke on the countertop. I got chills down my back, and Annie couldn't handle it. She begged me to take her somewhere else, and I couldn't get her to relax. I was okay, because I knew it was another sign Dawn had given up her place here so Annie could be okay. But, I knew it had been too much for Annie, so we got dressed and went out, over to the Pine Tree Lodge on Main Street, where we got a room for the night.

Annie was still edgy, so I didn't try to talk to her about what had happened. We lay on the bed together watching some garbage on the TV, then shut it down and went to sleep.

The next morning we got up early and went over to the Lensels' for breakfast, as we had agreed to do the day before. Annie didn't seem her usual glowing self. She obviously had things on her mind, but I didn't ask her what it was, figuring she would tell me when she was ready. Maxine had one of her usual hearty breakfasts going, eggs, bacon, pancakes, juice, toast, the works. But Annie barely ate anything. Maxine asked her if she was feeling okay.

"I'm afraid I'm not, Mrs. Lensel." Annie was speaking to Maxine, but looked at me when she said it. "Something happened last night to make it difficult for me to be here." Still she looked at me.

I asked her if she'd care to take a walk so we could talk.

"No, Jester, I think talking here with Dawn's family is the right thing. You see, Mrs. Lensel, your daughter, who must have been a special person, is still here. She made herself known to us last night. I'm sorry, but I can't deal with something so strong it still remains even now. It's too much for me."

238

I felt my chances with Annie slipping away.

"I'm sorry, I'm not stronger, Jester. I care about you, but I don't think I could replace the powerful love you and Dawn shared."

She got up quickly and went out to the porch. I sat still for a moment, all of them staring at me. I told them it was true, Dawn had been there last night, and described what had happened. Maxine said she understood, and whenever she had gone over to dust the place and putter around, she knew Dawn was there with her. "I truly believe she has been waiting for you to return, Jester."

I got goose bumps all over, and knew she was right. "If it's true, and I think it is, I can't stay there. I need to get on with my life. As much as I loved and still love Dawn, I have to move forward."

Maxine and her two sons quietly nodded their understanding. I got up and went to talk to Annie on the porch.

I told her I wasn't going to stay there either. I let her know I needed to break away and live my life in the present, not the past. She understood, she told me, but I could see things weren't the same. A block had been put between us, and it was not going to work anymore. We didn't have to say a word; it was understood. After a moment, I asked her what she wanted to do.

"I think I want to go back to Massachusetts, clear my head, and decide what to do next."

I offered to drive her back East, and would have been happy to, hoping things might clear between us, but she was having none of it. So, it was decided I would drive her down to San Francisco the next day, and she would fly home.

I insisted on getting her a first-class ticket to let her fly in style. She finally accepted. I went inside and told the family what was happening, and I would be back to visit after seeing Annie off.

It was settled. I was going to be on my own again. I was bummed over the way things had gone, to be losing Annie when I thought we could make a go of it. But it seemed life had put another kink in my trail. Annie and I went back to the motel. I know we both wanted to make love, but things were too awkward, so we just hung out together.

In the morning, we drove down to the San Francisco airport, luckily getting her a flight leaving in several hours with a first-class seat available. Sitting together in the boarding area, we didn't speak much, just held hands. When the flight started loading, I offered her some money for the trip, but she smiled, touched my cheek, and said no. A few minutes later, she was gone. I watched as the windows in the plane went by, but didn't see her face. I felt emptier than I had in a long time, but I knew what Annie and I shared in the short time we had been together had reconnected some loose wires inside me because of her loving ways. I wouldn't forget her.

The ride back to Monte Rio helped me clear my mind, as being on the road always did for me.

By the time I got back, I knew what I was going to do. I needed to get my butt out on the road again. I had decided it was time for another rig. I wanted to get a pick-up with a nice camper on the back so I would be self-contained. The jeep had been groovy, but its limitations had made themselves known, especially with someone else along on a long road trip. I guess I was getting older too, and wouldn't mind some comfort on my trips rather than waking up in a tent with sticks and rocks not noticed the night before making my ribs ache.

When I told George and Avery about my plans, George told me he knew an older man who had given up driving recently, as his eyesight had been failing him. He had a nice '80 Dodge pickup with an almost-new camper on it. I went over with George the next day after he had called the truck owner, who had said he would be willing to sell it. It was a clean truck-and-camper outfit and I didn't argue the price with the man, who was in his seventies. I figured he could probably use the money.

The deal made, I drove it back to the house with George following me in the jeep. When Avery and Maxine came out, I told them I had decided to give the jeep to Marla and the boys. Maxine had told me the old Travelall was on its last legs. At first Marla didn't want to take it, but I convinced her it was cool. Her boys were as excited as kids at Christmas, when it was settled. We transferred my gear from the jeep to the camper, which didn't take long.

After dinner, I went to spend the night at the cabin. Even though nothing obvious happened, it was definitely a charged atmosphere there. Before I went to bed, I talked to Dawn, asking her to forgive me for needing to let go. When I did, I got a tiny whiff of cinnamon and nutmeg, and then the cabin cleared, and was just the cabin again. I had been given my release, Dawn's blessing. Climbing onto the bed, I slept like a babe through the night, a peaceful, dreamless sleep.

At first, I was sorry I didn't dream of my little family, out of habit, I guess. But, you know, it was cool; I was okay. Life would give me whatever I needed. I knew it, same as I knew Dawn loved me unconditionally. But, as you know, when the accident date comes round, I'll spend it in mourning 'til the day I die. Just the way it is, brother.

I spent about a week visiting with my Monte Rio family, the Lensels, and with Marla, Todd and Evan. At this point I decided to call my folks, see how they were, and find out if they were up for a visit. My pop was glad to hear from me. He told me my mother's heart was worse and she was very weak. I told him I would head right on down to see them.

This trip would be a good trial run for the truck, and after being on the road for a while, I learned the Dodge with the camper on the back was definitely not as agile as the jeep. I had to learn its limitations, meaning I had to adopt a slower, easier-going driving style. I soon found the truck's happy groove on the road, and the rhythm felt good. It was during this trip I decided to go see if my old San Francisco acquaintances, Larry and Robin, were still on the commune outside Nevada City, California and found Wil, Chet's burnt-out brother there, as I mentioned before. After seeing Wil and having a short, but mellow visit with Larry and Robin, I continued on down the road, heading south toward my parents' place. I had left them out of my life for quite a while. I hoped it would be a good thing to see them again.

I was tripped out over having a home on wheels. It was all my old step van was, and set up a whole lot better. I liked not having to put up a tent. The camper was self-contained, with all that I needed neatly stashed away. It wasn't the bus, for sure, but, I no longer needed what the bus had provided. It made things convenient and simple. The camper was cozy for one person, and nicely equipped with all the necessities, but to tell the truth, I never used its built-in crapper. The thought of having to stop and dump my own byproducts did not appeal to me one bit. I could always find a place to lighten my load, especially when traveling through woodsy areas.

Not wanting to stay anywhere else, I drove on down to Southern Cal, making for a very long day. I got to my folks' place quite late, maybe midnight, and spent the night parked in my camper on the street in front so's not to wake them up. Around four in the morning, there was a hard knocking on my camper door.

I pulled my jeans on, and opened the door to be greeted by two policemen, their flashlights shining in my face. They asked me to step out, and then wanted to know what I was doing parked in front of this "residence." I figured one of the neighbors had made the call, not having seen my rig before.

After showing my I.D. and registration, and explaining the situation, I looked closely at one of the cops, and asked him if he had ever left town, or just decided it was not the scuzziest place in the world, as he had once thought. He asked if he knew me, and I told him we had played ball together in high school. I told him my original name and he smiled. His name was Terry Yost, and we had been on the football team together in school.

Looking me up and down, Terry said it was really something, how life had sent us in such different directions. He asked me if it would be okay to search my camper, and when I told him absolutely, he smiled and apparently decided maybe it wasn't necessary after all. I guess I did look rough and shaggy compared to his neatly trimmed self.

After visiting a few minutes, he had to get on patrol again, and suggested I park in the driveway next time. After he got into the patrol car with his partner, I asked him if he was married, and he told me yeah, and I wouldn't believe to whom. She was the girl he had dated all through high school, and they were still together after twenty-odd years. I told him a good marriage was a special thing, and he should feel blessed. He smiled and drove off in his cruiser.

I have learned over the years to be cool and not get cranky with cops, whether you know them or not. Makes no sense to do otherwise. It's like throwing rocks at lions, you dig?

About seven a.m., there was another knocking at the camper door, but when I opened it, it was my mother this time, and it was a shock to see her. Instead of being my normally plump mother, she looked painfully thin, and had an oxygen tank on wheels behind her with a plastic tube wrapped around her head and fitted into her nose. Her hair had gotten thin, and her color was not good. I did my best not to show my surprise at the way she looked, but she had picked up on it and smiled. "Sorry I scared you," she said. "It's not as bad as it looks." All I could do was nod.

We walked slowly into the house with me wheeling the oxygen tank along, and sat in the kitchen. My pop was still asleep. It took several minutes for mom to catch her breath, sobering minutes for me. Mom told me she was supposed to get a quadruple bypass, but none of the doctors in the area wanted to touch her, since she was such a bad risk.

My mother had always been an active person, so it was hard for me to see her this way, and it must have been terrible for her to be in such a condition.

My pop woke up an hour later, and came into the kitchen looking for a cup of coffee. I had made a pot so my mom wouldn't have to.

After my father and I greeted each other, we all sat around the kitchen table catching up on things.

My folks needed to know if I was okay after Dawn and Nathan had been taken from me. I told them I had some moments, but all in all I was doing alright. Then I started crying. I don't know exactly why, man, but out the water came. Maybe it was being with my folks and knowing mom was in such bad shape, I figured I would have another heavy loss soon. I tell you, man, it's a never-ending process.

While we were talking, I had a brainstorm. I asked my folks if they would like to go camping with me over the weekend. But, mom had to have an oxygen source at all times. She also needed to be within easy reach of her doctors. So any real journey was out. I offered to drive them up to Mt. Blakely, a local mountain hangout with lots of wooded hillsides and all, but mom couldn't handle any altitude either.

So, we hung out with each other, sitting on the back patio, sipping iced tea. I helped out with things while I was there. We talked some, mostly reminiscing about earlier times, and looked at the old family albums. I hadn't seen them for years, but as soon as I looked at them all the photos were familiar to me.

It was good spending time together. I apologized for not having stayed in closer touch and pop nodded, saying, "It's just the way life is, son."

Since none of us had been in touch with my brother for a while, we decided to give him a call. The folks had his phone number in Sweden. After several attempts to dial the odd number correctly, we made contact. I talked to my bro' a bit, but mostly the folks did, especially mom, until she ran short of breath.

When it was my turn to say good-bye, I looked at my mom a moment and suggested he might consider visiting if it was at all possible. But he was quite busy with his teaching job and couldn't plan a visit. He asked me if seeing the folks soon might be a good idea, and I tried to be tactful and said, "It sure would be." He was disturbed because he couldn't just fly on over, being so busy with his own life. We talked a few more minutes, catching up, and then signed off.

I could tell my brother was feeling the effects of being so far from his family. I know he would have loved to be with us more, but the path he chose in life made it difficult.

While Mom was napping, Pop asked me what I planned to do next and where I would go. "I expect you have another journey to go on. Seems it's what you do most of the time."

I told him I hadn't planned anything yet after the visit with them.

My father suggested I try my hand at prospecting, gold panning. "We did some panning on the trips we took after I retired. It's lots of fun. In fact, I still have some maps and books about it. You can have our gold pans and other stuff, since we won't be needing it anymore." It was my father's turn to cry. I put my hand on his shoulder and he sat there weeping.

Man, I was bummed. They had been married a very long time. I wondered how my old man would do when my mom left this world. Pop had been gone five years during World War II, but he and Mom had stayed true to each other. I knew he loved her as much as I loved Dawn, though the relationships were definitely different.

Near dinner time, my mom said she would kill for some Chinese food. It was forbidden due to her condition, congestive heart trouble and diabetes. I looked over at Pop, he looked at me and shrugged, so I took them out for dinner, and boy, did my mother enjoy herself. I figured she probably didn't have much time, so what the heck, she might as well have some fun in the life she had left. I did serve her the food so she wouldn't overdue it, which I was sure she would have otherwise. When we got back home, my dad thanked me. He told me he hadn't seen mom enjoying herself so much in quite a while.

I was there less than a week, when I started hearing the call of the road again. I had looked through the written material my dad had given me on gold panning. There were lots of places in Arizona where you could go prospecting with no hassles. I thought maybe I'd go see Gregorio while I was out there. He was no youngster either, so maybe it was a timely idea.

I left my parents home, telling them I would be back soon to see them again. Pop said he hoped I would. Mom said I better make it quick, and gave me a little hug. I had serviced the truck while I was there, so I just got in and split.

I didn't know if I could get into this prospecting thing, but the visit with my folks and my mother's poor condition had been a real downer, and a journey would help me blow the stink off. Life itself is definitely a trip and a half. If I'd had a doobie just then, I would have smoked it right down to the nub.

I drove California from west to east, crossing over the Arizona border in good time. There was a campground outside Wenden, Arizona in the gold-panning leaflets, so I headed there to see how it would go.

My dad had given me a tiny bottle with a few grains of gold in it so I would know how it looked. I had read up on the best places along creek beds to look. I got into it right away. Something about the whole scene, squatting down by the creek and running water over the dirt in the pan turned me on, took me away from all the sadness in life I had been smacked in the face with lately. I simply concentrated on the water, the air, and my panning.

After several hours of this reverie, there in the bottom of my pan were several pieces large enough to be picked up in my fingers. Gold! I had found gold! Man, I was hooked.

Every person who has ever struck gold must have had the same feeling. A chill ran down my back. I had to pan some more. I knew it could sometimes be disappointing, but I was hooked. I had plenty of money, so a chance to become rich wasn't why it turned me on.

Finding gold in a creek was a very cool thing. Maybe it was why they called it the gold rush! I certainly had the time to pursue this newest urge. Hey, maybe that was it! I was supposed to be a modern prospector, without the burro! Far out! A new lifestyle to add onto the others I had tried. I could camp out in my truck in the wooded mountains or sandy deserts. Why not? I figured I'd probably meet other like-minded people along the way.

Only time would tell where my latest interest might take me, maybe even Alaska again. I certainly knew the way.

I ended up visiting various campgrounds in Arizona, New Mexico, and Colorado. My life was wide open again. I never felt lonely while doing the gold search. I met lots of people, some of them good to connect with, looking, as I was, for the yellow stuff. Others, I realized right away, would much rather be left to themselves. But, we all had our own reasons for being out there. I did enjoy having a cup of java with the more sociable folks. It was a strange combination of obsession and relaxation at the same time.

I kept seeing people with gold-dredging systems at some of the larger creeks. At first it seemed out of place, almost gross, compared to the very Zen panning method. But, as time went on, it started to interest me, floating around under water, sucking up all the sand and gravel, sorting out the gold by gravity. I almost submitted to the urge for more advanced ways to find the yellow treasure, but finally brought myself down again. I wanted this to be a part of my life, not to overwhelm it.

I got myself back to panning, even though other prospectors tried to get me on the "proper track" to finding more gold. But I met some others who fully understood my position, preferring to pan only, though some had what was called a "dry washer" for shaking out the gold when no water was available, and I finally bought a ready-made one from a man in a camp outside Redwing, Colorado, who made and sold them. It was fascinating being able to find gold without water, though I preferred the sound and feel of a creek.

By the time I had spent a few months out on the land scrabbling for bits and pieces, dust and nuggets, I had almost four ounces of pure gold, with a quarter-ounce nugget the largest I had found, having bent down and picked it up at an Arizona creek bed where I saw it glittering. I also had a few small pieces of quartz with some nice color in them.

I was in Phoenix after a lot of time panning, my neck, face, and arms nut brown from being exposed to the hot desert sun. I decided to call my folks to see how things were. It had been more than a month since I had last done so. When my father answered the phone and recognized my voice, he started crying and talking so fast I couldn't understand him. After I finally got him calmed down, he told me mom was in the hospital in bad shape and could I please come. Her brother Bert had come up from San Diego. I told him to hang on; I would start back right away. It would take a few days of driving, but I would be there as soon as I could.

I fueled up the truck, and headed back to Southern California. I needed to be there with my folks, but in the back of my mind was an urge to run and hide in the hills or desert somewhere, to avoid more sadness and grief. I knew, though, I would never forgive myself if I did. It's not what you do to friends and family, you dig? I hit some high speeds heading back. An Arizona State Trooper stopped me and was going to give me a citation for doing ninety. I told him what my situation was, and apparently he sensed it wasn't just a B.S. story to get out of a ticket, 'cause he gave me a warning, ending by quietly suggesting if I kept it to eighty on the main roads, I'd probably be okay. It reminded me, cops were individuals too, some good, some bad. The only ones I ever had a real hard-on for were those two sheriffs who caused Hawk's death, and I never got a chance to do anything about it.

I got to my folks' place after a day and a half of driving without stops except to eat, pee, and fuel up. The truck hadn't failed me. I drove to the house, but no one was there, so I went to the local hospital where Pop had said Mom was. I was looking funky and probably smelled the same.

I know I got looks along the halls of the hospital. Even Pop and Uncle Bert stared at me from where they sat in Mom's room, keeping their vigil. I realized my "Find Gold or Die in the Sand" T-shirt was old, holey, and faded and my Levis were the same, the knees shot from kneeling on rough ground. "So what?" I thought. "It doesn't mean a thing."

I hugged my now-standing father, and shook Bert's hand, and then I went over to where Mom was lying on the bed, eyes closed, with all those tubes connected to her. She looked so small lying there she hardly made any shape in the bedcovers at all. I held her hand and waited. After a few moments, her eyes opened, and I know she recognized me and was glad to see me.

My mother and I could always talk about anything, and during my last visit when Pop wasn't around, we had talked about this time, which was sure to come. She told me even though my brother was far away in Sweden, if Pop and I were there, she'd be able to find peace.

Mom gripped my hand as tight as she could, moving her eyes from me to Pop and back again, until I knew what she wanted. Oh, brother, it hit me like a ton of bricks. She wanted to die without all the paraphernalia hanging out of her. So I called Pop over, along with Uncle Bert. She squeezed my hand several times, and looked around at the three of us. She took her free hand and tugged on the respirator tube. I took Pop and Bert aside and told them what was up. At first, my Dad couldn't respond, then he let go, the tension going out of him until he slumped. "We filled out forms in case of this," Pop said. "This is what she wants, so there's nothing I can do, God help me."

I found the doctor, and told him what was desired. He asked if we were sure, and I told him yes. He said he would be back in a few minutes. Five minutes later, the doctor came in, went over to my mom, took her hand, and quietly spoke to her. I saw Mom nod her head. The doctor turned to us and said he would take her off life support.

It was not pleasant for Mom to have the tubes removed, but she seemed relieved when she was free of them.

When the doctor left the room, we gathered around Mom, who said in a weak, rough voice, "I love you all and I'll always be with you." Looking at my uncle, she winked, then she looked at pop and said, "You are the love of my life, stop smoking."

Pop's tears were silently flowing and Uncle Bert couldn't say a word, but had his hand on Mom's arm. I told her things would be alright for her soon, no more pain.

She smiled a beautific smile, and was gone. No matter what it meant to us, she was free.

We stood there a moment, then fell into each other's arms and cried. A few minutes later, we had regained ourselves, and I went out and told the doctor she was gone. He came in and verified her passing with a nurse. He told us he would make the initial arrangements as they had been told to him.

Before we left mom, pop took a partial pack of Pall Malls and threw them in the trash can.

Out in the parking lot, I looked at my dad and uncle. "You know, if there is one thing mom would want, it would be for us to have a good breakfast." They both nodded their agreement, so I drove them in my truck to a coffee shop I remembered Dad and Mom loved to go to for breakfast.

It was a quiet meal, a memorial for mom, and then we went home and spent some time remembering. The rest of the day was no fun, with me calling the friends and relatives who needed to be told, while my father and uncle sat around, grieving.

I contacted my brother to give him the bad news. He knew, of course, that mom had been ill for quite a while, so, even though he was upset, he knew it was one of those things where she was gone, but at peace. The cremation was done two days later, and we received her ashes the next day. Bert had to return home soon, so we went to the local mountains and spread her ashes in the creek running through Mt. Blakely's main canyon. In the evening, we drove Bert to the airport, and then Pop and I went back to the house. Mom was only sixty-three, but she had lived a lot in those years. I wondered how Pop was going to be. Only time would tell, I guess.

I stayed with Pop, doing my best to help him make the necessary changes in his life. But, I knew it could only go so far. Mom was all around, you know? After about two weeks, he surprised me by saying he had to move, telling me, "I don't think I'd last long living here without your mother. It'd make me crazy."

I asked him if he'd thought about where he'd go. He told me he wanted to go see his sister, Rochelle, who still lived in Upstate New York. Pop had originally been from Rochester, New York. He wanted to see her and look around the area to see how it felt to be back there. With the money from his retirement and what he'd get for the house, he'd be okay. He told me, "What bothers me is not getting to see you much, but you travel all the time anyway."

I told him, whatever he decided, I'd help him with what had to be done. So, Pop called Rochelle and started talking to her, at which point he broke down, so I talked to my aunt, who is a sweet person. She said it would be wonderful if he came up to spend time with her. In fact, if he thought he could, it would be fine with her if he came to live there. Her husband, my Uncle Erwin, had passed away almost ten years before. Rochelle had never remarried. I guess the people in Pop's family married for life.

I gave him back the phone, and he and his sister talked for quite a while. I know it made him feel better, kept him from feeling so alone. Rochelle told him if he ever wanted to, he could come live with her. Pop and his sister had always gotten along, and her offer seemed to make him feel better.

So, it was settled. I would stay and help Pop sell the house, and then drive him back to New York State to be with Aunt Rochelle. He would be with someone who loved him, and hopefully he would find some peace.

It took about a month to sell my folks' house. It was a typical southern California ranch-style home, but Pop had kept it up and it showed well. Then we had an estate sale. He was amazed how good I was at selling. I told him he should have seen me in the San Francisco days, when I had my business. Anyhow, we made over a thousand bucks from the three-day sale. My folks had a lot of nice stuff, mostly heirlooms, from both sides of the family. But Pop had already stashed all he wanted to keep, so the rest could be sold.

When the time came, we rented a small, enclosed trailer, hooked it up to the truck, said good-by to their home of over twenty-five years, and split for New York. We had decided to take the southern route, as Pop had always loved the Southwest. I sure hoped the trip together would be good for both of us.

The first night, we camped over the Arizona line. We ate the simple meal I cooked in the camper, after which we sat outside on two folding chairs, sipping coffee, not saying much.

Pop asked me to tell him about some of my adventures. I told him it might not be such a good idea.

"Look son, I have no illusions about what things you have gotten into. I long ago gave up wondering why you got into drugs and God knows what else. You can at least tell me a good story."

So, I did. I told him all about Big Sur, how I got there and what happened, not leaving anything out. Once in a while he'd shake his head slowly back and forth, but mostly he just sat there listening.

When I was through, he said something to me I'll never forget, because it was so unexpected. He said, "You know, I don't think I could ever do the things you did when you were there, probably elsewhere too. You've got nerve. Have you got any more stories?" I told him I sure did, but it was getting late, We had plenty of time to talk while on the road, so it could wait till morning.

As we were getting settled in our cozy camper for the night, I got a bug in my ear. "Pop, how'd you like to meet someone special I know, who lives right here in Arizona? He's an Apache man named Gregorio, and he's an amazing person."

"Sure, why not, we could have an adventure together while we're at it."

So, come tomorrow, we'd go see if Gregorio was home. I wondered how it would go. I'd already started pondering what might happen, and wondered how my dad might handle it. I figured we'd find out soon enough.

The closer we got to Gregorio's place, the more I felt it was the right thing to do. I was hoping he might help my father heal from the major loss he had suffered, though I also wondered if anything could make it easier to deal with. When we made the turn-off for Gregorio's dirt road, my heart started beating faster. He was such a special person, you know?

I had a vision of the puzzle we were putting together, the jigsaw puzzle of our life, an overview, as if I were a spectator looking in. It all made sense in a random way. All the pieces of the puzzle were there to be put together by living it; there was no other way to do it. That meant the only way to see what it was all about was to put the last piece in place. 'Course it also meant your life would be at an end, so even if you were together enough to pay attention, you would never know until it was time to leave.

My pop had been quietly sitting as we drove down that magical dirt road to Gregorio's place, looking out the window at the desert, taking it all in. He never had been much for rapping anyway, but he was definitely quieter now.

We pulled into Gregorio's yard. He was sitting outside at the table, as though he was waiting for something or someone, maybe us. When we got out, I smiled and waved to him. But, it was my father Gregorio homed in on. He walked up to my dad and shook his hand, holding it for a while, looking at my dad's face.

Pop just stood there, like he was willing to accept whatever would happen next. Gregorio stared into his eyes for a long time. Taking my dad by the wrist, he turned to me and said I should go into the house to get some coffee and not bother them for a while. I saw him lead my dad around to the back of the house.

I went in and visited with Gregorio's wife, talking in the casual way we had in the past. Several hours must have passed. I actually dozed off sitting against the wall of their main room. Gregorio's wife wasn't inside when I woke up. I decided to let my curiosity rule me, and went out to see what was up. What I saw when I went around the back, I will never forget.

There under the singing bird tree, which was full, was Gregorio, his wife, and my dad. She was kneeling in front of pop, very close, with her arms extended, holding his arms above the elbows. She was softly singing in what I decided was the Apache language, a sweet song, or a prayer. He was staring at her with a blissful look on his face, tears flowing out of him. Gregorio was sitting to the side, facing them both, softly chanting, with a small rattle in his hand, gently shaking it. Although his song was different, the two songs seemed to blend perfectly.

I froze there, hoping not to break the wholeness of what was happening. After a few minutes, the scene started to fade away, the chanting and rattling. She slowly let go of my father's arms, and the atmosphere, like a dense cloud around them, evaporated. But my father didn't budge. He sat there smiling serenely and crying silently. Gregorio came over, motioning for me to come with him.

"I know of your father's loss, Jester. We have done a healing on him. He will sit there for a time longer, until he is ready to return. Nothing can make the loss go away, but he will be able to always stay on the positive side of what he and your mother had, so things will be easier for him until the time they will rejoin. He is a good man." Gregorio smiled a funny smile and said, "I wonder how he ever received such an unusual son."

Pop came out of his reverie an hour after Gregorio and his wife had finished the healing. Gregorio told me to sit outside and wait for Pop to call out, which he did. As I had been instructed, I took Pop down to the creek to wash his face. We stayed the rest of the day and the next. Pop never said a word to me about what had happened to him during the healing. I had the feeling he never would, and perhaps it was for the best. It was done for him alone, so who was I to intrude?

My father seemed happy in Gregorio and his wife's company. They chatted away, the three of them, like old friends. They were similar in age. In fact, it turned out Gregorio had fought in the Pacific Campaign of World War II, as my pop had, but not in the same places at the same times.

Not taking part in most of their conversations, I found an opportunity to suggest to Gregorio that it must have been difficult for him, being a healer, to participate in such battles as he did. I'll never forget what happened next.

Gregorio's pupils dilated completely again, as they did when he saw the person walking on his dirt road years earlier. This time though, he was looking at me. I started to feel queasy and dizzy, and I saw a scene in my mind, a vision. It was amazing.

There stood Gregorio in what seemed to be an old Mexican village, with other Apache men around him, blood splattered on his white shirt, a bright blue cloth wrapped around his forehead. There were a number of bodies lying on the ground. He had a look of total wild-animal fierceness on his face.

Then, he raised his head and gave out a tremendous howl. All the other Apaches joined in. It was so loud and startling, I snapped out of my reverie, returning to the present. Gregorio's eyes had returned to normal, but I would never see him in the same way again.

Gregorio said to me, "We all walk down many paths during our lifetimes, not always the one we finally settle upon. Sometimes to heal, one must remove the thing causing pain and suffering by giving it a dose of its own medicine."

He turned back to my dad and picked up their conversation where I had interrupted it. I went down to the small stream near their place and sat watching the water flow, figuring I had asked for enough trouble for one day.

The next day it was time to leave. Gregorio's wife gave us her traditional bag of Indian bread to sustain us on our journey. Pop gave Gregorio a fast hug, which startled him, but he patted my dad on the back and smiled. I shook Gregorio's hand, and told him I would try to see him again on my way back from taking Pop to Aunt Rochelle's. Gregorio said it was the right thing to do. His voice hadn't changed and he was still smiling, but I felt there was some underlying meaning there. He said, "You will see Walter again. Be alert."

He and his wife walked to their home and went inside, shutting the door behind them. On past visits, they had always stood in the yard until I was out of sight. I didn't feel as though they were shutting us off, but did wonder what it might actually mean. I sensed a finality to it.

Pop and I headed out down the dirt road still seeming to exist in its own time zone. Coming to the main highway we turned east, continuing our journey to Pop's new home. Driving along for about an hour in mutually acceptable silence, I finally asked him what he thought of Gregorio.

"I've never met anyone like him, but the only way my meeting him would work was as it happened these past few days. He is not a person to have a normal friendship with, but I now consider him a good friend, even though I know I'll never see him or his wonderful wife again. What they did for me will make living the rest of my life without your mom bearable, though I can't and won't try to describe what happened to me. Just accept it as a wonderful experience, if you can."

The rhythm of the road took over. We spent our days heading to New York State enjoying each other's company, the country we went through, and the people we briefly met along the way. There seemed to be some special energy surrounding us as we went, and people treated us respectfully, more so than I would have expected.

We avoided the larger towns, taking country roads whenever possible. Since my father was an experienced traveler, he made a good navigator. We became closer on the trip in ways not possible before, at other times. We even did some fishing together with the couple of rods I kept in a closet in the camper. My pop apologized to me for not having taken me fishing when I was younger. I put my arm around his shoulders and told him "As long as we're doing it now, it's okay."

All too soon, we arrived at our destination in Upstate New York. The end of summer had arrived, and the leaves were beginning to turn color.

Aunt Rochelle lived in a large two storey house with plenty of room. Uncle Erwin had built it when they were first married, because they planned on having a lot of kids.

Pop and Rochelle were affectionate with each other when we arrived. He smiled a lot and seemed relaxed, as if he'd reached a safe place to be, and could be at peace. I knew things were going to be okay.

I spent almost a week there, visiting and helping get things arranged. Aunt Rochelle was a great cook and baker. She made a wonderful apple cobbler, and one night, around midnight, I snuck down to the kitchen for another bowlful. Pop and Rochelle were already there, munching and quietly talking away. Unnoticed, I snuck back to my room, hoping there would be some cobbler left. I needn't have worried.

Seeing the two of them together made me feel good, knowing it was going to be okay. As I drifted back to sleep, a familiar pang tapped my heart. It would have been sweet if it had been Dawn and me sitting there in the wee hours, just talking little nothings. I dozed off right afterward.

One day, my pop helped me change the oil in my truck. I told him I would be leaving the next day, and he nodded. "Road calling out to you, is it?"

"Yeah, it is. I was thinking about heading back to Alaska. I don't feel my visit there was completed. Besides, if my good friend Walt is back there, I thought I might try my hand at jewelry making. Walt said he'd teach me if I ever wanted to learn."

"Son, I hope whatever you try in life brings you happiness."

"Thanks Pop, me too."

It wasn't easy leaving my father, even knowing he would be okay living with my aunt. But, my own life was poking me in the ribs, demanding my attention, so away I went. I didn't have a clear idea of what route I would take to return to Alaska, but first I'd go to Denver, to the address Walt left me on the note in Seward. So, heading west again, I set my sights on Colorado and whatever did or didn't wait for me there.

Driving west from New York State, I didn't feel the urgency I had in earlier travels. It was true I had put some years on, and maybe my age had something to do with it. Besides, I'd certainly had my share of adventures, more than many ever have. So, I wasn't actively seeking any more, though I had the feeling a few more were going to catch up with me before all was said and done. No, I cruised down the road, the natural flow carrying me along.

It was funny; a number of times I saw open country and settled areas that seemed familiar, even though I knew I hadn't been there before. It's like when you see someone you're sure you know, but you actually don't.

So, I hummed along in my faithful rig, feeling the air rushing by me, radio tuned to some local station, working out some things in my head. I always could think best while driving.

I have to say, Kansas didn't do much for me as far as keeping my interest in new places sparked. It was flat. But then, I stopped for a hitchhiker.

I don't pick up hitchers anymore, not the way people are these days. But, it seemed okay to give this one a ride. He was a middle-aged black man, and I didn't notice his unbathed condition 'til he tossed his beat-up old backpack in the cab before he slid in. The man was ripe, but I had been gamey myself a time or two, so I just accepted it. When I asked him where he was going, he said as far as I wanted to take him. Fair enough, but no actual destination?

"I'm following God's command to spread his word wherever I can."

Uh-oh, now what was I in for? But, he didn't preach me The Word as I thought he might, only passing the time making conversation. He apparently had been on the road quite a while, coming from East Texas to begin with, making his way around the Midwest, living off of people's kindness. The hitcher, Abe, seemed mellow, and with the windows open was bearable.

We passed by a slow-moving river on the back road I had chosen to drive. Coming to a stop, I asked Abe if he wanted to make use of the fresh water to bathe himself. I had soap, shampoo, and a towel he was welcome to use. As I expected, he took it the right way and accepted my offer.

"Would you care to read something I wrote while I clean myself up?"

"Sure Abe, why not."

After he had disappeared into the willows on the riverbank, I settled down a bit and started reading. It was a simple but direct piece of work discussing what Abe's idea of what God's plan was, a text for "everyman." It was intelligently written, and non-sectarian. I appreciated a lot of what he had to say, relating some of it to my own life. Now, don't get me wrong, I'm not a religious person, though if all of us practiced living a decent life, treating each other with kindness and love, I would be much happier.

I had just finished, when Abe came walking back. I went into the camper and brought out a shirt and pants I could part with and gave them to him to try on. They fit him, and he was grateful, and asked if I might have a pair of socks I could spare. Indeed I did. He made a small fire and burned his old stuff, telling me they were well past the point of redemption.

The weather turned colder and stormier as we continued down the road. We passed a sign announcing a small town coming up. I don't remember the name now. With some excitement in his voice, Abe asked me to pull over when we reached the town. "I do believe this is the next place for me to spread the word, brother."

I did as he asked, and as he was leaving the truck, I pushed a few twenties into his hand, letting him know I was okay money wise and I hoped it would help him get along. Taking the money, he suddenly grabbed my hand in his and started praying for my health and prosperity. I knew this was the only thing Abe had to give me, his sincere belief, so I let him do his thing. When Abe was done, I told him I hoped to see him again sometime. He smiled a beautiful smile, saying he was sure that someday we would meet again, and walked away toward the town. I sat there for a moment watching him go, then drove on.

As I headed down the road again, I considered my interaction with Abe. I thought to myself, "Perhaps he is doing God's bidding, a wonderful thing if it's true."

At that moment, the sun, hidden behind storm clouds until then, caught the edge of one. Rays of light shot out in such a magnificent display, covering much of the sky above me, I had to pull over to look in amazement. It lasted for about ten seconds, and then went out as if a switch had been flipped. If this wasn't a sign verifying there was far-reaching truth in what I had just thought, I don't know what would be.

I had to accept the fact my thoughts had been responded to. Anyway, it happened exactly as I'm telling it, and you can take it as you wish. Me, I know in my heart what it was.

The storm and heavy rain continued, so I camped by a small lake for the night, about twenty miles from where I had dropped Abe off. There was no one else there, more than likely because the weather was so rough. Me, I loved it, the way Nature has of reminding you how small and insubstantial you are by comparison. I sat in my camper sipping coffee, feeling the rig rock back and forth in time to the wind, listening to the rain coming in sheets against it. I also started hearing something else.

It was quiet singing or chanting, yet I could hear it clearly over the storm. It continued for some time, until I finally put my raincoat on and took a look outside.

At first I couldn't see much. Then I saw someone standing under a tall cottonwood tree, but who it was wasn't clear. Taking myself in hand, I walked toward the figure, thinking someone needed help. I got to a few yards away and froze in my tracks. In spite of the many strange and amazing things I had seen over the years, this did a job on me. I was stunned by who I saw.

It was Gregorio, dressed in what must have been traditional Apache clothing. He had a peaceful look on his face, the usual intensity gone. I stood there, unable to do anything, not knowing what to do anyway. Suddenly, the wind let up, though the rains kept on. I wanted to say something to him. But, what could I say? I knew he wasn't there in any normal way. He didn't even appear to be wet from the rain. In fact, I wasn't even one hundred percent sure it was him. I had experienced enough in my life to wonder. I heard his voice speaking to me, though his lips didn't move. He said, "My path here is over, but yours is still unfinished. Follow the open trail. Your life is still before you. Be strong." And then, he was gone.

I stood in the pouring rain, the wind picking up again, trying to find a way to accept what I had just experienced. Even knowing Gregorio and his abilities and powers, this was a lot to handle. I walked back to the camper, realizing Gregorio had come to say good-bye and was now gone. It felt good to know he thought enough of me to do this. But, I had lost another important person in this life. I crawled into my bed, pulled the covers over my head and fell into a deep, dreamless sleep.

In the morning, the sky had cleared and the wind was gone. There was an incredible freshness to the air. I made some coffee, and hit the road again. It's what Gregorio told me to do, and who was I to argue with such an incredible being as he was? It was as if I was given a real blessing the last few days, what with Abe, the sign from above, and Gregorio's appearance.

I considered what Gregorio had told me the night before. I had to admit life on the road always felt like the righteous way for me to go, but I usually didn't give it any deep thought. It seemed the natural thing to do. Now, I had been given strong confirmation this mobile life was truly my proper path.

I continued on my way to Denver. I arrived there several days later, and drove to the address Walt had left me.

When I knocked on the door of the nice old wooden house, I was greeted by a black lady older than myself who, without a doubt, was Emerald's mom. I introduced myself, asking if Emerald was at home. As soon as I gave her my name, she lost her smile and asked me what I wanted with her daughter.

"I'm actually wondering if Walt is still in town."

Just then, Emerald came to the door, saw me, and slipped past her mom to give me a firm hug. Her mom gave me one more hard look and walked away. Emerald said she hoped her mamma hadn't been too tough on me.

"No," I said, "But thanks for rescuing me in the nick of time."

Emerald giggled and suggested we go out for some lunch so we could talk.

Over lunch, Emerald had told me she and Walt had not been able to get it together. He had left for Alaska about two weeks back. There wasn't much else to say about it, so we quietly ate.

Over coffee, we talked about what we were going to do next. My answer was simple: on the road again. Emerald was going back to school, to become a legal secretary. Emerald a secretary. Always surprises in this life.

I drove her back to her mom's house. On the way, Emerald put her hand on my arm and suggested I stay around a while, to let her show me all the good things about Denver.

Call me a boy scout if you want to, but I had to back away. Walt was my good friend, as was Emerald, and I wasn't going to let myself get wrapped up in an emotional web; no way, brother. I gratefully declined, saying I was on my way to visit my people in Monte Rio and needed to keep rolling. I dropped a disappointed Emerald off at her mom's house, and said good-bye.

Hey, a man has to be faithful to his own beliefs, especially about the people he loves. Otherwise, man, life would be just a crock, at least to my mind, anyways. I knew if I got close to Emerald, it would put a ruin on my friendship with Walt and Emerald both. Turning the key, I shifted into gear and slowly drove away, headed west.

At this point in my reading about Jester's experiences, I knew his people were becoming more scattered, the ones not permanently gone from his life. I considered where I had first met him, alone in his camp by the river. I saw him as having a "trap line," to travel between places where his friends and relatives were, or had been. I knew he had made the road his ever-changing home, as nomads all over the world do. He had become a nomad, his modern means of transportation letting him cover greater distances faster than any traditional nomad ever could. The difference I saw, was while nomads traveled to get somewhere specific for business and socializing, Jester seemed to have a need to keep moving. Maybe he was running from something he could never escape.

But, I also had to wonder about him becoming lonely, and then dismissed such a thought as foolish. I had never met anyone who had such ease in meeting and becoming friendly with others, even those who might not seem so friendly at first. I finally decided Jester was right where he ought to be, living the life best suited to him. From his first hitchhiking trip to S.F., I envied him a bit, because even though such a life wasn't for me, it really worked for him, while most people tried to make do with the one they had. It was a lesson for me, which would eventually help me find my own way.

I decided my little white lie, telling Emerald I couldn't stay 'cause I was headed to Monte Rio when I had made no such decision, was actually a good idea. As I rumbled along the road, I decided to head west once again. Dawn had been back in my thoughts a lot more than usual lately. Maybe it was why Monte Rio seemed a good next stop.

The day Tie-Dye arrived, I was thinking so much of Dawn and Nathan, memories rolling by in my mind, I had to pull off the road awhile. I had been driving on automatic pilot for a few miles, which you know can't be too safe. Since I was just coming into a town in Utah, I pulled into the parking lot of the local supermarket to buy supplies and take a break.

Just outside the front door, there were two young girls with a cardboard box, obviously with animals of some sort to give away. What a symbol of American culture, giving away excess pets outside food stores. I didn't give them a second look as I went in to shop.

But, on the way out, I saw there were three puppies about ten weeks old, trying their best to get out of the box, and the girls were doing the same to keep them in.

Forgetting his mates, one of them connected with me, and came to the side of the box where he could stretch up and look at me. I couldn't tell what kind of mutt he was, but definitely a mutt. Besides, being just a pup, he hadn't changed into his final form yet. He was a many-colored pooch, splotches of color all over him, black, brown, even some mottled gray-blue such as on Australian dogs. Then he clinched the deal. The little fart smiled at me! He lifted his upper lip enough to show his tiny front teeth, narrowing his eyes at the same time. His floppy ears even tried to stand up, without much success. What a sketch! Then it came to me. Tie-Dye, I'd call him Tie-Dye with all those colors. Wait a minute, I wasn't looking for a pooch; what did I need with a dog? Too late.

Letting out my breath and knowing I was hooked, I told the two girls I would take him, and asked them to watch him while I went into the market again. The girls said he was weaned on Purina Puppy Chow, so I bought a bag, along with two medium-sized dog bowls.

I was only going to get the food and bowls, but I noticed this small black leather collar with trippy chromed studs on it. I paused for a moment, thinking how it was too bad all my leather tools were back in Monte Rio, and maybe I should get them out while I was there to make him a collar myself. Taking the easy way out, I dropped the ready-made collar into the cart.

I came out of the store and gave the girls two dollars, just because, even though the puppies were free. I put Tie-Dye into the truck with me and we began our life together.

I had never had a dog before. My old man never liked pets, dogs or cats, though my mom brought home a canary one day when I was about ten. Pop came home from work and stared at the bird, which was in a cage in the kitchen. "I thought we weren't going to have any pets," he said, giving Mom a firm look.

"Oh, WE don't have a pet, mister, I have a canary and I'm keeping it in my kitchen." First time I remember my mom backing him down. After an awkward silence, Pop grumbled something about hoping dinner would be ready soon, and went to sit and smoke in the living room.

So, this pup was my first dog. I had no idea what to expect from him, not knowing what owning a dog would be like. So, I didn't try to treat him as a dog. He was simply my bud. I began talking to him right away, as any other being sharing this life with me. We hit it off from the start. Soon as I got in the truck, he snuggled in where my right hip and the seat met, pushed his little snout up against me, and letting out a sigh, fell right to sleep, snoozing away for quite a few miles. Yeah, I thought, I've got a partner now.

I camped near a stream in Nevada for the night. While eating a couple of homemade chili burgers for dinner sitting out by a small fire, I watched Tie, as I was already calling him, sniffing around, checking out his surroundings.

I thought how good it would feel to be in Monte Rio. I missed my people and felt the need for some family around me. I'd had my fill of loss lately, and could use the company.

I didn't know if I'd stay in the cabin again. I would always hold Dawn's love close to my heart and Nathan, my good boy, but I felt it wasn't a good thing to keep the past so strongly alive. Truth to tell, after my go-around with Annie, I realized I probably wouldn't have a permanent thing with anyone again. No, Dawn had been the one for me.

Tie-Dye came galumphing up to me, looked at the camper, looked back at me, and yipped. Darned if the little dude wasn't telling me it was time to bed down for the night. Now, I had been sleeping in the overhead bed, but Tie whined so much, obviously wanting to stay close, that I set up the lower bed, and we continued the arrangement for all the years we traveled together.

I woke up to a puppy foot poking me in the nose early the next morning. I opened one eye just in time to get some quick licking and a dose of puppy breath. He wanted out. He had held his water and poop till morning, so I let him out to do his thing. I watched him from the camper until he came back, but I had to help him up the metal stairs to the door. He got a lift onto the bed and snuggled right down again. I lay down next to him, and he put his paw on my arm. I was learning how mellow a trip it was to have a dog.

Later, having eaten our breakfast before heading out, I let Tie check out the collar I had bought him. He sniffed it, and gave me a questioning look. I gently put the collar around his neck. It was long for him, but he would grow into it. Tie-Dye seemed to accept the collar, not whining or scratching at it. I told him he looked good in it. He yipped at me and the deed was done.

We headed on down to Monte Rio. It took several days to get there, and on the way I talked to Tie a lot, being the rapper I am. First time I had somebody to talk to who didn't have to answer back. He would sometimes fall asleep mid conversation, but it was cool. He was always glad to see me when he woke up. He taught me each day was brand new, and the events of the previous day were over and done with.

When we got to Monte Rio and I pulled into the Lensels' driveway, Maxine and Marla came out of the house, obviously glad to see me. "Look what the wind blew in!" said Maxine.

Marla added, "Must have been a strong wind, you've put some weight on, Jester."

"You haven't, Marla, you look great."

"Yeah, sure, sure. Hey, who's your friend?" Tie-Dye had put his paws up on the window frame and peeked out, curious about the new people. Marla and Maxine went over, already doing the puppy baby talk routine, but when they got a few feet from the window, Tie-Dye raised his hackles and made a determined attempt to growl at them. They stopped short, taken by surprise. Maxine looked at me and said, "Jester, you've got yourself a real dog there, don't you?"

"I guess so, Maxine," I said, surprised myself. I picked him up through the window, and took him over to them, telling him it was okay, they were all right. He sniffed them both and he did his smile thing at them, which made them crack up, and his tail started thumping me. But, I knew I had to make sure in the future, when he had grown, to let him know when things were cool.

Maxine told me George and Avery were away gathering some meat, and after I had visited a while with the girls, I asked her where they had gone and when. I knew I could set and wait for them, but decided to drive on up there and join them in the woods. It took a while to get to the turn-off, and I figured if I saw them heading back, I could flag 'em down.

I drove with my window open, which was my usual routine unless it was raining or cold, and I enjoyed the smell of the mountain air. Traveling, for me, was what it was all about, and the open window got me closer to the smells and the feel of the sun and wind on me. Tie enjoyed it too, his puppy head out in the air stream.

I got to the turn-off, and headed up the old logging road. It hadn't changed, except for being more overgrown. The trees and branches were making a lot of racket against the sides and top of the camper, but I took my time and figured we'd be okay. Tie sat there in the cab with me and didn't pay any attention to the noise.

When I came to where George and Avery had parked their truck, I pulled my rig in behind theirs. Seeing they weren't there, I left Tie in the front seat with the windows mostly rolled up, and started walking up the road. It did seem a little late for the boys to be hunting.

I hadn't gone more than one hundred yards, when I saw George and Avery sitting against a tree on the side of the road, smoking and drinking coffee from their ancient thermos, still sharing from the same cup with the broken handle. When I walked up to them, Avery smiled and told me it was about time I showed up. I asked them how it was going.

George said, "We're setting here waiting for the black bear we wounded to stiffen up and hopefully be dead by the time we find him."

"Yeah," said Avery, "he was kinda sneaking up on the ground stand George was settin' behind, waiting for a buck we've been after. I was in a tree stand about thirty yards away and glanced over in time to see this bear walking up on George from behind, so I waited for a shot and hit him good, scaring the crap out of George when I did."

"Sure did," said George. "The bear let out a huge roar when Avery hit him with the 30-30. Luckily he ran back the way he came. We watched him go, listened for a while, too."

George continued, saying, "I guess it's time to go find him now. It'll be dusk in about an hour and a half. Care to join us, Jester? Still got your old cannon?"

"Matter of fact, I do, boys. Let me settle my pup in the camper first."

"You got a dog, man?"

I took them over to the truck and opened the door. Avery reached in to pick up the pup, but Tie gave him the same greeting he gave the girls. Avery chuckled, not taking offense, telling me I had a "definite" dog there.

I went into the camper and got the Winchester out, along with the box of ammo I had for it. I settled Tie-Dye into the camper and told him to stay. He started to whine, but I gave him a firm look, put my finger to my mouth and went, "Shhhh, quiet boy. Stay."

Tie stopped whining, lay down, and stayed there.

"Yeah," said George, "he's a definite dog, all right."

The three of us walked quietly back to the place where they had shot the bear. I tell you, it was a trip being back in those woods. It had been a long while, and I had forgotten how perfect it all was. When we reached the place, we all three put rounds into our guns' chambers and went on alert. I added another to the 86's magazine just in case.

Avery said it was a good-sized bear, so we needed to be careful. We tracked the bear's blood trail about a quarter mile up a slight slope, covered with dense brush at its upper end. The blood trail had thinned out, but the bear was hard hit, and George and Avery could track a mouse on concrete.

Just ahead of us, the bear let out a loud bellow, betraying his pain and anger. We all stood ready. Suddenly all sorts of noise started coming from our right: sounds of heavy feet, and ground cover getting torn up. The bear was about sixty feet from us and coming on strong. We all swung around, but I touched off the first shot.

When the heavy bullet from my 45-70 hit him, he fell and lay still, except for one ear, which twitched several times. The three of us stood there, breathing fast and hard, as if we'd just run a quick mile.

We walked up on the bear, lying still as a stone. His eyes were open, but he wasn't seeing anything. We crouched around him for a while in silence. He was a beautiful animal, with long, glossy black fur. I was sorry he was dead, but knew he would be fully used, nothing wasted.

"Your old Winchester packs quite a punch," George said. I had put the bullet right between his eyes and he never knew what hit him.

"To tell the truth, boys, I was aiming for his chest."

"I don't care what you was aiming at, Jester, long as he went down before he got to us. The hide will be yours."

We field dressed the bear and dragged it up to the road. It was large, weighing about three hundred pounds dressed out, and we weren't about to carry it. Avery trotted down and brought back their pick-up. We got the bear in the bed of the truck, and covered it up with a tarp. Putting my rifle behind the seat, I followed them out to the road in my truck and headed back to the house.

About fifteen minutes from their place, a sheriff's car pulled them over. I drove past them slowly. Avery was driving, and when I went past he didn't even give me a look, so I kept going, knowing they could deal with this better and with less hassle by themselves. No sense stopping too and making the officer edgy, you know?

I got back to the house and let the girls know what had happened. Maxine asked what the deputy looked like, and when I described him, she smiled and said she knew the man and it would be all right.

Sure enough, the boys pulled up a few minutes later. George said, "It appears Deputy Shannon is going to be getting a free tune up on his Buick later in the week." We all looked at him for a moment and broke out laughing.

We went to look at the bear. Even in death, you could tell it had been a powerful animal.

Suddenly I got up and trotted over to the camper. I had forgotten about Tic-Dye. I opened the back door and there he was, looking upset, sitting next to a neat little pile of puppy poop.

I told him, "I'm sorry, man. It's my fault." He made a gruffing sound and came over to me. I picked him up and a moment later he was licking my face as if he'd never stop.

After cleaning up after him, I carried him over to the truck bed, and the minute he saw the bear he freaked, barking, snarling, and piddling on me. Taking him back to the camper, I finally got him calmed down, though he did whine and grumble for a while after. I'm sure the pup knew what a bear was by instinct, and reacted appropriately.

I never tired of spending time with my Monte Rio family. We never argued or conjured up any emotional distress as so many people do. We were functional as friends and family. It was understood we had all lost loved ones, but we still had each other. And even if I wasn't in their lives as regularly as they would have liked, our bond stayed strong.

There have been times on the road when some loneliness seeps in, not just for human companionship, but for the company of my family. I often feel them strongly in my mind and heart and have no doubt it is the same with them at times. We never discussed such things. Can you just hear me telling George and Avery I can feel them near me a long ways away on the road? Oh, they might accept that, but they'd never come right out and say it, and most likely pass it off with some remark such as, "probably weren't far enough away, ha-ha."

I spent several days at the Lensels' place. On the third day, over iced tea in the backyard, with no one else nearby, Marla said she thought it would be nice if I could stay at her place. The boys would be home on the weekend, and would love to see me. Marla sat looking at me, waiting for an answer. I was quiet for several moments, searching my feelings. Finally, I said, "I don't see why not, Marla. Do I have to do the cooking?"

"Not if you want to stay friends, Jester," she said, with a sweet smile.

Later, George took me aside and told me Marla's boys had gotten into a bit of trouble a while back, and were working at a camp up the road a ways, clearing brush and doing trail work as community service. They came home on weekends. "Heck, all they did was swipe some beer. Kinda dumb, though. Hard to hide a six-pack under your jacket. The new county judge is a hard-ass, too. The boys have a few weeks to go."

When I left the next morning to go over to Marla's place, Maxine stopped me at the front gate and told me Marla had been alone ever since Greg had passed. It was hard keeping the boys reined in. "She's a lovely person Jester. If anything happens, it's your business, but try not to make things worse, okay?"

I laughed and told Maxine I was only going over to have a friendly visit and nothing else. Marla was like family to me.

She smiled. "My Jester, always the boy scout."

I smiled back, shook my head, and left with Tie-Dye trotting next to me.

When I got to Marla's place it was about noon, and the sun was nice and warm. Her yard was even thicker with flower gardens than I remembered. In fact, she was in the back yard messing around in one. She didn't see me come up, so I watched her for a while. Guess Maxine's words had planted themselves in my brain. Marla was older than me, but it was true, she was a good-looking woman. Man, I thought to myself, just stop thinking.

I walked up behind her and said in a loud voice, "Hey, Marla!" Scared the bejeesus out of her. I think she actually jumped a few inches off the ground. Tie-Dye even barked.

"Thanks a lot, Jester! Made me drop all these seeds!" So, I knelt down to help pick them up. Next thing I know, I'm getting a soaking from Marla's flower-sprinkling pail. We wrestled around with the pail, then she ran and got the hose. In a few minutes, we were both soaked and laughing like crazy.

We were both standing close to each other, holding onto the end of the hose, the water running out of it. We stopped laughing and stood looking at each other, as would Bogart and Bergman, or Cooper and Grace Kelly. Marla said, "I think we better go in and dry off, don't you?"

"Aren't the boys home?"

"Nope, they decided to work this weekend for actual pay. They won't be home till Sunday night."

Jeez, man, the energy was starting to get heavy, you know? Suddenly a swirl of breeze whipped around us both, chilling us. I shivered, and I think Marla did too.

"Yeah, Marla, I think we better do that."

I figured it was best to take Tie-Dye over to the Lensel house. I told her I'd be right back. Mercifully, Maxine didn't admonish me about anything when I asked her to watch him for a while, but she did take notice of my wet condition, and I think I saw a bit of a smile.

Marla was waiting for me on the front porch, drying her hair with a towel. Watching her for a moment removed any hesitation. She was a fine woman. So we went in, and shared our feelings in many ways.

You already know by now, I talk all the live long day, but the time we spent that afternoon and evening, and the next morning, I kept my talking to a minimum, for a couple of reasons. We totally connected with each other, as if the world was minimized down to just us, so a lot of words weren't necessary, and I didn't want to spoil anything by talking too much.

It was a perfect time. We had both lost the ones we loved and were comfortable with each other. If I had to describe how it was, and of course I have to, I'd say those several days reminded me of a freshly baked, still-warm loaf of bread. You love the smell and warmth of it and can't leave it alone till it's all gone, and then wish for more.

We both knew it was necessary to settle down by the second afternoon, which wasn't easy. It was understood this was not a permanent thing. As I say, we knew each other. Marla was a homebody, almost never leaving Monte Rio, at least not since Greg had died. She knew I had the wanderlust. We had satisfied our mutual needs and could go easy now. It sure had felt good though.

The boys got home about six p.m. Sunday evening. It was far out how much they'd grown. They were glad to see me, but quickly realized something had gone down with me and their mom. It was their house and their mother. But, they were cool about it, and I caught them grinning at their mom and me once or twice. They wanted to know all about my travels, especially in Alaska, so I spent the rest of the evening jawing at them. The three of them got into the bear story, where Cary almost turned into grizzly food. Bear stories always make things interesting.

Evan and Todd had worked their butts off over the last week, so after dinner, they were going to call it a night.

"Guess you know all about our stupid problems by now," Evan said. Todd looked away when his brother spoke.

"Yeah I do, but you've probably already heard anything I would have to say about it. I figure this situation has shown you trouble is just that: trouble. The heavier the problem, the worse the consequences. I've been around you two enough to know how much you love your mom, so you don't want to cause her any more trouble, right?"

"That's for sure, Jester. Besides, there are some flaky dudes at the work camp. We wouldn't hang around them if we had a choice."

"All I need to know. You two get some rest. We'll visit some more while I'm here."

"Where you going to next?"

"Probably back to Alaska for a while, but it's not written in stone."

"Wish we could go with you, but . . ."

"I know, and if you didn't have to work off your mistakes, you might."

"Right."

"Right, and goodnight."

"Goodnight, Jester."

I joined Marla where she sat on the porch glider, enjoying the cool evening air.

"It has, without a doubt, been the mellowest weekend I've had in a long time, Marla. Thank you for everything."

"I hope you know it's mutual, Jester. It has been very sweet."

"Marla, what are the boys going to do after their community service is up?"

"I would like to get them into the junior college down in Auburn. They have a good forestry program there. Their cousin lives there and Evan could start there next term and Todd in the spring."

"Sounds great. How would that affect you money-wise?"

"Oh, it would be tight, but we'd make do."

"There's something I want to do, and I don't want any argument. I want the boys to be okay too. I'm going to deed the cabin over to you to sell or rent as you see fit to help out. I am never going to live there again, as I think you know, and this is a thank you for all you and Greg did for me when I needed help. We'll get the paperwork done before I head north."

Her eyes going all teary, she said, "I don't know what to say, Jester, so I'll just say thanks." With that, she leaned over and gave me a kiss. "Do you have to leave soon?"

"Yeah, I need to, Marla. Will you be okay?"

"As long as you come back to visit again."

"You can count on it."

I headed back over to the Lensels' to spend the night. When I got there, George and Avery were sitting on the front porch steps. This is how that went:

"Evening, Jester."

"Evening, George."

"Beautiful night."

"Yeah, Avery, it is. Think I'm gonna turn in for the night."

"Can't say's I blame you, Jester." says George.

"You must be tuckered out by now."

"Yup," said Avery, "Maybe it's a good thing the boys got home."

I stood there a minute on the porch, but couldn't think of a thing to say. I stared at the backs of their heads, until they finally cracked up, laughing like idiots.

"You are uncool, very bad men," I said, and went inside to sleep like a baby.

The next day, I went down to the local bank with Marla and did the paperwork to turn ownership of the cabin over to her. My life was now a mobile one, and I already knew it probably always would be, until I got too old to drive. We went to have lunch afterward, then back to her house where we parted as good friends.

I had planned to do as I always did, simply head up the highway to wherever my intended destination was, checking out what was along the way as I went. This time, though, before leaving Monte Rio, I decided to check and see what was up with Walt. So, I played phone detective, and found the number for the bar in Seward. I got the bartender friend of Walt's and asked him to give Walt a message to tell him I was coming up to hang out with him. But the bartender put the stops to my plan. He told me Walt had been there a while and then packed it in. "He didn't want to be there alone is what he told me," the bartender said. "He offered the place to me, 'cause I told him I'd take it off his hands if he ever wanted to sell. It's a great old building, you know?"

I told him yeah, I knew.

He said Walt had moved down to Washington State, near Olympia, to start again.

"Believe it or not, he was buying back his bus from the man up at Cooper's Landing, No one had ever bought the thing."

I said, "Guess it was still Walt's bus, no matter what."

"Whatever the story, he bought the bus from him, giving him back the Power Wagon which he had put a lot into, made it shine, so to speak, plus some cash. He brought the bus down here, and went over the whole thing. Had a lot of miles on it, but it seemed in great shape. A week later, he had turned over his place to me, had a farewell party with his friends here, and the next day, he was gone, headed south. It was about a month ago."

I thanked him for his help, and said I'd drop by for a beer sometime if I ever got back up there. But now, Alaska was out of my plans. It seemed Olympia, Washington was my next destination. I made a mental adjustment, and the next day, we headed north, Tie-Dye and me.

The weather had turned cold and rainy, and it followed us all the way up to Washington State. Once I got to Washington, it got even wetter. There's a reason the place is called "Squishington."

Tie was not happy when he had to go out and do his business. I wasn't either, especially when he came back into the camper soaked, and did his dog shake, getting everything wet. Can't be avoided when you have a pooch in a small place. It got so when he'd come back in, I'd have a towel ready and rub him down right away. Funny thing is, he did his shake afterward anyway, as if he refused to give up his right to complete dogness.

Olympia was in some gorgeous mountain country. Even in the rain, it was great being there. The smells in the forest were terrific. I left the passenger window partly open so Tie could trip out on it all, the overhang of the camper keeping most of the rain out.

The second day we were in the area, we woke to dry skies and sunshine, a nice reprieve. This was also the day I came across Walt. Man, it was so quick and easy, I almost wished it could have taken longer and been more of an interesting event.

Tie and I had finished our breakfast at the campsite, packed up, and stopped about fifteen miles outside Olympia to get gas. We pulled into the station, and damned if Walt wasn't there, doing the same thing to his bus. It looked as roadworthy as it ever had. I walked quietly up on him from the side and asked to see the license and registration for his vehicle.

He started to ask why as he turned and saw me. All the seriousness left his face and he said, "Guess I can never get away from you, can I, Jester?"

"Nope, Brother Walt, I don't think so." We shook hands, and then started laughing.

Then Walt's face got serious again. "It's good to see you man."

"Likewise, Walt, no doubt."

After talking a few minutes more, we drove out to his place. It was about a quarter mile off the main road, and had a roomy ranch-style house on a couple of acres. There was also a large storage shed and a nice workshop he had almost finished.

The whole spread was nestled between two wooded hills with a view out over a wide meadowland, with more hills on the other side. Walt had found the place in the classifieds while up in Seward, and after seeing some photos they had sent him, had agreed to purchase, putting down a good deposit and paying the rest off monthly.

"I've checked all the local regulations Jester, and I can have a store, no problem," he said. "Beautiful here, isn't it?"

I had to agree with him.

We heard some barking from my rig. I took Walt over to meet Tie. When Walt stuck his hand out and petted him, Tie didn't do his standoffish routine. A good sign. I let him out to sniff around and he got right to it, no worries. After giving me the tour, Walt suggested we go in and have some coffee and talk. "Better bring the pup in, though. Plenty of coyotes around here. Is he housebroken?"

Walt and I spent the rest of the day and evening filling in all the gaps. He told me once he had gotten to Colorado, he knew right away Emerald was already moving in another direction. She was quite a bit younger than Walt, and being the right-minded fella he is, knew he had to let her go her own way, proving how much he really loved her.

Toward the end of that first evening Walt, Tie-Dye, and I went outside to breathe in some evening air and let Tie clear himself for the night. We each did our thing. Just before heading in, I thought I heard a wolf howl in the distance. I looked at Walt who smiled and said the locals didn't mention to anyone about there being a few wolves around. Something about a Fish and Game program from a few years back.

All of a sudden, Tie let loose with some puppy howls. He did his best, but was so darned cute, Walt and I couldn't help letting out with a chuckle. Tie turned, and gave us an obviously offended look. Sharp little dog. As we let him in for the night, he blew some air through his muzzle, sounding like a cranky old man letting his feelings be known. He went over to lie down on the old blanket at the foot of the bed in what was to become my permanent room.

In the morning over breakfast, Walt suggested I consider becoming partners with him in the place. I asked him why.

"I never was much for having a partner, but I can see a number of reasons for joining up here. You can learn jewelry making if you meant what you said last night, so we can make something out of the place. You could do shows after you get good at it, which I'm sure you will, while I run the shop here. Truth to tell, Jester, I'm tired of the road, but I know you're not. Then too, there's the thing about neither of us being as young as we once were and this way, you'd have a permanent place to live whenever you want. I have money laid by, but if you decide to go halves, we could pay off the place so I won't have to put out all I've got. We'll share fifty-fifty, right from the get-go. Think it over."

"I don't have to, Walt. The whole thing sounds excellent to me. One thing, though, to make it safe for us both and no other reason, let's put it all in writing, so that no one can say otherwise."

We shook hands, had a shot of good whiskey and it was settled. Walt contacted the owner of the place a few days later, letting him know about our arrangement. As with so many things in my life which were meant to be, there were no real obstacles presented to us, as if what we were doing was a part of the natural flow of things, the next proper step in our lives.

The next few months were filled with me getting set up and settling in at the place. But, right after I agreed to being there, Walt also started showing me the basics of jewelry making. It was great. I enjoyed all the processes he showed me. I understood each material has its own requirements for being worked. Wood, stone, metal, and leather, each one had its own rhythm. I got into working with soft metals and stone quickly. Apparently my hands were still good, so anything I put them to, I could accomplish.

Walt was pleased I learned so quickly. It meant I could help out working with basic pieces so he could work on custom orders. It was all going so well that at the end of four or five months I could work on many things by myself, even though I still had a lot of questions. During that time, I did several shows in Washington and one in Oregon with work Walt had done. With what I had learned, I could sit and work at the shows as Walt had. I found selling the jewelry was no different than selling the leather, as far as dealing with people was concerned. I did miss having someone with me, though Tie-Dye was good to have there. He had learned to be mellower with strangers. The few he growled at, he must have had a good reason.

When we were at the Washington homestead, we went several times a week to a small cafe about six miles up the road toward Olympia, usually for breakfast. There were two waitresses there, one named Evelynn. She was easy to look at and had a classic, brassy professional waitress's attitude. I figure you can always tell the difference between someone who works at a restaurant taking orders and bringing food to the tables and a real waitress. Evelynn was definitely the latter. Several times we saw her put a customer in their place, once walking a slightly drunken local out, no problem.

Walt had apparently taken a real shine to her. It seemed to be mutual. But, they had both paid some dues in life, and weren't pushing anything. Finally, though, Walt asked her out and they started dating. When it got to the point where they were getting real close, they would usually go to her place, but often I would come out of my room in the morning to find her cooking breakfast, always for the three of us, which I appreciated. Things seemed cool with all of us.

About four months after they started going together, Walt told me they planned to get married and asked me if it was all right if she moved in. Without hesitation, I said it was cool with me. I was glad Walt would have a woman in his life. But I knew things would change. They had to change. It was a natural fact of life. I knew I would have to give them some space, at least for a while, so they could get settled in with each other.

A month later, they had a pleasant ceremony with about a dozen people at the Justice of the Peace in Olympia. Except for me, and Walt of course, all the others were Evelynn's circle of friends and family.

About a week after Evelynn moved in, I told Walt my feet were getting restless and I felt the need for the open road. Naturally he picked right up on my real reason for leaving, and told me it was fine, but I should remember it was my home, too, so, if there was any other reason I was going away, it wasn't necessary. I assured them it was okay; I simply needed to travel. I had planned on going to visit my dad, who I checked in with about once a month. He always asked me if I was going to visit sometime, and finally I said yes.

Tie and I hit the road about two weeks later. We would have left sooner, but my truck had started smoking, so I had gone to see a mechanic recommended by one of Evelynn's customers.

The mechanic, Ernie, and his place, were covered with grease and various other stains associated with mechanical work, but after talking to him a while, drinking coffee out of an incredibly funky coffee mug, stained and cracked, I realized he was the man to deal with.

He asked me if I wanted more power than the original engine had put out, and I told him I was mostly interested in reliability and decent mileage. He smiled, and told me he could make it happen. I left the truck with him, and he drove me back to our place.

A week later, he called me to say he had finished my rig, and would drive it over that afternoon.

I said that was far out.

He paused and said, "Whatever."

Ernie was a homegrown Washington kid, so using my old slang must have set off bells and whistles in his mind.

I heard the truck roll up before I saw it, and Tie had begun barking before I heard it. Tie had grown, filling out into a handsome pooch. He took right to Ernie, ending up with the top of his head and his semi-erect ears having friendly grease stains all over them.

The truck sounded healthy, better than it used to. Turned out Ernie had installed a Hemi engine in it he had taken from a late '60s Dodge he'd had sitting around for a while. Besides doing a rebuild on it, he had put on a different intake manifold and four-barrel carb, but had set it up so that it would get decent mileage. "Long as you don't put yer foot in it, that is," Ernie said. Ernie asked for only six hundred and fifty dollars for the whole deal, but I gave him eight, and was glad to do it. I gave him a ride back to his place.

Man, did it pick up and scoot! I saw what he meant by not putting my foot in it. It was downright rude, the way it spun its tires and roared ahead.

"You could use some better mufflers on it, too, but that's not life or death," Ernie had said. "These are kind of noisy." he said with a wink.

"I think I'll stick with these, Ernie."

"I kinda thought you would."

After a few days of breaking the engine in, I took the truck back to let Ernie retighten some important nuts and bolts. He figured since I was heading out soon, it was important to check things over. Not to worry, he had done a great job.

After saying so long to the newlyweds, Tie and I headed east, destination Upstate New York. I stayed north heading across. The new engine actually gave me several miles per gallon more than the old one, if I took it easy and stayed within sight of the posted speed limit. But even at eighty, it purred along. Tie and I enjoyed the ride. It only took about four and a half days to get to New York, the fastest trip I had taken over a long distance, except when I went to my folks' place when mom was bad off.

Nothing out of the ordinary happened on the trip east. It was funny, but things felt different to me. Though I was still happy to be on the road, it was nice to know I had the Washington home to fall back on. Walt had been right about that.

My father had gotten older faster than I expected. He looked a lot smaller than he had the last time I'd seen him. It was good to see him again, though. He seemed at peace. What Gregorio and his wife had done for him was apparently a wonderful healing.

Rochelle talked to me after dinner. Pop had gone to bed about seven, which he did regularly, according to my aunt. She told me she could often hear him shuffling about early in the morning, making his breakfast. Apparently he spent a lot of time in the enclosed back porch during the day, sitting with a cup of coffee.

She said, "At first, I thought he was talking to himself, but one day, when the window between the house and the porch was open, I realized he was talking to your mother. It was as though there was a real two-way conversation going on. I was worried at first, but realized he was pretty normal otherwise, so it was okay. He does seem happy, doesn't he?"

I told her I thought so too.

I spent two weeks visiting, and several times I drove Pop downtown to shop. My father had been brought up there until he was about sixteen, before my grandparents moved downstate for business reasons. But, there were many people who still remembered him. It was as if he had only been away on an extendedY trip. When he introduced me as his son, I was immediately welcomed too.

I invited pop on a ride up into New England, just for fun. He thanked me for the offer, but he didn't feel up to the long ride I had in mind.

I had already taken him for a ride in the truck to several nearby old towns he remembered, just cruising around, him with his arm around Tie, pointing out different places. Sitting on the back porch with him after dinner one evening he said to me, "You know, your mom has seemed so close to me lately. I know Rochelle thinks I'm getting nutty, thinks I'm talking to myself, but your mom and I have wonderful conversations together. It makes things so much easier for me. I know I have Gregorio and his wife to thank for this. The only thing to make it better is to actually be with her again."

"Pop, when that feels like the most important thing, it'll happen, and I'll be happy for you, both of you."

"I know that, son, and I understand that's how it will be."

I decided to take a ride into New England anyway. I told my dad and aunt Rochelle I would be back in a week to ten days, and went on my way. It was a groovy journey.

I went through bits of Vermont, New Hampshire, and Maine. The trip actually took me about a dozen days. The old land there, the settled countryside, was different than anywhere else I had been. In many places, it was as if passing from one picture postcard to another, through farm country settled a few hundred years ago.

I only stopped at one country antique store, knowing how easily I could get burned there, but on the back wall behind the counter was what appeared to be an original Pennsylvania rifle, which I only verified later. But it looked so good, I could picture it sitting on pegs in the living room in Washington, or better yet, on a shop wall there. It would be for Walt. For Evelynn, I bought an old embroidered sampler, nicely framed and dated 1854, signed Nancy Colclaugh, who had done a beautiful job on it. I got the price of the rifle down to what I hoped was a fair one. I knew enough not to pay the asking price, but the shop keeper wouldn't budge on the sampler, so I said okay anyway. The man wrapped the rifle carefully, and would ship it out the next week, properly insured, along with the sampler in a separate box. I had no doubts they would arrive in good condition. After visiting the shop, I decided it was time to head back to my aunt's.

When I arrived back in New York, there were a number of cars in the driveway. I knocked on the front door, which was opened right away by a man who told me he was Uncle Louie, my father's brother. "Your father's gone, leaving us in his sleep two nights ago. Your aunt called me and I came right up from the city. I'm so sorry you had to return to this."

Uncle Louie gave me a hug and I could smell the booze on him. I had heard stories about Uncle Louie as a kid, his legendary drinking. I guess time hadn't slowed him down much.

I didn't freak out when I learned of my dad's death. I'd had a feeling after our last conversation he was close to the end. He had told me when

I was visiting, his life had been full and he was wanting for nothing but my mom's company. I had mentally prepared myself for the inevitable, but wasn't expecting it quite so soon.

I thanked my uncle for coming, and then went to see my aunt. She was not in great shape, but we talked and it seemed we were both of a same mindset about it. She said he had seemed so content the last few weeks, almost as if he had reached the point where he was ready.

Pop had been taken to the nearby funeral home. I called there and told them to let me know when they were finished, so I could come say good-bye to my father privately.

You know, I had long ago decided dead bodies are not people anymore. They are just a reminder of who the person was. The spirit being gone, it was only necessary to pay respects. But, when I stood over him, my hand on his, and said what I needed to say to him, I lost it, man. I had become so much closer to my father since my mother's death, it was as if losing a friend.

After I had cleared out my feelings, I found the funeral director to ask him for the details of the procedure, what had been planned. Pop was to be buried the following day after a simple ceremony, next to his parents in the family plot at the local cemetery, with a headstone picked out by my aunt and me. I paid the director, and left.

After I got back to my aunt's home, I went up to Dad's room and found his address book. It was the one he and mom had filled with the names of many, many friends and relatives over the years. I found my brother's number, and went downstairs and called him. I had phoned him after mom had passed, and now it was time again. When he answered, I took a deep breath and told him we were orphans now. We both started crying on the phone same as the last time, and it took a minute to get it together. We talked for a while about nothing specific, just to stay connected, the feeling of brotherhood helping us to deal with the loss of our father. I told him all the final things had been taken care of and not to worry. We vowed to keep in closer touch, but we both knew even though we meant it, we would go back to our lives and live them the same as we had been, just more alone now.

The rest of the experience in New York was slightly unreal, as those kinds of times can be. At the meal after the ceremony, I was given sympathy from lots of people I had never met. Several of my pop's cousins were there also. Uncle Louie made a real scene, freaking out during the meal. He had been into the liquor cabinet a lot, and broke out crying, yelling, and groaning, and then he fell into an armchair, passed out cold, snoring loudly almost immediately. Several of us carried him to the guest room he was staying in and shut the door.

Tie was in the fenced backyard, and when I went to give him food and water he seemed to sense my mood. When I sat down in a chair in the yard, he laid his muzzle on my knee and whined. He was a good dog.

Talking to my aunt later, she told me I could have anything of my dad's I wanted, but there wasn't anything I needed. I had my memories, some of the best being the most recent. I told her to keep whatever she wanted for sentiment and to give to charity or have a yard sale with the rest. But, before leaving his room, I spotted the belt I had given him. I took it, rolled it up, and put it in my pocket.

The next day, I lingered only long enough to get my things together and say good-bye to my aunt and a few of Pop's old friends who had been so cool to me.

Warming up the truck, it was back to Washington State. I wanted to get into jewelry making full bore, to be creative and gain something, to balance out the losing end of life.

I took it easy going back. Tie and I took about seven days this time, and stayed at some nice campsites along the way.

The only glitch was at a stop in Idaho, not far from the Washington border. Along about midnight, Tie started quietly growling while we were bedded down in the camper, which woke me right up. I told him to be quiet. I could hear voices outside. The camper doorknob rattled. Tie started whining. I shushed him again. Remembering Frank's old .45, I leaned over, and took it out of the drawer I had put it in after his daughter had given it to me. I had never used a semi-auto pistol before, but knew the basics. Pulling back the top of the gun and releasing it, I chambered a round. Getting myself set, I popped open the door and flipped on the exterior light with the pistol pointed out the open door. I saw two faces with wide eyes staring back. They stood still, frozen in place. One of them had a beer bottle in his hand.

I said, "You boys picked the wrong truck to mess with, dontcha think?"

The two men disappeared, gone in an instant. I didn't even hear them running away. The pistol did have a sizeable hole in the end of the barrel and I guess they weren't too drunk to notice.

Shutting the door again and turning out the light, I sat up a while till I figured they were long gone, put the .45 back in safe mode and slipped it under my pillow, just in case. I snuggled back down in bed again, Tie right next to me. He had been sleeping on the floor, but not for the rest of the night.

"I guess we showed 'em, eh, Tie?"

He made a tiny growl, agreeing with me, I'm sure.

Dozing off, I thought, "Frank, I guess you're still backing me up. Thanks old friend."

It was good to get back to the place, definitely like coming home. But when I got inside, after Walt came from the shop to greet me, something was different. None of Evelynn's stuff was around. I asked Walt if anything was up.

After a brief pause, Walt quietly said, "Evelynn and I parted ways. Things didn't work out after all."

"C'mon Walt, what happened man? You two seemed to be having a good time of it."

"Can't I just tell you I value real friendship over a lot of other things and we can let it go?"

"No."

"I can see you won't let loose of this until you root it all out, so here it is. Evelynn told me a little while after you left, she thought it would be better if I bought you out, since she didn't think you'd be happy here with her in residence. We went around about it until I saw things probably wouldn't be so nice for me around here either. I figured except for the loss of certain physical activities I don't see as the only priority in life, I'd be better off without her. So, after a whole night of back and forth, we said our farewells. Not exactly friendly, but not as bad as I expected. I had to pay her off, but it was worth it. Brother, Evelynn turned out to be a prize-winning nag!"

"I'm sorry it didn't work out for you Walt, but long as you're okay, I guess it's all cool, except for one thing."

"What's that, Jester?"

"We'll need to find a new place to have breakfast."

Things settled down to a regular routine at the place after that. Evelynn did stop by one time to pick up a few things she had left there. I asked her to wait, and went and got the sampler I had bought her, which showed up with the old rifle about a week after I got back.

"I got this for you in a shop in New Hampshire when I was back east, Evelynn. I'd like you to have it."

Evelynn gave me a hard to figure look. "I don't think it would be appropriate, all things considered," she said.

"I didn't get it for you for a particular reason, just wanted to get you something."

"Okay, thanks."

Evelynn headed out the door and just before she got in her car, she turned, looked at the both of us and said, "I hope you two have a good life together."

Walt let out a sigh of relief as we watched her storm away in her car, raising a cloud of dust.

As I said, things settled into a good routine. Walt and I did a lot of jewelry work together. He made some new contacts and was also beginning to sell on the Internet. Things were going right. I went down to Monte Rio every three months or so. Marla and I stayed good friends, but never got as close as we did that one memorable weekend.

The boys did go to school in Auburn, California. George and Avery got nailed for poaching by a gung-ho new officer in Fish and Game. They didn't do any time, but had their guns confiscated and had to pay substantial fines. Funny thing was, they couldn't get a hunting license for two years, as if they planned on getting one anyhow. The one big drawback to the whole business was it forced them to find a new hunting area.

During my visit there, when I found out what had happened I bought them both brand new Marlin 30-30s. When I gave them their guns, they were both at a total loss for words, a rare thing. George actually gave me a quick man hug.

Back at the Washington spread, Walt and I sometimes took hikes in the beautiful forests around our place. Only once did I suggest we go hunt for a deer, for fresh game meat. We went, though Walt only came along for the ride, telling me he had already done his share of hunting. I had seen lots of sign on hikes I had taken. I had learned a lot from George and Avery, more than I realized, but also, I could sense things in the woods.

We got ourselves in a good place to set and wait for a buck, and about five in the afternoon, along comes a deer, as I thought one would. I waited until he had his head down to browse, slowly brought the Winchester up and was close to pulling the trigger when Walt whispered in my ear, "You know, we do have some steaks in the freezer. We could come back some other time and see how this buck is doing in his territory."

I slowly lowered my rifle, turned toward Walt and said, "That would be a cool thing to do, wouldn't it." So, we watched the buck until he drifted away, and we went home. I still have the model '86, but haven't hunted with it since.

Things went fine for about a year. We did shows here and there, kept making jewelry, kicking back and generally staying mellow. Tie had tangled with a porcupine. He came out okay but lost the sight in his left eye. He had learned his lesson, steering clear of them from then on.

One morning, I woke up and knew I had to head out. I held on for a week, but Walt picked up on it. Finally he told me he knew it would happen eventually, and was surprised I had been able to stay put for so long. We talked about things and figured it would be okay for the both of us. I had a home whenever I needed it.

Walt told me I should go someplace I hadn't been before. I decided, even though I'd been there briefly in the past, I wanted to check out Nevada. Tie and I packed up, said good-bye and headed out. It didn't actually take long to get there, but there was a lot of desert to explore. I still had my prospecting gear and did some panning here and there. I finally arrived at the Carson River and really took to the place. There was something about the area where you and I met that drew me. I've spent a lot of weeks there, relaxing, panning, and meeting folks. It's good for me, man. When I'm there, I'm not in much of a hurry to head somewhere else. Must be a good place for me, spiritually. After Gregorio passed, I didn't have much desire to go to the Southwest, so I guess the Nevada desert and the Carson River took its place somehow.

In fact, Tie is buried there. Yeah, he passed the year before I met you there. He had been getting weak in the joints, aches and pains. One morning, I let him out while I made breakfast. He came back to eat, but then wandered off while I did some panning. After a while, I went looking and found him peacefully lying under a sage bush. He had gone. He was old, and I never found a snakebite or anything, so I guess it was simply his time. I'll never get another dog. Tie was my dog.

My friend, I hope the words I've given you to this point will hold you for a while. I am finding it harder to write things down, and besides, I've told to you most of what is worth hearing. Life hasn't been particularly exciting for some years now. It's okay, because I'm not as up for adventures as I used to be. Sitting around with folks sharing our thoughts and experiences is more my speed now. But, I will try and get to see you if I come your way again. Until then, take good care of yourself.

Jester

The way Jester's "letter" ended caught me off guard. I suppose I expected the stories to just go on and on. I went over all the writing I had put together from him. The wealth of experience he had shared made me realize I had no reason to be disappointed. But, the fact I might never hang out with him again bummed me out. Bummed me out? I guess knowing Jester had a definite effect on my life.

I edited and added the new information to my compilation of his stories and stashed them away for a while, not certain how I would go about sharing them with people, which was definitely the thing to do. I went back to my normal life. I had become a pit boss in the club and things had improved for me financially, but I couldn't get away as I used to. I figured the Carson River was getting along without me just fine, but I missed it.

One Saturday in June, my wife was off with friends at the mall and I was sitting, relaxing after mowing the lawn. I heard a vehicle with a noisy engine outside, but instead of going by, it stopped and shut off. I heard the sound of two doors slamming shut, one after the other. A minute later, there was a knock at the front door. A chill ran down my back. Getting up, I went to open it.

When I did, there before me was Jester, not looking much different from when I had last seen him. With him was another man who I knew immediately.

I said, "For Pete's sake, hello Jester." and shook his hand. Before Jester could say anything, I reached out and shook the other guy's hand. "You must be Captain Walt. I'm pleased to finally meet you. I hope you brought your bus so I can check it out."

Walt turned to Jester and with fake irritation, said, "Man, did you tell this young fella all about me?"

"Heck, Walt, I told him everything!" Grinning at me, he added, "Well, almost everything."

Finis

Made in the USA
San Bernardino, CA
31 May 2015